OUT OF THE ASHES

OUT OF THE ASHES

RITA POTTER

SAPPHIRE BOOKS

SALINAS, CALIFORNIA

Book ISBN- 978-1-952270-84-0

Editor - Tara Young
Book Design - LJ Reynolds
Cover Design - Fineline Cover Design

Sapphire Books Publishing, LLC
P.O. Box 8142
Salinas, CA 93912
www.sapphirebooks.com

Printed in the United States of America
First Edition - March 2023

This and other Sapphire Books titles can be found at
www.sapphirebooks.com

Rita's other books

As We Know it Series

Upheaval

Survival

Betrayal

Stand Alone

Broken Not Shattered

Thundering Pines

Whitewater Awakening

Dedication

For Terra, who loves the 1980s more than anyone I know.

Acknowledgment

I can't believe I'm writing acknowledgments for my seventh book. It gets harder and harder to say anything unique and interesting with each new release.

I'd like to thank Chris and everyone at Sapphire Books who took a chance on me and continues to let me write the stories I want to tell.

I want to thank Tara, who makes it fun working with an editor. I always look forward to your comments. Sorry that I seemed to have forgotten the rules of capitalization in this manuscript. Shouldn't I have learned those in fourth grade?

As always, thanks to my work flock, who make my days good enough that I have the energy to write at night. Thanks to my family and friends who continue to support me in this endeavor.

A special thanks to the sapphic writing community and the friends I have made along the way—from my GCLS classmates to the friends I made at the Queer Word Writer's Retreat, to my Sapphic Lit Pop-up Bookstore friends.

Thanks to Jae, who taught me more about writing than anyone and who has continued to support me as I continue to grow.

A special shoutout to my beta readers Michele, Cade, and Nan. Words can never express how much better you've made my books. I thank you from the bottom of my heart. And, Nan, we'll see what everyone thinks of Cano's name.

And to Terra, who has graciously let the last couple of years be all about my writing, including all our travel. Thank you for living up to the nickname you earned in DC—Terrafirma. Next trip is for you—Italy, here we come.

Oops, I almost forgot, for Chumley, the best cat in the world. He told me to say that.

And of course, to my readers, who continue to buy my books and let me tell my stories. I appreciate you more than you know.

Author's Note

The events depicted in this novel are based on real-life events. Whenever possible, the author stayed true to the historical account. The main characters of this book are completely fictional.

Cano's Map

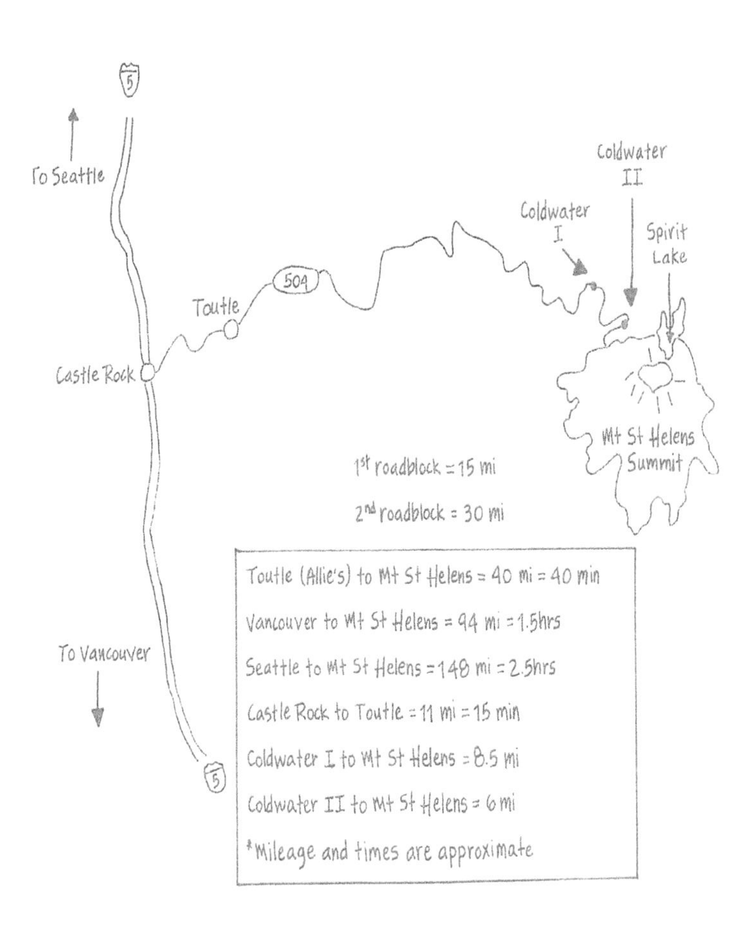
5
To Seattle
Coldwater
II
Coldwater
I
Spirit
Lake
504
Toutle
Castle Rock
Mt St Helens
Summit
1st roadblock = 15 mi
2nd roadblock = 30 mi
Toutle (Allie's) to Mt St Helens = 40 mi = 40 min
Vancouver to Mt St Helens = 94 mi = 1.5hrs
Seattle to Mt St Helens = 148 mi = 2.5hrs
Castle Rock to Toutle = 11 mi = 15 min
Coldwater I to Mt St Helens = 8.5 mi
Coldwater II to Mt St Helens = 6 mi
*Mileage and times are approximate
To Vancouver
5

Chapter One

Days until eruption: 58
Friday, March 21, 1980
Menlo Park, California
United States Geological Survey

"Hey, Cano, did you hear the news?" Johnny Garcia greeted her with a huge smile when she entered their office.

Nova "Cano" Kane glared. *Morning people sucked.* She dropped her helmet on the floor next to her desk. "I haven't even had a cup of coffee yet, so how the hell would I have heard any news?"

"It's a doozy." His dark bushy mustache curved up with his smile. The glint in his deep-set brown eyes was even more pronounced than usual.

"Did Julie and Randy finally get caught doing it in the storeroom?" she asked before she left the office in search of her first cup of coffee.

"No!" he called after her. "Get your coffee and get your grumpy ass back here."

She smirked as she walked down the hallway toward the staff lounge. It shouldn't give her so much pleasure to irritate Johnny, but it always did. By the time she returned, he'd be chomping at the bit to fill her in on the gossip. Maybe she should take her time getting back.

She grunted a hello to those she passed in the

corridor. Her coworkers knew not to engage her in conversation first thing in the morning. Before she could swing open the door, the rich aroma of her favorite Maxwell House brew welcomed her. She sucked in the scent as she entered the tiny room. *Heaven.* Even better, someone had left doughnuts on the counter.

Coffee first, then doughnuts. She made a beeline to the coffeepot. Once she'd poured a cup, she grabbed two creamers and a packet of sugar. The sugar went in first followed by one and a half creamers. She brought the half-empty creamer cup to her lips and threw it back like a shot of whiskey.

She licked her lips while she inspected the doughnuts. Why didn't they come with labels? Jelly-filled doughnuts disgusted her, and even worse was the yellow custard filling. The snot-like consistency made her gag.

Before she flipped the doughnuts over, she stole a glance at the door. Nobody was around. She plunged her index finger into the first, and it came out covered in red jelly. She sucked the sticky goo from her finger before she moved on to the next. *Strike two.* Yellow slime coated her finger. *Yuck.* When she couldn't find a napkin, she wiped it off on her jeans, not willing to put the repulsive stuff in her mouth. On the third doughnut, she found what she was searching for—fluffy white cream. She quickly flipped the other two doughnuts over, hoping nobody would notice the punctures.

Armed with coffee and doughnuts, she meandered back to the office, deciding to let Johnny wait a little longer. He was bent over his desk and pretended to be hard at work, but he didn't fool her.

No doubt, she could outlast him, so she plopped into her chair and picked up the file folder she'd left the night before.

"Jesus." Johnny threw down his pen. "Aren't you even going to ask?"

She stifled a grin. He'd not lasted thirty seconds. She pretended to be engrossed with the file before she dropped it to her desk. "It looked like you were busy, so I didn't want to disturb you." Cano gave him her best innocent look.

He narrowed his eyes, obviously trying to discern whether she was messing with him. The story he'd been anxious to share won out. "Did you see the report from U-Dub yesterday afternoon?"

She stiffened. When would she stop reacting this way whenever anyone mentioned U-Dub? "Nope."

"I thought one of your former colleagues might have called you about it."

Was he baiting her? Or was it just typical Johnny, innocently stepping in it? "I don't hear much from anyone there anymore. I graduated in seventy-four." She feigned calculating on her fingers, even though she knew exactly how long it had been. "Six years ago. Plenty of time to lose touch."

His eyes widened. "You've been here that long?"

"Nah, I stuck around Seattle for a year and a half before I decided to grace you with my presence."

"It's such a pleasure to be in your squalor." He pointed to the stacks of paper and books that spilled off her desk and filled the nearby chairs.

She turned her nose up at his immaculate desk. His neatly stacked color-coded files were the most offensive. "I'm glad I can bring a little personality to your little anal-retentive corner of the world."

He squinted and pursed his lips, an expression she'd seen many times. Would he take her bait? He stared for a couple more beats before he shook his head. An indication he wouldn't play her game of exchanging insults, at least not today. "With your love of volcanoes, I still can't believe you don't stay in touch with anyone."

"Don't you have big news? It has to be more interesting than my time at U-Dub."

"You studied with some of the premier volcanologists in the country, yet you rarely talk about it." He fixed her with his fatherly gaze, one he used often with her.

"If you're going to dwell on my college experience, never mind." She needed to do something to slow her racing heart, so she grabbed a pile of books. Somewhere in the stack was the presentation she'd been working on for the local high school. She'd been asked to speak about the U.S. Geological Survey and had been agonizing for days how she could make it interesting to a bunch of hormone-infused teens.

"You're kidding me. You're not even curious?"

"Tell me if you want. I'm not begging." She pulled out her crumpled notes and ran her hand over them several times to smooth them.

"What if I told you it's about your favorite volcano?"

She stopped herself from jerking her head up, not wanting him to sense her interest. If he did, he would draw this game out forever. "Mount St. Helens?" she said, finally looking up.

He grinned. "Didn't you do your master's thesis on it?"

He knew she did. She glanced at the wall where

the eight-by-ten photo of the snow-covered mountain hung. At first, she'd despised it since most of her classmates scattered to exotic locales to do their research. Mauna Loa and Kīlauea in Hawaii, Mount Vesuvius in Italy, Krakatoa in Indonesia, while her finances forced her to stay close to Seattle. Sometime during her research, her feelings changed, and she'd fallen in love with the volcano that had been dormant since 1857.

"You know she's my baby," Cano said.

"Well, your baby burped yesterday." Johnny chuckled at his own cleverness.

"What?" She met his gaze.

"Earthquake at three forty-seven p.m. Magnitude four-point-one."

"Why the hell didn't you tell me?"

He threw up his hands. "I've been trying to since you walked in, but you needed your stinking coffee."

"Has there been any more?" She leapt from her desk and paced their tiny office. "Are we sending anyone?"

He shrugged. "That's all I've heard."

"Who told you?"

"Spenser."

"Is he sending someone?"

"Maybe."

"What the hell? He has to let me go."

Johnny grinned. "I already put your name in."

She picked up a paperclip from her desk and threw it at him. "Jackass."

He caught it and launched it back at her. "You're welcome."

"I'm sure they'll choose Johnston, but there should be room for me, too."

"David's already there. He was doing some work at U-Dub."

Her chest tightened. In her excitement, she'd temporarily forgotten the university, or more accurately, the professors at the university. But this was *her* volcano; surely, she couldn't let the past get in the way.

"Are you okay?" Johnny asked. "You've got that look on your face again."

"I don't have a look." She scowled. "I'm just worried that Spenser won't let me go."

"Have you pissed him off lately?"

"Depends on how you define lately."

"He's your boss." Johnny groaned. "Why do you insist on making trouble for yourself?"

"Wasn't my fault." She crossed her arms over her chest. "The dumbass messed up the calculations on the project we were working on, so I pointed out his mistake."

Johnny scrunched up his face. "And did you call him a dumbass?"

"Of course not. I called him an idiot."

"Ugh." Johnny slapped his hand against his forehead. "You have to stop doing shit like that."

She shrugged. "Maybe he'll want to get my ass out of here for a while."

"That might be your only saving grace." Johnny raised his eyebrows. "Or..."

"Or what?" Somehow, she didn't think she'd like what he was about to say.

"You could ask him nicely." He ducked his head as if waiting for her to throw something else at him.

"Or I could just quit. Go up there on my own." She gave him a half smile.

"Why do you always have to act so cool about everything? Nonchalant. Maybe go in there and tell him how much this means to you, instead of acting like nothing matters."

She waved her hand at him. "I'm not into begging anyone. He chooses me, or I figure out a way to do it on my own."

"Always like to do it the hard way, don't you?" He shook his head. "More doors will be open if you're an official member of the USGS."

"You're wounding me." She thumped her hand against her chest with an exaggerated motion. "You mean Spenser and the Geological Survey have me hostage?"

"I don't think I'd be that dramatic, but all the amateurs are going to flock there like flies to shit. Having credentials will get you into places you otherwise couldn't go."

"Fine, but if he says no, it's on you. And I refuse to beg." With a grunt, Cano rose from her desk and grabbed a pad of paper and pen. She'd better get it over with before she changed her mind. Without another word to Johnny, she turned and opened the door.

"Just don't call him a dumbass," Johnny called. "Or an idiot."

Chapter Two

Days until eruption: 58
Friday, March 21, 1980
Menlo Park, California

Cano leaned into the curve and accelerated as she powered through. Riding her motorcycle was her therapy. It always helped clear her head. More than ever, she needed it. Her conversation with Spenser was short. He'd obviously made his mind up before she came in. His quick yes caught her off guard.

Walking toward his office, she'd convinced herself that she'd be forced to storm out in a rage. His smirk told her he got satisfaction from catching her by surprise. He'd even agreed to let her stow her motorcycle in the equipment trailer. The theory that her boss wanted her out of the office seemed more likely than she cared to admit.

He'd dismissed her for the rest of the day, so she'd have the weekend to get her affairs in order. *Right*. Her affairs consisted of throwing a few clothes in a suitcase, but she decided not to tell him that.

He'd logged the assignment for two weeks, but she'd likely be away for much longer if Mount St. Helens continued to rumble. Even though Cano wanted to leave right away, Spenser decided Monday morning was soon enough. She'd told him she'd never forgive him if she missed something. His only response was to shrug before he returned to the report he was reading.

She wasn't looking forward to the thirteen-hour drive, especially being paired with "Gabby" Grant. Even though she'd coined the nickname, she wasn't the only one who used it. She'd have to feign sleep, so she wouldn't have to listen to him drone on about his precocious children.

When she'd left the USGS building, instead of going east toward her apartment, she'd opened her throttle and went west toward the preserve area. After driving the curving roads for over an hour, she'd not been able to shake her unease at returning to the University of Washington, but the call of Mount St. Helens was too great to ignore.

Guilt gnawed at her as she sped past the lush scenery. Johnny had invited her to have dinner with him and his wife, Rosaria, but she'd declined under the pretense of packing. He'd only laughed and winked. Somehow, he had the impression she was as fast with women as she was with her bike. Possibly, she'd led him to the erroneous conclusion. It wasn't her fault. He was a scientist, so he should have analyzed the data better.

She roared back into Menlo Park. The closer she got to her apartment, the more the heaviness in her chest increased. Tonight, she feared, would be one of those evenings that she dreaded being alone. She should probably savor it since she'd likely be surrounded by more humanity than she cared for in the coming days.

She gunned her engine as she rumbled through her neighborhood. On residential streets, motorcycles were expected to keep their speed and noise down, but she believed quite the opposite. She wanted to make a splash so her neighbors could mark her arrival home. With practiced ease, she cut her bike hard and went into a sideways skid. At the precise moment, she twisted the throttle and shot forward in front of the two cars parked outside her apartment. She'd made a deal with the couple next door and shared the spot with them. They got to keep both of their cars nearby, while she had a place to nestle her bike, which she hoped would prevent a thief from targeting her baby.

After she pushed her bike onto the kickstand, she flipped her wrist and cut the engine. With one foot on the ground, she swung her other over the bike. She took a couple of steps back to admire it. *1973 Triumph Hurricane.* Beulah was a beauty. Her bright orange finish, with the yellow stripe along the side, glistened in the sunlight. Cano stepped forward and ran her fingers over the smooth surface. This was the only girl she needed. The only one she could rely on.

Her neighbor waved from his front door. She needed to tell them she would be gone for a while but decided she'd slip a note into their mailbox before she left. With a quick wave, she ducked into her apartment. When she pulled off her helmet, sweat plastered her hair against her head. She rifled her hand through it, splaying it in every direction and left it that way. *It'll dry quicker.*

The apartment seemed quieter and more depressing than usual. The only decoration, if she could call it that, was the lone picture hanging on the wall, a replica of Dali's *The Persistence of Memory.* It had been a gift. She stared at the melting clocks in the desolate landscape, something she did often. It made her feel something but not always anything good.

She shoved her thoughts away. What was her problem? Soon she'd be back in Washington seeing her baby, Mount St Helens. It would probably be a false alarm just like Mount Baker had been. *Baker.* Now wasn't the time to think about that, either. *Get a move on.* She'd get her packing done tonight, so she'd be ready come Monday morning.

Chapter Three

Days until eruption: 58
Friday, March 21, 1980
Seattle, Washington
University of Washington
Department of Geological Sciences

Dr. Allison Albright dropped her head to her desk. Although she loved her office, today, the walls felt as if they were closing in on her. Her surroundings were stereotypical academia, with three overflowing bookshelves, colorful geological posters strategically placed on the walls, and a small sitting area where she met with students. In her anxious state, she'd straightened all the files on her desk and even dusted the furniture, but the tightness in her chest remained.

She sighed. A couple of minutes of rest, and then everything would be fine. The tingling in her legs had worsened since last night, but it was the fatigue she hated the most. She hadn't experienced this level of exhaustion in over three years, and she didn't like it.

The last thing she wanted was to be found slumped over on her desk, but she couldn't even manage to lift her head. Maybe she should get up and lock the door and take a little nap on the couch. That would require standing, though. *Shit.* She'd lie here a little longer; surely, it would pass.

"Allie!" A loud voice jolted her awake. "Oh, god. Are you okay?"

Allie lifted her head and hoped she didn't have a spit string hanging from her mouth. She squeezed her eyes shut and opened them wide a couple of times to get better focus. "Jesus, Fran, you scared the shit out of me."

Fran Carlson glared down at her with her hand on her shapely hip. "That makes two of us. I wasn't expecting to find you passed out on your desk again."

Allie narrowed her eyes, going for her best glare. "I was *not* passed out on my desk. Stop making it sound like I'm snockered. I was just resting my eyes for a minute."

"Sure. And I'm a natural blonde." Fran flipped her wavy platinum blond hair with her well-manicured hand. It was their running joke whenever Allie tried to stretch the truth.

"Possibly, if you learned to knock, we wouldn't be having this conversation." Allie subtly swiped her hand across her lips. *Good.* No discernible spit strings.

"Sorry, *Professor.*" Fran put her fingertips against her bosom and put on a contrite expression.

"Cut the crap. And stop calling me Professor." Allie grimaced when she sat up straight in her chair. Her muscles weren't cooperating with her today nor did it appear that Fran planned on it, either.

"Yes, Dr. Albright."

Now Allie knew Fran was worried. It was the only time she intentionally goaded her. Fran had been the first friend she'd made eight years ago when she came to teach at the University of Washington. A thirty-one-year-old female professor of geology caused quite the sensation in 1972. It was a profession dominated by men, so she'd been viewed as suspect. The men, while respectful, didn't know how to interact with her, so they kept their distance. Fran, on the other hand, was thrilled to have another woman in the department.

Allie sighed. Better to get the conversation over with than continue along the path they were traveling. "What's wrong?"

Fran shrugged. "I just came in to see if you needed anything before I went home." She kept her face impassive, but the concern in her eyes gave her away.

Allie nodded. "I see." She put her hands on her desktop and pushed up with all her might. Her legs wobbled, but they held as she brought herself to a standing position.

Fran rushed around the desk and stood inches from Allie but didn't touch her; instead, she held out her elbow. With her platform shoes, Fran towered over her. Sometimes, Allie hated being so tiny, but in this situation, it worked to her advantage.

She thought of waving off Fran's offered arm, but the shaking in her legs made her reconsider. Her cane was tucked into the closet since she'd not had to use it in some time. Heat rose up her neck, and her jaw clenched. *Damn it.* Now wasn't the time for this.

Reluctantly, she threaded her arm through Fran's and allowed herself to be led to the couch. Fran gave Allie just enough support to help her onto the seat cushion and then stepped back.

Allie's chest filled. Fran was perfect. Too bad she was one hundred percent straight with a handsome husband. Allie didn't chastise herself anymore for these thoughts. When they'd first become friends,

Allie had been mortified when she caught herself checking out Fran's shapely calves as she sashayed down the hallway in her form-fitting dress.

Fran studied Allie before she sat a few feet from her on the couch. "What are you thinking about?"

"Your legs," Allie said without hesitation.

"Again?" Fran flashed her a smile.

Allie laughed. Early on in their friendship, over way too many beers, Allie had confessed her impure thoughts. Her intention was to alleviate her guilt, certainly not to hit on Fran. Somehow, Fran knew it and never took offense. The conversation only served to deepen their friendship. That was eight years ago, and in that time, they'd only become closer. Allie couldn't imagine life without Fran.

"You're pretty smug, aren't you?" Allie said.

"They're my best weapon." Fran stretched out one of her long legs and twisted it from side to side. The strap of her platform shoe hugged her slender ankle as she flexed her foot. "And if I can distract you with them for a few minutes, all the better. I can't stand to see the pain on your face."

Allie looked down at her own hands. She knew Fran would eventually turn the conversation serious, but she wasn't sure if she was ready for what Fran would say. *The best defense is a good offense*. "Thank you. You're the best friend I've ever had."

"Are you going to get all sappy on me?" Fran swiped at her eyes, pretending to wipe away a nonexistent tear. "You're gonna mess up my mascara."

"Oh, heavens, we can't have that." Allie smiled. "I think the last twenty-four hours has taken its toll."

"Work or personal?"

"Probably a little of both." Allie sighed. "A four-point-one near a volcano isn't something to sneeze at."

"Do you think it could blow?"

"It's too early to tell. We don't want a repeat of Mount Baker."

Fran's jaw tightened. "In more ways than one."

"I can't go there." The tightness had returned to her chest. "I've got to find a way to manage it all."

"Maybe you should take a sabbatical." The words tumbled out of Fran's mouth quickly, and then she stared down at her lap, suddenly extremely interested in her deep red fingernails.

At first, Allie bristled but then took a good look at her friend. Her best friend. The flamboyant woman with the bangle bracelets, hoop earrings, and wild print dress was afraid. With Fran's larger-than-life persona, it was easy to forget how sensitive she could be underneath.

Allie put her hand on Fran's arm and waited for Fran to meet her gaze. "I know you're only trying to protect me, but I have to learn how to manage my stress, not run away from it."

"Stress is one thing. But an erupting volcano and the eruption of Cano is pushing it."

"Clever wording but not helpful." Allie shook her head with a smile, closed her eyes, and let her head fall against the back of the couch. "It's too early to tell if either of those eruptions is going to happen. Besides, if Mount St. Helens blows, I don't want to miss it."

"And if Cano shows? Do you want to miss that?"

"There's no indication that she'll be here."

"You really think anything could keep her away?"

"Ugh. I don't know." Allie lifted her head and

opened her eyes. "It's her volcano, but she knows I'm here, so hard telling which will win out."

"Or maybe it'll give her an excuse to come back."

No. It was that thought that kept her up half the night and left her exhausted today. She'd done well with only minor relapses, but if she wasn't careful, this could lead to a major setback.

As if reading her mind, Fran said, "It's already started to take a toll, and she isn't even here yet." Fran's eyes filled with sadness. "You've been doing so well. Remember how..." Her mouth fell open.

"Go ahead and finish," Allie said. When Fran didn't, Allie went on. "Yes, I remember how bad it got. I thought I'd never...I wondered if I'd ever be able to live on my own again. But I've been out of that damned wheelchair for nearly three years, and I'm not going back." Allie rubbed her legs, hoping to keep the numbness at bay.

"Damned right. You've managed your MS as well as anyone could hope." Fran nodded toward Allie's legs. "This is the first time in forever that I've had to help you get around. When's the last time you've used your cane?"

"It's been a while." Allie didn't want to think about how far she could fall if she let her Multiple Sclerosis get the better of her again. It terrified her. "I just need to stay disciplined and follow my plan. And no stress."

"Easy. Now that you put it that way, why should I worry?" Fran grinned, but it soon faded. "By the looks of you, we need to get you home."

"I'll be fine. I can get myself home."

"Nonsense. Ben's picking me up at four thirty." She glanced at her watch. "Which means he'll be here shortly, and we're taking you home. You can stay with us if you'd like."

"No." Allie wanted to decline all help but knew it was better if she stifled her stubbornness. "I'll take you up on the offer for a ride, but I want to sleep in my own bed." She paused. *Did that come out too harsh?* "But thank you. I appreciate the offer."

Fran stood and held both hands out to Allie.

A battle raged in Allie's head before she finally said, "I think I need my cane out of the closet." The words left a bitter taste in her mouth. But she couldn't let this send her into a spiral. Being a prisoner to her body was frustrating, but she wouldn't fall victim to it. In her support group, she'd learned MS patients had a higher level of depression than the general population. She refused to be one of the statistics.

Fran returned with her cane but continued to hold it in her hand. "Can I at least help you to your feet?"

No doubt, with the aid of her cane and enough struggle, she'd be able to rise to her feet, but at what cost? She needed to preserve her strength and get a good night's sleep. Allie held out her hand.

Fran smiled and took it.

"You know I'm going to beat this. Then I can have a real life," Allie said as Fran pulled her to her feet. "With modern medicine, they have to find a cure."

"I'm praying for it." Fran sighed, an indication she was measuring her words. It was a conversation they'd had before. "In the meantime, you have a *real* life. You live on your own. You're funny, intelligent, caring, and an amazing friend. And one hell of a cook." Fran rubbed her stomach for emphasis. "And most impressive, you're well respected in your career, which is a feat considering you're a young woman in a man's world. That takes some *cojones* to pull off, and—"

"Stop!" Allie let go of Fran's hands and gripped her cane. With measured steps, she walked across the room. The tingling was better, but she still felt unsteady. She reached her desk and rested her butt on it before she spoke. "Hooray for me. I'm nearly forty and live on my own. Living the dream." She knew her words came out biting, but she needed to feel sorry for herself for a bit.

"That's all you got out of what I just said? Let me know when you're done with your pity party," Fran said.

Ugh. She hated that phrase. She wanted to bite at Fran, but how could she when she knew Fran was right?

"I didn't mean that." Fran clapped her hand over her mouth. "I'm so sorry. I wasn't thinking. I shouldn't use it on you."

"I'm the perfect person to use it on." Allie ran her fingers through her long hair. "Feeling sorry for myself doesn't become me."

"Not really, but you have a reason." Fran's eyes filled with unshed tears. "I'm so sorry."

"No." Allie waved her hand. "I'm not myself today." The thought of Nova's potential return was affecting her more than she cared to admit, but she wasn't ready to tell Fran. Allie smiled. "And I hate whiners."

"Oh, honey, you're far from a whiner. You're one of the most courageous people I know."

"Enough!" Allie glanced at the clock. It would

still be at least fifteen minutes until Ben arrived. She couldn't remain perched on the corner of the desk for that long with her weakened legs. *Damn it!* She shuffled around behind her desk and sat.

Fran watched her from the other side of the room but remained silent.

"I'll get my spunk back. I'm just tired today," Allie said.

"When's your next support group?" Fran asked.

"Wednesday."

"That should help."

The hopeful look on Fran's face made Allie smile. How could she explain that sometimes the group made her feel more alone? "It's a weird disease. On some level, we have similar experiences, but on others, our symptoms manifest so differently." She wouldn't bring up the biggest reason she felt so isolated from the rest, although likely Fran knew.

Fran studied her. "You look so sad. What else is going on?"

Allie shrugged. "I'm just being silly."

"You're lonely," Fran said as a statement not a question.

Why did she have to be so damned astute? She wouldn't lie to her friend, so she gave a slight nod.

"Dr. Pappas would love to change that," Fran said in a seductive tone.

Allie glared.

"Sorry. I know you aren't into men, but it would be so much easier."

Allie took a deep breath. How many times would she have to explain to Fran that sleeping with Papas had been a mistake? They'd come far in the decade since Stonewall, but they had a long way to go. "I know you don't understand, but it's how I'm wired."

"I've upset you." Fran's face fell. "I don't mean to."

"I know," Allie said and meant it. "I know you accept me, but when you say things like that it makes me wonder if you truly do."

"Oh, god." Fran marched across the floor. "I love you just the way you are."

Allie didn't want to alienate her best friend, but she'd made it her mission to educate those receptive to learning. Despite her low energy, the conversation had to happen. She took a deep breath and blew it out before she spoke. "I know you love me, but I'm not sure you understand me."

Fran's brow furrowed. "It's not that I don't understand. It would just make things easier."

"It would be easier for me to be with someone I have no feelings for?" Allie asked, trying to keep the judgment from her voice.

"No, that's not what I meant."

"What did you mean?"

"I dunno." Fran shook her head and looked away. "Just forget I said anything."

"Come on, Fran. Our friendship is built on honest communication. Just say it."

Fran shook her head so hard that her earrings slapped against her cheek. "I realize the error in my thinking. It's just...no, never mind."

"Just what?"

"I want you to be happy!"

Allie narrowed her eyes. "And you think putting me with a man would do that?"

"See, I told you, my thinking was off."

"Your thinking came from somewhere. Just tell

me."

"Now I've backed myself into a no-win situation." Fran dramatically threw up her hands, and the bangles on her wrists clanged together. "If I don't tell you, you'll be mad that I'm not communicating, but if I do tell you, then you'll be even madder. See? No win."

Allie knew she shouldn't push, but her curiosity had been piqued. "Just say it."

"Just remember you made me." Fran crossed her arms over her chest. "I don't want you to spend the rest of your life without ever having found love. There, I said it."

"And I won't find love with a man, so your logic is faulty."

"That's why you're the professor, and I'm just the secretary."

Patience. When Fran became stressed, she fell back on self-deprecation at her level of education. Never mind that Fran was one of the smartest women she knew. "You're holding back. Spit it out."

"I've done the math."

Allie leaned back in her chair. That answer came from left field. Her mind raced through the possible meaning, but she came up empty. "Care to explain the equation?" Allie hoped her attempt at math humor would lighten the heaviness in the room.

"You have MS."

When Fran didn't continue, Allie said, "I'm aware." She tilted her head and studied Fran, trying to make sense out of the conversation. "Can you elaborate?"

"Finding a partner that...that's willing to..." Fran's face scrunched up as if she were trying to pass a large bowel movement. If the conversation weren't so serious, Allie would laugh, but she suspected Fran wouldn't find it humorous.

"That's willing to take on the burden that I'll likely become?" Allie said.

"No! That's not what I said."

"But it's the truth," Allie said, her voice low. Her shoulders sagged. Fran was right, she wasn't exactly a catch. "The pool of candidates goes *way* down."

Fran nodded. "But it's on them, not you. You're beautiful, intelligent, funny, courageous, and anyone would be lucky to have you."

Allie smiled. "Thanks." She knew how hard it had been for her friend to speak the truth. Realization finally descended. "And since lesbians make up such a small percentage of the population, you're worried about the size of the pool. Not a lot of options."

Fran shifted her gaze to the floor. Her cheeks blazed. "It's their loss."

"Come here." Allie tried to push herself up from her chair, but her strength wasn't there.

Tentatively, Fran stepped around the desk but stayed an arm's length away.

"Now get me out of this chair, so you can give me a hug."

Fran smiled and blinked back tears. She easily helped lift Allie out of her seat.

Allie wrapped her arms around Fran, enjoying the comfort of her embrace. She rested her head against Fran's shoulder and fought back the tears that threatened. Fran was the crier not her.

When they separated, Allie remained standing. Ben should be here soon, and she wanted to be on her feet when he arrived. She grabbed her cane in her left hand to support the side that had always been her weakest. "So we're clear on why I'm not interested in Martin?"

"Yes."

"Good. Besides, he's got a savior complex."

"Savior complex? Is that a thing?"

"He wants to ride in on his white horse." Allie crinkled her nose. "And save the sick damsel in distress."

"Eww. Are you serious? Did he really say that?"

"In so many words." Allie glanced toward the ceiling, trying to remember their last conversation. "He said he wants to help me and take care of me. Like that would make me agree to a date."

"Has he ever met you?" Fran said, her eyes wide. "You're the most stubborn, pigheaded person I know."

Allie put her hand against her chest. "Aw, thanks. That warms my heart."

Fran laughed. "You know what I mean. I certainly don't see you playing the role of the damsel."

"Exactly. This disease might make me rely on others more than I'd care to, but I'm not looking for anyone to rescue me."

"No doubt. Although, you could get a little better at letting people help you."

Allie waved the back of her hand toward Fran. "Pshaw. I'm letting you drive me home, aren't I?"

"My mistake." Fran wrapped her in another hug. "You've been reformed."

Chapter Four

Days until eruption: 58
Friday, March 21, 1980
Menlo Park, California
Cano's home

Cano fastened the latch on her suitcase and pulled it off her bed. She dumped it on the floor next to her black leather jacket and helmet. Why did packing always seem so monumental when it only took her a half hour? It was simple when most of her wardrobe consisted of a pair of jeans and a T-shirt. She'd gotten adventuresome lately and bought red, blue, and green tees to go with her black and white ones.

She'd packed a few pairs of black slacks, her new parachute pants, some button-down shirts, and a sweater in case she needed to attend a professional meeting. Never mind the shirts were Allie's favorites.

She glanced at the clock over her dresser. *Perfect.* Just enough time to heat up dinner before she watched *The Facts of Life.* She wandered into the kitchen and pulled open the cupboard next to the stove. The cans were neatly lined up. She chuckled. Johnny would never believe it, gauging by her desk. She hated for her cans to be out of line or mixed. Soups should be with soups. Stew with stew. Pasta with pasta. It was a simple formula. A can of ravioli caught her eye. She opened it and dumped it into a pan.

She found a lone beer in the back of her refrigerator. Hard telling how long it had been there, but she needed it tonight. She pulled off the tab and took a big gulp. After two more swigs, she let her head fall back against the cabinet door. Butterflies danced in her stomach. Soon she'd be in the presence of the two greatest loves of her life: Mount St. Helens and Allie. Her chest clenched. Which one would burn her the worst?

Sizzling from the stove pulled her from her thoughts. The ravioli had started to burn. That was what happened when she cooked everything on high. She tried to scrape the ones stuck to the bottom of the pan loose without ripping them open.

With a flick of her wrist, she cut the flame and pulled the pan off the stove. She poured the contents into her awaiting bowl. Two of the ravioli were torn open and beyond repair, so she tossed them into the garbage can. *Shit.* Some of the ravioli guts from the damaged ones had gotten on the others. She carefully wiped them off with a paper towel.

With her beer in one hand and ravioli in the other, she went to the living room. She set the bowl on the rickety TV tray and walked to her television. Once she turned it on, she waited for the picture to slowly fill the screen. Before the picture had completely materialized, she turned the dial to NBC before she sat. The familiar strains of *The Facts of Life* theme song made her bob her shoulders. She loved the snappy tune.

She plucked the *TV Guide* off the end table. *Pathetic.* She'd memorized her entire TV schedule for each day of the week, only needing the guide to tell her about the episode. *Dieting. Should be a good one.* Hopefully, Blair doesn't think she needs to diet.

But when will Blair decide she needs to find herself a good woman? Cano laughed at her own joke, nearly spitting out the ravioli in her mouth. Yep, she'd sunk to a new low. Here Johnny thought she was out on the town picking up the ladies, while all along, she was immersed in her television.

Beyond pathetic. She tossed the *TV Guide* across the room. Now she could add lack of maturity to her growing list of flaws. Her life had been settled, but this trip threatened to turn it upside down.

During the commercials, she glanced around her sparse surroundings. Other than the Dali replica on the wall, there were no other personal effects, not even a stray knickknack. If someone broke in, they might assume it was abandoned. How had her life become this? When everyone at work thought she was living large and boogieing down night after night, she sat alone in her living room. She took a swig of her beer, trying to recall the last time she'd stepped foot into a discotheque.

The memory flashed, but she was saved when the commercials ended. It was for the better. She couldn't let old memories invade her thoughts, or it could send her into another spiral.

Cano had just finished cleaning up her dishes when the phone rang. She stared at it for a second. Nobody ever called her. Maybe she should just ignore it, but it might be Gabby Grant or Spenser calling her about Monday.

"Hello," she said into the receiver.

"Are you going to miss me?" Johnny's cheerful voice said on the other end of the phone.

With that line, she realized he was probably her only friend, if she could call him that. "Not as much as you'll miss me," she answered, putting as much bravado in her voice as possible.

He laughed. "I might just clean your desk while you're gone."

"You do, and I'll haunt your ass."

"Whoa. You planning on sacrificing yourself to the volcano gods? You know you have to be dead to haunt someone, don't you?"

"I was thinking more like astral projection."

"Astral projection, I'm good with that. Better than letting Mount St. Helens swallow you up."

"Do you really think my baby is going to erupt?" Cano put the receiver under her chin and backed up to the kitchen counter. With both hands on the surface, she hoisted herself up and let her legs dangle.

"I can't say, but that's why I'm calling." He paused. "Um, you rushed out of here so quickly that I didn't have the chance to tell you to be safe."

Cano put her hand against her chest. How sweet, he was concerned for her, but she couldn't let him know she was touched. "Rosaria put you up to calling me, didn't she?"

He laughed. "You know you're impossible. Why can't you let someone show you they care about you without you becoming a smartass?"

Good question. "Part of my charm."

"You don't fool me," Johnny said, his voice serious. "Something happened at U-Dub. Don't think I don't notice your reaction every time someone mentions your professor—Allie."

Damn it. Why did he have to be so astute? Probably raising teenagers helped him in that department. She sighed. She'd never talked to anyone about her time with Allie, and at times, she wished she could.

"I heard that sigh," Johnny said. "Tell me what's going on, Cano."

Maybe she could tell him a little. "Yeah. Allie and I had a relationship. It didn't work out." *There!* She'd opened up.

A few seconds passed before Johnny said, "That's it?"

"What else do you want?"

"Maybe a little backstory."

"Sure." Cano tried to keep the defensiveness from her voice. "We had a fling. She's ten years older than me, and she ended up with MS. Not exactly conducive to a long-term relationship. So I left Seattle and ended up here."

"You did not just say that." Johnny's voice was harsh. "*Not exactly conducive to a long-term relationship*. That's cold."

Cano's chest tightened. Cold was the only way she knew how to handle her feelings about Allie. Act like it didn't matter. Pretend that leaving Seattle wasn't the biggest regret of her life. She couldn't let Johnny know, or he would want her to talk about it. *Nope.* Talking about it was something she wouldn't do.

She cleared her throat. "What happened in Seattle is in the past. I'm perfectly happy here." She glanced around her stark kitchen as she said it. Was she lying to him? Not intentionally. She'd been numb for so long, it felt almost like happiness, or at least it was the absence of pain. Same thing, *right?*

"Why do I feel like there's so much more

you're not saying?" After several beats, without her responding, he said, "Are you still there?"

"Yeah, I'm here. You think too much. I'm good. My life is good. And I'm going to Washington to see my volcano."

He sighed into the phone. "Fine. If that's the way you want to play it, then okay. But know your nonchalant act isn't working with me. You can't keep running away and hiding from the things that cause you pain. Sometimes, you have to face your demons."

What the hell? "You know me, I'm living the dream. Chasing the ladies. You're just jealous because you're an old married man."

"I've let you think that I believe it, but I never have." His voice was filled with sadness. "Maybe I haven't been fair to you." He cleared his throat. "Rosaria's been at me for a long time to say something. I guess the time wasn't right until now."

"Wow. That's a lot to unload on me right before I leave." She'd balled her hand into a fist, and her fingernails dug into her hand. "I don't run away from shit, and there's nothing I need to face in Seattle. So whoever's been spreading rumors about me needs to knock it off. Next time you hear it, tell them to cut the crap."

"I didn't mean to make you mad."

She bit her lower lip. Hard. The pain shut down the angry thoughts rushing through her mind. He meant well, so she shouldn't unload on him. "I know you weren't trying to cause harm. I suppose I'm edgy about the trip and being cooped up with Gabby Grant for fifteen hours."

"You can make it in fourteen if you drive fast," he said. She suspected he was trying to lighten the mood to offset the tension sizzling through the phone lines.

"I plan on feigning sleep most of the way."

"You could tell him you have narcolepsy."

"Brilliant." She smiled now they were on safer ground. "That's why I like you."

"Wow. I'll take it. That might be the most sentimental thing you've ever said to me."

"Shut up, or I'll take it back."

He chuckled. "I better leave you on a positive note. The kids were wanting to talk to the old man. Won't be long before they fly the coop, so I better get to it."

"Thanks for calling. I really do appreciate it." And she meant it. Nobody else cared enough to send her off.

"I'll miss your sloppy ways. And I'm going to say this one last time and then shut up. Whatever created such a tight grip on your heart, I hope you find some answers on your trip."

Hmph. "The only answer I need to figure out is whether my girl is going to blow." Her stomach roiled. What a loaded comment. Which girl was she referring to?

"Okay," he said softly. "Just be safe and call me every now and then."

"Will do. And say hi to Rosaria and the kids."

"Okay. Goodbye, Cano."

"Bye."

The line went dead, but she sat on the counter staring at the receiver for several minutes. What the hell had that been about? She never suspected that Johnny didn't buy the persona she'd created. *How many others hadn't, either?*

Chapter Five

Days until eruption: 58
Friday, March 21, 1980
Seattle, Washington
Allie's home

Goose bumps covered Allie's entire body as the cold water cascaded over her. She scrubbed her hair, deciding to forgo rinse and repeat. In the past, she loved scalding hot showers, but MS had taken that away from her, along with so many other things.

Stop. Feeling sorry for herself was unlike her, but every now and then, she slipped. Tonight, her insides were as cold as the outside. She needed to get a grip. One bad day didn't have to send her into a downward spiral.

She turned off the water and held the grab bar as she stepped out of the walk-in shower. It was one of the many home modifications that allowed her to live independently. She lowered herself onto the raised toilet to dry herself.

Even though her body didn't work as well as she wanted it to, she'd remained trim and fit. Most days, nobody would guess the damage inside. When she was able, she exercised regularly, hoping to stave off the disease. The fight could be tiring, but normally, she waged the battle. Tonight was one of the rare instances when her fight had left her.

She ran the towel over her damp hair. Blow drying it sounded like too much work, so she rubbed harder. Likely, it would be uncontrollable in the morning if she left it wet, but she didn't care. She didn't plan on leaving the house this weekend unless something significant changed. After the earthquake on Thursday, it had been quiet today. A team would monitor the seismic activity over the weekend and promised to keep her in the loop.

Once dressed, she used her cane to rise from the toilet seat. She finished pulling her pants up and threw her towel into the hamper. The hallway in the ranch-style house was designed in a circular path. It allowed her to get to any room quicker. Her parents had thought of everything.

She stopped at the hall closet and put her hand on the doorknob. For several seconds, she stood while an internal battle raged. She'd not opened it for a long time. She glared at the door as if it were the closet's fault.

No, not today. She pounded the tip of her cane on the wooden floor and continued walking slowly toward the kitchen. The wheelchair remained behind the closed door.

The savory scent of tater tot casserole filled the kitchen. Fran had insisted on throwing it together when she and Ben brought Allie home. And she literally had. Allie had never known anyone to be able to put a meal together as quick as Fran could. She had it prepared, in the oven, and was out the door in less than half an hour.

The timer said there was still ten more minutes, although the heavenly smells told her stomach she should pull it out now. Instead, she eyed the bottles of wine in her wine rack. A nice glass of merlot would hit the spot, but she never drank when she suffered a setback. Wine was yet another thing MS had stolen from her.

The weekend would drag on forever if she stayed in this mindset. She needed to find something to perk her up. Maybe a good book. She left the kitchen and wandered to her bookshelf in the living room. A dog-eared copy of *Rubyfruit Jungle* caught her eye, so she snatched it from the shelf. Was she up for it? Her gaze traveled the rest of the bookshelf before landing on the spy thriller she'd recently bought. *The Bourne Identity.* Probably a better choice than reading about lesbians.

She carried both books to the end table and set them next to the *TV Guide.* She could never remember what was on. Most times, she preferred reading, but a little noise might do her good. She flipped the pages to Friday night and let her finger trail down the listings.

The Facts of Life. It was settled. She loved that show but never remembered what day it was on. She read the episode description. *Interesting.* She'd watch it before she settled in to read.

Allie's meal was finished and the TV show over. She'd picked up *Rubyfruit Jungle* but had only gotten a few chapters in before she set it down. *Nope.* Reading about lesbians only brought Nova to mind.

She put both hands against her forehead and covered her eyes with her palms. With her thumbs, she massaged her temples. Maybe she just needed to go to bed. Tomorrow would be a better day.

She strained to get off the couch, but with one final push, she was able to stand. It looked like she'd be using her armchair this weekend. The last thing she wanted was to call Fran because she got beached on the sofa. She considered carrying her book when she took her dishes to the kitchen to save a trip, but she thought better of it. Her cane would be her friend this weekend.

Once settled in bed, she wondered how long she'd be able to stay awake to read. She'd put *Rubyfruit Jungle* back on the shelf and cracked open her spy thriller. Surely, nothing in it would remind her of Nova.

She sighed, dropped the book on her chest, and her first meeting with Nova flooded her thoughts.

March 13, 1974
University of Washington
Department of Geological Sciences

Allie splashed water on her face and stared into the mirror. She could do this. It was her big shot, so she couldn't let nerves get in the way. She'd been teaching undergrads at the University of Washington for the past two years and had been itching to teach a graduate-level course.

Granted, her big break came at the expense of Dr. Foreman's burst appendix, but that meant she'd only have a few classes to prove herself. *Metamorphic Processes.* She'd spent the entire weekend preparing for the class and was as ready as she could be.

She gazed at her youthful face in the mirror. Would the older students take her seriously? As a petite blond woman, she'd battled it her whole life, so this shouldn't be anything new. She didn't consider herself pretty, but others had, which made it even more difficult to be respected in a predominately male profession. She just needed to walk into the classroom with confidence.

Tying up the staff bathroom any longer wouldn't endear her to the rest of the faculty. She took one more glance at herself in the mirror and ran her hands down the length of her dress. She'd had multiple compliments on it. *Crap.* She wasn't looking for compliments. All she wanted was for her lecture to be well received. Maybe she'd chosen wrong. She loved her turquoise dress, but maybe it was too bright. Should she have chosen one that the hemline was below the knee, not above?

Stop. She doubted if any of her male colleagues would have locked themselves in the bathroom and fretted about how they were dressed. How counterproductive. Her thoughts should be focused on her lecture material. Abruptly, she turned from the mirror and pushed open the door. *Enough.* She had a class to teach.

When she entered the classroom, she scanned the faces of the ten students, all male but two. It was much different than her undergrad classes that often numbered more than a hundred. Strangely, the smaller group made her more nervous. In a large class, it was easy to find a few engaged students and play to them. With only ten, the odds were less that she'd find those connections.

All attention was on her, so she confidently

strode to the front of the classroom and placed her notes on the lectern. Dr. Foreman had insisted she take attendance, which was something she never did in her classes. At least it would give her a way to break the ice. A chill that seemed to be getting colder each moment she fumbled with her notes.

"Good afternoon," Allie said to the faces that stared back at her but didn't return her greeting. "As you have probably heard, Dr. Foreman will be unable to teach for the next few weeks, and I've been asked to step in. I'm Dr. Albright. Allison Albright, but I prefer Allie."

At least the students held a hint of interest in their eyes, unlike many of the undergrads. "Dr. Foreman has asked that I take attendance. When I call your name, I'd like you to tell me a little about yourself."

She rattled off the first few names without incident. The students seemed engaged and readily shared their career aspirations. *Good.* She moved to the next name.

"Nova Kane," she said. As soon as the words were out of her mouth, she frowned. *Shit.* Had Dr. Foreman pulled a prank on her? She'd never seen any evidence that he had a sense of humor, so this surprised her. She began to move on when a voice interrupted her.

"The name's Cano." A dark-haired woman gazed at her with soft hazel eyes. She wore a leather jacket that hung open to reveal a white T-shirt. *Tough girl* was the first thought that came to Allie's mind. A young woman used to having to prove herself in a man's world.

Allie wavered on how to respond. She decided

on, "Thank you, Ms. Kane, please tell me a little about yourself."

The time flew, and Allie felt it had gone well, except for Nova "Cano" Kane, who didn't speak the rest of the class period. She'd not exactly glared at Allie, but her intense gaze tracked Allie as she moved around the room.

After she finished her lecture, she said, "Ms. Kane, would you please see me after class? The rest of you are dismissed. Unless you want me to keep you for the last five minutes."

The students shot out of their seats in answer.

"Don't forget to read chapter eighteen for next week," she called to their retreating backs.

Nova took her time gathering her notebook and pen. Allie suspected it was her way of showing she was in control of the meeting. When she finally did rise, Allie's eyes widened. Sitting, Allie hadn't been able to see how tall Nova was. She must be at least five-eight, six inches taller than Allie. Nova sauntered to the front of the room.

"You wanted to see me?" Nova said with a cocky smile. "Did I do something wrong, Teach?"

Allie's back stiffened. What an arrogant piece of work. But she couldn't let a student get under her skin if she wanted to prove her worth to the department. "I was about to ask you the same question. You didn't seem as if you wanted to participate in class. I wanted to find out if there was something wrong."

"Yeah." Cano locked gazes with Allie. "I don't have much to say to someone who insists on calling me by the wrong name."

"I see." Allie pursed her lips. "Nova is such a beautiful name, though."

"Not if your last name's Kane."

Allie couldn't deny that logic. "Nova Kane *is* a unique name. How did your parents come up with it?"

Without missing a beat, Nova said, "Too much bootlegged booze. Prohibition didn't stop them. I suspect they fried their brains out, or they were drunk when they named me."

Allie narrowed her eyes and did a round of quick calculations in her mind. "Nice try. Unless you're a lot older than you look or your parents were drinking when they were children, the math doesn't work."

Nova smirked. "Damn. I've used that line on a lot of people, but you're the only one who's figured it out. I've gotten a few puzzled stares, but then they roll with it."

"I'm not as naïve as I look."

Nova let her gaze trail up and down Allie's body before it settled on Allie's face. "Good to know."

Allie hoped the heat rising in her cheeks didn't show on her face. She needed to get a handle on this conversation. "So how did you get your name?"

A shadow crossed Nova's face but disappeared as quickly as it came. She put on an easy grin and shrugged. "My parents were assholes. They thought it would be cute."

"At least they didn't name you Candy," Allie said, hoping to lighten the mood.

"That's my sister."

Allie's eyes widened. "Seriously?"

Nova burst out laughing. "I had you going." Her sullen face transformed. For the first time, Allie noticed how attractive Nova was. Despite her tough persona, her features were soft. Her eyelashes unusually long and thick, and her perfect unblemished skin had a hint of color despite the season. It was her crooked smile that won the day.

Allie returned the smile. "You got me."

"They learned their lesson after they had me."

"And what lesson might that be?"

"Don't give your kid a messed-up name if you don't want to spend a bunch of time in the principal's office. People picked on me, and I fought back." Nova flashed a mischievous smile. "They learned. My baby brother's name is Robert."

Underneath the swagger and leather, Allie sensed there was a wounded child still fighting the battles from her youth. Likely, Nova's bravado was an act to keep people at bay. "So how did you get the name Cano?"

"My grandma." A genuine smile lit Nova's face. "She claimed I'm stubborn, so the only way to stop the fighting was to find me a new name. Most people think it's just a play on my last name, but it's not. As a kid, I was fascinated by volcanoes." She winked. "Obviously, I still am. Anyway, Grandma started calling me Cano, and it stuck."

Allie smiled, warmed by the tough girl. "So you spell it with a C, rather than a K?"

"Yep. C-A-N-O."

"I still think Nova is a very pretty name."

"I'll make you a deal." Nova took a step toward her. "You can call me Nova if you let me take you out for a cup of coffee."

Allie took a step back. Was Nova hitting on her? *Shit.* Her first taste of teaching a higher-level class, and it was already spinning out of control. She needed to establish her role quickly before things spiraled. "I'm your professor, so that's out of the question."

"I won't tell if you won't." Nova wriggled her eyebrows.

"Absolutely not," Allie said. "How about we compromise? I'll call you Ms. Kane."

"You're only filling in, so I'll just bide my time until Foreman returns." She smirked again. "In the meantime, to show that I'm negotiating in good faith, I'm okay with *you* calling me Nova." Without another word, Nova turned and walked toward the exit.

Allie watched her strut from the room, her gaze never leaving Nova's perfect ass. *Ugh.*

Chapter Six

Days until eruption: 55
Monday, March 24, 1980
Seattle, Washington
Holiday Inn

Cano dropped her suitcase on the floor and flopped onto the hotel bed. Thirteen hours in the car with Gabby Grant had nearly done her in. The man literally never shut up. Even when she turned on the radio, he just talked over it.

She rubbed her temples, hoping to rid herself of the headache building behind her eyes. The nondescript hotel room looked like any other hotel room she'd ever stayed. *Home sweet home.* She chuckled. It actually had more decoration and warmth than her own house. How sad was that?

Reluctantly, she sat up. She'd promised to call Johnny when she got in, and it was already after nine p.m. She yawned. If she didn't make the call soon, sleep would win out. Besides, she wanted to know if there'd been any other earthquake activity while she was on the road.

She picked up the receiver and dialed.

Johnny picked up on the first ring. "Hello."

"Sitting on top of the phone?" Cano asked.

"Of course. Been waiting on your call." She could hear the smile in his voice.

"Tell me what my baby has been up to today while I was in hell."

"Come on. Grant's not that bad."

"I know every fucking spelling word his precious GiGi spelled in her winning bid at the eighth-grade spelling bee. Every damned one," she said for emphasis.

Johnny groaned. "How many words did she have to spell for the win?"

"Eight thousand. At least it seemed like that many. The man droned on and on and on. Do you know how to spell onomatopoeia?"

"Did you just swear at me?" Johnny laughed. "I don't even know what the hell it means."

"I do. At least I do now. It's the naming of a word based on the sound associated with it."

"Ouch. I'm a scientist not a linguist. I have no clue what that definition even means."

"Words like cuckoo and sizzle. The word sounds like the sound it describes."

"Ah, kinda like plop."

"Exactly," Cano said with enthusiasm and then groaned. "I need de-nerded. Now I'm talking about a spelling bee. Quick. Talk to me about science."

"Yeah, because that's so less nerdy."

She chuckled and flipped open her notepad. "According to what I got this morning before we left, Saturday had one moderate quake followed by a series of smaller ones. Have they confirmed whether those were aftershocks or separate quakes?"

"Yes. From what we're being told, they were separate."

"Then Sunday was four?"

"Nope, the latest information says six."

Cano scribbled out the four and wrote six next to

the date 3-23-1980. "Okay, so what happened today? I've not heard anything."

"Reports are that there were fourteen today."

Cano whistled. "My girl is heating up. Any other buzz?"

"People are starting to take notice. Several teams are either making their way there or in serious talks to send someone. Johnston is at U-Dub already. We let him know to expect you tomorrow."

Her pulse raced at the mention of U-Dub. She was strictly here for Mount St. Helens not Allie. "I have a funny feeling about this." Goose bumps rose on her arms. Could she trust her instincts, or was having Allie nearby causing her reaction?

"Never doubt your gut."

"I know. I just hope we don't end up with egg on our faces like we did with Baker."

"Just remember, better safe than sorry."

Cano fought the excitement churning inside of her. As a volcanologist, she lived to see an epic eruption, but then guilt gnawed at her. Her desire to see an eruption didn't justify the devastation and destruction that a volcano could cause.

"Fighting yourself?" Johnny asked, obviously sensing what her silence meant. "It's the curse all volcanologists have to wrestle with."

"Yeah." Cano sighed. "I have to keep in mind we want it to be like Mount Baker. No eruption, even though we thought there would be. Why can't the public and politicians understand it was good for us to be wrong? It would have been much worse if we were right, and nobody heeded our warnings." She shuddered at the thought.

"Laymen underestimate the power of nature.

Especially when it interferes with the almighty dollar."

Cano shook her head. "So true. Hopefully, we don't run into that here."

"Sure, you keep thinking that if it helps you sleep tonight."

"You're so supportive." Cano chuckled. "Speaking of sleep, I'm beat. I should get to bed."

"Sweet dreams of onomatopoeia and other spelling words dancing in your head."

"Stop! I'm hanging up on you now." Cano grinned.

"Goodbye," he said, still laughing on the other end.

She quickly stripped out of her clothes and sniffed them. Satisfied that they didn't stink, she folded them and put them into one of the drawers. She wanted to avoid the laundromat for as long as possible.

She pulled a pair of shorts and T-shirt out of her bag and took them to the bathroom. A shower would have to wait until morning. The pile of washcloths caught her eye. At least she could wash her face. She waited for the water to warm before she ran the cloth under the stream. As she lifted the fabric toward her face, the color on her left arm drew her gaze.

Her tattoo always made her smile. *Thank you, Janis Joplin.* As a kid, she'd wanted a tattoo like her uncle's, but her parents had told her that girls didn't get tattoos. Then in the early seventies, Joplin got one on her wrist to symbolize women's liberation. Her parents still hadn't approved when she'd showed up with her entire upper arm covered with an erupting volcano.

She paused and examined the orange and red

lava flowing down the sides of the rocky volcano. Eight years later, she still thought it was badass.

After finishing in the bathroom, she pulled the sheets back and collapsed onto the bed. Her limbs were heavy. Tomorrow would be a big day. She tried to keep her thoughts on Mount St. Helens, but they drifted to the tiny blond woman who stole her heart six years earlier.

March 13, 1974
University of Washington
Department of Geological Sciences

Cano slid into her seat near the back of the room. Metamorphic Processes wasn't one of her favorite classes, especially having to listen to Dr. Foreman drone on in his monotone voice. She needed to get to the library to finish up a paper that was due tomorrow, so she just wanted to get this over with.

She sighed. As much as she loved learning, she was ready to be done. Only two more months. *Graduation. Commencement.* What the hell did commencement mean anyway? She'd have to look it up. She pulled out her notebook and wrote it on the top corner of the page.

The geeky guy sitting next to her turned in his seat, and his eyes widened. When she turned to see what had caused the reaction, her eyes widened, too.

Wow! A tiny woman strode to the front of the classroom. She couldn't have been much over five feet, but her presence made her appear much taller. *And those legs.* Her snug blue dress hit her above the knee, showing off her shapely calves. Who was this angel with long blond hair and dark brown eyes?

She soon found out, as Dr. Allison "Allie" Albright introduced herself to the class. Dr. Foreman's appendicitis was Cano's gain. She just might enjoy Metamorphic Processes after all.

After a rocky start, with Dr. Albright calling her Nova and then Ms. Kane, Cano pushed it aside and focused on her new instructor. Not only was she easy on the eyes, but she was also bright and made the subject interesting.

Normally, Cano participated in class, but she found herself mesmerized by Dr. Albright. There was an eloquence, a grace, to the small woman. Cano had started to answer one of Dr. Albright's questions but found she was tongue tied, so she gave up trying. Instead, she sat back and feasted on the beautiful woman who animatedly talked about the earth's crust.

At the end of class, Cano's heart raced when Dr. Albright asked her to stay after. Cano was a master of nonchalance, so she took her time making her way to the front of the classroom. She fought the urge to wipe her sweaty palms on her pants leg. Dr. Albright didn't need to know the effect she was having on Cano.

The conversation was a blur. Not only was Dr. Albright beautiful, but the scent of sandalwood and lavender permeated the air. Cano's senses were on overload just from the sight and smell of Dr. Albright. What would she taste like? Cano's face heated. *Stop.* She didn't want to think about how she would taste or how her smooth skin would feel under Cano's fingertips.

She needed to pull it together before she made an ass of herself, so she put on her best cocky smirk.

Turn the tables on Dr. Albright. The conversation grew easier as she talked about her name.

With her confidence somewhat restored, Cano stepped forward and locked gazes with her professor. "I'll make you a deal. You can call me Nova if you let me take you out for a cup of coffee." Where the hell did that come from? Did she just hit on her professor? *Damn it.* What was she thinking?

The shock on Dr. Albright's face matched Cano's own shock. Hitting on a professor was daring, even for her. Dr. Albright recovered quickly and politely rebuffed Cano. The right thing would have been to quietly slink away, but staring into Dr. Albright's intelligent eyes emboldened Cano.

Cano made her interest clear before she abruptly turned away. She wanted to turn around to see if Dr. Albright continued to stare, but she didn't look back.

Her heart raced. What in the hell just got into her? As soon as she cleared the door, she swiped her sweaty palm down her pants leg.

Chapter Seven

Days until eruption: 54
Tuesday, March 25, 1980 (Morning)
Seattle, Washington
University of Washington
Department of Geological Sciences

Allie frowned as she pulled her car to a stop. She hated having to use the handicap parking, especially when she was feeling better. The extended weekend had been just what she needed. Despite the continued seismic activity from Mount St. Helens, she'd listened to Fran and stayed home an extra day. Something told her Mount St. Helens would prove to be a marathon not a sprint, so taking care of herself would pay off in the long run.

She considered moving her car into a regular parking space; instead, she cut the engine. Now wasn't the time to be stubborn. Today would likely be a long one, so being close to the building when she left tonight would be welcome.

All weekend, she'd been able to keep her emotions in check, but now her chest ached. There was no guarantee that Nova would be here; besides, her focus needed to be on geology not biology.

She took a deep breath before she stepped from the car. When the wind hit her, she pulled her jacket closed. It was beginning to warm, but there was still a nip in the air. She'd become more aware of temperatures since her diagnosis. Both hot and cold seemed to wreak havoc with her mobility. Chilly days sparked more muscle spasms.

She'd just reached the door when the rumble of an engine caught her attention. *Motorcycle?* Involuntarily, her shoulders stiffened. She fought her desire to turn and look. What if it was Nova? She slipped inside the building and peered out through the glass, hoping she was obscured from the outside.

When the bright orange motorcycle with a yellow stripe roared past, her heartbeat quickened. The distinct look of the three tailpipes flaring down the side and sweeping up across the tire caused her breath to catch. No doubt, it was a 1973 Triumph Hurricane, just like Nova rode.

Stupid. That didn't mean it was her. Many people owned a Hurricane, but the rider did have a similar build to Nova's. She shook her head. This craziness needed to stop, or she would suffer a serious setback. If Nova showed up, they'd have to behave professionally. She stood taller and straightened her jacket before turning from the door.

When she arrived in the basement, the volume in the room overpowered her. It was more like a frat party than a seismologist's lab. She half expected to see a keg rolled out.

"Would someone get that damned phone?" someone called out.

It was as if the phones were playing a symphony with the sound coming from multiple directions at once. *What the hell?* She'd never heard anything like this in their quiet little lab.

She glanced around the room, looking for a

place to escape the frenzy. Fran waved at her from across the expanse of flurried activity.

Allie waved back and made her way toward Fran. She was stopped several times by one of her team members who excitedly shared the details of the latest seismic activity. A cluster of her colleagues sat bent over their notepads, frantically scribbling calculations. Allie wanted to join them, but she needed to make the rounds before she could sit down. Most of the team had spent a better part of their weekend here, so she owed it to them to listen to their excited theories.

Twenty minutes later, she finally made it to Fran, who stood leaning against the wall in a pose reminiscent of a fashion model not a department secretary.

"They drug you down here, too?" Allie asked Fran.

Fran smiled and shook her head. "No. I brought some coffee and bagels down to feed the hungry masses. I hung around, figuring you'd be here soon. I'm hiding over here, so they don't try to make me answer the phones."

As if on cue, several phones started ringing again.

"What the hell's going on?" Allie asked.

"Reporters. Looking for the next big quote. The dean's been down here three times already, reminding everyone not to say anything stupid to the press."

Allie's eyes widened. "He said that?"

"I'm paraphrasing."

Allie grinned. "In other words, he reminded everyone to choose their words wisely should they be asked for a statement, so as not to cause undue panic."

"You should be the dean. That's almost word for

word. But you know someone's gonna say something outlandish or at least half-baked."

"Inevitably, someone will say something off script. I swear, one day, the man's head is going to explode." Allie pointed over her shoulder. "Sorry I kept getting waylaid."

Allie stifled a chuckle as Fran tried to discreetly study her. If anyone else had looked at her like that, she'd have taken their head off. Fran got a pass. "Would you stop checking me out?" Allie wriggled her eyebrows. "People will start to talk."

Fran's eyes widened before a smile lit her face. She flicked her wrist at Allie. "You're obviously feeling better."

"Yes, like I told you the half-dozen times you called this weekend."

Fran gave a quick shake of her head and glowered. "Surely, it wasn't that many times."

Allie shrugged. "Surely."

"But look at you." Fran put her hands on Allie's shoulders, held her at arm's length, and studied her. "You finally decided to wear your power suit. Any particular reason?"

Allie brought her arm across her midsection and grasped her other arm just above the elbow. Of course, Fran would see through her. She'd bought the pinstriped suit on one of their shopping trips over a year ago, but she'd yet to wear it. Allie decided to ignore the question and focus on her job. "From the sounds of it, the department will fill up before too long. A couple of the guys said that the USGS is sending teams from all over."

"Any specific USGS personnel you're thinking of? You know that outfit just might turn a few heads."

Allie pulled harder on her left arm, drawing her shoulders in tighter.

"Okay, okay. Stop trying to cover yourself up. I'll quit talking about Cano." Fran's eyes held concern. "Looks like the long weekend did you good."

"It did." The tension in Allie's shoulders released. Her health was a much safer topic. "I took it easy. Read the new Robert Ludlum novel. *The Bourne Identity.*"

Chapter Eight

Days until eruption: 54
Tuesday, March 25, 1980
Seattle, Washington
University of Washington
Department of Geological Sciences

Cano sped through the parking lot and slid into an empty spot. Her heart raced. The blond woman walked into the building. *No.* She'd been jumping at shadows, or more accurately, petite blondes since she'd left the motel. It was the third woman this morning who had made her heart skip a beat. She'd drive herself crazy if she kept this up.

Besides, the woman moved much too briskly. By now, Allie was likely in a wheelchair. It was a little over a year ago Cano had heard that Allie had won an award from U-Dub, which meant she was still on the faculty. Cano hadn't stuck around to hear the details, though. It was too painful. It could have been a lifetime achievement award for all she knew. Maybe Allie's MS had forced her into retirement.

Cano's chest tightened with guilt, which always happened whenever she thought too much about Allie and her condition. No matter how many times she tried to reason it away and accept it wasn't her fault, remorse clawed at her.

She yanked off her helmet and bent down so she

could check out her hair in the tiny rearview mirror attached to the bike's handlebar. A few errant strands stood up on top of her head. She put her fingers in her mouth, wetting them before she pushed the unruly hairs back into place. So this was what it had come to? Her standing in the middle of a parking lot primping, just in case she ran into Allie.

Damn it. Mount St. Helens was the reason she was here. The only reason. She looped the chinstrap from her helmet over the handlebars and left it hanging. Standing upright with her shoulders squared, she breathed in deeply and let the fresh air enter her lungs. Before she made her way across the parking lot, she pulled the zipper of her leather jacket down. As she walked, her familiar strut came back. She could do this.

Nostalgia hit her when she entered the building. Always aware of the energy surrounding her, Cano immediately felt the electric force radiating throughout the building. More people than she'd remembered during her time here scurried through the corridors. Had something else occurred with the volcano? She slowed her walk and listened in on the conversations around her.

Instead of going straight to the basement where she suspected most of the action would be, she decided to walk the corridors. It was where she'd spent nearly eight years of her life. Where she'd grown up, fell in love, and had her heart broken. *Damn it.* She wasn't a college kid anymore. At thirty years old, she couldn't be getting all dewy-eyed just walking the halls, or this would be a long couple of weeks.

As soon as she entered the lab, she scanned her surroundings. Her gaze landed on a petite blond woman with her back turned. Cano's breath caught. Surely, it wasn't Allie. The short woman wore a pinstriped black business suit that hugged her small frame and curved out around her hips. Cano had always loved the feminine curve of Allie's body. The shoulder pads, which seemed to be the style, caused the woman's waist to look even smaller.

With her gaze locked on the blonde, Cano casually strode toward her. A couple of former classmates from her time at U-Dub greeted her. She said hello but kept moving. She had to know who the woman was. When she got within ten feet of the blonde, her gaze shifted to the woman standing in front of her. Cano's heart sank when Fran met her gaze. *Shit.* She couldn't hide now.

She heard the blond woman say, "So, I spent the weekend with Jason Bourne, and I loved it."

Cano's stomach lurched. She'd know that voice anywhere. She blinked back tears. The first words she heard from Allie's mouth in four years were about her lover Jason. *Great.* Maybe she could turn around and get the hell out of here.

"Well, look who's here," Fran said and glared at Cano.

Too late. Cano jutted out her chest and held her head up. She wouldn't let either of them see her sweat.

The words caught in Allie's throat. By the look on Fran's face, Allie knew exactly who stood behind her. Should she turn or wait? She searched Fran's face for an answer but only saw contempt in her expression. This could get ugly fast if she didn't get between the two.

Allie turned. Nova pulled up short, her eyes wide. Their gazes met. So many thoughts rushed through her head, she hoped none of them showed on her face. She should speak, but words escaped her.

Nova flashed her crooked smile and said, "Hello, Dr. Albright." She nodded toward Fran. "Fran."

Okay. That was how she was going to play it. "Hello, Ms. Kane." *Score.* Nova visibly winced. She held out her hand. "It's nice to see you again."

Nova froze for a beat, but then her hand shot out. "You as well."

Nova's larger hand engulfed hers. *Crap. Bad idea.* Why did she offer a handshake? The warmth from Nova's hand radiated through her body. She needed to let go, but she wanted to continue holding on.

Was Nova blushing? *No.* Probably windburn from riding her motorcycle in the still chilly weather of Seattle. And what was with her hair? Nova had always kept her dark hair short. It still was short on top, but it was long in the back. Allie couldn't help but stare at the fringe that curled up at her collar. *Interesting.* Allie wasn't sure what she thought of the strange new hairstyle.

Other than her hair, she looked almost the same. Still in her leather jacket, with a T-shirt underneath, rounded out by faded blue jeans. Always the rebel who dressed the part, regardless of where she was.

Fran stepped up when the two continued to stare. "Hello, Cano. Long time no see."

Allie realized she still held Nova's hand, so she released it as if she'd been holding a snake. Nova recoiled at Allie's reaction. *My god, we're too old for this.* She needed to get control of the conversation.

Before Allie could speak, Nova said, "So you

have a new beau, huh?"

What? Did Allie hear her right? Where would she have gotten the impression that Allie was seeing someone, especially a man?

"Jason?" Nova said and squinted. "The guy you were talking about when I walked up."

Allie laughed, but then bit her lip when she recognized the pain in Nova's eyes. Without thinking, she grabbed Nova's leather-clad arm. "No. We were talking about Jason Bourne."

"Is that his name?" The volume in Nova's voice rose, and she took a step backward, breaking contact with Allie.

Allie moved forward. "He's a character in the book I'm reading. A new one by Robert Ludlum. Jason Bourne. It's an action thriller. He's a spy. Well, not really a spy. He's, well, he's lost his memory." She needed to shut up, but instead, she continued. "And then he meets this woman...and well..."

"Do you think you might want to take a breath?" Fran said and moved up beside Allie. Fran's protective pose wasn't lost on her. She doubted that Nova missed it, either.

This whole meeting was getting more awkward by the minute, but Allie didn't want it to end, either. *Pathetic.* She couldn't let her emotions churn out of control like this, or her body would likely rebel.

Nova opened her mouth to speak, but a loud shout from the men gathered around the seismograph cut her off. *Saved by the bell?* Allie wasn't so sure, but whatever was going on needed immediate attention.

Their gazes met one last time before they turned toward the commotion. Did she detect sadness in Nova's eyes, or was it just wishful thinking?

Chapter Nine

Days until eruption: 54
Tuesday, March 25, 1980
Seattle, Washington
University of Washington
Department of Geological Sciences

Come check this out," one of the geologists sitting in front of the seismograph machine called out.

Cano watched as Allie walked away from her. Pain tore at her heart. She wanted to chase after Allie, but instead, she stood slack-jawed and said nothing. Sensing someone watching her, she turned and met Fran's gaze.

A look of compassion filled Fran's eyes, but when she caught Cano's gaze, the softness hardened. Fran turned away and followed Allie.

Cano's first instinct was to run. Get out of here. This was Allie's world not hers, and she didn't belong. The room full of monitoring equipment, charts, and various printouts strewn all over the tables used to be her home, but it wasn't anymore.

The conversations increased in volume. Something had them revved up. Cano slid closer to the group but avoided getting near Allie, which was easy with all the commotion. She stood off to one side but could still listen in on the exchange.

"Look at this reading." A man holding a long printout pointed at the squiggly on the paper. "The frequency and intensity of the earthquakes seem to be increasing."

"Has anyone done any calculations on these?" Allie asked as she bent over the man's shoulder.

Cano grinned. Just like Allie, taking charge. She stared at the confident, small woman, searching for any signs of the MS that had ravaged her body. Allie's mobility seemed much better than when Cano left nearly four years ago. *Remission?*

"We were just about to ask for volunteers to do that, Dr. Albright," the man said. "I knew you'd want to be part of it." He smiled up at her.

Allie put her hand on his shoulder. Cano winced, wishing Allie's hand was on hers. *Stop.* She was acting like a lovesick teenager not a respected geologist. She would never make it through the next couple of weeks if this was how she was going to feel. Her heart just might stop beating. More likely, it would erupt from her chest like the volcano she was here to study.

While lost in her thoughts, Cano missed the conversation between Allie and the seismograph operator. When she tuned back in, Allie handed a sheet of paper filled with handwritten notes to Fran.

"Can you get us copies of these? A lot," Allie said to Fran.

"I'm on it." Fran turned and marched toward the door.

Her platinum blond hair flew out behind her, looking more like she belonged in a shampoo commercial than the basement of the geophysics department. At least Cano would get a reprieve from her disapproving stare.

Cano eased her way toward the others now that Fran had left the room. She hoped to get a glance at the readings everyone was so interested in.

"We had fourteen quakes yesterday," the geologist said. "Something tells me we'll get more today."

"Wishful thinking or evidence-based?" the tall man standing next to Allie asked. He smiled down at her. "Allie, um, Dr. Albright prefers data over hunches."

Cano bristled. She didn't like the way he leered down at Allie or the familiar way he talked to her.

Allie backed up a step. She almost had to in order to meet his gaze. "No. Dr. Pappas, I appreciate hearing a scientist's visceral feelings. We can then test it against the data." After Allie delivered the line, she shot a glance in Cano's direction before she quickly looked away.

Dr. Pappas's cheeks reddened. "Of course."

Take that, Dr. Pompous. Mature. She'd have him in a headlock in a few minutes, giving him a noogie if she didn't get her emotions under control.

Allie had always respected Cano's gut feelings. Many scientists would have shamed her for her less-than-scientific methods, but Cano's sixth senses were rarely wrong. Now her senses told her that Dr. Pompous would love to get into Allie's pants. Her stomach lurched. Or had he already?

She needed to get fresh air. *Now!* She kept her gaze on the floor as she made her way toward the exit. Her cheeks burned, and bile rose in her throat. She pushed through the door and ran headlong into the person entering. "Shit. I'm so sorry," she muttered and looked up into Fran's confused eyes. *Great.*

"Whoa." Fran put her hand on Cano's shoulder

to steady her. "Are you okay? You don't look so good."

Cano shook her head. "I'll be fine. I just need to get the hell out of here." Cano trotted away, not caring she'd probably given away too much. She needed to escape more than she needed to appear cool.

Fran moved alongside Allie and bent down so her mouth was only inches from Allie's ear. "What the hell's going on?"

"Huh?" Allie looked up at Fran's concerned frown. Once she registered the emotion on Fran's face, she said, "Why don't you hand out the papers? We can talk about this in a minute." Allie motioned to the other side of the room. "Over there."

Fran nodded. "Hot off the presses." She held up the copies. "Get them while they last," she teased.

The scientists circled Fran like sharks. Fran made a point to hand one of the pages to Allie, knowing she wouldn't be able to reach the forms Fran held over her head.

Allie studied the data. The seismic activity was increasing, but what did it mean? The same had happened with Mount Baker, but it had turned out to be a PR nightmare. Would the same thing happen here?

Once they had data in hand, the geologists scattered to various tables around the room. Some chose to sit in groups, while others found a corner all to themselves. The volume in the room increased again, so Allie raised her voice and said, "Let's make sure we look at the data from all angles."

"Hear! Hear," someone called out.

The geologist manning the seismograph machine

said, “Are we thinking Mount Baker or Lassen Peak?”

“Good question,” Allie said. The last volcanic eruption in the continental United States had been at Lassen Peak in California in 1915. Would Mount St. Helens be the next? “That’s why we get paid to do what we do. The powers that be are going to want some answers.”

“And they’re not going to want a repeat of Baker,” Dr. Pappas said. “Right, Dr. Albright?”

She bit her lip. He was obviously still upset by her rebuke of him earlier. “Dr. Pappas is correct. Because of Mount Baker’s lack of eruption, we’ll likely be faced with an added level of skepticism and scrutiny from the bureaucrats and politicians, which means we have to do an even better job of parsing the data.” She waved her hand over her head. “I’ll shut up now, so we can get to work.”

Gazes dropped to the tables, and the only sounds in the room were the scratching of pencils and the needle scraping against the seismograph’s paper.

Dr. Pappas made a beeline toward her. “I’m sorry. I think we should talk,” he said.

Allie shook her head. “Not right now, Martin. We have calculations to do.” She nodded toward Fran, who stood against the far wall. “Plus, Fran informed me I have a pressing matter to attend to.”

“I hope everything is all right.” He gave her his best impish smile.

She wanted to vomit. The only person who could get away with a smile like that was Nova. She glanced around the room. Speaking of, where had she run off to? Allie had intentionally not looked in Nova’s direction in fear she’d be unable to intelligently form sentences. Now she’d lost sight of her. Allie’s gaze became more frantic searching for the familiar face.

"Are you okay?" Martin said. "Is it an episode?" He stuck out his elbow. "Here, take my arm, I can lead you to a table."

"I don't need to be led to a table." Allie tried to keep the impatience from her voice. "I need to talk to Fran. I'm fine."

He narrowed his eyes and tilted his head. He was a handsome man, but he did nothing for her. She wished he'd save his energy for someone who would appreciate his advances.

"Okay." He nodded slightly. "I'll be around if you need me."

"Thank you, but that's not necessary." She lifted her hand to pat his arm but thought better of it. Without saying anything more, she turned toward Fran.

Allie monitored her own walking. Her legs seemed to be moving well. So far, so good. The next few weeks would be a test of her resilience, so she needed to watch herself carefully. When she reached Fran, she knew her emotions had a grip on her since all she wanted was one of Fran's patented hugs. It might take away the horrible feelings swirling in her chest. Likely, those sensations had nothing to do with her MS.

Fran smiled and put her hand on Allie's shoulder. "Having a rough go at it?"

Damn it. Her eyes filled with tears. Obviously, she couldn't handle kindness right now. *Mount St. Helens. Mount St. Helens.* That would have to be her mantra if she wanted to get through this without bursting into tears.

Fran squeezed her shoulder but didn't pull her in

for a hug. She knew better than to do so in a room full of scientists who would discount her as an emotional female if they saw any sign of tears.

Allie blinked several times, and her eyes cleared. "Where's Nova?"

Fran shrugged. "I'm not sure. She shot out of here like something bit her in the ass."

"I see. Did she say anything to you?"

"Just I'm sorry."

Allie narrowed her eyes. "She apologized to you?"

Fran held up her hand. "No, no. I mean not that way. She ran into me coming through the door. She apologized for bumping into me."

"Oh." Allie heard the disappointment in her own voice. Had she wanted Nova to apologize to Fran? *Nonsense.* That wouldn't make sense.

"That's an interesting response." Fran put her hand on her hip and looked down at Allie. "Want to explain?"

Allie let out a sigh. "I'm not sure I can. Seeing her has brought up so much." Allie's hand trembled, so she slid it into her pants pocket. She didn't want Fran to see it.

"What needs to happen?"

Allie shrugged. "I wish I knew. Maybe I should go find her. Talk to her."

"And say what?" Fran's voice held an edge.

"I don't know." Allie snorted out a breath through her nose. "But we can't walk on eggshells all week or month or however long this is going to take."

"Dr. Albright," one of the scientists called out and waved his arm.

She looked up and met his gaze.

"When you have a minute, I'd like to show you something." His eyes sparkled as he held up the paper.

She smiled. "Be right there." She turned to Fran. "Duty calls. If I know Nova, she'll be back."

Dumbass. Cano had just made a fool of herself, running out of the basement like a frightened five-year-old. She needed to toughen up or go back home to Menlo Park. *No!* She wouldn't run. At least not this time.

She'd circled the campus a couple of times, walking fast to ensure her elevated heart rate had a physical reason, not just an emotional one. The crisp clean air filled her lungs and began to relax her. She slowed her pace, no longer afraid she might throw up.

Allie looked great. Beautiful. Cano knew she'd missed Allie, spent every day missing her, but she didn't realize quite how much until she laid eyes on her today.

It was obvious, though, that Allie had moved on. She was so calm, cool, and in charge, not a tongue-tied babbling idiot like Cano. In typical Allie fashion, she'd calmly taken charge, given instructions to her team, and had them working on the data, while Cano ran out of the room without making any contribution.

Funny. Cano was the cocky one, but it was Allie with ice water in her veins. She hadn't even seemed rattled to see Cano. If Allie could do it, surely, she could. Her resolve hardened. Mount St. Helens was her volcano, and she deserved to be here. Imagine if it blew, and she'd tucked her tail and scampered home. It would haunt her forever. One regret was enough, she wouldn't add another.

On her third pass around the campus, she slipped into the student union. Time to take charge of the situation and stop being afraid of Allie.

Allie bent over her notebook and studied the numbers. *Shit.* Angrily, she scrubbed at the page with her eraser. It was her job to proof out the data she'd been given, but her concentration was off. Maybe if Nova returned, she could focus again.

She put her hand over her eyes and rubbed. All she needed to do was center herself. With her hand still covering her eyes, she closed them. She drew in a deep breath and slowly blew it out. This technique had been a lifesaver when she struggled to accept that her limbs sometimes wouldn't cooperate with her. The next breath she held even longer, until she had to let it escape. One more, then she'd be ready to try again.

"Looks like you could use this," a familiar voice said.

Nova. Allie pulled her hand away from her face and looked up at Nova's soft eyes. "What could I use?"

Nova thrust out a cup of coffee. "Decaf, one sugar, one Sweet'n Low, and one creamer."

"You remembered." Allie took the coffee from Nova.

"Yep." Nova nodded. "Your tastes haven't changed, have they?"

Allie sensed the double meaning in the sentence. She met Nova's gaze and held it before she said, "Nope. I still like the same things."

"That's good to hear." Nova gave her a half smile, but her eyes still held pain. She nodded toward a man who'd just walked in. "Looks like Grant's here. He's the one they sent me with. We still need to catch up with Johnston to work out a game plan. So I better let you get back to your numbers."

"Thanks for the coffee." Allie smiled and held up the cup. "I found a place that sells the best coffee beans."

"Nearby?

"Downtown in Pike's Place Market."

"They only sell beans?" Nova took a sip of her coffee.

"Unfortunately. I keep telling the owner he needs to sell brewed coffee, too. So far, he hasn't listened."

"I'll have to check it out. What's the name of this place?"

"Starbucks."

Nova crinkled her nose. "Even if they have the best coffee in the world, that's a stupid name for a coffee joint. Nobody will ever remember it."

Allie flipped her hand at Nova. "I think it's catchy. Just wait. One day, it will be a household name."

"Sure. We'll see about that."

"Mark my words."

"Words marked." Nova smiled. "I better leave you to it."

"Thanks again for the coffee. I think we'll all need it before the week's over. I might even have to switch to caffeinated."

"No doubt." Nova turned, but she stopped and looked back over her shoulder. "Any chance we can catch up sometime while I'm here?"

Allie's heart raced. "I'd like that."

"Great," Nova said, her smile still guarded.

Chapter Ten

Days until eruption: 54
Tuesday, March 25, 1980 (Evening)
Seattle, Washington
University of Washington
Department of Geological Sciences

Allie sat in her office chair, happy to be away from the throngs of people gathered in the basement. As the day progressed, more people crammed into the basement, and it would probably only get worse, especially after the day's seismic activity.

A tap on her door brought her out of her thoughts. "Come in."

Fran poked her head inside. "It's just me."

Allie relaxed against the back of her chair. "Thank god. I'm about talked out."

"It was crazy down there, wasn't it? It's starting to thin out now. I think everyone has their marching orders. Have you decided what you're going to do?"

Allie shook her head. "I don't want to be stuck here in the basement. But I'm not sure how my body will hold up in the field. Damn it. I want to at least see her for myself." Allie dropped her head to her desk. "Argh."

Fran chuckled. "Aren't you the melodramatic one?"

"Seriously, Fran. There's something going on in that mountain. Twenty-two earthquakes in an eight-hour span. That's nearly three an hour. And five of them were within one hour."

"But what does it mean?" Fran frowned. "Is it gonna erupt like really soon?"

"That's the five million-dollar question. We thought it was imminent with Mount Baker, and then nothing really happened." Allie bit her bottom lip and shook her head. "She could heat up or cool down. A big blast is such a rare phenomenon that we don't have the data to be predictive." Allie pointed at the file on her desk. "At least with that activity, I hope someone will take us seriously."

"Sounds like someone already is. There's a big meeting in Vancouver tomorrow."

Allie nodded. "Yep. Decisions need to be made."

"Are you going?"

"Nah."

"They cut you out again?" Fran raised her voice. "When will the dickheads realize you're as talented as them? Probably more so, which is why they don't want you there."

"Down, girl." Allie made a calming gesture with her hand. "While I appreciate your loyalty, the dean invited me. I turned it down."

"Why?" Fran asked, wide-eyed. "I thought you wanted a seat at the table."

"I do. Just not with the politicians and bureaucrats."

"Could be more volatile than the volcano."

Allie smiled. "Exactly. That's why I said no. Plus, being packed into a room like sardines is not my idea of a good time."

"Who all's going to be there?"

"From what I've heard, Forest Service, Emergency Services, the Department of Natural Resources, and of course, the USGS. I'm sure there's more."

"Do you think Cano will go?"

"It's doubtful her boss will send her." Allie chuckled. "She'd tell the bureaucrats to go fuck themselves if she didn't like what they had to say."

Fran smiled. "True. But maybe they need someone to tell them that. It makes me nervous that a bunch of politicians might interfere in the decision, instead of leaving it to the experts."

"Me too. But unfortunately, that's the way it works."

"The dean had me book a block of rooms in Vancouver, so I'm assuming the action will be moved there."

"Likely, since Seattle's two and a half hours away from Mount St. Helens. Being in Vancouver will shave at least an hour off travel time."

Fran smiled. "Want to hear a good one?" Fran didn't wait for Allie to answer. "The dean apparently thinks I'm a dumbass. He reminded me three times that it was Vancouver, Washington, not Canada."

Allie groaned. "Doesn't he realize that you're the glue that holds us all together?"

"Apparently not." Fran shook her head. "Any thoughts of joining them in Vancouver?"

Allie grinned but didn't speak. She'd been sitting on her news and wanted to prolong it a little longer.

Fran tilted her head and narrowed her eyes. "I know that grin. What aren't you telling me?"

"Since you asked." Allie smiled broader. "Remember that weekend I took you and Ben to visit Silver Lake?"

"You shit." Fran propped her fist against her hip. "Your parents' little summer house in Toutle. It's a lot closer to Mount St. Helens than Vancouver is."

"About half the distance." Allie flashed a cheesy grin. "And I have the keys. I figure I can spend some time there on the weekends, so I don't have to drive back and forth."

"It's like right on top of Mount St Helens."

Allie rolled her eyes. "It's not right on top of it."

"Close enough."

"A little over half an hour."

"But still. Your parents are going to let you borrow it?"

"Yep."

"No way. Their precious Allie can't stay that close to a volcano."

Fran was right, her parents were protective, or more accurately, overprotective, which had only worsened with her MS diagnosis. "I had to do a little convincing." Allie held up her hand with her thumb and index finger a few centimeters apart.

Fran raised her eyebrows. "A little. How come I'm not buying that?"

"I might have mentioned that if I couldn't stay in Toutle, I'd probably have to stay in a tent around Spirit Lake."

"You're horrible."

Allie shrugged. "What can I say? I want to see it for myself, and I'm not sure all the traveling back and forth will be the best for me. The last thing I want is to be laid up while everything is going on."

"All's fair in love and volcanoes," Fran said with a smirk. "Speaking of...what about Cano?"

"I can't believe you just made the transition from love and volcanoes to Nova."

"Oops. Sorry." Fran gave her a sheepish smile. "But do you have any plans to see her? Talk to her?"

"Nothing concrete."

Fran winced. "I'd hoped you'd say no."

"She asked if we could get together. I didn't see a reason not to."

"I could give you a few."

Allie glared. "Don't. Besides, it might not happen. After she asked, things got crazy with all the seismic activity, so we didn't really have any opportunity to make plans." Allie shrugged, hoping she came off as nonchalant. "She'll probably forget anyway."

"Not likely," Fran said. "I saw the way she looked at you."

Chapter Eleven

Days until eruption: 53
Wednesday, March 26, 1980
Vancouver, Washington
U.S. Forest Service Building

Cano pulled off her leather jacket, something she didn't like to do in these settings. Her jacket gave her confidence, and without it, she felt exposed. But the heat in the room continued to climb, and sweat trickled down her back.

There were at least three dozen people crammed into the conference room. Just when she thought they couldn't possibly fit anyone else, another person pushed their way in. She couldn't complain, at least she had a seat at the table. Well, not quite the table but around the perimeter, which was good since she'd been given strict orders not to say a word.

The team from the USGS in Denver was taking the lead, but her boss wanted representation from their office in Menlo Park. With her reputation for being a rebel, it surprised her that he'd given her the nod. David Johnston, one of the rising stars in the Menlo Park USGS office and fellow U-Dub graduate, decided to stay back at the university, so the only other choice was Gabby Grant. Getting chosen over Grant wasn't a major endorsement, but if things continued to heat up, it would only be a matter of time before more of her colleagues poured in. Then she'd certainly not be allowed to attend.

She studied the others relegated to the edge of the room. Mostly reporters. The excitement that rippled through the press was electric. Cano sat back and listened to the chatter amongst the news hounds.

When the leader from the Forest Service stood, a hush fell over the room. Cano sat up straighter when the meeting was turned over to Donal Mullineaux from the Denver office of the USGS. He and his partner Dwight "Rocky" Crandell had been studying Mount St. Helens for two decades, and Cano had followed their work since she'd been introduced to it at the University of Washington.

She listened intently, a little starstruck, as he laid out the history of Mount St. Helens. The reporter next to her scribbled in his notebook as Mullineaux pointed out that in the past millennium, Mount St. Helens had erupted approximately every hundred years or so, and the last eruption was in 1857. She stifled a smile as the reporter counted on his fingers and looked up in horror when he'd finished the math.

When asked what type of damage could occur should the volcano blow, Mullineaux didn't hold back. Cano was so engrossed in his speech that she nearly missed the elbow poking her in the side.

She glared at the reporter when she turned to him.

Her withering gaze didn't deter him. "What did he just say? Pyrotechnics?"

She shook her head and whispered, "Pyroclastic."

He scribbled out the word he'd written and put his pen back on the paper. He lifted the pen and leaned over. "Can you spell that?"

She motioned for his pen and notebook, scrawled pyroclastic on the page, and handed it back to him.

"Did he say something about a hurricane?" he whispered.

She leaned in. "The force of a hurricane, except the atmosphere is full of red-hot rocks, gas, and ash."

"How did he say it can kill people?"

She sighed. She wanted to hear what Mullineaux had to say, but she knew the reporter wouldn't stop until he got his answers. "The hot dust can get in your lungs and cause suffocation, the hot cloud can cause burns, or the force of the blast could just rip you apart."

The color drained from the reporter's face, and he leaned against the back of his chair. Now maybe she could listen to Mullineaux in peace.

The tension in the room had increased in the short time she'd been talking to the reporter. Mullineaux laid out where the danger could lie. While the area was sparsely populated, the Spirit Lake resort was nearby, and the Weyerhaeuser Company was logging only a few miles from the volcano.

A red-faced man threw up his hands. "For Christ's sake, it hasn't blown in over a hundred years, don't you think you're overreacting?"

Cano marveled at how patiently Mullineaux fielded the angry questions and explained why they needed to shut down part of the mountain. She would have just told them to fuck off, which was why she wasn't allowed to sit at the table.

The longer the meeting went on, the factions became clearer, and the scientists seemed to be outnumbered. Cano bit down on her lip and put her hands under her legs. *Don't say anything. Don't say anything.*

"Do you know how much revenue will be lost?" one of the politicians asked. "We're heading into warmer weather and camping season. The resort owners will want to open their cabins. And surely, you don't expect the Weyerhaeusers to shut down their logging operation."

"Do you know how many jobs will be lost?" another man said and pounded his fist on the table. "My constituents won't stand for it, and neither will I."

Here goes. Money and politics were in full force, pushing the scientists' backs against the wall.

A reporter a couple of chairs down from her called out, "Are we going to have a repeat of Baker?"

There it was. Cano's jaw clenched. She'd been waiting for someone to drop Mount Baker into the conversation.

Another reporter pointed at the representative from the Forest Service and then looked down at his notes. "In 1975, wasn't it your department and the Geological Survey that nearly put all of the restaurants, resorts, and hotels out of business around Mount Baker?"

"We took the necessary safety precautions to keep the citizens of the area safe," the Forest Service representative answered.

"No, by opening the sluice gates on the dam, you fundamentally drained the lake." The reporter held his notebook up and read, "The Geological Survey issued this statement the following spring, *There was no clear evidence of a forthcoming eruption.* By then, the businesses were decimated because of your inability to do your jobs."

One of the men, who'd been getting louder as the meeting went on, crossed his arms over his chest and said, "You mean to tell us that we as a nation can send a man to the moon, but you can't predict if a volcano will erupt or not?"

Mullineaux attempted to explain that despite the advancements in science, they'd still not been able to pinpoint the exact conditions.

Cano's jaw clenched. Didn't these people understand that a volcano was a complex system that still needed years of research to come closer to unlocking the secrets?

Another man cut Mullineaux off to spout his own brand of nonsense about the incompetence of scientists.

Cano couldn't listen to this any longer. She got to her feet. "We're damned if we do and damned if we don't. Err on the side of caution, and nothing happens, we're called idiots, but God forbid if we don't take precautions and people die. Then we're vilified. I can't listen to this shit any longer."

She stomped toward the door and didn't look back.

Once outside, she breathed in the crisp air. More than anything, she wished she had her motorcycle. It had been too long of a drive from Seattle with the weather still not giving way to spring to ride here. If she'd been thinking, she would have pulled the trailer with her, but she'd left it back in Seattle.

She marched to the truck. No sense sticking around. Might as well get back to U-Dub. Likely, in the next couple of days, she and Grant would be reassigned to Vancouver, but for now, she wanted to get far away from the idiots at the meeting.

It frightened her that the politicians might prevent them from taking the safety precautions necessary, but she still had faith in Mullineaux and his team to get the bastards to do the right thing.

The truck roared to life, and she threw it into gear. The meeting played in her head as she pulled out of the parking lot. When would people understand that scientists didn't have crystal balls, and it wasn't as simple as adding two plus two and getting four? A volcanic eruption was complex.

As she drove and thought, the angrier she became. She needed a distraction, so she turned on the radio. *Big mistake.* Her chest tightened as the first refrain of *I'm Sorry* by John Denver filled the cab of the truck. It had been her wallowing anthem after she and Allie broke up. She must have listened to it a thousand times.

The smart thing to do would be to turn it off; instead, she cranked the volume and sang along, letting her tears roll freely down her cheeks. Why did everyone have to tie what happened at Mount Baker to what was going on here? It just intensified all her feelings, and her mind wandered to the past as she drove.

March 13, 1975
Whatcom County, Washington
Mount Baker

"This is so exciting," Cano said over her shoulder as she bounded up the side of the mountain. She pulled up short when she realized Allie lagged behind. "Are you okay?" she called.

Allie stopped about twenty yards away and dropped the case of equipment she was carrying.

Cano left her own load and hurried back to where Allie sat on the ground. Allie's knees were drawn to her chest, and her head was buried in her hands. With a gentle touch, Cano ran her hand down Allie's long blond hair. "What's wrong, babe?"

Allie shook her head. "I think this load is just too heavy for me."

Cano narrowed her eyes when she glanced at the case. Hadn't she taken the heavy one? Maybe they'd gotten mixed up. She grabbed the handle and yanked, nearly flinging it down the mountain. *What the hell?* It had to weigh less than ten pounds.

Allie still hadn't removed her hands from her face, so Cano studied her. Something had seemed off with Allie the last couple of weeks. She'd slept more and seemed to get fatigued easily. Cano had written it off as work stress, but now looking at the small woman sitting on the ground, she knew it was something more.

Chapter Twelve

Days until eruption: 53
Wednesday, March 26, 1980
Seattle, Washington
University of Washington
Department of Geological Sciences

Allie crinkled her nose as she pulled the top piece of bread off her turkey sandwich. *Gross.* It had been sitting so long the mustard seeped through, making a soggy mess of the bread. She tossed the piece of bread into the garbage and folded the rest over to make a half-sandwich.

Her appetite was gone, but she knew she needed to eat something. Not getting proper rest and poor nutrition was a sure way to make her condition worse. Even though the offensive bread was gone, it lingered in her mind, making the rest of the sandwich distasteful. Maybe she should hold her nose while she ate, like she did as a kid.

"What the hell are you doing?" Fran said when she burst through the door without knocking.

Allie shot her a defiant glare, continued to plug her nose, and swallowed the bite in her mouth. "What does it look like I'm doing?" She held up her mangled sandwich. "I'm eating."

Fran walked closer to her desk and nodded. "I see. Want to tell me why you've got your fingers up your nose?"

"Geez, I don't have my fingers up my nose." Allie bit off another piece of sandwich and chewed, still not releasing her nostrils.

Fran edged closer to the desk. "Is there something wrong with your sandwich?"

Allie swallowed. "It got soggy." She crammed another bite in her mouth.

"And apparently you don't like mushy sandwiches."

It wasn't lost on Allie that Fran was talking to her as if she were a small child. She felt like an overtired toddler who was just looking for a reason to throw a tantrum. "Soggy bread sucks." She chomped down on the sandwich.

Fran checked her watch. "Lunch was delivered four hours ago, probably why the bread is sodden."

"Really?" Allie temporarily removed her hand from her nose and put it against her chest. "I never would have thought of that on my own. Thank you for enlightening me." *Yep. Insolent child.* She quickly grasped her nose again before taking another bite. She'd almost finished the damned thing.

Fran bit her lip, obviously stifling a giggle. "Would you like me to leave you to pout in peace, or do you want to talk about it?"

Allie shoved the rest of her sandwich in her mouth and chewed slowly. She tried to work up anger at Fran but instead found herself holding back a laugh. Not a good idea with a mouthful of food. Chewing faster, she hoped to swallow before it bubbled to the surface. As she tried to force down the last of her sandwich, she couldn't hold back. She let out a half-snort and half-laugh, causing her to choke.

Fran looked on with amusement and slid Allie's can of pop closer to her.

Allie snatched the drink and took a huge gulp. Her eyes watered as she fought against another coughing fit.

Fran picked up a napkin from the desk and handed it to Allie. She gratefully accepted it and dabbed her eyes before she put the napkin over her mouth and coughed deeply.

Once Allie no longer feared she would start another round of coughs, she said, "I'm sorry. Why do you put up with me when I get so bitchy?"

Fran sat in the chair across from Allie's desk. "For one, because I love you. Two, I know you don't mean it. And three, it cracks me up." Fran flashed a toothy grin.

Allie smiled. "I deserved that. I'm sorry."

"For god's sake, you act as if you screamed at me. You let fly a ridiculous sarcastic comment every now and then." Fran put her hand in front of her and shook it. "Scary, scary. You make me tremble. Stop with the apologies and tell me what's going on."

"Did you see the headline in the *Oregon Journal*?" She pushed the paper toward Fran.

"Eruption seems imminent," Fran read. "Ouch. Where'd they hear that?"

"Someone from Portland State. I'm not sure what he was thinking. Great way to start a panic."

"Let me get this straight. A quote from some guy at Portland State caused you to get in a fight with your sandwich?"

"Yes."

"Nice try." Fran smiled. "Let me guess. Cano."

Just hearing Nova's name caused Allie's chest to

tighten. "I wasn't expecting to react this way. It was so long ago."

"Four years isn't that far past."

"Seems like another lifetime to me. So much has happened, but just seeing her, and now..."

Fran leaned forward. "And now what?"

"I thought maybe we'd get the chance to talk." Allie reached across her chest and grabbed on to her opposite arm. She squeezed as if she were giving herself a hug. The gesture calmed her. "Stupid, I know."

"Am I missing something? Why can't you still talk to her? Or are you thinking it's better if you don't?"

"You haven't heard?" Allie sat up taller in her chair. "It was the big buzz in the basement at lunch." She crumpled the sandwich wrappers on her desk and tossed them into the lunch sack. "Hence why my sandwich is gross."

"Sorry, hon. The dean had me running all over today. Press releases. Lining shit up for visiting scientists. You name it." She gazed at the door. "He's probably looking for me as we speak. I had to sneak out for a little break. You'll have to tell me what I missed."

"The odds are ten to one that Nova will be sent back to Menlo Park. At least, that's the latest betting line I heard before I escaped to my office."

Fran scrunched up her face. "What did she do now?"

Allie couldn't help but smile. Fran knew Nova too well. "Pissed off some of the powers that be in Vancouver. Rumor has it, she told someone off and stomped out."

"Sounds like Cano. Anything in particular set

her off or just Cano being Cano?"

"From what I've gathered, it happened right after they started talking about Baker."

"Ah, I see. Doesn't surprise you, does it? Baker seems to set both of you off."

Allie let out a deep breath. "Don't remind me."

A loud bang on her door interrupted them. Before Allie could answer, the door flew open.

The dean poked his head in, and his gaze landed on Fran. "There you are, Fran. I've been looking all over for you."

"Here I am." She raised her hand and shot Allie a look.

After Fran left, Allie sat back in her chair and let her thoughts travel back to Mount Baker.

March 13, 1975
Whatcom County, Washington
Mount Baker

Allie lifted her head and looked up at Nova's concerned face. She kept her arms wrapped around her knees as she sat on the cold ground. No matter how hard she'd pushed to keep up with Nova, she'd fallen behind. Suddenly, she'd felt as if something was squeezing her around her abdomen. The sensation frightened her, so she'd dropped to the ground.

Now she was embarrassed. Nova had picked up the equipment bag Allie carried and nearly flung it over her shoulder. Apparently, it wasn't as heavy as it seemed to Allie.

The last few months she'd been so tired, but

today, it was as if her limbs barely worked. She'd not wanted to be a downer and dampen Nova's enthusiasm, so she'd forged on. Obviously, not the best choice.

Nova knelt and put her hand on Allie's knee. Her hazel eyes, so full of compassion, made Allie's heart skip a beat. She could get lost in those eyes forever. She pushed the thought out of her head. Now wasn't the time or the place to be thinking this way.

Nova must have noticed Allie's look because she grinned and said, "Are you undressing me with your eyes again?"

Allie laughed. Leave it to Nova to bring levity to the situation. Allie was scared and suspected Nova was, too, but she wouldn't show it. At least not in front of Allie.

"Busted," Allie said, deciding to play along. She pretended to glance around. "Do you think anyone would catch us if I stripped you down right here?"

Nova's eyes sparkled, and she nodded toward a group of scientists setting up equipment. "They're too into Mount Baker to notice anything we do. I say we go for it."

Allie laughed. "I think I've just got myself overly tired." She let go of her knees and stretched out her legs.

Nova reached out and rubbed Allie's thigh. Allie flinched at the unpleasant sensation.

Nova pulled her hand back as if she'd been burned. "Uh, sorry. Um..." A hurt look crossed her face before she smiled. She glanced over her shoulder at the others on the mountain. "I didn't mean to out you."

"No." Allie grabbed Nova's hand. "It's not that, sweetheart. It felt weird. Tingly. It kinda hurt."

Nova's eyes narrowed. "Do you think I should take you to the ER?"

Allie vigorously shook her head. "Absolutely not." Her chest tightened. Her body was frightening her, but Nova didn't need to know that. "We're here to check out Mount Baker. I've probably just exhausted myself."

Nova studied her. "Are you sure?"

"Definitely. You forget, I'm ten years older than you."

"Nine."

Allie grinned. It was a conversation they'd had often. Nova insisted their age difference wasn't a problem since it was still in single digits. "Nine and a half," Allie shot back her typical response.

Nova brushed the hair off Allie's face. "I still think you're beautiful...even if you are an old lady."

"Flirt. You say that now, but I'll be thirty-five soon. It'll all be downhill from there."

"I'll take my chances," Nova said with a smirk. "Feeling better?"

Allie nodded. The tightness around her midsection had subsided. Her legs still tingled but not as badly as they had. "I think I'm ready to tackle our research."

"Maybe we should call it a day. I can come back tomorrow and collect the data we need."

"Nonsense. I'm good. Just get your young butt up and help this old lady off the ground."

Nova sprang to her feet. "Yes, ma'am."

Nova reached out her tattoo-covered arm. Another reason Allie loved her so much. She'd always had a thing for the bad girls. She gripped Nova's forearm and let herself be pulled to her feet.

Chapter Thirteen

Days until eruption: 52
Thursday, March 27, 1980
Seattle, Washington
University of Washington
Department of Geological Sciences

Allie sipped on her coffee as she listened to her coworkers debate whether the meeting in Vancouver had been successful.

"They closed the mountain above the tree lines," one of the scientists said. "That's a good start."

"They didn't go far enough, if you ask me," another replied.

Allie wanted to ask if anyone had any further information on Nova's situation, but she was afraid to ask for fear they'd become suspicious. Maybe she could do it inconspicuously. "Who won the bet yesterday?" She hoped it came out casual, even though butterflies danced in her stomach.

"Bet?" One of the men narrowed his eyes.

"With Cano." *Wow.* That sounded weird to her ears. She never called her that, but likely, many of the men wouldn't know who she was speaking of if she said Nova.

Grant, Nova's coworker, laughed and held up his hand. "I won a nice chunk of change."

That didn't tell her anything. "And you bet

how?"

"Oh," he said. "I knew the boss would never pull her. She's too talented. But I heard he chewed her ass *hard.* She can be such a dumb shit sometimes. Never knows when to keep her mouth shut."

The tightness in Allie's chest released. She bit her lip. It would do no good to voice her thoughts about who could stand to keep their mouth shut. The irony would no doubt be lost on him. "Why isn't she here then?"

"Drove up to Mount St. Helens," he said. "She left at the crack of dawn." He glanced at his watch. "She's probably there by now."

Allie's eyes widened. "She rode her motorcycle?"

"No. Boss let us rent a second truck, so we both have one. Last I heard, the roads up to the mountain aren't cleared, so we need our four-wheel drive." Grant laughed and shook his head. "Still can't believe she had the audacity to ask him to rent another truck. Right after he got done chewing her ass."

Allie smiled. *Typical Nova.* She wanted to ask him more questions but noticed the other scientists had grown quiet listening to their exchange. None of them, except for Johnston, knew about their relationship or that she was a lesbian. She'd like to keep it that way, so she said, "What's everyone working on today?"

Allie had spent the morning with her team, analyzing the data and building a game plan. When lunch was delivered, she'd taken her sandwich back to her office.

She glanced at the pile of student reports she

needed to grade, but she pushed them aside and stared at her overflowing bookshelves. A twinge of guilt nibbled at her. Normally, she wasn't the type of professor who turned her teaching duties over to her teaching assistant, but likely, her students would see much more of her TA, Madeline, the rest of the semester. It wasn't like she was shirking her duties for nothing. This could turn out to be a once-in-a-lifetime event.

A sharp rap on her door tore her away from her thoughts. Fran burst into the room. "Something's happening," Fran said breathlessly. "David asked that I come and get you."

"Johnston?"

Fran nodded, still trying to catch her breath.

"What's going on?" Allie tossed her lunch sack in the garbage.

"Reporters from a Portland radio station were flying over Mount St. Helens when they saw steam and ash. They're claiming a crater's opened up on top."

Allie jumped to her feet. "Are they getting any activity in the basement?"

"Better. The reporters called and invited someone from here to fly over with them. The guys downstairs decided Johnston should be the one to go."

Allie tried to hide her disappointment. She would love to be the one going. "Good choice. David knows his shit."

"That's why I'm here. He's getting ready to head to the helicopter pad now, and he asked me to see if you'd like to go with him."

Allie's heart raced. Was she hearing right? David was asking to take her along.

Fran grabbed Allie's arm and shook her. "Are

you listening? He wants to know if you want to go."

"Hell yes," Allie said, finally reacting. "But I have to go to the bathroom first."

Fran laughed. "Well, hurry up. You don't want to miss out because you had to pee."

Chapter Fourteen

Days until eruption: 52
Thursday, March 27, 1980
Skamania County, Washington
Mount St. Helens

Cano's breath caught in her throat as she stared up at the majestic mountain. *Overused word? Perhaps.* But Cano could think of none other when she gazed at the snow-covered peak. Most of Mount St. Helens was white at this time of year, but as spring and summer came, the snow would melt to expose more of the gray rock.

Timber scaled part way up toward the peak. Where the tree line ended, only a few rocky areas could be seen through the snow. Goose bumps rose on Cano's arm but not because of the cold. Just looking at Mount St. Helens had that effect on her.

"Are you going to blow?" Cano whispered.

Some of the roads had been treacherous. Eventually, as the weather warmed, the plows would make it up this high, but today, she preferred four-wheel drive to go farther.

All morning, she'd traveled around the area, taking pictures from as many angles as she could. Hopefully, the campus had a lab to develop film. She wanted to capture the essence of Mount St. Helens in case she blew. Hard telling how it might change the face of the mountain she loved.

Her chest tightened. She'd done good all morning. In small snippets of time, she'd been able to focus all her attention on her job. Inevitably, her thoughts returned to Allie as much as she tried to hold them at bay.

Cano had known it would be hard seeing Allie again, but she wasn't prepared for how much it hurt. It was as if a corset had been cinched around her heart, and slowly, someone pulled the strings tighter.

She felt a lot like a volcano herself. Inside, an earthquake of emotions was rumbling just under the surface, and it wouldn't take much for her to erupt. Yesterday had been a perfect example. She'd been stupid and impulsive. Worse was that she could have jeopardized being allowed to stay. Her normally short fuse was even shorter.

When she'd called Johnny last night, she'd had to sit through his fatherly lecture. Did she want to risk her chances? *Blah, blah, blah.* She had to learn to control her impulses. *Blah, blah, blah.* She hadn't said it out loud, but she'd wanted to.

She lightly slapped her cheek. *Focus.* Dwelling on Allie would get her nowhere but frustrated. She wasn't sure what she'd expected to be able to do driving around the mountain without a plan or equipment, but something had called her here. Laying eyes on Mount St. Helens would normally bring her peace. Remind her of how small and insignificant she and her problems were.

Earlier, she'd jealously watched a news chopper fly around the peak. They circled several times before they shot away. It wasn't necessarily the smartest thing to fly over a volcano experiencing seismic activity, but it would be exciting to get a closer look. From overhead, they'd be able to detect things they were unable to see from the ground.

She sighed, turned away, and climbed into the rental pickup. She'd taken more than enough pictures here. Her hope was to take more from the Timberline parking lot. It was the farthest road up the mountain, so it would still be covered in snow.

Cano patted the dash. "Let's see how well your four-wheel drive works."

The pickup bounced along the narrow road. As the path became more snow-covered, driving took her entire attention. Earlier, while gaping at the mountain, she'd almost landed the truck in a ditch. Then surely, she'd be sent back to Menlo Park. *Hmm.* Did she secretly want to be sent away to escape Allie? If she were a psychologist, she might think that. What other explanation was there for her increased level of reckless behavior?

While there had been other tracks on the road that should have clued her in, she was surprised when she came around the bend. It seemed as if everyone had the same idea she did. Several news vans were scattered around the parking lot. Cameramen and reporters milled around. Some appeared to be doing a live show.

So much for quiet. She stepped from the truck and took a deep breath. Nothing beat the crisp clean air in the mountains. Her breath crystalized as she let it out. *Refreshing.*

She sauntered over to one of the news crews. "What's going on?"

The reporter met her gaze and studied her as if sizing her up. "How'd you get through the roadblock?"

Shit. If these vultures realized she was a volcanologist, they'd descend on her. The last thing she could afford was to make another scene. She'd surely be pulled out then.

Cano put on her best cocky smile. "I wanted to see what was going on, so I told them I was a member of the press." She chuckled for good measure.

The reporter laughed. "A helicopter from Radio KGW was flying over and spotted a plume of smoke. Said a crater opened. We're here to see what's up."

Cano's heart raced. Was she starting to blow? If so, this wasn't the best place to be, but she wanted to know more. "Have you heard anything else?"

"Apparently, Emergency Services is pissed. Called up the station and told them to stop creating a panic. Said this is a minor explosion not an eruption."

Just as Cano started to speak, a helicopter flew toward the mountain. The reporter excitedly pointed and called to his cameraman. Soon all the reporters were tracking the flight.

She jogged back to her truck and pulled out her camera. She might as well get a picture of it for herself.

Chapter Fifteen

Days until eruption: 52
Thursday, March 27, 1980
Skamania County, Washington
Above Mount St. Helens

What a thrill. Allie leaned over David to get a look below. From the ground, Mount St. Helens loomed large, but from above, it was so enormous she couldn't make out the peak.

She always loved when her students had the opportunity to see the summit from the air. They looked around confused and asked her where the peak was. She had to explain that the top spanned miles across, and from above, it appeared almost flat, not like the point they saw from the ground.

It was beautiful. The snow-covered top showed no signs of melting, but it was only March. The pristine white snow looked different here. *Cleaner.* No human footprints disturbed the smooth surface, and they were too high up for her to detect the animal tracks that likely marred the surface.

The reports were accurate. A crater had opened on top of the mountain. She estimated it to be between two hundred and two hundred fifty feet across. Although small in terms of an active volcano, still something to be concerned about.

The helicopter dipped, and Allie's stomach

dropped with it. Now she was thankful she'd eaten a tiny lunch. As they made a second pass, the mountain made her forget her nervousness at being in a helicopter over an active volcano.

She and David were soon embroiled in a scientific conversation, which left the news reporters to gape in stunned silence.

One of the reporters called out over the *clack, clack, clack* of the helicopter blades. "We need to touch down somewhere, so we can do an interview. Imagine how the footage will look with this scene in the background."

The man sitting next to the pilot held up a map. "Looks like the Timberline parking lot would be a perfect place. It's the last stop before you have to get out and climb."

The energy in the helicopter was electric as everyone excitedly pointed to the steam and ash being released from the mountain. There was no guarantee that this would lead to anything more. Many volcanoes spewed like this for years, releasing a little pressure at a time and never having a big blow. Although, this was something new for Mount St. Helens. At least in the recent past.

Allie leaned back in her seat and stared at the breathtaking terrain. She wished Nova could be here with her. Allie smiled to herself, imagining the giddy response Nova would have to the experience. As *tough* as she pretended to be, she still had a childlike wonder. One of the many things Allie loved about her.

Stop! Allie purposefully engaged in a conversation with one of the reporters to shift her mind. *Ridiculous.* During an experience of a lifetime, she was daydreaming about a former lover. She needed to get her priorities in line.

After a couple more passes, the pilot turned and darted off to the north. As they approached Timberline, Allie spotted the pickup truck amongst a sea of news vans.

Her heart raced. *Nova?* She sighed. She already reacted to every motorcycle; now would she respond the same to every pickup?

Cano watched with interest as all the news crews scrambled to get pictures of the approaching helicopter. It had flown a couple of passes around the summit before veering away. Now it looked as if it were going to land.

She jumped into the bed of her pickup. A helicopter landing with the mountain in the background would make for a cool picture.

As it approached, she noted KING-TV on the side. More news crews, she thought with envy. It was the scientists and researchers who could benefit from having access to such equipment.

She zipped up her leather jacket as the helicopter began its descent. Snow kicked up in all directions and created a mini whiteout. The copter touched down, and the blades slowed. When the doors lifted, a man with a large camera hopped out and rested it on his shoulder. He trained it toward the door's opening and backed up.

From the distance of about thirty yards, she heard the cameraman call out, "I'd like to get a shot of you coming out of the helicopter. Ladies first. Dr. Albright, if you please."

Cano slid from the bed of the truck and moved

to the front. Had she heard right? No, she just had Allie too much on the brain. She edged closer to the landing spot. Although aware of the patches of deeper snow, she trudged through, never taking her gaze off the helicopter door.

Another reporter who'd exited with the cameraman held his hand up toward the opening. A gloved hand took his, and a tiny woman wearing a long black wool coat hopped from the opening. She staggered slightly, but the much larger man steadied her.

"Over here," the cameraman called. "Give me a big smile."

The woman turned. Long blond hair cascaded from under the stylish knit cap. And then the woman flashed a smile.

Cano's heart caught in her throat. Her thoughts raced, but her instinct took over, and she brought her camera to her eye and snapped several shots as the cameraman slowly backed up, shouting instructions.

Her gaze never left Allie, even as the herd of reporters scrambled toward the helicopter. David Johnston materialized beside Allie, but Cano hadn't seen him emerge.

Allie didn't seem to be paying attention to any of the action around her, either. Her mouth had dropped open, and her gaze locked on Cano.

Surprise! But was it a good one or a bad one? Cano wasn't sure, but all she wanted to do was rush to where Allie stood. Instead, she casually took her time placing the camera back in the truck. For good measure, she pulled on her gloves before strolling to the group gathered around the helicopter.

The cameraman turned and recorded her journey toward them. *Great.* She couldn't afford to do anything stupid like yesterday, or she'd surely get pulled back to Menlo Park.

She plastered on her best smile as she approached. David was the first to greet her since Allie still stood slack-jawed.

"Fancy meeting you here," Cano said with a chuckle.

"We could say the same," David said. Before he could say more, the cameraman swooped in and began snapping pictures.

It was a perfect time to make her escape from the throng. She jogged to the edge of the parking lot. Maybe from a different angle, she could see something. She squinted at the peak but still couldn't make out any volcanic activity from here.

As she continued to stare, she felt someone move up beside her. A hand touched her sleeve. Even through layers of leather and cloth, the touch sent goose bumps up her arm. Somehow, she knew whose eyes she'd look into when she turned.

She steeled herself and took a deep breath, not sure if she was ready to meet those brown eyes. It felt as if her head turned in slow motion, although she suspected it was her mind playing tricks on her.

Allie looked up at her, their faces only a foot from each other. Cano hadn't been this close to her in nearly four years, and her body reacted. She almost wanted to laugh. Leave it to her. Most people's hearts fluttered, or their loins ached. *Nope.* Her armpits poured sweat, and it dripped down her sides. No amount of deodorant could conquer her reaction to Allie.

Allie narrowed her gaze, obviously aware that something churned inside of Cano's head. "I'm afraid

I can't interpret that look."

Cano shook her head. "Just me being stupid."

"How so?" Allie's voice was cautious.

Should she be honest? She'd always been nothing but truthful with Allie, so she wouldn't hold back now. "My armpits are running like a leaky faucet."

Allie's eyes twinkled, and she put her head back and laughed. "Oh, god, you still react that way?"

Cano glowered.

Allie bit her lip, obviously trying to stop her laughter once she saw the serious look on Cano's face.

Cano couldn't hold it in any longer. She burst out laughing, too. "Only with you." She lifted her arm and pretended to sniff. "Deodorant has worked fine up until now."

Allie laughed. It was Cano's favorite sound, and she wanted it to go on.

Cano held her thumb up to her mouth and talked into it as if it were a microphone. "We're here with Cano Kane at Mount St. Helens. Tell us, Ms. Kane, how has your deodorant held up under the pressure of a possible eruption?"

Cano turned her head and brought her makeshift microphone back to her mouth. "Well, Mr. Reporter, my deodorant held up very well through a volcanic eruption." Cano shook her head and gave a sorrowful look. "Then Dr. Albright came along, and my pits have never been the same."

Allie laughed and clutched Cano's arm tighter. They were still chuckling and creating more outlandish interview answers when one of the reporters made his way to where they stood.

"Um, David is about to give his live interview," the reporter said. "We thought maybe you'd like to come over and be an audience. Looks good on the newscast."

"Sure," Allie said, wiping the tears of laughter from her eyes. She turned to Cano and held out her arm. "Join me?"

Cano's deodorant couldn't keep up when she glanced down at Allie's arm. Joining Allie was what she'd like to do more than anything, but was this a good idea? *Idiot.* It was a simple request to watch a colleague give an interview, not an invitation into Allie's bed.

"Certainly." Cano took Allie's arm.

As they walked across the snow-covered parking lot, Cano noticed that at times Allie held on a little tighter in the slickest spots and the deepest snow. Other than that, Allie moved well. Much better than Cano had expected.

They arrived as the reporter was giving David last-minute instructions. "Just be natural. I'm going to just let you talk. Tell us what you see. What your impressions are."

David nodded.

"Okay. We are live in three, two, one..."

The light on the camera flicked on, and the reporter began his introduction.

Cano watched, fascinated by the entire process. She'd never been around an event like this, but she suspected that this would become the new norm if Mount St. Helens continued to spew. It was evident that David was ecstatic to be here, but the reporters seemed equally as excited. They were possibly witnessing what could be a historic event.

The reporter turned the microphone toward David. David bounced on his feet, his long lanky body barely able to contain his enthusiasm. He looked over his shoulder at the volcano and grinned when he turned back. "We're standing next to a dynamite keg. We just don't know how long the fuse is."

Ouch. Cano scanned the faces of those gathered. Many turned wide-eyed toward the mountain. Reality set in with David's words. Leave it to David to get right to the point. He wasn't one to mince words or make people feel better with false assurances.

A selfish thought raced through her head. Maybe David's interview would take her off the hook with their boss. The media would likely focus more on his dynamite keg comment than her stomping out of yesterday's meeting.

While David was an expert in volcanic gases, not seismic activity, the reporters were more interested in the previous few days. Earthquakes they could understand, while gases were too obscure.

As the interview wound to a close, David said, "If it were to explode right now, we would die."

Priceless. Cano was surprised the reporter didn't drop his microphone and run.

He quickly signed off and motioned to his crew. "We have enough. I think it's time to move out of here."

He didn't need to tell the crew twice. They'd already begun tossing equipment into the helicopter, and the pilot had fired up the engine.

Allie leaned over close to Cano. "Leave it to David to clear a room."

Cano smiled. "He's clearing an entire mountain. Impressive."

Allie's eyes danced as she laughed.

Without thinking, Cano blurted out, "Let me take you home."

Chapter Sixteen

Days until eruption: 52
Thursday, March 27, 1980
Near Mount St. Helens, Washington
Timberline parking lot

Allie stared at Nova but didn't speak. The frenetic activity around them faded as Nova's words reverberated in her head. *Let me take you home.* What was she asking?

Cano shifted her weight from one foot to the other and rubbed her hands together. "I know flying isn't your favorite thing." She motioned over her shoulder at the pickup. "I'm heading back to Seattle, and I wouldn't mind having company."

How should she answer? She wanted to spend time with Nova, didn't she? Laughing with her earlier had been the best thing. Her heart felt light and free, but what would the long-term consequences be?

"Never mind." Nova took a step backward, and her gaze shifted to her feet. "Have a safe trip back."

"Wait." Allie grabbed Nova's arm before she turned away. "Sorry. You just caught me off guard. It wasn't a no."

"Then it's a yes?" Nova looked up, her eyes full of hope.

Allie's chest clutched, making it hard for her to breathe. "It's not a yes, either."

Nova's shoulders slumped before something flickered in her eyes, and then she stood taller. "Then it's a definite maybe? I'll take it."

Allie laughed. *Damn it.* Why could Nova always do this to her? Her insecurity hidden under her false bravado was possibly the sexiest thing about her. At least from Allie's viewpoint.

"Definitely a hard maybe," Allie replied.

Nova smirked. "What do I need to do to move it into the yes column?"

What, indeed. Without giving it much thought, Allie blurted out, "No talking about the past. We can talk about Mount St. Helens and catch up like old friends. But nothing about the past."

Nova nodded. "Fair enough." She smirked. "Just so I don't break the rules—"

"When have you ever been known to follow the rules?"

"True. That's why I want to make sure I get them ingrained in my noggin." Nova tapped her head several times. "It takes a while to sink through this thickness."

"Trust me. I know." Allie winked.

Nova leaned back, stuck out her chest, and studied Allie. She brought her hand to her chin and gave her best professorial look. "Was that a violation of the rules? I believe you just invoked my past."

"Dork." Allie playfully pushed Nova's shoulder.

"Hey now. I just need to make sure. I don't want you to jump out of the truck going fifty-five because I'm in violation."

"Let me tell David I'm going with you." Allie took a step forward and froze. The ice-covered patch in front of her taunted her. Her earlier good mood plummeted. She turned back to Nova. "Maybe I should just go with David."

From the look on Nova's face, Allie's words had landed like a slap. Nova stared at Allie for several seconds before she glanced at the path in front of her. Nova's eyes regained their spark. She held out her arm. "What do you say we walk over to David together and tell him that you're going with me?"

Allie's shoulders relaxed. Nova truly was one of the most caring people she'd ever known. Sadness swept over her at the thought. She'd already agreed, so it wouldn't be fair to change her mind now. Besides, it was *only* a three-hour drive. Nothing more. *Sure.* Whatever she needed to believe to get her through.

"Thank you," Allie said and took Nova's arm.

Cano was glad to be behind the wheel since the first ten minutes of the drive had been awkward. She was able to feign concentration as she made her way to the highway.

After the initial discomfort, it didn't take long before they fell into an easy conversation. Their scientific excitement took over, and they'd spent the first half of the drive speculating on the likelihood of an eruption.

It felt like old times. Cano wasn't sure if it would make it harder or easier when she dropped Allie off. It was a reminder of how empty her last four years had been. She'd not let anyone into her life since. *Fucking MS.*

Cano shook her head. She needed to enjoy Allie and not go down that black hole. *Stay in the moment.*

"Are you okay?" Allie asked.

"Um, yeah. Just contemplating your last theory," Cano lied.

"It was so brilliant it left you speechless?" Allie smiled.

The smile made Cano's heart leap. It wasn't just her straight white teeth that made her smile so appealing, but also the way her eyes twinkled and the tiny dimple in her left cheek. *Focus.* "Yeah, that's it."

"Do you think you'll stay in Seattle, or will you get moved to Vancouver?"

"I could end up back in Menlo Park if I don't watch myself."

"I heard about your outburst." Allie chuckled. "I had the movie of it playing in my head. Down to the look of indignation on your face."

Cano replicated the look and turned to Allie.

"That's it." Allie pointed and bounced in her seat. "I knew it."

Cano smiled at Allie's enthusiastic response. It always warmed her heart when she could bring levity to the more serious woman. "I'm glad my near suspension makes you so happy."

"He almost suspended you?" Allie's eyes widened.

Cano shook her head. "No. I just got my ass chewed for half an hour. I didn't know Spenser knew some of the words he used. I guess you could say I'm on probation."

"Then you better stay out of trouble." Allie rubbed her hands together. "You never answered whether you'll stay in Seattle or go to Vancouver."

"My guess is we'll end up in Vancouver. Closer. It wouldn't surprise me if the orders are in by the time we get back. With the volcanic activity today, they might even send a few more people." Cano wrinkled her nose at having to play nice with others.

"Don't look so excited about it," Allie teased.

"I'm already having to put up with Grant, so you can't blame me."

"True. I'll give you that much. Nice guy, but he makes me tired with his incessant chatter."

"Try being in a van with him for fourteen hours."

"Ugh. No thanks. Anyone you hope will get the nod to join you?"

Cano gave Allie a sideways glance. Was she fishing or was it an innocent question? "Johnny," she replied.

"Johnny? Who is he? Or should I say she?"

Warmth spread across Cano's chest. Maybe Allie had been fishing. Did that mean she still cared? Cano had been hesitant to ask about Allie's life, but she'd just kicked in the door. "He. My mentor. Johnny Garcia. I guess you could say he's my best friend, too." Cano put her hand to her forehead. "How pathetic is that?"

"Why do you say it's pathetic?"

"He's a fifty-year-old man with a wife and three kids. Not exactly someone I have a ton in common with."

"Father figure?"

"God knows I need one."

"Your parents aren't that bad. I always thought they were kinda sweet."

Cano thought of calling Allie for a violation of the rules but decided against it. "Anyone that names their kid Nova Kane automatically gets one strike against them. Just on principle."

Allie chuckled. "Yeah. That was a bit of an...

um...interesting choice."

Cano snorted. "To put it nicely. They've been on me lately, wanting me to come back to Arkansas to live. My annual visit is plenty. Enough about my parents." Cano wasn't sure how she wanted to word the next question or if she wanted to know the answer. "How's life with your parents?"

Allie paused for several beats. "They're good, but I don't live with them anymore."

Cano's heart dropped to her stomach. What did that mean? "Oh. I just thought. Um...just that you...."

"I moved out a couple of years ago."

Another stabbing pain rocked Cano's chest. Who did she live with and was it appropriate for Cano to ask? The easy conversation was suddenly becoming more difficult.

"I live on my own," Allie offered.

Cano let out a deep breath. "That's wonderful. So things are going okay with...with your MS?"

"Better." Allie shrugged. "I have good stretches and bad stretches. As much as I appreciate all my parents have done for me, I needed to be on my own."

Cano nodded. She felt better now that she could breathe. "I can understand that. You're doing okay on your own?" She didn't want to know if there was someone *special* helping Allie.

"I have help."

Cano felt Allie's gaze but stared out the windshield. "That's great." *Shit.* That sounded robotic even to her.

"Fran and Ben are the best."

Oh, good. Still no mention of a girlfriend. Or boyfriend. She couldn't help thinking that after watching Dr. Pompous fall all over Allie. "Does Fran still hate me?"

Allie pointed. "That's pretty close to a rule violation."

"What? I asked if she *still* hates me. In the present tense. If you'd like, I could rephrase and say, does she hate me?"

"She never hated you."

Cano returned the gesture and pointed at Allie. "Foul. We can only talk about whether she hates me in the present."

"She does not hate you in the present. Is that better?"

"Much." Cano smirked. "I didn't feel much love coming from her the other day. I thought she was going to throw me to the ground and stomp me."

"I would have protected you."

Cano fluttered her hand in front of her face as if fanning herself. "My hero." She turned to Allie and met her gaze. "You do know you just confirmed she was about to stomp me."

"I did no such thing!" Allie's voice rose an octave. "I simply stated that should she have decided to stomp you that I would have intervened on your behalf."

"I could take her." Cano winked.

"Doubtful." Allie touched Cano's leather jacket. "You might look the part, but straight women can be vicious. Don't let her Farrah Fawcett hairdo and platform shoes fool you."

Cano laughed. "Trust me. I figured out long ago that I didn't want to cross her."

"Foul." Allie pointed and pretended to blow a whistle.

"You're just mad that I called a foul on you

earlier."

"Maybe." Allie crossed her arms over her chest and pretended to pout.

They pulled into the university much too soon. Cano had caught herself going well under the speed limit to prolong their time together, but now they were back. She would likely be moved to Vancouver, so it would be hard telling when they'd get another opportunity to talk.

As much as she wanted to discuss what had happened four years ago, she hadn't violated Allie's rules. Cano reminded herself that there was still hope.

"This has been nice," Allie said, pulling Cano from her thoughts.

Cano drove into a parking space next to the only car in a handicap parking spot. She turned to Allie and smiled. "It has been. Thank you."

Allie's shoulders sagged as she gestured toward the car. "I guess you figured out what car was mine."

Cano wanted to lie and tell her it was a coincidence, but she'd vowed long ago never to lie to Allie. She averted her eyes. "Yeah. I just figured."

"Very good deductive reasoning." Allie put on a smile, but it didn't reach her eyes. "I left my purse inside. I didn't think I should take it on the helicopter."

Cano turned off the truck and pushed open the door, excited to spend a little more time with Allie. "I'll walk you in."

"You don't have to."

"I want to. Besides, I'll just go back to my hotel and watch television. It's Thursday, so I should get there in time to catch *Mork & Mindy*." *Ugh.* She'd just given away that she had the television schedule memorized.

Allie pushed open her office door and gasped. "What are you doing in here?"

Fran laughed. "Hiding from the dean and waiting for you. I wanted to see how..." She abruptly stopped when Nova stepped in behind Allie. "Hello, Cano," Fran said with an edge to her voice.

"Fran. Nice to see you again." Nova shot her a smile.

Fran nodded but didn't return the compliment. She turned back to Allie. "Nice drive?" Sarcasm dripped from her words.

"Beautiful day." Allie smiled, refusing to let Fran bring down her elation. *Oh, god.* She was feeling almost euphoric. That didn't bode well. "Any particular reason you wanted to see me?"

Nova wandered over to Allie's bookshelf and studied the titles.

"You might want to hear this, too, Cano," Fran said with a raised voice.

"Huh?" Nova turned back. "What do I need to hear?"

"David's interview has attracted attention. The dynamite keg comment has already created a stir," Fran said. "We're getting calls from around the country. People are beginning to believe she could erupt."

"Are they going to invoke any more restrictions?" Allie asked. "What they've done so far is inadequate."

Fran nodded. "Emergency Services has told anyone within fifteen miles to evacuate."

"And the loggers?" Nova asked.

"They were pulled today," Fran confirmed.

"Thank god." Allie put her hand against her chest. "I've been worried."

"Let's see how long it lasts." Nova said. "The mighty dollar will win out."

"Possibly," Fran said. "But with today's activity, things are changing. The USGS is mobilizing. There's talk of setting up a camp near the mountain to monitor it. I've been tasked with keeping a list of all the geologists pouring in from all over the country."

Allie's pulse quickened. While nobody wanted a destructive eruption, as a scientist, the thought of an eruption caused an adrenaline rush. "Does the dean plan on having people here all weekend?" Allie asked.

Fran held up a file. "Yep, that's the other reason I'm here. I need to get people signed up for their shifts." Fran winked. "I wanted to make sure you got your slot first."

Allie shot Nova a smile. "The perks of having Fran as a best friend." Allie took the file from Fran.

"Well…um…I should probably leave you ladies to it," Nova said. She shoved her hands into her pocket and rocked slightly from side to side.

Allie fought the urge to run to her and give her a hug goodbye. It would be a big mistake. Without Fran glaring at them, she might have thrown caution to the wind. "Thank you so much for bringing me back."

"Yeah. Much better than riding back in a helicopter." Fran rolled her eyes.

Allie shot her a look. "The helicopter ride made me nervous," Allie lied, hoping to save the situation. "Nova was gracious enough to help me out."

Nova's eyes twinkled at the lie. "It was my pleasure." And then she was gone.

Allie stared at the empty doorway and willed herself not to cry. She suspected Fran would be merciless anyway without adding tears to the equation.

"Do I even want to ask?" Fran said as soon as the door closed behind Nova.

Allie walked to her desk and flopped into her chair, not trusting her legs anymore. Did she want to answer? Even if she did, she wasn't sure what to say. It had been one of the best days she could remember, but for some reason, she didn't think Fran would understand.

"Are you just going to sit there and stare?" Fran said in a raised voice.

Allie shrugged. "I'm not sure what you want me to say."

"Tell me that I'm imagining the gleam in your eyes."

"Okay, you're imagining the gleam."

"Is it true?"

"You didn't tell me it had to be true. You just said to say it."

"Ugh." Fran slapped her hands on top of her head and pretended to pull her hair. "This is so not good."

"What? Me having a gleam in my eyes?" Allie knew she shouldn't bait Fran, but she couldn't help it. She hadn't felt this alive in so long. It felt good.

"You know that's not what I meant." Fran put her hand on her hip and glared down at Allie. "I want you to have a gleam. Just not one created by Cano Kane."

"When's the last time you've seen a gleam there?" Why was she challenging Fran when she knew Fran was right?

Fran's eyes softened. "Oh, honey, you know I love you. But she broke your heart once. I don't want to see it happen again."

"Maybe I broke my own heart." Allie snatched the file off her desk. "I need to sign up for my shifts."

Fran opened her mouth and then closed it. She stared at Allie for several beats before she turned away. "I'll be at my desk. Drop the sheet off when you're done."

Once Fran cleared the door, Allie dropped her head to her desk.

Chapter Seventeen

Days until eruption: 48
Monday, March 31, 1980
Seattle, Washington
University of Washington
Department of Geological Sciences

Fran's shoes clicked on the polished floors of the corridor. While Fran always shortened her stride to accommodate Allie's gait, adrenaline pushed Allie forward, forcing Fran to hurry to keep up.

Since her trip with Nova, Allie hadn't had any significant problems with her MS. In fact, she'd felt good all weekend. When she wasn't working in the lab, she'd gotten outside to enjoy the weather.

"Tell me again why we're sprinting," Fran said.

"Harmonic tremors."

"Harmonic tenors? You're risking my falling off these heels for a musical concert?" Fran pretended to wobble on her shoes.

"Nice try. I've seen you disco dancing in shoes higher than those, so I think you can keep up with a five-foot-two woman without breaking anything."

"Fine. But why are we rushing off to hear harmonic tenors?"

"*Tremors.* Not tenors."

"What in the hell are harmonic tremors? And

why are we running because of them?"

"The earth is shaking in rhythm."

Fran chuckled. "Mother Nature putting on a concert with your girl Helen?"

Allie shook her head but smiled. "It typically signifies the movement of fluid underground. Molten magma or gases."

"Magma? Is that kinda like lava?"

"Exactly like lava, except for the location." They arrived at the elevator, and Allie punched the down arrow. She hit it several times before Fran casually put her hand over Allie's and pulled it away from the button.

"Oh, kinda like soda is called pop in some parts of the country?" Fran said.

Allie laughed. "No."

Fran scowled. "You said it's called something different depending on the location."

"The molten rock *under* the earth's surface is called magma. Once it breaks through the surface, through a vent or volcano, it's called lava."

"It's like a caterpillar turning into a butterfly?"

The elevator doors slid open. "Not exactly, but I'll let you go with it."

"So does that mean she's gonna blow?"

"We can't say for sure. Unfortunately, there's still so much we don't know about volcanic eruptions." Allie naturally slid into teacher mode. "We still haven't determined the best predictors for when a volcano will erupt."

Fran waved her hand in the air. "Even with this whole building full of machines measuring stuff?"

"Yes." Allie smiled. The elevator door pinged open, and they stepped out. "We know some of the things to watch for, but we don't know what finally pushes a volcano to erupt."

"Like the seismic activity?"

"Exactly. That's one of the biggest indicators, but we saw with Mount Baker our predictions were wrong. David has been studying how gases might be an indicator. We simply don't know enough or have enough data since every eruption is different."

"The dean is fuming at some of the things the press is saying. I keep hiding the newspapers from him."

Allie laughed. "Smart. It might keep him from yelling at us." She let out a deep breath. "People act like we should have a crystal ball and be able to predict exactly what's going to happen."

Fran stood up straighter and put on a haughty expression. "Today the scientists had a breakthrough," Fran said in her best reporter voice. "They are now predicting that the situation will worsen, improve, or stay about the same."

Allie laughed. "God, that's almost what some of the reporters wrote, isn't it?"

"Afraid so."

Allie shook her head. "Will people ever respect the word of scientists?"

"Doubtful."

Allie sighed. "Sad but true."

Days until eruption: 48
Monday, March 31, 1980
Seattle, Washington
Holiday Inn

Cano fell back onto her hotel bed, fully clothed. She should change into her pajamas but didn't have the energy. Besides, she was still cold from tromping around outside all day. Maybe after she warmed up, she'd undress.

Lying on top of the covers wouldn't help her shake the chill that had settled in her bones, so she tried to slide under the bedspread without getting up. *Damn it.* She only managed to tangle herself in the blankets.

Shit. She rolled off the bed and straightened the bedding before she dived underneath. Now she just felt weird, being covered up with her blue jeans still on.

Jesus. The lumpy mattress and thin pillows were bad enough, but now everything felt off. She let out a loud breath and pushed back the covers. If she hurried, she could get into her flannel pajamas before she got any colder. As she hurried to her suitcase, she glanced at the thermostat.

No wonder. What idiot turned it down to sixty-two? She twisted it to seventy-five and grinned. One of the perks of being in a hotel, she didn't have to pay the electric bill. She stripped out of her clothes and tossed them on the floor. She'd pick them up later once she warmed up.

The soft red and black flannel pants slipped over her legs. Maybe it was her imagination, but she already felt warmer. She pulled on her favorite T-shirt. Allie had bought it for her at the KISS concert Cano had taken her to on their second date. The shirt was frayed around the collar and was threadbare in a few spots, but she'd wear it as long as she could.

Cano smiled at the memory. She'd spent more time watching Allie than the stage. Once Allie had gotten over the makeup and crazy costumes, she'd surprised Cano and danced with reckless abandon. It had made Cano realize there was more to the straitlaced professor than met the eye, and from then on, Cano was hooked. By the end of the evening, Allie had declared Gene Simmons her favorite. She'd jokingly said she had a thing for the bad boys or girls.

Cano shivered, not sure if it was from the cold or the memory, but her body's reaction brought her back to the moment. She peeled off her socks and dashed for the bed. With a practiced leap, she slipped between the covers and pulled them over her head.

Warmth spread through her, and her teeth stopped chattering. She should read the report on the nightstand, but that would require her to take her arms from under the blankets. Instead, she snuggled in deeper.

A loud ring pierced the air, causing her to jump. *Damn it.* She didn't want to talk to anyone. It was probably Spenser calling her to chew her out for something. Or it could be Allie.

Cano snatched the receiver. "Hello."

"Ya miss me?" Johnny's familiar voice rang out.

"Ugh, if I knew it was you, I wouldn't have answered."

"I see. The tough girl has to keep her image." He chuckled. "Don't worry. I won't tell anyone how bad you missed me."

"In your dreams." Cano would never admit she missed him, even though she had.

"You ain't my type. How many times do I have to tell you that?"

"And to what do I owe this unpleasant surprise?" Cano teased.

"I've got some good news and some better news."

"All right. I'm starting to like this call. Hit me with it."

"The good news is I've been chosen to join the team at Mount St. Helens and should be there by Wednesday."

"Is this an April Fools' joke?" Cano asked.

"It's March 31."

"I thought you might be doing it a day early to throw me off the scent."

"That's not how it works." Johnny groaned. "Leave it to you to bend the sacred rules of April Fools'."

"Wow. So it's a sacred holiday?" Cano grinned.

"You know it."

"While fascinating being taught the rules of April Fools' Day, if that was your good news, what is the better news?"

"I'll get the chance to meet this professor of yours."

Cano groaned. "Apparently, you don't know the definition of good and better."

"It's good and better, at least in my world."

"You live in a warped world, Johnny Garcia."

Johnny chuckled. "So you ready to talk about something really exciting?"

"And what would that be?" Cano asked with hesitation.

"Harmonic tremors."

"Now you're speaking my language. Finally, a conversation I can get behind."

They talked for another ten minutes, until

Rosaria's voice sounded in the distance.

"Coming," Johnny called. "Dinnertime. I best be going. What's on your agenda tonight?"

Cano glanced at the report on the nightstand. "I'm gonna read Rocky Crandell and Donal Mullineaux's report from 1978. See if I can glean some insight."

"Which paper is that?"

Cano picked up the report and took a deep breath before she read, "*Potential Hazards from Future Eruptions of Mount St. Helens, Volcano, Washington: An Assessment of Expectable Kinds of Future Eruptions and Their Possible Effects on Human Life and Property.*"

"Wow. Now I've probably missed dinner after listening to all that."

Cano laughed. "No doubt. It's no wonder that nobody ever reads scientific papers."

Chapter Eighteen

Days until eruption: 44
Friday, April 4, 1980
8.5 miles northwest of Mount St. Helens
Coldwater observation post

Trees whizzed past as Cano accelerated out of the curve. Even though it wasn't quite the same in a pickup, she still loved traveling the Spirit Lake Highway. State Route 504. The Douglas firs, hemlocks, and red cedar stretched toward the sky. Driving this close, she couldn't see their tops.

Cano hoped soon she'd be sailing along on her bike. At this time of year, it was as if she traveled the seasons backward as the elevation rose. When she'd passed through Castle Rock, spring was evident by the buds on the trees and the flowers popping along the roadside. Once she'd cleared the sheriff department's roadblocks near Elk Rock, it was as if she'd traveled back in time to winter.

At over four thousand feet elevation, it was no surprise that snow lined the road. The state had finally plowed Weyerhaeuser's 3490 and 3533 roads. They led to the platform above Maratta Creek where the USGS's Coldwater observation post had been set up four days ago.

This would be her first time to visit the camp since she'd been relegated to the basement at U-Dub for the last few days. Cano suspected it was her punishment for being *too* outspoken. After four long days of recording and analyzing data, she'd finally been let loose to work in the field.

She roared around another curve and slowed when she reached the turnoff that would take her to her destination.

When she arrived at the camp, she was surprised to discover it empty. The scientists were likely out setting up more monitors around the base of the mountain or making a supply run.

It didn't bother her to be alone; in fact, she enjoyed the quiet. She knew it was unlikely to be peaceful for much longer. With more geologists pouring into Vancouver every day, they would likely descend on Coldwater soon.

Cano's chest tightened. She'd checked out of her room in Seattle this morning. Since giving Allie a ride on Monday, they'd spent little time together. While Allie's team focused on the seismic activity, Cano's team concentrated on gases. Now it would be nearly impossible to see Allie since Cano would work between Coldwater and Vancouver.

Cano stood at the edge of the camp and gazed out over the expanse. A chill ran through her as she stared at the volcano. Even though she tried to focus on the mountain, her thoughts kept going back to Allie.

"Hello?" a voice called.

Cano jumped at the sound. She whirled around as Johnny strolled up. "Jesus. Don't you knock?"

"Jesus doesn't have to knock, and neither does Johnny." He flashed her a huge smile. "You were a million miles away. What were you thinking about?"

"Nothing," Cano said too quickly.

"I see." He smirked. "The lovely professor."

She glowered but didn't respond. "Where is everyone?"

"Coming later. They're having a meeting in Vancouver." He held up a box. "I offered to set up the new radio. And volunteered you to unload the van."

"What kind of radio?"

"A better one, so we can keep in touch with Vancouver and U-Dub."

Maybe she could stay in touch with Allie after all. Her face warmed. *Sure.* The rest of the team would love her sitting around the tent like a teenager talking on the radio to her girlfriend. *Wishful thinking.* She certainly couldn't call Allie her girlfriend.

"Did you bring everything?"

"Yep. I told them not to hurry because you'd love to unload everything and get it set up."

"You're an asshole."

He laughed as he ran a box cutter along the packing tape. "I saw the truck when I pulled up, so I wasn't expecting it to be you."

"Who'd you think it was?"

He shrugged. "Wasn't sure. Figured you'd have your bike."

She swatted at the snow and ice pellets in the air. "Sure, I want to ride in this shit. But spring is just around the corner, and I'll have Beulah out soon enough."

"Just don't go places you shouldn't. We don't need you riding up the mountain or trying to outrun an eruption."

Cano held her hands out in front of her, pretending to grip handlebars. She flicked her right wrist to indicate twisting the accelerator and said, "Vroom, vroom."

"Ugh." Johnny pulled a radio that was still wrapped in plastic out of the box. "I don't need to watch you ride your imaginary motorcycle. I have a radio to build, and you're being disruptive."

"Speaking of being disruptive, did you hear the governor appointed a Mount St. Helens watch group and declared a state of emergency?" Cano asked.

"I did. Some of the boys in Vancouver were surprised." Johnny turned over the box, and pieces cascaded onto the tarp he'd laid down. "Apparently, Dixy Lee has a reputation of not wanting to put too many regulations on commerce."

"Radio said they've evacuated hundreds of people."

Johnny snorted. "Good luck with that. Word has gotten out, so I suspect our volcano will attract flies to shit. It'll be like bailing a leaky boat. As soon as some people are evacuated, others will sneak in."

"True, but the governor had to make a show of doing something after Tuesday's activity." Cano peered at the mountain. "I heard my girl spit ash sixteen thousand feet. Some rocks as big as three feet wide. Are they bringing any of the samples here?"

"That's what I heard. We should be getting them in the next day or two."

"Good. Means I won't have to sneak out there and get my own."

Johnny shook his head. "Speaking of fools, did you hear about the damned fool who had a helicopter take him to the peak to get samples?"

"I did." Cano laughed. "I heard he employed good old-fashioned scientific ingenuity. Apparently, he used a ladle attached to a yardstick to scoop up the ash."

"No way. You're full of shit."

"Seriously. That's what Allie told me."

Johnny clasped his hands to his chest. "Of course it's true if Allie told you." He batted his eyelashes. "She knows everything." He pretended to swoon.

"Shut up." Cano glowered. "Any idea when the time-lapse camera will get here?"

Johnny shrugged. "Maybe it's with the supplies I brought."

"Really?" Cano's eyes widened.

"No, dumbass." He laughed. "Do you think the powers that be are going to entrust me with a twenty-five thousand-dollar camera?"

Cano whistled. "Holy hell. Is that really what it cost?"

"That's what they said at the meeting. It's a sixteen-millimeter camera that'll take pictures twice a minute."

"That is so cool." Cano couldn't hide her smile.

"And you call me and my radio geeky?" Johnny motioned toward the tent. "Speaking of, I need to get it set up. And you have boxes to lug."

"Fine," Cano grumbled. "But I'm doing it under protest."

"If you get your boxes unloaded, you can scout the best location to set up the camera."

"Now you've given me motivation." She turned and strode toward the van as Johnny disappeared into the tent.

While she carried boxes, her thoughts drifted back to the past and her time with Allie. Something that seemed to be occurring all too regularly.

September 11, 1975
University of Washington
Medical Center

Cano's right leg bounced up and down as she sat with Allie in the examining room. The crisp white and silver in the room added to the cold sterility, but it was the antiseptic scent that caused her gag reflex. For Allie's sake, she'd kept it at bay, but the longer they sat, the more overpowering it became.

Allie put her hand on Cano's knee, stopping it from continuing to rhythmically bob. Their gazes met. Allie had been quiet and reserved all morning, while Cano had been practically ricocheting off the walls. Another example of the difference in their personalities. Stress caused Cano to act out, while Allie withdrew.

A quick rap on the door was followed by Dr. Antioch, who stepped into the room. Cano stretched her neck to look up at him. He must stand at least six-foot-five. His crew cut had more gray than black, which was the only sign of his age. His boyish smile made him appear much younger.

He reached out his hand to Allie. "Allison, so nice to see you again." He turned to Cano and took her hand, as well. "Ms. Kane."

Cano grunted a *hello*. Why did he insist on calling her Ms. Kane? Allie got to be Allison. She would settle on Nova if he didn't want to call her Cano.

He sat on a stool that she suspected had been intentionally lowered, so he didn't tower over his patients. She marveled at how he'd maneuvered his legs behind him, so his knees didn't jut into his face.

"How have you been feeling?" Dr. Antioch asked.

"Okay," Allie replied.

He nodded and gave her a knowing smile. "In doctor speak, *okay* translates to not so hot."

Allie smiled. "Perceptive."

Cano shifted in her seat but fought the urge to allow her leg to bounce again. The social niceties were enough. He needed to get on with giving them answers. He was the fifth doctor Allie had seen. Finally, the last doctor referred her to Dr. Antioch, a neurologist."

"We've been able to rule out several possibilities."

Allie nodded.

Cano listened without speaking, feeling invisible in this setting.

"Among them, lupus, vitamin B12 deficiency, fibrositis, myasthenia gravis to name a few."

"That's very good, Dr. Antioch," Allie said. "It's great that you've determined what it isn't, but—"

"Have you figured out what it is?" Cano blurted out.

Dr. Antioch nodded. "I can understand your frustration."

"It's been nearly six months since I started showing symptoms, so you're right, this has been frustrating." She glanced at Cano. "For both of us."

"Indeed." The doctor steepled his hands together. "After we analyzed your cerebrospinal fluid and took a CAT scan, I believe you're suffering from MS. Multiple Sclerosis. Do you know much about the disease?"

Allie grimaced. "Yes. I've been doing some research of my own."

Blood pounded in Cano's ears, making it difficult for her to focus on the doctor. She blinked, knowing she needed to hear what he said.

"Then you know that MS is tricky. Not every patient exhibits the same symptoms."

"So you're not sure?" Allie said in a small voice.

Dr. Antioch pursed his lips. "Based on your symptoms and the tests, my professional opinion is that it's MS. You're exhibiting many of the common indicators."

"But not all," Cano blurted out.

"You're correct. Allison doesn't exhibit every symptom, but most patients don't. But she shows enough signs, coupled with the test results, that I am confident in my diagnosis."

Allie nodded.

"I suggest you avail yourself of all the resources we have at the university. Our team of specialists can provide you with excellent information about your condition, as well as things you can do to combat the disease."

Cano dropped her gaze to the floor. This couldn't be happening. She wanted Dr. Antioch to shut up and leave. If only she and Allie could talk it out, everything would be okay. Faulty logic, she knew, but she wasn't ready to hear this.

"It's my understanding that there's no cure," Allie said in a controlled voice.

"You're correct. We're constantly discovering new things about the condition and hope this will allow us to manage, if not cure, the disease."

Cano scowled. It sounded like a load of bullshit to her. "How long has MS been around?"

"It was first defined in 1868."

Cano threw up her hands. "So they haven't figured it out in over a hundred years, what makes you think a cure is right around the corner?"

Allie shot her a withering glare before turning back to the doctor. "I apologize for Nova's outburst. This is quite a lot to take in. What about medications?"

"Yes. I will prescribe you a steroid that has been known to help other patients." He smiled. "Your emotional health is important, too. We have wonderful support groups, not just for the patients, but for their *friends* and family, as well."

"Thank you." Allie bit her lower lip. "Anything in particular I need to do or not do? Anything that makes it worse?"

"Stress," he said immediately. "Stress is bad for everyone's body, but for someone with MS, it can be more problematic. Getting proper nutrition, exercise, and rest will always help."

Allie nodded.

"Do you have any further questions?"

"How will it progress?" Allie asked. "What can I expect?"

Cano wasn't sure if she wanted to hear the answer.

Dr. Antioch rubbed his chin. "That's one of the problems with this disease. It doesn't follow a typical course with every patient. You could go into remission for weeks, months, or years. There is still so much we have yet to learn."

Cano clenched her jaws together, knowing Allie wouldn't appreciate it if she unleashed her thoughts on Dr. Antioch.

"Any other questions?" Dr. Antioch asked.

Allie shook her head. "Not that I can think of at the moment."

The doctor smiled. "That's typical under these circumstances. We've found that patients need to go home and absorb everything they've been told. Read through all the materials. A couple times. And then don't hesitate to call if you think of any further questions."

He paused and met Allie's gaze. "I'd like to do a follow-up appointment with you in two weeks. See how everything is going and see if I can answer any questions that may have come up."

When Allie didn't say anything more, he stood and reached out his hand.

Allie's hand looked small in his. *Frail.* Cano couldn't allow herself to think this way. Allie would beat this thing. Despite being tiny, she was a tiger and wouldn't let this defeat her. Cano's shoulders relaxed. *Yeah.* Allie wouldn't let this stand in her way.

Chapter Nineteen

Days Until Eruption: 42
Sunday, April 6, 1980
Toutle, Washington
41 miles west of Mount St. Helens
Allie's cottage

The fresh breeze billowed in through the open windows. There was still a nip in the air, but Allie didn't care. After being cooped up all winter, she welcomed spring.

The house still held a musty scent, but the breeze would sweep it away. If not, the bleach she'd brought to disinfect the place should do the trick.

She dropped the last box on the kitchen counter and leaned against it. Unloading the car had worn her out. Who was she kidding? The last week had worn her out. Like all the scientists at the university, she'd been working long hours. The heavy bags under her eyes confirmed it. And likely, it wouldn't get any easier. They might get a few stolen hours to relax, but that would be it. Mount St. Helens wouldn't take the weekend off, so neither could they.

At least fortune had smiled on her this week. She'd be able to stay in Toutle for the duration. The dean had given her the assignment she'd wanted—field instructor. Various groups of students would filter in and work under her guidance. They would likely learn more in a few short weeks than they'd learn in the classroom in a year.

She'd rest for a spell and have a light lunch before she drove up to USGS's observation camp. She'd been itching to check it out. Of course, she wouldn't admit why. Besides, it was unlikely that Nova would be there anyway since many of the USGS team was working out of Vancouver much of the time.

Allie shook her leg, sensing a slight tingling, but nothing too serious. She'd need to keep an eye on her health and not let herself get rundown. The location of the cabin was perfect. Should she begin to feel tired while in the field, she could be back at the cottage in a little more than half an hour.

She whistled while she unpacked her groceries. Her other boxes would have to wait until later. The place was small but cozy. The kitchen was one of the largest rooms. On one side, closest to the doorway to the living room, a large table took up nearly half the kitchen. Luckily, the work area was designed for efficiency and didn't require a lot of space. The refrigerator was only a step from the stove, which was a step down from the sink. She'd prepared many a meal here. The most memorable were the ones Nova had helped her make.

Small spaces and Nova were never a good combination since she was like a rambunctious puppy who was curious about everything. Every time Allie turned around, she'd bump into Nova. Eventually, Allie hit on a genius solution.

She'd assigned Nova a designated spot where she was expected to stay. Then Allie would bring her assignments. Cut up onions. Grate cheese. Stuffed peppers. Given a purpose and made to stay in one spot, Nova stopped bouncing off her like a pinball.

Allie shook her head, reached into the sack, and pulled out a loaf of bread. Her thoughts had been going to Nova too much lately, which, Fran reminded her, wasn't a good thing.

Damned MS. Would they still be together if she'd never gotten the terrible disease? She absentmindedly spread mustard on her bread as she remembered that horrible day her life changed forever.

September 11, 1975
University of Washington
Medical Center

Allie was numb. She'd already guessed at her diagnosis, but she hadn't been ready to hear it from Dr. Antioch. Her theory had gone from speculation to reality, and it felt like a gut punch.

Nova walked beside her across the parking lot but remained silent. They'd only been living together for six months. Would this news change that?

Nova unlocked the passenger side door and opened it. Allie bristled. She could open her own damned door. *Relax.* Nova always held the door for her. An old-fashioned notion Allie hadn't been able to break her of.

Allie climbed into the passenger seat, and Nova gently shut the door. When Nova slid into the driver's seat, she slammed her door hard, shaking the entire vehicle.

"Sorry," Nova muttered as she started the engine.

They'd driven several blocks in silence before Allie said, "What are you thinking?"

Nova's face reddened. "I think this sucks."

"Granted." Allie hid her smile. "Maybe you could elaborate."

"Antioch's a quack." Nova's knuckles were white as she clenched the steering wheel. "We need to get a second opinion. You're too young and healthy to have MS." She swallowed hard after she'd said MS.

"I'm thirty-five, which fits right in the range."

Nova shot her a glance. "We need to get a second opinion. Have someone run better tests. Something."

Allie shook her head. "I don't think a second opinion is necessary."

When they pulled up to a stop sign, Nova turned. "You knew." She said it as a statement not a question.

Allie averted her gaze. "I suspected."

"Why didn't you tell me?"

A horn blared from behind them. Cano's hand shot up, but Allie grabbed it.

"Don't flip him the bird." Allie held Nova's hand. "You shouldn't take out your frustration on some innocent soul."

"Innocent?" Nova punched the accelerator, and the car lurched forward. "Someone who lays on the horn like that is far from innocent."

Allie squeezed Nova's hand and continued to hold on. "I hoped I was wrong. That's why I didn't tell you. I thought I'd just gotten myself panicked."

"But it doesn't make sense. They're doctors, for god's sake. If it's been around since the eighteen hundreds, they should know more. Have a cure."

Allie grinned. "I think I've heard something like that before."

Nova shifted her gaze from the road and met Allie's. Confusion danced in her eyes. "Heard what before?"

"What the journalists have been saying at Mount Baker for the past six months. We're geologists. Volcanologists. Why can't we predict if the volcano is going to blow? Shouldn't we be able to pinpoint exactly when it will happen?"

"That's different." Nova's brow wrinkled.

"How so?"

"Because...because...." Nova took both hands off the wheel and threw them over her head in an exaggerated motion. "Because that makes us look bad."

Allie laughed. It felt good. Even during the toughest times, Nova could always make her laugh. "Damn right. How dare I be logical when you're throwing a fit?"

"Exactly."

"Would you put your hands back on the wheel?"

Chapter Twenty

Days until eruption: 42
Sunday, April 6, 1980
Spirit Lake Highway
Near Coldwater Observation

Allie slammed on the brakes, just missing the fool who'd run across the road in front of her car. Her heart thumped at the near miss. The young man glanced in her direction, shrugged, and gave her a cheesy grin before he continued to the other side of the roadway.

She'd been on the road for forty-five minutes when the drive should have only taken her thirty. It was more like Daytona Beach during spring break than an out-of-the-way corner of the world in Washington. She doubted the area had seen this many people during the previous decade.

She met what must have been the fifth news truck. She'd heard the Timberline parking lot had become an informal gathering place for reporters. Judging by the traffic, it was likely true.

She pulled to a stop in front of the barricades and waited for one of the National Guardsmen stationed there to come to her window. His furrowed brow told her that he'd had about enough of the constant stream of traffic.

When he approached the vehicle, she put on

her best smile. She rolled down her window and said, "Good afternoon."

He grunted what she would take as a greeting. "Ma'am, this is a restricted area. You'll have to turn around."

She held out her ID. "I'm a geologist from the University of Washington. I'm on my way to the Coldwater observation camp."

He glanced from her to the ID and back again. Without a word to her, he called out, "Stan, move the barrier."

Another man rushed to the yellow blockade and pulled it aside. He motioned for her to drive through. She went to thank the guardsman, but he'd already turned away. Nerves were apparently frayed, although she couldn't blame the men if today's crowd was any sign of what they'd been dealing with.

Her hands shook as she drove on. The adrenaline from nearly running over the man in the street and the tension from the guards must have stirred up her system. She left her window down, hoping the fresh air would clear her head.

By the time she'd made the short drive to the camp, she felt better. She'd prefer no one notice her reaction, or they might share it with the dean. The last thing she wanted was to be pulled back to the university.

As she drove the final stretch of road, her gaze landed on the van and pickup parked near the camp. Her heart raced. She was almost certain it was Nova's truck.

The sound of a car engine grew louder as Cano bent over the makeshift table. She'd been at Coldwater camp most of the day, and they'd had a stream of visitors. She wished they'd all go away and leave her alone, so she could focus on her analysis of the rock samples.

Scientists were the worst. They all wanted to excitedly share their theories on the volcano, even after she'd told them she had work to do. This latest visitor would be Johnny's problem; she'd had enough.

"Hey, Johnny," she called. When he didn't answer, she called louder.

He peeked his head out of the tent flap. "What are you bellowing about?"

"This one's yours." She motioned toward the car that had almost made it up the road.

"I'm busy."

"Don't care. If I have to talk to one more person, I'm going to lose my pleasant disposition."

"Then I feel sorry for the poor sucker who just pulled up." A car door slammed, and he glanced toward the newcomer. He smiled. "Sure. I'd be happy to greet our visitor."

Cano narrowed her eyes. He'd turned much too agreeable. She spun to see what had brought on his grin. She froze. Without thinking, she brought her hand to her chest.

Allie greeted her with a smile. "Clutching your pearls or heartburn?"

Cano glanced down at her hand that remained on her chest. Heat rose up her neck. "Um…you surprised me."

Johnny moved up next to Cano and shot her a sideways glance. She wanted to laugh at the calculating look on his face and knew the moment he'd put the pieces together. He lunged forward and held out his hand. "You must be Dr. Albright. I've heard so much about you."

Shit. Now she had to run interference before he did or said something embarrassing. He'd already reached Allie and clutched her hand in his.

"Please, call me Allie." Allie smiled. "I wasn't expecting such a warm greeting. Let me guess, Johnny."

"Johnny Garcia, at your service." He held her hand for another beat before letting it go.

Her smile widened, and she glanced at Cano before meeting Johnny's gaze. "I'm so happy to meet you."

Cano pulled up beside Johnny. "How come I'm not liking this?"

Johnny smiled and held up his arm to Allie. "Cano just got done telling me that she was out, and it was my turn to handle our next visitor. It must be my lucky day."

Allie took his arm. "Sounds like Nova is in one of her moods. Will you show me around the camp?"

"It would be my pleasure."

They began to walk away before Cano found her voice. "Very funny, you two. Johnny, get your ass back here with Allie."

Allie turned to Johnny in mock horror. "Does she always treat you this way?"

He hung his head and looked up with his big brown eyes. "Afraid so."

Allie patted his back. "You poor thing."

"Would you two stop it?" Cano said, raising her voice. They were having way too much fun making her squirm.

Johnny and Allie burst out laughing at the same time.

"I'm glad the two of you can find amusement at my expense."

Johnny nudged Cano in the ribs before he said to Allie, "Now that I've met you, I can see why my girl Cano is so enamored."

"Jesus," Cano said. "Would you stop already and go back to work on your stupid radio?"

"It's all fixed, so I have plenty of time to show this lovely lady around the camp."

"I surrender." Cano threw up her hands.

Johnny smiled at Cano before he turned to Allie. "How was the drive up?"

Allie shook her head and sighed. "It's a zoo out there. I almost hit a man. He ran right out in front of me."

"It's unbelievable," Johnny said. "People are treating this like a tourist attraction. No sense taking your kids to Disneyland when you can visit an active volcano."

"They even have souvenir stands." Allie shook her head. "I stopped at one just to see what they're selling. People will buy anything."

"I've gotta pick up something for the kids. They'll get a kick out of it."

"I'm sure." Allie's smile went straight to Cano's heart. "Plus, the media is swarming. I passed several news vans."

"One of the locals compared the road up the mountain to downtown Seattle at rush hour," Cano said.

"Yes! He's right," Allie said. "It took me forever

to get up here. I'm hoping Vancouver sends out guidance soon to keep people from being at the wrong place at the wrong time."

Johnny nodded. "Last I heard, the Forest Service is scrambling to put out a red zone map. They need to get it out soon."

"Rocky Crandell is supposed to draw up a map. Apparently, based on various scenarios. I've been working on one of my own," Cano said.

Allie shuddered. "It gives me the chills to think what could happen if she blows."

"Let's just hope our equipment and analysis picks something up, so we aren't caught flat-footed," Cano said.

"Or that she ends up like Baker and never erupts," Johnny added.

Allie nodded. "Speaking of equipment, I'm ready for a tour."

Johnny moved toward the large tent. "I'll show you what's inside. Then I'll let Cano give you a tour of the grounds."

"Sounds good." Allie smiled. "Are you going to join us, Nova?"

"No way. I've been listening to him ramble on about fixing that stupid radio of his for the past several days. I can't hear about it again, or I might have to throw myself into the crater and sacrifice myself to the volcano gods."

Johnny shook his head. "Your loss." He motioned toward the tent. "Shall we?"

"Looking forward to it." Allie moved up next to him.

Johnny glanced over his shoulder at Cano with a smug smile. "At least someone has taste."

After they disappeared into the tent, Cano held up her trembling hand. *Jesus.* She needed to get a grip. Unexpectedly seeing Allie must have sent adrenaline coursing through her.

She'd wanted to join them but decided against it. Maybe if she practiced what she'd show Allie, her nerves would steady. She walked around the tent, giving a mock tour to no one. On her third pass, she'd perfected her presentation. Was she cracking up? If Johnny and Allie came outside, they'd think she'd lost her mind as she pointed like a game show hostess showing off the latest prizes.

Cano shoved her hands into her pockets and collapsed onto a folding chair sitting outside the tent. Her head fell back, and she closed her eyes, letting the sun warm her face.

"I guess you won't be getting the rest of the tour," Johnny said. "Looks like Cano's asleep on the job."

Cano opened her eyes and glared. "You've been in there rambling for so long, it just about lulled me to sleep." Cano got to her feet.

"Johnny was a fascinating tour guide," Allie said. She turned to him and smiled. "Thank you."

He grinned. "It was my pleasure, but now I have data to record, so I'll leave you with Cano. I apologize in advance." He winked at Cano.

Smartass. No doubt, he was leaving them alone on purpose. Before she could respond, he ducked back inside the tent.

"I guess it's just you and me," Allie said with a smile.

Cano grinned and swept her arm out. "Where would you like to begin?"

"Surprise me."

"Adventurous. I like it." Cano walked to a barrel surrounded by several chairs. "Here we have our fireplace."

Allie laughed. "Fireplace, huh? Looks like a burn barrel to me."

"One person's burn barrel is another person's hearth."

"I see." Allie peeked into the barrel. "Looks like you're out of fuel."

Cano pointed to a pile of wood stacked next to the tent. "We've got plenty of fuel. Hopefully, we won't go through it all. Warmer weather should be just around the corner."

"Spoken like someone who's itching to ride her motorcycle."

Cano clapped both her hands over her heart. "Yes. I almost brought Beulah today and said screw the weather. But Johnny talked me out of it. He's such a downer."

"I might have a solution for you." Allie's eyes danced.

"Really? I'm intrigued."

"Remember my parents' cottage in Toutle?"

"Sure." Cano's eyes widened. "Would they let me park my bike there?"

"I would."

Cano's shoulders slumped. "They aren't exactly my biggest fans. Are you sure they wouldn't slash my tires?"

"They're not that bad. Besides, they aren't staying there. I am."

"What? You mean—?"

"Yep. I've been named the field instructor for the

university. They'll be bringing out groups of students for me to give hands-on experience." Allie's smile lit her whole face. "I'll get to be closer to the action, and the cottage saves me from having to make the drive back and forth from Seattle. It works perfect."

"Congratulations." Cano's heart raced. This changed everything. Allie would be around the mountain and Coldwater a lot. "Definitely well deserved. You were the best professor I ever had."

Allie shook her head and laughed. "You had me for six whole classes when Dr. Foreman's appendix burst. I don't think you have enough data to critique my body of work."

"Seven." Cano bit back a flirtatious retort to Allie's mention of her *body* of work.

"I stand corrected." Allie smirked. "Still, I think you're biased."

Cano shook her head. "Nope. Anyone that can make Metamorphic Processes exciting should be named teacher of the year."

"Thank you." Allie's eyes danced, and she bit her lip. "I'm looking forward to being in the field. It's been a while."

Cano's chest tightened. She wondered if Allie had done any field work since their time at Mount Baker. It wasn't a topic she planned to broach, so she said, "When do you start?"

"I just moved my stuff in today. I haven't even unpacked. My first group of students should be here on Tuesday."

"So you're going to be...um...be—"

"Hanging around here more," Allie finished Cano's sentence.

Watching Allie teach was one of Cano's greatest

pleasures. It never got old, witnessing the skeptical, sometimes condescending, looks turn to admiration as Allie's intelligence and wit won them over. Would Cano be able to concentrate on her own work when Allie was around? She stared at Allie with what she suspected was a dumbfounded look, but she couldn't muster any other reaction.

"Are you okay with that?" Allie asked, the hesitation evident in her tone.

"Yes!" *Seriously.* Apparently, Cano was going to show all her cards up front. "I mean, yes, I was just surprised since you'd not mentioned anything before now."

"It all happened so fast."

Butterflies danced in Cano's stomach. Having Allie closer was both exhilarating and terrifying. So far, they'd done well. No animosity. In fact, the opposite. Cano was drawn to Allie, but did Allie feel the same?

"Are you sure you're all right?" Allie asked. "It's not often you're speechless." She playfully swatted Cano's arm.

"Um, yeah. Sure." Cano needed to get control of the conversation. "You wouldn't mind if I parked my bike there?"

"I'll even let you have the garage."

"Thanks." Even though Cano had warning bells going off in her head, having her bike nearby would be amazing. "You just made my day."

"Because you have a place to park your bike or because I'll be here?"

Cano swallowed hard. Was Allie flirting? *Crap.* She needed to find her swagger. Cano grinned and raised her eyebrows. "Both."

Allie's eyes widened in surprise before she smiled. "I see you haven't lost your cockiness."

"It's how I survive."

"I remember."

The conversation was going down another path Cano wasn't ready to tread. "Shall we move on with our tour?"

"Definitely."

Cano took Allie to the area where she'd been analyzing rock samples. They stood shoulder to shoulder as Cano ran her finger along the striations on the rock. Back on firmer ground now that they were talking about science, Cano forgot her earlier nerves.

"And you said Johnny would talk my ear off about his equipment," Allie said. "We've been engrossed in this rock for at least half an hour."

"No way." Cano glanced at her watch. "Shit. How did that happen?"

"Time flies when you're having fun."

"Remember that time at Baker when—"

Allie pointed. "Rules violation."

"Oh. The rules still apply? I thought it was just for our drive."

Allie shook her head. Her eyes held pain. "The rules still apply."

"Okay." Cano held up her hands and took a step back. "I'm sorry."

"Not your fault." Allie dropped her gaze. "I think it's better if we keep the rules in place. Don't you?"

Talk about a loaded question. How should she respond? "Whatever makes you the most comfortable." Cano suspected the response wouldn't be well received, but it bought her time to come up with another answer.

"Ah, we're back to this, are we? Let me make all the tough choices." Allie's voice held an edge.

That's the way you always wanted it, Cano thought but knew better than to say it. She didn't want the conversation to spiral any further. This was her chance to repair the damage of the past. "I understand how that might've come out," Cano said, trying to keep her tone as emotionless as possible. "But that wasn't my intention."

Allie's face reddened. "When did you become such a grownup?"

Cano grinned, seeing an opening to lighten the moment. "I turned thirty at the end of December, so I'm no longer a kid."

The hard line in Allie's jaw softened. "I see. I suppose we better get you signed up for the AARP."

"Do you have your card on you, so I can get the number off it?"

"Smartass."

Crisis averted. Cano didn't want tension to build between them again. Eventually, they'd need to talk about the past, but for now, she was happy to reconnect. "Are you ready for the highlight of the tour?"

"You mean there's more?" Allie feigned surprise. "After seeing the hearth and the rock samples, I'm afraid I might not be able to handle any more thrills."

Johnny picked that moment to emerge from the tent. "What's that? Cano, are you out here giving Allie thrills?"

Heat rose up Cano's neck. Damned Johnny.

"Yes, she is," Allie said and pretended to fan herself.

The heat continued up Cano's neck to her

cheeks. *Please don't let it show.*

Johnny pointed and laughed. "I think we've embarrassed her."

"She's already showed me *her* fire and *her* rocks." Allie said with a smirk full of sexual innuendo.

"Oh, lordy." Johnny turned to Cano. "Haven't I told you that you can't go around showing your fire and your rocks to the ladies?"

Allie burst out laughing and was joined by Johnny. Cano tried her best to bite back her laugh but soon joined them.

When the laughter subsided, Cano said, "You guys are regular comedians. Just for that," she gently poked Allie's arm, "I might not show you the highlight."

Allie clasped her hands together and moved toward Cano. "Please. If I promise to be good."

Johnny chuckled. "I'll leave you two to work this out." He turned back toward the tent.

"Wait. What did you want?" Cano asked.

"Oh, yeah. I just got done talking to the guys in Vancouver. After the three explosions yesterday, the Geological Survey is bringing in more scientists. Looks like we might have a regular party here soon."

Cano groaned. "Yippee. I can't wait."

"I was just telling them on the radio, Cano is such a people person she'll be thrilled." Johnny chuckled.

Allie bit her lip. "Aren't you two a little concerned?"

"About?" Johnny asked.

Allie turned and gazed at Mount St. Helens. Clouds drifted past the snow-covered peak. "We're dealing with a volcano that might erupt. The harmonic tremors were a game changer to me. If magma is flowing, she could blow. She's pretty isolated, but as more and more people flock in, the risk for lost lives goes up."

"Don't forget the loggers," Cano said and pointed toward the west. "They're back to felling trees up to the timberline. Couldn't be more than five miles from the summit."

"Tourist season is coming," Allie added. "Spirit Lake has cabins all over it. The resort owners are going to be clamoring to open up."

"Speaking of resort owners, did you hear about Harry Truman?" Cano asked.

"Didn't he die in the early seventies?" Johnny said.

"Not that Harry Truman. The old geezer who's refusing to evacuate." Cano shook her head. "I saw him on TV the other day. He's run the Mount St. Helens lodge for over fifty years and says he's staying."

"And they're letting him?" Allie asked, her eyes wide.

"What else are they going to do?" Cano said. "The press is making him out to be a hero. The rebel who refuses to give up his freedom. I don't think anyone has the political will to snatch some old guy from his home."

Allie put her hand against her forehead and shook her head. "This is going to turn ugly, isn't it?"

"Likely," Johnny said. "People could die if the wrong moves are made."

"This conversation is a ray of sunshine," Cano said. "Can we talk about something else?"

"Let's," Allie said. "How about we finish our tour?"

"That's my cue," Johnny said. "I'll let Cano

continue to *thrill* you."

Allie laughed, while Cano scowled at Johnny's retreating back.

"Let me show you my favorite spot." Without thinking, Cano took Allie's hand. She froze when she realized what she'd done.

Allie squeezed Cano's hand but didn't let go. "I'd like that."

Cano's chest swelled as she walked with Allie toward the edge of the camp and the time-lapse camera.

Chapter Twenty-one

Days until eruption: 39
Wednesday, April 9, 1980
Toutle, Washington
Allie's cottage

Allie straightened the sparse living room for the third time. She'd hurried home after she'd finished with her students, so she could prepare for dinner.

She rolled her eyes. *So domestic.* This shouldn't be a big deal. Dinner with a friend. She'd made dinner plenty of times for Fran, so it would be no different. Besides, it was only polite to provide a meal when Nova dropped off her bike. It wasn't like she invited her for the sole purpose of getting together. *Yep.* Keep thinking that way, and maybe she'd believe it.

The beef stew boiling in the pot filled the house with the smell of thyme and rosemary. The aroma made her stomach rumble. Her abdomen had been in knots most of the day, so she'd eaten little.

For the past two days, her legs had been tingling a little more than she'd like. She knew she was pushing too hard, but there was so much to be done. Having Nova for dinner would force her to slow down, instead of spending the evening working on lesson plans.

Luckily, Fran wasn't around, or she'd be all over her. Fran and Ben planned on driving down on

Saturday, so Allie had better get enough rest. If not, Fran would pick it up in a heartbeat.

She hadn't told Fran about dinner with Nova, knowing she'd get Fran's patented disapproving glare. Sure, Fran was protective, but Allie could handle herself, couldn't she?

Allie didn't have time to dwell on it. She needed to get out of her grubby clothes and into something more appropriate for a dinner guest. She'd tried on several outfits. At first, she'd chosen a bright blue silk shirt and a pair of black slacks, but she feared it would be too dressy for entertaining at home. Instead, she'd settled on a simple black button-down shirt with a nice pair of blue jeans. Casual would be a better statement to make. Besides, Nova would be coming from the camp, so she'd be in her work clothes.

Allie picked up the necklace for the third time. She loved the piece and still wore it often, but would it give Nova the wrong idea? They'd found it in a little shop in Seattle that sold handmade jewelry. It had been made from lava stone and had quickly become Allie's favorite.

She fastened the clasp around her neck. No way would she start altering the way she dressed. *Sure.* That sounded tough. Forget about the multiple times she'd changed her clothes.

She ran a brush through her hair and considered putting it up before she quickly discarded the idea.

A door slammed out front, causing her to jump. She glanced at her watch. *Right on time.* She took a deep breath and made her way toward the front of the house.

As soon as Nova knocked, Allie threw open the door.

"Shit." Nova jumped and nearly dropped the large bag clutched in her hand. "Um, sorry. I wasn't expecting you to answer so soon. Here." She thrust out the bag, and her face reddened. Before Allie could take it, she pulled it back. "Um…I mean I brought you something. For dinner. Well, not for dinner because you made dinner, but as a complement to dinner. I mean dinner doesn't need a complement because I'm sure it's delicious."

Allie stifled a giggle and held up her hand. When Nova stopped rambling, Allie said, "I have an idea. I'm gonna shut the door. You knock again. And we'll start this all over. How's that?"

Nova nodded.

"But this time, I'll wait for a count of ten before I answer. Does that work for you?"

Nova nodded again.

Allie shut the door and waited. No knock came. She moved to the window and peeked out. Nova had her eyes closed and looked to be taking deep breaths. Allie's chest filled. Anytime Nova got nervous, she'd stop and take a few breaths. *So sweet.*

Allie waited. Soon a knock came. *One, two, three, four, five, six, seven, eight, nine, ten.* She opened the door and grinned. "Nova, it's so good to see you." Allie pretended to look at her watch. "But you're late."

Nova's eyes widened. "But I was here…and..."

Allie burst out laughing. "Sorry, I couldn't resist."

The tightness in Nova's jaw relaxed, and she laughed. The tension disappeared as they laughed together.

Allie reached out her hand. "Please, come in."

When Nova stepped into the house, Allie finally

got a good look at her. Allie's theory had been wrong. Nova must have changed at the camp because she wore a soft gray sweater with a pink oxford shirt underneath. Her black pants were pleated in the front, accenting her slender waist.

"I brought something for you," Nova said, holding up the bag in her hand. She moved closer to Allie to hand it to her.

Cano's cologne filled the air. "You smell good." Allie took a deeper whiff. "What is it?"

Nova blushed. "It's a new cologne I'm trying out. Polo."

Allie leaned forward to take the bag and made another exaggerated inhale. "That's yummy." *Oh, god.* Did she just say that out loud?

Nova grinned. "Are you talking about me or the beef stew that's making my mouth water?"

Allie wasn't going to bite, so she said, "Beef stew, how did you know?"

"I'd know the smell of your beef stew anywhere." Cano smiled and nodded toward the sack. "Aren't you going to see what I brought? Just be careful when you open it."

"Let's go ahead and take it into the kitchen."

When they entered the kitchen, Nova put her hand against her chest. "Oh, my god, it smells even better in here."

Allie set the bag on the counter and carefully opened it. She stifled a smile when she saw the familiar floral paper. She wouldn't recommend putting flowers in a bag, but it was the thought that counted. Allie lifted them out carefully.

"I hope they didn't get smashed." Nova's voice was full of concern. "I bought them in Vancouver this morning and tried to keep them alive at Coldwater."

"They'll be fine." One side of the wrapping was pressed in; hopefully, they weren't crushed. As she lifted them out of the bag, she bumped the baggie full of water attached to the bottom of the bouquet. Before she could react, the bag plummeted to the floor, sending water splashing in all directions.

"Oh, shit. Shit." Nova grabbed a towel from next to the sink and dropped to the floor. "That was so stupid of me."

"It's okay. It's just water."

Nova sopped up all the water she could until the towel was saturated. Allie tore paper towels off the roll and handed them to her.

"It's all over your pants, too." Nova blotted Allie's pants leg but abruptly stopped. A look of horror crossed her face. She backed away, jumped to her feet, and handed the towel to Allie. "Um…you might want to use these to dry off."

Why? I kinda liked you doing it. Allie stopped herself from saying it aloud. It wouldn't be fair. Besides, Nova was already rattled enough. Allie took the offered towel. "Just relax. It's okay."

Nova let out a long breath. "I seem to be making a mess of things."

"Nonsense." Allie picked up the bouquet and peeled the paper away to reveal a splash of orange and yellow. "Oh, Nova, they're beautiful. You got my favorites."

"Tiger lilies to match the color of lava and the sunflowers to match your hair."

"Aren't you poetic today?"

Nova reddened again. "There's something else in there, too."

"Let me get these in water first." Allie pulled a vase out of the cabinet and did her best to rearrange them after their less-than-ideal travel arrangement. Satisfied, she turned back.

Nova had picked up the sack and held it out to her.

"Oh, my." Allie pulled out a box of Ding Dongs.

"I know you like Twinkies, but I thought the Ding Dongs were a little classier."

Allie bit her lip. She'd almost forgotten Nova's childlike excitement over simple things. "Thank you. This will go perfect with the stew."

"There's wine, too." Nova shifted her gaze to the bag. "That Barefoot kind. Isn't that what you drink?"

"It was."

"Oh, shit. Was?" Nova ran her hand through her hair. "Damn it. You aren't supposed to have wine with your...uh...um...condition."

Allie held up her hand with her thumb and forefinger a couple of inches apart. "I can have a little."

"Oh, good." Nova shifted her weight from one foot to the other.

Nova seemed to be floundering, even though Allie found it adorable. *No.* One didn't think of her friend as adorable, did she?

"Why don't you set the table?" Allie pointed to the dishes she'd laid out earlier. Giving Nova a task might put her at ease. "I've got to throw the bread in the oven."

"Bread? That fluffy flakey stuff you always made?"

"Straight from Pillsbury." She held up the familiar blue roll. "I'm afraid I can't take any credit for it."

Nova picked up the plates. "I'm all over this."

"Wait."

Nova stopped in her tracks and turned. Her eyes wide. "What's wrong?"

Allie pulled open a drawer. "I got you a present, too." She held out the bag.

Nova's eyes lit up. "Is this some of those coffee beans you were telling me about?"

"Yep. Starbucks."

"Can we have some with our dessert?"

"Ding Dongs, wine, and coffee. Sounds like a feast."

Chapter Twenty-two

Days until eruption: 39
Wednesday, April 9, 1980
Toutle, Washington
Allie's cottage

Cano leaned back in her chair, her stomach full. She'd always loved Allie's stew and could never stop at one helping, even though she should. "I haven't had a meal like that in years."

Allie gave her a shy smile. "It's not like it's gourmet. It's just beef stew."

"Well, it's the best beef stew I've ever eaten."

"Thank you. By the way you're slumped over in your chair, you won't be ready for dessert any time soon."

Cano groaned. "Ugh. Don't mention food." She patted her belly. "I think I've gained ten pounds in just this one meal."

"Why don't we go in the living room where you can get more comfortable?"

Cano rose from the table and picked up her bowl.

"I'll clean up later," Allie said.

"Nope. You cooked. I help clean up."

Allie stood but didn't move to pick up her dishes.

"Is everything all right?" Cano stiffened. Had she done something wrong? Being here with Allie felt so normal. So familiar. She'd spent the last four years missing it, so she didn't want to do anything to mess it up.

For a second, Cano thought Allie's eyes had turned misty, but it must have been the light. Allie opened her mouth to speak but closed it.

Cano's heart raced. She'd blown it, but she didn't know how. "Did I say something wrong?"

Allie grabbed her dishes from the table. "No, no. Not at all. I was having a *moment*, but I'm okay now."

"Can I ask what kind of moment? So I don't cause another one."

Allie smiled. "You didn't cause it. It's just been nice so far. Nice having you here." Allie met Cano's gaze. "After you left, I guess I never thought we'd be here again. Doing this."

Allie's words were like a punch to the gut. *After you left.* The words reverberated in Cano's skull. She needed to come up with a response. One that wouldn't come out defensive but would stop the path the conversation was going.

Cano decided on a lighthearted reply. "Is that a foul?"

Allie narrowed her eyes for a split second, but then a smile broke out on her face. "Yep. I withdraw my statements. Does that keep me from getting whistled for the infraction?"

"Yep. At least this time, but you're on probation." Cano gave her a crooked smile.

"Just for that, I'm gonna make you wash the dishes." Allie walked to the sink with a pile of plates.

Cano watched her, enjoying the way her jeans hugged her buttocks. If anything, Allie had gotten even more beautiful over the last four years.

Allie turned. "Let's go. These dishes aren't going

to wash themselves."

Cano took a deep breath. "I'm on it." Would this make things better, or would she experience the pain all over again?

Allie sipped on the wine Nova had brought. She hadn't felt this relaxed in a long time. She sat on one end of the couch with her feet pulled up under her, while Nova sat on the other with her long legs stretched out onto the coffee table.

It was nice having Nova here. Their conversation was easy and familiar. They'd only had to call foul twice when the conversation got dangerously close to talking about the past. Now they were deep into a discussion about Mount St. Helens, which kept them on safer ground.

"How long do you think they'll keep up the restriction?" Cano asked.

Allie shrugged. "Probably not long enough. It's only been a week since Governor Dixy Lee Ray signed the emergency declaration, and I'm already hearing grumbling about it."

"What kind?"

"The sheriff moved the roadblock farther down the mountain, but someone didn't like it and complained to Dixy. She ordered him to put it back closer to the mountain."

"That's crazy. Nobody needs to be up there."

"Tell that to the Weyerhaeuser Company. Apparently, they've been given permission to continue logging."

Nova shook her head. "Why? Can't they log somewhere else for now?"

"You'd think. But it's not just them. The cabin owners are getting antsy, too."

"I thought people would be scared after Tuesday's eruption lasted an hour."

"That's part of the problem. People think it's going to be like the volcanoes that rumble and have mini eruptions every now and then. Kinda like Hawaii."

Nova shook her head. "So short-sighted. Maybe we need to get mouthy like that old guy Harry Truman."

"That's a plan. Are you volunteering?" Allie smirked at the thought of Nova speaking her mind. "You'd be yanked back to Menlo Park so fast, you wouldn't know what hit you."

"Johnston keeps opening his mouth, so it saves me from being on the radar."

Allie took another sip of her wine. She pulled her legs out from under her and stretched them out on the couch. "What did David say now?"

"He told a reporter that the mountain will *just go boom! Maybe with no warning.*"

"He's right."

"No doubt." Nova frowned. "But then Mullineaux was quoted as saying that the probability of a big eruption is very low."

"Did he really say that?"

Nova shrugged. "Who knows, but the press likes the *drama*. One scientist against the other. Makes for an interesting story, but they don't understand how many variables we're looking at. I'd think they'd want to err on the side of caution."

Allie snapped her fingers. "That reminds me. I have to show you the draft of a map I got from Vancouver." Allie set down her wine glass and swung her feet toward the floor.

Nova jumped up. "I'll get it. Where is it?"

Allie's jaw tightened, but she forced herself to relax. Nova was being kind. Not making a commentary on her capabilities. "I left it on my desk in the spare room."

Nova disappeared but returned with a deep crease in her forehead as she studied the map. "Are you kidding me? They think this will protect people?"

Allie's heart rate increased when Nova sat on the couch beside her and put the map between them. Nova's finger traced the uneven borderline around the mountain. Allie always loved Nova's hands. They were big and strong with prominent veins.

"Did you hear what I just said?" Nova asked.

"I'm sorry. I missed it." She needed to stop gaping and pay attention.

"I said, look at the border on the northwest. What are they thinking?"

Allie put her hand next to Nova's on the map but was careful not to touch her. Afraid of how either might react. "Apparently, they didn't want to infringe on private property."

Nova jabbed her finger at the map. "It's less than three miles from the summit. The other areas are ten, which I think is still too close. But three miles? If she blows, anyone there might as well kiss their ass goodbye."

"It scares the hell out of me." Allie shuddered.

Nova put her hand on top of Allie's and then stiffened. "Um...I just..." She pulled back.

Nova's hand had felt good covering hers—reassuring. Allie suddenly became more aware of how close they were sitting. Strangely, it didn't feel sexual but comforting. She wanted nothing more than to feel Nova's touch again, but she knew it wasn't fair. Instead, she patted Nova's arm a couple of times and then stood. "I think it's about time for dessert. Are you ready for some Ding Dongs?"

"I thought you'd never ask," Nova said with a smirk. Allie saw the sadness behind her eyes but said nothing.

"Two Ding Dongs, coming up."

Cano glanced at the clock. *Shit.* It was nearly eleven. The evening had been nearly perfect, except for the awkward moment when she'd put her hand on Allie's, but Allie had handled it with grace and not made her feel bad.

Cano stretched. "I better think about heading out, but this has been great." She rose to her feet.

"It has." Allie smiled and rose, too. "I have one question I've been wanting to ask you since I first saw you."

Cano's back stiffened. *Shit.* This didn't sound good. "Okay," Cano said tentatively.

"What in the world is this?" Allie pointed to the long hair at the back of Cano's head and touched the curls that rested on Cano's shoulder. "You've always had short hair."

Cano turned from side to side. "Do you like it?"

"Um...well..."

"You hate it." Cano nervously pushed the hair off her shoulder.

"It's different." Allie drew out the word different.

"It's called a mullet."

"Mole it? Named after an animal?"

Cano's forehead wrinkled. "Animal?"

"A mole." Allie put her hand on her hip.

"No. Mullet." When Allie continued to stare at her blankly, Cano said, "M-U-L-L-E-T. Mullet."

"Oh. Mullet."

"Yes."

Allie touched Cano's hair again, the look of confusion still on her face. "So other people are wearing their hair like this, too?"

"A few. It's gonna be all the rage."

"God, I hope not," Allie said under her breath.

Cano pointed. "I knew it. You hate it."

"Hate's a strong word. It'll just take a little time to get used to."

"And then you'll love it. Everyone will be wearing their hair like this."

"Sure they will." Allie smirked. "Lesbians far and wide will be clamoring to style their hair that way."

"What can I say? I'm a trendsetter." Cano swiped her hand through her hair and pushed it back.

Allie touched the hair on Cano's shoulder. "I do like the way it curls up at the bottom."

"See it's growing on you already." Cano grinned.

Allie smiled. "Are you working at Coldwater tomorrow?"

"No." Cano crinkled her nose. "They're making me attend a stupid planning meeting in Vancouver."

"Your favorite thing. An endless meeting."

"You know me too well." *Ugh.* Was that bringing up the past? She braced for Allie to call a foul.

Allie's cheeks flushed. "Would you like to take the rest of the Ding Dongs? I'd offer you the leftover stew, but I doubt it would do you much good at the hotel." A mischievous smile played on Allie's lips. "And I won't be responsible for you crashing because you're eating it on your drive back."

Cano smiled. This time she refrained from saying, *You know me so well.* "Thanks. But the Ding Dongs were a gift, so they're all yours."

Allie put her hand against her chest in an exaggerated motion. "A gift I will treasure forever."

Cano laughed. They'd moved toward the front door as they talked, and Cano's hand fell on the doorknob. Her chest tightened. Was this it? Had this been Allie's way of putting closure on their past? Her grip tightened on the knob. She wanted to beg Allie to let her come again, but instead, she patted her stomach with her other hand. "The meal was amazing."

"Beats hotel food?"

"Beats most food. You know how much I always loved your cooking." Cano held up her hand. "I know, foul."

Allie grinned. "I'll let it pass since you were complimenting me."

"Whew. I dodged a bullet on that one." Despite the lighthearted teasing, their discomfort was evident. The tension was denser than volcanic ash. She inwardly smiled at her geological humor.

"Are you going to be at Coldwater on Friday?"

"I better be. I can't sit in meetings two days in a row."

"Well, maybe...." Allie fidgeted with the bottom of her shirt, and her voice held a note of hesitation. "I have the leftover stew that needs to be eaten. And *The Facts of Life is on.*"

Cano let go of the doorknob, hoping she didn't leave sweaty prints on it. She stopped short of wiping the moisture on her pants leg. "Is that an invitation?"

Allie smiled and stood taller. "Yes. It is." Her

voice was filled with renewed confidence."

"Then I accept. Especially since you're luring me with *The Facts of Life*. I love that show."

"It's good, but sometimes, the girls are just too damned sweet."

Cano smirked. "You think they need a bad girl?"

"Exactly."

"Maybe one that rides a motorcycle?" Cano couldn't help herself, knowing she was bordering on flirting.

"I think a motorcycle-riding girl would be perfect. Stir things up a bit."

Cano nodded and pursed her lips. "Might be interesting. Give Blair a run for her money."

"Maybe that's exactly what Blair needs."

"I couldn't agree more." Cano's insides danced, but she fought to keep her cool exterior. Were they still talking about the television show or something else? Her senses told her it was time to make an exit. She wanted to hug Allie good night but thought better of it. She'd leave that entirely in Allie's hands.

As if on cue, Allie put her hand on Cano's arm and looked into her eyes. "Nova, I can't tell you how nice this was. I'm so glad...it's just nice."

"I agree." Cano knew it was impossible, but she swore she could feel the heat of Allie's hand through her leather jacket. She needed to get out of here before she said or did something stupid. She twisted the doorknob. "I'll see you Friday."

Allie smiled. "Friday it is."

Cano willed herself to step from the house. She glanced over her shoulder and waved but kept moving toward her truck.

Chapter Twenty-three

Days until eruption: 35
Sunday, April 13, 1980
Toutle, Washington
Allie's cottage

Allie gave the bowl one more shake before she wet her finger and stuck it into the mixture of spices. She tasted it and frowned. *Not quite right.*

She grabbed the jar of cumin and shook a generous amount into the rub. It was her secret ingredient. Nova had never been able to guess, no matter how hard she tried. In typical Nova fashion, she'd dreamed up elaborate ways to figure it out. She hadn't succeeded.

Nova had come the closest when she'd *borrowed* a motion-activated camera from the university and rigged it up in the pantry. Luckily, Allie had noticed the blinking light peeking out from behind a box of rice before she revealed any secrets.

Just to be sure, Allie sampled the concoction again. Satisfied, she poured the contents of the bowl onto a cookie sheet. One at a time, she put a pork chop on the sheet and flipped it over several times as she used both hands to grind the rub into the meat.

Allie was thankful for the distraction. All morning, she'd wondered if this was a good idea. *Too late now.* Allie scooped up the spice jars and put them back on the shelf next to the sink.

Had the shower just turned off? Allie cocked her head and listened. The door to the guest bedroom, where Fran and Ben were staying, clicked shut. She needed to move fast. She covered the meat with foil and slid the tray into the refrigerator. The potatoes and vegetables would have to wait until after she got cleaned up.

She threw open her bedroom closet and scanned the offerings. The lime green sweatshirt caught her eye. Nova loved bright colors. *Stop.* She was not dressing for Nova, but still she grabbed it out of the pile. The less colorful sweatshirts mocked her from the shelf, so she slammed the door.

She pulled a pair of Calvin Klein jeans from her dresser. The ones she knew molded to her body as if they were custom tailored. After selecting her undergarments, she approached the bedroom door and opened it an inch.

Clear. The guest bedroom door was still closed. Allie made a dash for the bathroom and slipped inside. Juvenile, maybe, but she wasn't ready to have a conversation with Fran about Nova.

Perhaps after she'd showered, dressed, and put on makeup, she'd be more prepared. *Oh, god.* At that moment, she realized she intended on putting on makeup for a backyard barbecue. *So?* She glared at herself in the mirror. She felt more confident when she looked her best. What was wrong with that?

She turned on the shower, and while it warmed, she slipped out of her clothes and put them in the hamper. *Shit.* She needed to do laundry.

Her routine was off with Nova's visits on Wednesday and Friday. She smiled. Friday night had been nice. They'd watched *The Facts of Life* and then played gin rummy. In many ways, it was more intimate than a date. *Damn it.* It was *not* a date. It was two old friends hanging out.

Yep, maybe this was a bad idea. She pulled the shower curtain back farther and stepped in. The warm water cascaded down her face. She forced herself to focus on the sensation of the drops bouncing off her skin.

She'd nearly reset her thoughts when the bathroom door creaked open. Allie wiped the water from her eyes and moved a corner of the curtain away.

Fran sat on the closed toilet lid.

Allie pulled the curtain closed. "What the hell are you doing?"

"We need to talk."

"Now? Did you happen to notice I'm in the goddamned shower?"

"Yep." Fran's voice held a hint of amusement, but she'd yet to laugh.

"And that's acceptable in what world?" Allie did her best to put indignation into her voice, even though she was holding back a giggle.

"In the world that you are trying to avoid me. Two can play at your games."

"And what games might I be playing?" Allie had returned to washing herself. She put a dollop of shampoo in her palm and rubbed it into her hair.

"Yesterday, telling me you invited Cano to the barbecue while we were in the car with Ben and then faking being tired last night so I couldn't grill you about it. I saw the light under your bedroom door. I know you were in there reading one of your smutty books."

"First, Rita Mae Brown's books are not smutty, unlike those Harlequin romances you read."

After several beats without Allie saying more, Fran said, "And what's second?"

"I don't have a second."

"Then you can't have a first."

"Can if I want to." Allie scrubbed her hair, enjoying the scalp massage.

"Ahh," Fran held out the word. "I get it. You think if you distract with firsts without seconds, it'll save you from the conversation we need to have."

"I'm not sure there's any conversation *needed* here."

"Well, I think there is. And I don't intend to leave my throne until we have it. So you can stay in there and get all pruney, or you can talk to me. The choice is yours."

"Is pruney a word?"

"Nice try." Fran chuckled.

"Fine." Allie evenly distributed the conditioner through her hair. "Lecture away. Let's get this over with."

"Do you know what the hell you're doing?"

"Yep, I'm conditioning my hair." Allie stifled a laugh, imagining the irritated look on Fran's face.

"Yep. You're going to be one big prune by the time Cano gets here."

"It's not like you've never seen me naked." It was true. During her worst times, Fran had helped her dress when she struggled to do it for herself.

"Well, I'd rather not have this conversation with your naked ass."

"Does that mean I just have to moon you to get you to go away?"

"Keep it up, and I'll drop my pants and stick my butt into that shower."

"Hmm, I'm not sure you should be offering up that lily white globe of perfection to a lesbian." Allie bit her lip, barely able to contain her laughter. She only wished she could see Fran's face. Every now and then, she'd turn the tables on Fran, and this was one of those times.

"Jesus Christ. You're incorrigible."

"Yes." Allie did a dance in the shower, making sure to splash water, so Fran would know what she was doing. "I got an incorrigible."

"I'll make a deal with you."

"Sounds interesting." Allie rinsed the conditioner from her hair and squeezed out the excess water.

"I'll let you finish your shower in peace. And then we'll talk while you put on your makeup."

"Who says I'm wearing makeup?"

"I'm not even going to justify that with an answer. Is it a deal?"

"Fine. Deal. Now get the hell out of here."

Chapter Twenty-four

Days until eruption: 35
Sunday, April 13, 1980
Spirit Lake Highway, Washington

Cano and Johnny needed to make a run up to Coldwater before the barbecue, so she sped past the exit toward Toutle. Just being this close to Allie caused her heart to race. *Dumbass.* She needed to get this under control, or the cookout would be a disaster.

"Whoa," Johnny said from the passenger seat. "We're not in the Blue Flame."

Cano turned and narrowed her eyes. "Huh?"

"The Blue Flame." Johnny slapped his knee. "I thought you were into speed considering that motorcycle of yours. You don't know about the Blue Flame?"

Realization dawned. "Oh. You're talking about the rocket car. The one that set the land speed record in the Bonneville Salt Flats."

"What other Blue Flame is there?"

"The one they claimed to have spotted in the crack in Mount St. Helens." Cano let up on the accelerator now that they were past Allie's exit. "Back at the end of March. They thought it was possibly burning gas. Remember?"

"Of course I remember, but they haven't seen

any flame for almost two weeks."

"I thought maybe they had since you brought it up."

"I wasn't talking about those flames."

"I know that now, but can't you see my confusion?"

"Okay, fine." Johnny nodded. "I'll return your need for speed card. Just as long as you know what the Blue Flame is."

"Know it." Cano waved her hand as if motioning toward a display. "I had posters of it all over my dorm room. October 23, 1970."

"Hopeless." Johnny shook his head. "And people still wanted to be your friend?"

Cano glared.

When he realized she didn't plan to respond, he said, "So what should I expect today at this shindig?"

"Shindig? I would hardly call it a shindig."

"Then what are you calling it?"

"A cookout."

"Shindig sounds more interesting."

"Did you tell Rosaria that you were attending a shindig?"

"Maybe." He defiantly stuck out his bottom lip. "This is the first time I've had time off since I got here, so I can call it a shindig if I want to."

Cano snorted. "I'd hardly call it time off since you're going right back up to Coldwater after the cook…um, shindig."

"See, it sounds better." Johnny gave her a smug look. "So tell me about it."

"I expect you to protect me from Fran."

"No way. From what you've told me, I'm way outmatched."

"True."

"Why does she hate you so much?"

"Because she loves Allie."

"You mean...um...they...." Cano caught Johnny's blush out of the corner of her eye. "Doesn't she have a husband?"

"For god's sake. Get your mind out of the gutter."

"I don't know how this lesbian stuff works."

Cano laughed. "Fran's a mama bear and would protect Allie with her life, so I can't dislike her, even though she seems to hate me."

"But you knew her, Fran, before. Did she hate you then?"

"I knew her. She was Allie's best friend when the two of us met, so she's always been in the picture. I think she liked me enough, until Allie was diagnosed with MS."

Cano's chest tightened at the memory. She felt Johnny's gaze on her, but he didn't speak, so she continued. "The only thing that made leaving Seattle bearable was knowing Fran would look after Allie." Cano swallowed hard. She wouldn't cry in front of Johnny.

"Isn't it going to be awkward being around Fran today?"

"Probably." Cano took her gaze from the road and shot Johnny a cheesy smile. "But you'll be there."

"I plan on hiding behind you." Johnny chuckled. "Fran sounds too scary for my sensitive soul."

Cano laughed. "No worries. I'll just grin and bear it. I respect Allie too much to cause any trouble."

"You're ruining your reputation." He shook his head. "The bad girl isn't so bad after all."

"Shh. Don't tell anyone." She glanced at Johnny

and was surprised to see the fatherly concern in his eyes. She quickly turned her attention back to the road.

They'd almost made it to the roadblock, which was good because she didn't want to have this conversation any longer.

Cars lined the side of the road as people parked to take pictures of the volcano in the distance. A lone guard leaned against the barrier. He looked bored and slightly annoyed as he approached the truck.

A smile lit his face as he got closer. "Cano, what the hell are you doing here on a Sunday?"

"I was about to ask you the same thing, Tom. Isn't it Zachary's birthday this weekend?"

He beamed. "It was Friday. Had the party on Saturday. They grow so fast. I still can't believe he's five."

"Then I'll ask you again. Why aren't you at home with that sweet family of yours?"

"Sunday's overtime, so I couldn't pass it up."

"I suppose not with another mouth to feed on the way."

He smiled again. "I can't believe you remember all my ramblings."

"I've got my fingers crossed for a girl." She motioned toward Johnny. "You ever need any advice, this is your man. He's got three teenagers."

Tom's eyes widened. "I don't even want to think about their teenage years."

Cano pointed at Johnny. "And he still has a full head of hair."

Tom ran his hand through his thinning hair. "Afraid I'm not going to be so lucky." He held his hand through the open window. "I'm Tom."

Johnny took his hand. "Johnny. It's nice to meet you."

Tom pulled out his wallet and was showing Johnny a picture of his son when a loud ruckus interrupted their conversation. Two couples appeared to be in a heated exchange.

Tom shook his head. "Duty calls. It was nice meeting you, Johnny. Don't be a stranger next time you come up."

"Sorry. We have a cookout to get to or we'd stay," Cano said.

The voices got louder.

"No worries. I best let you through."

"Been making friends, huh?" Johnny said as they drove on toward Coldwater.

"He's a good guy." Cano smiled. "We met when a carload of idiots were hassling him, wanting to go through the roadblock. I pulled over to keep an eye on them. I had doughnuts with me, so after he'd gotten rid of the morons, I shared them with him. Ever since, I usually stop and chat when he's working."

"You're always full of surprises."

Cano bristled. "Just because I gave a guy a doughnut?"

Johnny snickered. "You don't need to put on the tough girl act with me. I know underneath that leather jacket is a heart of gold."

Cano snorted and said under her breath, "It was just a fucking doughnut."

"Anything you say, Lone Wolf." He made a motion as if zipping his lips. "I won't ruin your reputation."

"Yeah, okay." Cano shot Johnny a look. "Let's talk about something pleasant, like volcanoes."

Before long, they pulled up to the camp. Cano killed the engine and hopped out of the truck. "I want to check on the camera. Make sure the film and batteries have been changed."

"I'm gonna slip into the tent and see who's here," Johnny said.

Cano walked to the edge of the incline, stopped, and stared up at the mountain. This was one of the first clear days in a while—no cloud cover. Something seemed off. She squinted. The north face of the mountain looked different. Was it just the snow melting or shifting because of the quakes? She must be seeing things. With all the monitoring equipment, it would surely pick up any changes.

With a final glance, she turned away. Mount St. Helens was a beauty, but she had the potential to be devastating. Cano chuckled. Those words could be used to describe Allie, too. For now, she'd take her chances because the last week had felt so good. God, she'd missed her. She shook her head. *Enough.* The camera wasn't going to check itself.

Once finished, she walked toward the tent. She should go inside and be social, but the crisp clear air held her back. She felt better than she had in years. Alive. But eventually, she'd have to leave the mountain and go back to Menlo Park. Away from the mountain. Away from Allie.

Johnny pushed through the large tent flap. *Perfect timing.* She needed to get out of her own head. Another man followed Johnny outside. She'd met him before but couldn't remember his name.

"Cano," the man said with a large smile.

Shit. "Hey. Nice to see you." Hopefully, he wouldn't figure out she'd forgotten his name.

Johnny stepped toward her, his back to the man, and winked. "Harry said he wanted to come say hi to you."

"Well, I'm glad you did, Harry." Cano smiled. "What are you working on?"

"I've been analyzing some of the seismic tremors. We've been getting quite a few." Harry shook his head. "Weird, but they're becoming so common that I don't even think about it when they happen."

"Right." Cano pointed at Johnny. "Remember the other day when Allie brought her students for a tour?"

Johnny laughed. "Oh, god, you should have been here, Harry. I'm showing them around, and the next thing I notice, they've all gone white as a sheet."

Cano shook her head. "And Johnny here was clueless. The ground had been rumbling for at least five minutes as he explained the different types of eruptions to them."

Harry laughed. "Those kids must have been pissing themselves."

"They were too scared to piss," Cano said. "Johnny thought they were riveted by his speech when they were too fucking afraid to move."

"The university is gonna send you a bill for their psychotherapy," Harry said.

"No doubt." Johnny laughed. "I hardly notice it anymore, unless it's a big one."

"Speaking of," Harry said. "Feels like we're getting a little movement. I should probably get back inside and see if I can get information from U-Dub."

"Thanks for stepping out and saying hi, *Harry*." Cano was sure to say his name again to cement it into her brain.

"My pleasure." He turned to Johnny. "You're coming back to relieve me tonight?"

"Sure am. Came to pick up my van since Cano won't be coming back with me."

Cano glanced down at her feet. Was it her imagination or was the tremble getting worse? Without warning, the ground began to shake more violently. The tent swayed, and her truck rocked.

"Shit. It's a leg spreader," Johnny said as the earth continued to shake.

After a few more seconds, it stopped.

"What the hell is a leg spreader?" Cano asked.

"You've never heard that saying?" Harry asked.

Cano shook her head. "Afraid not."

Johnny nodded toward his feet. "Leg spreader is when you spread your legs farther apart, so the quake doesn't knock you over. Gives you better balance."

Cano smiled at Johnny's bowed legs. Sure enough, he looked like he was sitting on a horse. "I learn something new every day."

"You gonna be okay on your own up here?" Johnny asked.

"I'm fine." Harry waved him off. "How big do you think that one was?"

"Damned close to five-point-oh," Cano said. "Least that's my guess."

Chapter Twenty-five

Days until eruption: 35
Sunday, April 13, 1980
Toutle, Washington
Allie's cottage

Thunk, thunk, thunk. Allie picked up speed as she chopped through the onion. Several years ago, she'd taken a cooking class, and her favorite part had been the knife skills. Too bad nobody was around to witness her proficiency. *No.* It was to her advantage that she'd convinced Fran to help Ben clean the grill. She loved Fran, but she needed a little time to herself.

She pushed the finished onion aside and snatched another. *Thunk, thunk, thunk.* The pungent scent threatened her eyes, so she stood taller to get her face as far from the onion as possible.

Their talk, or more like Fran's lecture, had gone better than expected. Allie had simply listened and nodded, knowing arguing would prolong the monologue. In fairness to Fran, she'd not been too harsh and in the end promised Allie that she'd be cordial during the cookout. More than anything, she wanted the rift between Fran and Nova to heal.

At this point, she'd settle for civility. She hoped Johnny would act as a buffer. Fran was a charmer and wouldn't want Johnny to see her in anything but a positive light.

She scooped up the potatoes and onions and placed them into foil pouches. One for each person. She drizzled the mixture with oil and salted and peppered them. One of the packets, she added more pepper and earmarked a corner to signify it was for Nova.

She smiled to herself. Fran would go into a sneezing fit if she accidentally got the one loaded with pepper, which would give her another reason to be angry at Nova.

At the thought of Nova, her stomach lurched. *Relax.* The more natural she behaved, the more it would put the others at ease. If she was uptight, it would ruin everyone's time. She took a deep breath and then another.

Without Johnny in the truck to distract Cano, the drive from Coldwater to Allie's seemed to stretch on forever. Allie's face kept flashing in her mind. They'd spent Wednesday and Friday evenings together, and it was the best time Cano had had in four years. Despite the others being there today, she hoped the magic would continue.

Dumbass. Get a grip. Allie was just being nice and wanted to put the ugliness of the past behind them. Nothing more. Cano needed to take it for what it was and be grateful that at least Allie no longer despised her.

Despised may have been too strong of a word. But now, maybe, they could talk every now and again, instead of going four years with no contact. That was all she should be hoping for, not creating some ridiculous reconciliation fantasy in her mind. Too much had happened. Too much hurt to ever overcome.

Her eyes began to well. *No.* This was not the way she wanted to go into the *shindig*. That thought brought a slight smile to her lips. The fun, devil-may-care Cano needed to be the person at the party today, not the angsty brooding one.

Besides, there was plenty of volcano news to talk about, she thought as she flicked her blinker for the turn to Toutle. She glanced in her rearview mirror. Johnny was right on her bumper. Had she been so lost in thought she'd been driving like an old woman? *Ugh.* Johnny would surely have something to say about that.

She pulled up along the curb in front of Allie's house, and Johnny pulled in behind her.

"What the hell was that?" Johnny said as soon as he stepped out of his van.

"What?" Cano glared, daring him to say more.

"While I'm in the truck, you drive like a bat out of hell, but then when I'm not, you drive like an eighty-year-old woman on her way to church. If I didn't know better, I'd think you were trying to scare the bejeezus out of me with the white-knuckle trip up the mountain."

"You are such a drama queen." Cano slammed her truck door. "I wasn't driving that fast, or slow, for that matter."

"The hell you weren't. I looked at my speedometer. You got all the way down to forty-five at one point."

"I was being safe."

Johnny laughed.

As he did, the front door of the cottage flew

open.

Show time.

"Welcome," Allie called from the front porch.

A huge smile lit Johnny's face, and he walked toward the house. "Allie. So good to see you." He flipped his thumb over his shoulder. "I've had enough of dealing with her crazy ass."

"Nice." Cano hurried up the walkway, not wanting to be too far from the action in case Johnny decided to say more.

Allie laughed and leaned in toward Johnny when he reached her. "I completely understand."

"Nice," Cano said again and put on her best scowl.

Allie led them into the house. "Ben and Fran are out back, firing up the grill. I don't know about you, but I'm starving."

Cano smiled. *So far, so good.* There didn't seem to be any tension in the air.

"I'm surprised you haven't heard my stomach growling." Johnny patted his belly. "Cano's told me all about your pork chops, so I've been thinking about them for the last two days."

"Yeah. He's been going through withdrawals, being away from Rosaria's cooking."

Allie looked over her shoulder. "Is Rosaria your wife?"

Johnny beamed. "The love of my life. Been married going on thirty-two years."

Allie stopped and put her hand on his arm. "No way. You must have gotten married when you were five."

Johnny laughed. "Got married right after we graduated high school in 1948."

They reached the kitchen, and Cano set the bag

on the counter.

"Congratulations." Allie put her hand on her chest. "You've restored my belief that love can last forever." Allie's face froze before she plastered on a fake smile.

Ouch. That hurt more than Cano wanted it to. She picked up the sack. "Are you going to check out what's in the bag?"

Relief washed over Allie's face. She fluttered across the room toward the package, showing a little more enthusiasm than was necessary, but Cano was okay with it if they could put the awkward moment behind them.

Just as Allie reached for the bag, the back door rattled open. *Oh, goody. Here we go.* Cano braced herself as she turned toward the sound.

Fran stood larger than life with her platinum hair and her fake tan. Cano couldn't deny she was not only pretty, but also had a commanding presence.

Fran smiled and walked toward Johnny with an outstretched hand. "You must be Johnny."

"Yes, ma'am." He took her hand. "And you must be the lovely Fran."

"Lovely." Fran glanced at Allie. "I like this man already."

Cano stepped back and pushed herself against the counter, wanting to stay as invisible as possible.

No such luck. Fran turned to her. "Cano. It's nice to see you." A genuine smile reached her eyes.

Shit. She'd prepared herself for hostility. If not outward, at least veiled, but she sensed none. She couldn't stand gaping like a kid caught with pee dripping down her leg. Cano put on her easy smile. The one that got her through life. "It's nice to see you, too. I've been looking forward to today all week."

Before Fran could respond, Ben pushed open the door. "What's going on in here? I've been waiting to throw the food on the grill."

"Hold on," Allie said. "We still need to open the sack Nova brought."

"It's Löwenbräu," Cano blurted out, suddenly feeling self-conscious about her gift.

Allie pulled a twelve-pack from the bag and handed it to Cano.

Cano ripped the box open and pulled out a distinctive green bottle with golden foil on the neck. "I had one a couple months ago. It's...um...like fancy beer. From Germany."

She gripped the top and twisted. Pain seared in the palm of her hand. *Fuck.* It wasn't a twist off. She rushed to the refrigerator and pulled the magnetized bottle opener off the side. She popped the cap and handed the bottle to Allie.

"Thanks," Allie said with a half-smile.

Cano hurried back to the case and popped the caps off more bottles and handed them around. Maybe she should have asked if everyone wanted one, but it was too late now. She pointed to the label. "See, it's a lion. Somebody told me Löwenbräu means lion's brew, but they might have been blowing smoke up my ass."

The others politely nodded and smiled as she rambled.

She needed to stop acting like a raving lunatic. This was such a stupid gift. "It's okay if you try it and hate it. I mean, you don't have to drink it or anything. You can pour it out. Or just give it to me, and I can finish it, so you know it doesn't go to waste or anything. Well, I can't drink all five at once, but maybe like save it for later. I just thought maybe it would be like celebratory or something."

Shut up. She shoved the bottle against her lips and sucked in a big gulp.

Allie finally came to the rescue. She held up her bottle. "To good friends and Mount St. Helens."

Everyone, except Cano who had a full mouth of beer, echoed Allie's words.

Shit. Should she spit her beer back in the bottle? Would she jinx the toast if she didn't? *No.* She could work around it. She raised her bottle several ticks late since the others had brought it to their lips. She muttered through her mouthful of beer an unintelligible garble of words that was supposed to be a repeat of what Allie said. Then she shoved the bottle against her lips and let a small amount of liquid into her already full mouth.

A couple of drops of the beer dribbled out of the corner of her mouth and rolled down her chin. She swallowed hard, hoping she'd caught up with the toast. Nonchalantly, she wiped her mouth with her shirtsleeve.

The others muttered about how tasty the beer was, but the blood pounding in her ears made it difficult for her to focus on the remarks.

This day would turn out disastrous if she didn't calm down. She turned back to the sack, snatched out the other twelve-pack, and put it into the refrigerator.

"Do you think the Supersonics are going to repeat last year's championship?" Ben asked Johnny, apparently losing interest in her ramblings.

"I think they'll get past the Bucks," Johnny said. "But even if they do, I'm not sure they have enough firepower for the Lakers."

"It doesn't seem fair that they can have Kareem and Magic on the same side of the court."

Fran waved her arms and pointed toward the door. "Out. Sports talk is not allowed in the kitchen."

Cano breathed a sigh of relief. It appeared that everyone was ready to move on from her embarrassing display.

The men filed out of the house, while Fran went to the refrigerator and pulled out a large tray. "I'll take this out."

"I can handle it." Allie's voice held a note of tension. "I'm the one that put them in there in the first place."

Fran frowned. "I know you can. I was being nice. Sheesh."

"Ah, you can understand my confusion then." Allie winked.

"Ha ha. Very funny." She playfully shoved the tray into Allie's hands. "You can take them out yourself after that comment."

Allie laughed and passed the tray to Cano. "Here. I'll put you to work."

Fran threw her hands up. "Seriously? You bust my chops, then you have Cano carry them out."

Allie smirked. "I'll let you take the potato packets." Allie piled several foil-wrapped packages onto another tray.

"Gee thanks." Fran snatched the tray.

"And I'll bring along the lion's brew." Allie smiled at Cano and winked.

Allie nudged her plate with a half-eaten pork

chop toward Nova. Ben had cooked the meat to perfection, but her appetite was off today. Likely because she'd allowed herself to get stressed about the party.

She shouldn't have been. It was perfect so far, even with the Löwenbräu incident. She'd found Nova's wordy discourse adorable. Her cheeks heated. How many times did she have to remind herself thinking of her friend as adorable bordered on inappropriate?

Nova leaned over. "Aren't you hungry?" she whispered and searched Allie's face.

Allie considered a lie but settled on the truth once she realized Fran was too deep in a discussion with Johnny about the best way to grow potatoes to listen in. "I think I got myself a little nervous about the party. You know how that messes with my appetite. Especially now."

Nova frowned, her expressive hazel eyes full of concern. "Are you going to be okay?" She shifted her gaze toward Fran and spoke quietly.

"I will be as long as I don't get caught not eating." Allie gave Nova a conspiratorial smile.

With a quick flip of her wrist, Nova switched Allie's plate with her own empty one and winked. "I'll never turn down more of your pork chops. I think I've about figured out what's in the rub."

"Really?" Allie raised her eyebrow.

"Yep."

Allie patted Nova's hand. "You keep thinking that."

"What are you two whispering about over there?" Fran asked. She gazed at Nova's plate with narrowed eyes. "I thought you loved Allie's pork chops. You haven't even finished it."

"That's because she's too busy trying to guess my secret spice." Allie smiled. "I told her to eat it and stop trying to deconstruct it."

The furrow in Fran's brow lessened but was still evident.

Nova cut off a bite and lifted it with her fork. She placed it on her tongue and rolled it around in her mouth. Her lips puckered, and she made a sucking motion. With her mouth still full, she said, "The flavor is right on the tip of my tongue."

"Literally." Allie laughed at her own joke.

Fran shook her head. "Give it up, Cano. You'll never guess it, and she'll never tell you."

Whew. Good save.

Allie mouthed, *thank you,* when Fran looked away.

"Allie, did Cano tell you that she almost punched a reporter the other day?" Johnny said.

Allie turned toward Nova and tilted her head. "You did what?"

"Great. Thanks, Johnny." Nova glared at him.

"I've got to hear this story." Fran put her elbow on the table and rested her chin in the palm of her hand.

"We're all ears." Allie mimicked Fran's gesture.

"It wasn't my fault." Nova's cheeks reddened. "He wasn't listening."

"I see. Go on," Fran said.

"I try to avoid reporters," Nova said.

"Yeah, because she doesn't want to get her ass sent back to Menlo," Johnny said.

"Who's telling this story?" Nova shot him a look.

"Just helping fill in the details."

Nova ignored him and continued. "The reporter

cornered me and said he wanted to get a better scientific understanding of volcanic eruptions. Said he didn't want the same old cookie-cutter article. He wanted to *really* dive into the science. I fell for it. Little did I know he was a moron."

Allie bit back a smile. She loved to listen to Nova's stories.

"He starts talking about all the ash coming out of the volcano. And how dirty it's making everything look." Nova nodded and held out her hand palm up. "Now I'm agreeing with him that it does do a number on the snow. Then he asks what's burning inside the volcano to create so much ash."

"And this is when it started going downhill," Johnny said.

"Are you going to let me finish?" Nova asked.

"Go ahead." Johnny motioned to the table as if giving Nova the floor.

Nova sneered at him before continuing. "Anyway, I tell him that nothing is burning. That it's a common misconception that laymen have about ash. He looks at me as if I've grown a second set of eyes before he asks how ash could be misconceived."

"I'm wondering the same thing," Ben said, finally joining the conversation.

Nova nodded in his direction. "I get that it's confusing. I thought this guy really wanted to understand, so I explained what volcanic ash really is, and then he—"

"Wait. Don't leave this layman hanging," Ben said.

"Sorry." Nova met his gaze. "Volcanic ash is created when rock or magma is pulverized during an explosion, not because of fire. The ash is comprised of tiny fragments of rock and volcanic glass."

Ben nodded enthusiastically. "Hmm, interesting."

"I'm still not seeing where the punching part comes in." Allie searched Nova's face, looking for clues.

"I'm thinking the reporter is understanding," Nova said. "So I tell him, that's why people need to be so much more careful of volcanic ash. He just shrugged and gave me this condescending eye roll."

"As soon as I saw that shit, I moved closer," Johnny said.

"Smart man." Allie winked at him.

Nova ignored them both and continued. "Anyway, he says, 'Then it shouldn't be any worse than the ash from a wildfire then, right?'" Nova's mouth dropped open, and she pointed to it. "So I'm giving him this look. Hoping he'll figure out I think he's an idiot."

"I'm pretty sure he did," Johnny said. "Probably why everything started going downhill fast."

"Then he says, 'By that slack-jawed look, I'm taking it you don't know the answer either.'" Nova's eyes widened. "At this point, I'm still trying to hold it together. And in my calmest voice…"

"Most patronizing tone," Johnny added.

"I explain that while wildfire ash is not good because it coats your lungs with burned organic gunk from the air..."

"Very scientific term—gunk," Johnny said.

Nova shot him a look. "I tell him that I'd much rather have that gunk in my lungs than broken-up slivers of rock and glass."

Fran's face contorted, and she put her hand on

her chest. "Eww. That grosses me out just thinking about it." She took two deep dramatic breaths. "I'm having trouble breathing."

"You would," Allie said. "If too much gets in your lungs, it basically suffocates you."

"Stop!" Fran put her hands over her ears. "You're freaking me out."

"Sorry," Allie said in a loud voice, so Fran could hear through her covered ears. "We want to hear the part about why Nova nearly punched him."

Fran slowly lowered her hands. "Yes, please. No more talk of suffocating ash."

"The son of a bitch turns toward Johnny and mutters under his breath, 'Why did I bother talking to a female when they don't know what they're talking about?'"

Allie's jaw went slack. "Jesus. It's 1980, not 1950."

Fran pounded her fist on the table. "You should have punched him."

"Trust me, she would have if I hadn't stepped between them and escorted her out of there."

"See." Nova pointed toward Fran. "Smart woman. Fran would have let me."

"I wasn't protecting him. He deserved it." Johnny glanced around the table, and his gaze locked on Allie. "But I didn't want you to get sent back to Menlo. This is where you need to be."

Allie's heart raced. The look in Johnny's eyes said more than his words. Allie patted Nova's hand. "Yep. We wouldn't all be sitting here enjoying such a wonderful day otherwise. Besides, you're needed...at the volcano," Allie quickly added.

Chapter Twenty-six

Days until eruption: 35
Sunday, April 13, 1980
Toutle, Washington
Allie's cottage

Cano pushed her Triumph Hurricane out of Allie's garage and swung her leg over the seat. She let the bike roll toward the street, maneuvering between the cars parked in the driveway.

The others were gathered around Johnny's van, saying their goodbyes. He clutched the bag of leftovers to his chest as if he were holding a suitcase full of money.

Cano glided over to where they stood.

"Where's your helmet?" Fran pointed and scowled.

"Oh, shit." Cano raised her hand to her head. "I forgot." She kicked down the stand and got off her bike. She jogged up the drive and said over her shoulder, "Be right back."

Her chest tightened. Was that concern from Fran? She couldn't remember the last time she'd had so much fun with a group of people. Her time alone with Allie had been the best, but this was a close second.

She snatched her helmet off the shelf and put it on her head. Laughter drifted up the driveway. She could hear the lilt of Johnny's voice. He'd seemed to enjoy himself, too.

This was what she'd missed. Her world in Menlo Park had gotten small. Other than an occasional dinner with Johnny and his family, she spent most of her time alone in her apartment, or she rode her motorcycle for hours on end. Granted, she'd become a more skilled rider because of it, but it didn't keep her warm at night. *Shit. Too far.* She needed to stop having these thoughts.

She sauntered down the drive, enjoying the sounds of laughter. Fran thrust her hip out and raised her hand into the air. A perfect mimic of John Travolta's signature move in *Saturday Night Fever.*

Johnny was next to join Fran, soon followed by Allie and Ben. Halfway down the drive, Cano broke into the Travolta strut. Allie was the first to notice and turned her gaze on Cano.

Allie let out a wolf whistle, causing the others to turn and watch. The one thing Cano could do was dance. She missed the nights she and Allie closed down the discotheques.

After such a nice day, she felt free, so she brought her hands in front of her and circled them several times as she neared the end of the driveway. She thrust one leg behind the other as she turned her strut into a full-blown dance move. Travolta had nothing on her. She spun a couple of times for good measure as she neared the van.

When she got to within a few yards from the others, she crossed her arms over her chest. *Why not?* She hadn't tried this move in some time, but she felt frisky. She dropped to her knees and popped back up.

Her gaze never left Allie, who stood clapping to the imaginary beat with the rest. Cano dropped to her knees and popped up two more times, before she ended with several exaggerated hip thrusts before pointing her finger toward the sky.

The group erupted in cheers, and Cano's back stiffened, her face suddenly hot. What the hell had gotten into her? She hadn't let loose like this in forever.

Fran was the first to speak. "Holy hell, Cano. You keep dancing like that, and you might just turn me lesbian."

"Me too," Ben said.

Everyone laughed, and Johnny thumped her on the back. "I'll be damned. You're just full of surprises."

It was Allie's reaction Cano was most interested in, so she waited with her breath held. What would Allie think? Would she think it another example of Cano not being able to take anything seriously, or would Allie appreciate her free spirit?

A huge smile spread on Allie's face. *Good sign.* Allie grabbed Cano's arm and raised it in the air like a referee at a boxing match. "The winner of the first annual Toutle impromptu disco street dance goes to…Nova Kane."

Cano hammed it up and hopped around like one of the overexuberant contestants on a game show.

Once the frivolity finished, Johnny said, "I better get going. I don't want to be late for my shift."

Allie put her hand on his arm. "You be careful. The harmonic tremors were back on Thursday. Could mean the magma is on the move."

Johnny nodded. "Trust me, I have no intention of being on the mountain when she blows."

Allie gazed at Cano with concern. "You be careful, too?"

"I will. I'm just going to follow Johnny up the

mountain until it gets too cold. Then I'll turn around and hightail it back down."

"Wouldn't it be better to ride around here?" Fran asked. "Where it's warmer and not so curvy?"

Allie snorted. "Never gonna happen. Nova loves the curves."

Fran snickered and eyed Allie from head to toe. "I guess she does."

Allie's face turned crimson, but she didn't respond.

Adorable. Cano thought of making another comment, but she thought better of it. The less she said, the better.

Johnny waved his hand. "Fran, stop picking on Allie. She's been a delightful host." He stepped up and held out his hand. "Thank you for an amazing meal and a great time."

"Oh, no," Allie said and pulled Johnny toward her. "We're huggers."

"Damned right," Fran said.

After a round of hugs, Johnny jumped in his van, and Cano slid onto her bike.

Just as Cano went to turn the engine over, Allie put her hand on Cano's arm. "Drive safe."

Cano gazed into her gorgeous eyes and nodded. "I promise."

Chapter Twenty-seven

Days until eruption: 35
Sunday, April 13, 1980
Southbound on Interstate 5

Cano glanced at the clock on the pickup's dashboard and yawned. She'd just turned onto Interstate 5, which meant she'd be on the road for another forty-five minutes. That was what she got for staying at Allie's so late. She smiled. It was worth her bleary-eyed trek back to her hotel in Vancouver.

Cano hadn't made it to the roadblock on her motorcycle before the cold became too much. Living in California, she hadn't had much occasion to drive in the lower temperatures. She'd waved goodbye to Johnny and turned back. With the sun sinking into the horizon, the last ten minutes of her ride had chilled her to the bone. Even through her leather gloves, her fingers had become tiny blocks of ice.

Allie had been awaiting her arrival and invited her in for hot chocolate. Several hours later, close to midnight, she'd finally left.

Cano's arms still tingled from when Allie hugged her good night. It was the first hug they'd shared, and Cano feared her heart would beat out of her chest. The feel of having Allie in her arms had been indescribable. And then there was the smell—the smell of sandalwood and lavender. It took all of

Cano's willpower not to bury her nose in Allie's hair and inhale.

The entire day had been nearly perfect. Fran had treated her well. She almost seemed to like Cano again. Having Johnny there made it extra special. She'd even gotten in a motorcycle ride, but spending time with Allie had been the highlight.

Damn it. She missed Allie in so many ways. A stabbing pain hammered at her chest as she remembered how bad things got after Allie's MS diagnosis.

October 4, 1975
Seattle, Washington
Allie and Cano's home

"Would you stop looking at me like that?" Allie said with a raised voice.

Cano froze and looked away. It had been nearly a month since Allie's diagnosis, so Cano was getting used to Allie's angry outbursts, but she still hadn't figured out a way to handle them.

"Do you think standing really still and ignoring me will make me forget you're there?" Allie said, her voice even louder.

"Uh-huh." Cano shifted her weight from one foot to the other but made no other move. "If it will stop you from getting angry at me."

"I'm sick of you looking at me with fear and *pity.*" Allie's face reddened.

"It's not pity." Cano met Allie's gaze. "It's concern."

"Pity. Concern. Not much difference." Allie shrugged. "But is it fear?"

"No. Terror. Pure terror." Cano wasn't sure if the truth was the best response, but nothing else seemed to work, so why not try it?

When Allie didn't respond, Cano took a chance and glanced toward where Allie sat on the couch. Allie's lip trembled, and tears welled in her eyes.

Cano fought against her desire to run to Allie and offer her comfort. She didn't want to make the wrong move. Moments like these made her understand the phrase *walking on eggshells.*

Cano gave Allie a questioning gaze but still didn't move closer. "Can I...um...may I come sit next to you?"

Allie's head bobbed up and down, and she patted the sofa cushion next to her. Cano moved quickly, not wanting to give Allie time to change her mind. She sat a few inches from Allie, making sure not to touch her.

"I won't bite." Allie's voice wavered as she spoke. "I promise."

Cano let out a huge sigh and covered the gap between them. She placed her hand on top of Allie's and waited.

After sitting this way for several minutes, Allie said, "I'm so sorry. I know I've been impossible to live with." Tears streamed freely down her cheeks.

"It's okay." Cano's heart broke. She loved Allie so much—so deeply—but she was at a loss how to help her. "You've got a lot to deal with. I understand."

"No! I can't use that as an excuse. You have a lot to deal with, too. I'm not being fair."

Cano shook her head adamantly. "It's not the same. You *have* to deal with it. You don't have a choice."

Allie's hand that had been trembling in Cano's stiffened. "That's right. But *you* do." Allie's soft voice hardened again.

Shit. What had she said wrong now? *Eggshells.* There was a landmine in the conversation, but after a month of little sleep and tons of worry, Cano struggled to figure out what it was. "Yeah, I could walk out tomorrow, but—"

"Just go then." Allie turned her body away from Cano and rested her head against the arm of the couch.

Cano didn't care if Allie got mad again. Her words cut through Cano like a jagged knife. "You know that's not what I meant." Throwing caution to the wind, Cano snuggled against Allie's back and wrapped her arms loosely around her. She wanted to give Allie the option of escape, even though Cano wanted to wrap her in a gigantic hug and never let her go.

At first, Allie stiffened, but she soon relaxed and melted against Cano. Allie put both hands on Cano's forearms where she held her. "It's bad enough that I'm older than you, but now I'm a burden, too."

"Nonsense," Cano said, but her mind raced. She was twenty-five years old, soon to be twenty-six, what did she know about handling something so serious? Being with Allie could possibly change her entire life. There would be things they would never be able to do together. The active life they planned was likely gone. What would it look like now? She wanted the vibrant Allie she fell in love with back.

"What are you thinking?" Allie asked.

Fuck. Loaded question. Cano couldn't admit her doubts. Allie was fragile enough without Cano making it worse. Cano tightened her grip on Allie and said, "About how beautiful you are and how much I love you."

"You won't leave me?" Allie's voice came out in a near whisper.

Could Cano make that promise? Her heart raced, and she hesitated for a split second, wanting to choose her words carefully. She loved Allie more than breathing, but making a proclamation when she felt cornered like this was tough.

"No. Don't answer that. It wasn't fair for me to ask." Allie hugged Cano's arms tighter. "I love you, Nova."

"And I love you, too." Cano moved even closer against her back. "I want to show you." They hadn't made love since the diagnosis. Cano's stomach roiled. She'd approached Allie several times but had been rebuffed each time. She braced for another *no.*

"Please," Allie said in a husky voice.

Cano almost asked if she was sure but bit back her question. Somehow, she didn't think it would sit well with Allie. *More eggshells.* "The bedroom?"

Allie nodded.

Cano backed away from Allie and stood. She held out her hand as Allie struggled to rise from the couch.

The pain and frustration on Allie's face stabbed into Cano's chest, but she wouldn't let it derail them now. She needed to make love to Allie. They both needed it.

Once Allie was on her feet, Cano moved forward and put her hand on Allie's cheek. "You are the most beautiful, the most amazing woman I have ever met. And the bravest. We'll figure it out."

Allie leaned into Cano. “Shh. Stop talking. I want your mouth busy somewhere else.”

Cano smirked, thankful to have Allie back. “That can be arranged.” Cano took Allie’s hand and led her toward the bedroom.

Chapter Twenty-eight

Days until eruption: 31
Thursday, April 17, 1980
Vancouver, Washington
U.S. Forest Service Building

Cano crumpled the french fry container and tossed it into the empty bag. She pulled the Styrofoam box off the dash, opened it, and removed the gigantic burger. Her teeth sank into the lukewarm sandwich. That was okay. Cold fries were unacceptable, but she could handle it in her burger.

As she stared out the windshield, she saw several of her colleagues enter the building. She chewed slowly to delay going inside. The meeting wasn't scheduled to start for another eight minutes, so she'd stay in her truck as long as possible.

Despite wanting to eat slowly, she discovered her sandwich was nearly gone. The past few minutes, she'd obviously been eating it unconsciously. Her thoughts had been far away—well, at least in Toutle.

She'd only seen Allie once since Sunday's get-together. They'd crossed paths on Monday at Coldwater, but the rest of the week, Allie and her students were working around Spirit Lake. They were monitoring the markers that had been placed throughout the lake. Allie hoped that the changes in water levels might give an indication of what was happening within the mountain.

Tonight, though, Allie had invited Cano for dinner, so she wanted to get this meeting over as quickly as possible. A room full of geologists and a bulge on the side of Mount St. Helens didn't bode well for a short meeting.

A sharp rapping on her side window caused her to jump and nearly spit out her last bite of sandwich. She angrily spun toward the window. Whoever the idiot was could have caused her to choke.

Johnny stood with a sheepish grin on his face and mouthed, "Sorry."

Cano rolled down her window. "What the hell? Are you trying to give me a coronary?"

"It's show time." Johnny pointed toward the building.

"Ugh, don't remind me." Cano glanced at the clock. "Still have three minutes."

"Get your ass out here. I'm not going in alone."

"Fine." Cano squeezed on the burger container and enjoyed the satisfying sound of the Styrofoam cracking.

"Would you stop being a child?" Johnny shook his head.

"What?" Cano tried for an innocent look.

"I've eaten with you enough to know you like to play with the Styrofoam containers." Johnny laughed. "You get that goofy smile on your face every time it squeaks and cracks."

"Don't take away all my fun." Cano scrunched the box one last time before shoving it into the sack. "I love Styrofoam."

"Shit's bad for the environment. I wouldn't get too attached."

Cano clutched the bag to her chest. "They'll have to rip it out of my bloodied fingers before I give it up."

Johnny shook his head. "Stop being a drama queen. And stop stalling."

"Fine." Cano threw the bag onto the floor of the pickup and rolled up the window.

Days until eruption: 31
Thursday, April 17, 1980
Toutle, Washington
Allie's cottage

Allie smiled at the red-faced Nova, who'd been spewing nonstop since she'd walked in the door fifteen minutes ago. With a little persuasion, Allie had gotten her to sit on the sofa and had brought her a cold brew.

The beer sat untouched on the end table. Allie pulled her feet up underneath her on the couch and studied Nova. *Damn.* She was adorable when she got so fiery.

Allie willed herself to pay attention to Nova's words, instead of ogling her. Allie nodded at all the right times but couldn't get a word in, let alone a question.

"So half the idiots don't want to admit we have a serious problem." Nova took a deep breath and finally reached for her beer.

Allie waited a few beats to make sure she wouldn't start back up again before she said, "So the bulge on the north side is definitely getting bigger?"

"Yep. I noticed it on Sunday. Well, I noticed something looked off. But in the last couple days, it's..." Cano held her hand out and made a curving motion with her hand. "It's obvious that there's a bump...a bulge coming off the side."

Allie bit her bottom lip. "Did you hear anything about the head of the USGS that came in from D.C.?"

Cano nodded. "Apparently, Mullineaux took him up to the Timberline parking lot on Sunday. I heard the guy took one look at the bulge and said it was terrifying, and he just wanted to turn around and leave."

Allie whistled through her teeth. "Whoa. That's concerning."

"No doubt." Nova shook her head. "And the press has been all over a local guy, a geologist, who told them that being at Timberline was like looking down the barrel of a gun."

"Ouch."

Nova ran her hand through her hair and took another long drink. "I can't say I disagree with him."

Allie's shoulders tensed. Nova wasn't one to overreact. If she thought something bad could happen, Allie believed her. Besides, as the days went on, Allie had become uneasy herself. "But the geologists in Vancouver aren't as convinced?"

Nova threw up her hands. "Nobody wants to get it wrong. Hell, Johnston is the only one I see willing to speak up. Somebody from USGS told the reporters that we have enough instruments to know hours or possibly days before a major event happens. What the hell is his problem?" Nova's red face drained of color. "I'm telling you, Allie, something bad is going to happen up there." Nova met Allie's gaze, her eyes full of pain. "People could die."

"I know." Allie looked at the floor, not wanting

to hold Nova's gaze.

"What's going on?"

Nova could always read her. She'd not wanted to tell her what she'd heard from Fran, but it was too late now. "I talked to Fran today. Things aren't much better at the university. I'm not sure if it's political or what, but a spokesman for the university is calling the earthquakes moderate."

"Jesus." Nova put her hand against her forehead. "Telling the reporters something is moderate is the same as telling them it's no big deal."

"I'm aware. There's lots of pissed off people at U-Dub, including me. I'm just not sure what we can do. Maybe we're wrong."

Nova blew out her breath. "Do you believe that?"

Allie shook her head. "No. But what if it's like Mount Baker?"

"Baker didn't have a damn bulge sticking out the side."

"True. But I'm afraid people are getting complacent. The media is starting to lose interest, and I've heard the roadblocks aren't that effective anymore."

"I've heard the same. Half the time, I don't even see guards anymore."

Allie stood. "Want another beer?"

"Please. You got any Doritos?"

"They'll spoil your supper." Allie put on her best stern look.

"Which means you do have some, or you would have just said no." Nova grinned.

Allie laughed. "Fine." She ducked into the kitchen and grabbed another beer for Nova and the unopened bag of Doritos. She settled on a can of soda for herself, mindful of the stiffness she'd recently experienced in her muscles.

When Allie returned, Nova had a huge grin on her face. She nodded toward the bag of chips in Allie's hand. "You just happen to have those laying around?"

Busted. They had always been Nova's favorite, while Allie could take them or leave them. She narrowed her eyes. "Maybe I had a craving for them."

"Sure, I'll go with that." Nova's smirk said she knew the truth.

"Back to the roadblocks," Allie said, ignoring Nova's Cheshire cat grin. "With all the logging side roads, people are getting too close anyway."

"True. At Coldwater, I've seen several climbers on the mountain, and a news crew landed on the crater the other day and shot some footage. It's crazy."

"Now, in light of the bulge, I'm going to pull the students farther from the summit. We can work on data and rock analysis anywhere. I'm responsible for them." Allie put her hands on top of her head. "It scares the shit out of me."

"Sorry." Nova leapt from her chair. "I shouldn't have brought it up."

Allie glanced up at Nova and recognized the panic in her eyes. "Whoa. It's okay."

"You were nice enough to invite me for dinner, and I'm unloading on you." Nova moved toward Allie but suddenly stopped in the middle of the room. "I shouldn't have brought any of it up. It was wrong."

"It's okay," Allie said again. She stood and took a step toward Nova. "I'm not fragile."

Nova stared at Allie. Her gaze swept from Allie's head to her toes and back again. "But your...um...your MS. Stress is bad for you."

Allie stiffened. She didn't need Nova's pity. She

bit her lip. This past month, renewing their friendship, had been nice, so she needed to tread carefully, or it could all collapse again. "I've learned to manage. A lot has changed in four years."

Nova winced.

Shit. Allie took another step toward Nova, so they were standing only a foot apart. She stopped herself from putting her hand on Nova's arm. "I didn't mean that the way it came out. I've learned to live with it better. I've had to."

Nova's eyes filled with sadness. "Because I wasn't around?"

Allie shook her head. "No. Because I needed to learn to care for myself, so I could get out of my parents' house." Allie stood taller. "And I did it."

"Would you take it wrong if I said that you're the strongest woman I've ever known?"

"No, I won't. Thanks." Allie grinned at the same time she blinked back tears. She put both hands on her chest. She struggled to breathe. The words threatened to open the floodgates.

"Are you okay?" Nova lightly put her hand on Allie's arm.

"I think I needed to hear that from you." A tear streaked down Allie's cheek. "The last four years, I've believed you thought me weak."

Nova's eyes widened. "God, no! How could you think that? If it were me, I probably would have curled up in the corner and given up."

Allie's chest tightened. Should she tell Nova that she'd thought about it many times after Nova left for Menlo Park? *No.* They weren't ready for that conversation. Maybe they never would be. Allie didn't want to do or say anything that would jeopardize the friendship they were rebuilding.

Allie wiped the tears from her cheeks. She needed to turn the evening around. "Damned volcano." Allie stepped back and fanned her hand in front of her face. "It's got me emotional, thinking about what could happen if she blows."

Nova stared at her with confusion. "But you were—"

"No!" Allie knew it had come out too forcefully, but now wasn't the time to talk about this. "We had a deal. For this to work, no talk about the past. We're getting dangerously close to a foul."

"You're right." Nova held up both hands and stepped back. Fear was evident in her eyes.

Guilt rushed through Allie. It wasn't fair to Nova, but nothing good could come of revisiting the past. "Go wash up. I'm going to put you to work chopping vegetables."

"Yes, ma'am." Nova gave her a giant smile.

Allie's heart raced, so she turned away. She didn't want to be drawn into that smile. The past threatened to resurface, and she couldn't have that. The memories were just too painful. They could be friends. It was for the best.

Cano didn't want to leave. It had been another perfect evening. She'd arrived on edge from the meeting in Vancouver, but spending time with Allie had erased it all. They'd laughed so hard while they watched *Mork & Mindy*. Not so much about the episode, but at their disagreement on whether it was funny or not.

Cano found the show funny and Robin Williams hilarious, while Allie groaned at the over-the-top humor. At one point during the commercial break, Allie stood and did an impersonation of the frenetic Mork. Tears streamed down Cano's cheeks from laughing so hard. It had always been one of her favorite things about Allie. When she broke out of her calm, controlled persona, Allie left Cano in stitches.

The evening had flown by too fast. Cano stood by the front door, while she waited for Allie to return from the kitchen with a care package of food. While she waited, a thought assailed her, likely inspired by watching *Mork & Mindy* earlier.

She envisioned spreading out like a starfish and clamping her hands and feet on each side of the doorframe to prevent herself from leaving. It would be something Mork would do. Cano laughed at the images flashing in her mind.

"Entertaining yourself?" Allie said, entering the room carrying a large bag.

Cano grinned. She had no intention of telling Allie her thoughts. Instead, she said, "Just thinking about Mork." Which wasn't a complete lie.

Allie shook her head. "My IQ dropped ten points just watching it."

"Just wait. I'll have you loving it before long." Cano held out her hand and split her fingers apart in Mork's signature handshake.

"I will not indulge you."

Their gazes met, and Cano melted into Allie's rich brown eyes. Without thinking, she took a step forward and reached out and put her hand against Allie's cheek.

With their gazes still locked, Allie moved closer.

As Allie's face drew nearer, Cano's heart raced. They were only inches apart when Allie stumbled backward.

"Oh, shit," Allie said, retreating several steps. "No. I can't."

A stabbing pain radiated through Cano's chest. "But...you have to feel—"

"No! I will *not* feel anything. Ever." Allie took another step back.

The words battered Cano. *Ever. Ouch.* Cano let out a slow breath, while she fought to keep her tears at bay. She'd blown it. It had been so good to have Allie back in her life, but now it was all toppling. There had to be a way to save the moment. "I'm sorry."

"I think you should just go, Nova," Allie said in a formal voice, the playfulness of earlier completely erased.

Cano wanted nothing more than to plead with Allie, but she knew by Allie's demeanor that nothing she could say would make a difference. Cano let her head drop, and she stared at the floor. "I didn't mean for that to happen."

"I know you didn't, but I need for you to leave."

"Okay. Um...I don't want this to ruin our friendship."

"Please." Allie pointed toward the door. "Go."

"Thanks for a great evening." After Cano said it, she realized how ridiculous it sounded. "I'll see you later."

Allie didn't answer, but Cano needed to escape. She turned and threw open the door but was careful to close it gently behind her. Part of her wanted to run screaming to her truck, while the other part of her wanted to stand pounding on the door until Allie let her back in.

She settled on walking slowly; her leaden limbs refused to allow her to move any faster. Cano didn't even try to brush away the tears that spilled down her face.

Allie wanted to retch. Once Nova shut the door behind her, Allie rushed to the bathroom. She needed to sit before she fell, but she also needed to be somewhere she could vomit.

She sat on the toilet seat. Her heart raced, and a wave of dizziness washed over her. When taking several deep breaths didn't help, she lowered her head between her legs. Now all she needed was a paper bag to prevent herself from hyperventilating.

The wave of nausea passed, but her stomach still roiled. She should straighten up the house; instead, she stumbled to the bedroom. With her clothes still on, she collapsed onto the bed. She nestled into the safety of her blanket fort and thought of another time she'd done the same.

October 4, 1975
Seattle, Washington
Allie and Cano's home

Tears streamed down Allie's face onto her pillow. She angrily swiped at them. The last thing she wanted was for Nova to see her like this. Suddenly cold, Allie rolled over and pulled the covers around herself.

She glanced at the alarm clock on her nightstand. Nova had been gone for a while. She probably wanted to get away from Allie. Had she gone to the spare bedroom to sleep after Allie disappointed her?

Allie's thoughts were interrupted when Nova appeared in the doorway. No longer naked, she'd put on an oversized T-shirt and a pair of shorts. Allie stared, not sure what to say.

"I got cold." Nova pulled on her T-shirt in explanation.

"Uh-huh, so did I." Allie pulled the blanket up to her chin.

"Um...did you want me to grab your clothes?" Nova looked everywhere but at Allie.

"Yeah, sure." Allie's stomach lurched. Nova didn't even want to see her naked anymore. Who could blame her? Nova probably hated Allie's malfunctioning body as much as she did.

Nova pulled a sweatshirt and pair of sweatpants from the drawer and held them out to Allie.

Yep. Nova wanted to cover every square inch of her. Allie snaked her hand from under the covers and snatched the clothes from Nova.

"I thought since...um...since things aren't working so well that you might be...uh...cold," Nova stammered. "I can get you something else if you want."

"These are fine." Allie blinked back tears. Still under the covers, she put her feet through the leg holes of the pants and slid them up her thighs and over her hips.

"Do you think we should...maybe...um...." Nova looked down at her own feet. "Talk about it?"

No! Never! Allie ducked under the covers so she could pull the sweatshirt over her head and then popped her head back out. Nova still didn't look at her, which was just as well. "What's there to talk about?" Allie's tone came out more defensive than she'd intended. "My body is worthless, so let's just say it like it is."

"No, Allie." Nova moved toward her and reached out to touch her cheek.

Allie flinched, and Nova stumbled backward as if she'd received an electric shock.

"I'm sorry," Nova mumbled. "I should just..."

A dull ache filled Allie's chest. It was a feeling she'd grown accustomed to the last few weeks. She wasn't being fair to Nova, but she just wanted to crawl under her blanket fort and never come out. "Yeah, you should go."

Pain registered in Nova's eyes as Allie finished her sentence. Nova nodded but didn't speak. When she reached the door, she turned back. "I love you, Allie. More than anything in this world. We'll figure it out." And then she was gone.

Allie fought her urge to scream at the top of her lungs. *Why?* Less than a month ago, she was on top of the world. Life was perfect. She loved her career, their home, and she especially loved Nova. They were supposed to grow old together but not like this.

Allie pulled her hand from under the blanket and glared at it as if it were responsible for all her woes. This was the first time they'd made love since she was diagnosed, and her body had let her down. She wiggled her fingers. The feeling had started to come back in them, so why did they have to go numb right in the middle of pleasuring Nova?

Her clumsy attempts had been embarrassing. It started when her fingertips had gone numb, so she fumbled around, unsuccessfully trying to find Nova's clitoris. She'd not thought of how important it was to have full sensation in her fingers to find the right spot. Even if she had found it, which she highly doubted, her fingers were stiff, and no matter how hard she tried, she couldn't make them move fast enough.

She closed her eyes and choked back a sob. In the end, she suspected she'd hurt Nova when in her frustration she'd pushed harder, hoping to bring her to a climax; instead, Nova had cringed and pulled away. Oral sex hadn't gone any better as the stress of the situation gripped Allie's body.

"Fuck," Allie said aloud to no one. "Fuck," she said it again louder. She wanted to scream it and never stop screaming it, but she pulled the covers back over her head and hoped sleep would take her soon.

Chapter Twenty-nine

Days until eruption: 18
Wednesday, April 30, 1980
Vancouver, Washington

Cano was quiet as she walked with Johnny toward the restaurant. As they got nearer, the smell of charred meat assailed her. Normally, she found the smell mouthwatering, but today, it made her nauseated. She doubted it was the scent but who she expected to be inside the restaurant tonight.

It had been almost two weeks since she'd nearly kissed Allie, and she hadn't been back to her house since. They'd spoken twice on the phone, but the conversations had been short and uncomfortable. At Coldwater, they'd run into each other a few times, and that had been even more awkward. Cano's heart ached, and she found it hard to concentrate, even on Mount St. Helens.

Tonight, several scientists were getting together for an informal meeting, away from the press and the decorum of the meeting room. Where it seemed few wanted to speak their minds for fear of being on the record and later being wrong.

Cano didn't care if she was on the record. The bulge in the mountain was unnatural, and she planned on getting her point across tonight.

Johnny held open the door for her, and she

slipped inside. The harried hostess met them near the door and led them to the backroom where several tables were pushed together to accommodate the group.

Cano scanned the room, and her shoulders dropped. Maybe Allie wasn't coming after all. She usually arrived early to everything, and it was already fifteen past the hour.

The boisterous group called out greetings to her and Johnny, and before they could even sit, a waiter descended for their drink orders. *Nice.* The service was obviously good here. Several others who were already seated called out for refills.

Gabby Grant had stopped Johnny, so he was wedged between Grant and another geologist from the USGS in Denver. Johnny gave her a pathetic look, almost pleading with her to throw him a life preserver.

She shrugged and gave him a pitying smile before she went around to the other side of the table. Should she sit near Allie's other coworkers from the university in hopes that Allie was still coming or to at least get information on her whereabouts?

There were a couple of chairs available, so she slid into one. The volume in the room grew louder as the scientists debated the probability of Mount St. Helens erupting and what kind of damage it might cause. Cano half listened but kept her eye on the entrance since Allie's coworkers said she planned to attend.

Cano scooped up salsa with her chip. She needed something to keep her hands busy, so she'd eaten way too many already. Allie would tell her she was going to spoil her dinner, but right now, she didn't care. She'd begun to worry about Allie; it wasn't like her to be so late.

Maybe she'd decided not to come and hadn't told her coworkers, which was also unlike her. Cano rubbed her aching chest. What if she'd gotten sick? Maybe she'd had a flare-up of her MS. *Damn it.* Stress tended to cause it, and after what Cano had nearly done, likely she was highly distressed.

Her thought was interrupted when Allie walked into the room, or more accurately, shuffled into the room. Cano nearly gasped but held back. Allie's normally perfectly styled hair was windblown. It looked cute but certainly not her norm. Her pale face was gaunt, and with each step, pain showed in her eyes. It was the cane clutched in Allie's hand that most concerned Cano. From what she'd observed, Allie tried to avoid using her cane in public as much as possible.

Cano fought the desire to rush to Allie, knowing she'd refuse her help. Their gazes met. Cano squeezed her hands into fists, and her fingernails dug into her palm, but she remained sitting.

Several others at the table noticed Allie's arrival and threw greetings in her direction. She politely nodded and said a few words to each before she made her way farther into the room.

Cano glanced at the empty chair next to her. Would Allie take it, or would she choose to sit somewhere else? Cano didn't realize she was holding her breath until Allie passed the last potential seat before she came to the one next to Cano.

As Allie got closer, Cano had no doubt that Allie was in pain and was struggling to walk the final distance to the chair. Maybe Allie would be pissed, but Cano couldn't stand by and watch her struggle any longer.

Cano rose from the table and covered the distance between them in three strides. She subtly held out her elbow and willed Allie to take it. Allie glanced down at Cano's offering before locking her gaze on Cano's.

After three beats, Allie grasped Cano's arm and leaned against her. The poor woman was exhausted, Cano thought, but she was putting up a brave front.

They walked deliberately toward their seats. Allie's gaze darted around the room. Cano suspected it was to ensure none of the others noticed her predicament. Taking Allie's lead, Cano also scanned the crowd. *Good.* None seemed to be paying attention to them.

When they arrived at their place at the table, Cano helped lower Allie into her chair. Allie smiled up at her with a mixture of sadness and gratitude.

Cano leaned down. "Want anything to drink?"

"I could use an iced tea."

"Appetizers?"

Allie shook her head and patted her stomach. "I'll pass. I've not been very hungry lately."

"You need to eat to keep up your strength." Cano gave her a concerned look and hoped it didn't come off condescending.

"I'll order something for dinner. Maybe a nice piece of fish." Allie smiled. "I think that will be more nutritious than fried whatever," Allie pointed at a plate of a greasy fried assortment, "and will sit in my stomach better, too."

"True." Cano waved for the waiter and gave him Allie's drink order before she continued. "Looking at the fried carnage on the table, I'm thinking he'll be around to take dinner orders pretty soon."

Cano sat in her own chair and moved it a little closer to Allie without getting into her space. Seeing Allie in this state always brought out her protective side, but she had to be careful because she knew how much Allie hated it.

Allie patted Cano's hand. "Stop worrying about me." She motioned with her head toward the rest of the table. "We're here about Mount St. Helens, not me."

Cano smiled and squeezed Allie's hand before she took it back. The tightness in her chest lessened for the first time in nearly two weeks. Allie's actions told her that their near kiss hadn't destroyed their renewed friendship. With that knowledge, Cano tuned into the heated conversation going on around her.

Scientists could be a messy lot, Allie thought as she scanned the table. It looked as if a pack of hungry wolves had descended on dinner, leaving food strewn everywhere. She imagined it was because they were too focused on their scientific discussion to pay heed to simple things like social graces and table manners.

She glanced at her plate and smiled. Maybe she wasn't a real scientist since her area was pristine. She'd nearly finished her salmon and vegetables, while she'd pulled the foil back over her half-eaten baked potato.

It was the most she'd eaten in two weeks. Apparently, having Nova sitting beside her helped her appetite. She pushed the thought from her mind and listened in on the conversation.

"At least the governor did something," one of

her colleagues from the university said.

"You call that something?" Grant said. "You guys from academia are all the same. She's a Democrat, so of course you'll give her the benefit of the doubt. But her order won't do shit."

"Grant has a point," Nova said. "They actually moved the roadblock a couple miles closer to the summit, which is crazy. And on top of that, the red zone is fourteen miles out to the east and the south but only four miles on the northwest side."

"Where the goddamned bulge is," Johnny added. "How short-sighted is that?"

A geologist from the Denver USGS entered the conversation. "That's where the national forest bumps up against the Weyerhaeuser land. They have no political will to mess with the logging operation."

"Are they going to have the will to keep the resorts and cabins around Spirit Lake closed when the season starts heating up?" Johnny asked.

"Right now, Spirit Lake is included in the closed zone," Allie offered, although she knew that could change if pressure mounted. "And I hear Harry Truman still refuses to leave his cabin."

Allie's colleague shook his head. "The dude's nuts. The place must be covered in ash by now. I saw the statistics a day or two ago that said there's been over two thousand earthquakes so far. I can't imagine how scary that must be being that close."

"I've seen him on the news." Johnny smiled. "The guy's a character."

"We all have," the USGS geologist said with a groan. "The media loves him."

Nova chuckled. "He said he's been on the mountain for fifty-four years and plans on being there another fifty-four."

Johnny laughed. "He has to be in his eighties. I guess he'll be the oldest living man in the world. Is it true he came here after giving up bootlegging in the twenties?"

Allie nodded. "That's what I heard. Colorful guy. One of the pilots said the mountain is starting to scare him, but he'll never leave. He's become too much of a celebrity to back down now."

"That's a shame." Nova shook her head. "I'm afraid for him."

The others around the table nodded.

"The bulge certainly isn't getting any smaller," Allie's colleague said. "Last I heard, it's a mile wide now. The north flank is three hundred feet higher than it was two months ago."

Johnny whistled. "That ain't normal. Something's gotta give."

"But the quakes are dying down," the Denver USGS scientist said. "We haven't had a harmonic tremor since April 12."

Neither have I, Allie thought. Why did she pick strange times to find amusement? Her harmonic tremors had last occurred April 12 but had turned chaotic ever since Nova nearly kissed her. Since then, she'd been left with chaos herself.

Nova was speaking, so Allie tuned back in.

"Last calculations show the bulge is swelling about one and a half yards a day." Nova's brow furrowed. "Everyone needs to take notice."

"But with the earthquakes being quieter, who knows?" Allie's colleague said.

"I know." Nova's voice came out loud. "It's not natural to have a giant bulge in a volcano. We're sitting here talking about it like it's a goddamned sporting event. You realize people will die if they're too close to her. And with the red and blue zones as they are, they will be too close."

Allie put her hand on Nova's leg and patted it. She'd heard from Fran that Nova had been stirring up some of the wrong people with her conviction. The last couple of weeks, Nova had been vocal about the potential dangers. Allie didn't want her to be sent home, but she didn't want anyone to die on the mountain, either.

"Johnston's been throwing around comparisons to Bezymianny," Allie's colleague said.

Nova threw up her hands. "I've been saying that ever since the bulge was discovered, but it appears that nobody cares what I have to say. Hell, they don't seem to care what David has to say, either."

"I'm not all that familiar with Bezymianny," Grant said.

Allie squeezed Nova's leg and gave her a pleading look. Grant got under Nova's skin already, but not knowing about one of the more spectacular recent eruptions would be sacrilegious in Nova's book.

Johnny's calm voice cut off what surely would have been sarcasm from Nova. "It's the volcano that erupted in Russia in 1956. Earthquakes started in September 1955, and just like our girl, it spewed a little over three weeks after."

"I do remember now. I just didn't recognize the name." Grant pointed and nodded.

Johnny smiled at him as if to say, you get a gold star, before he continued. "Then she quieted for a few months. Still some earthquakes but stayed relatively calm until out of the blue she erupted at the end of

March in fifty-six. Devastated everything within a twenty-mile radius."

"Just like Mount Pelée, it was a lateral eruption." Nova locked her gaze on Grant with a twinkle in her eye. Allie braced for what was about to come out of Nova's mouth. "You know," Nova said in a voice someone would use for a bedtime story, "most volcanoes go boom and shoot stuff straight into the sky." With an exaggerated motion, she threw up her hands and splayed out her fingers in a gesture that looked more like exploding fireworks than a volcano. "But," Nova drew out the word, "in this case, the bad volcano shot all its goo out the side." Nova flung her hand out in front of her toward Grant and opened it as if releasing something into the air. "So the shit blasted everything in its path, destroying acres and acres and all living things in its way."

Nova's voice was singsong, and Allie half expected her to say, *And they all died unhappily ever after.*

Across the table, Johnny stifled a laugh as Grant nodded enthusiastically. Allie shot Nova a sideways glance and mouthed, "Enough."

Nova guiltily dropped her gaze to the table and tried for a contrite expression, but Allie wasn't buying it.

Grant continued to nod, apparently none the wiser. "Yeah, yeah. Now I remember."

Nova groaned under her breath so only Allie could hear it and then plastered on a smile. "I'm so glad I could be of use."

Allie decided it was time to move on before Nova caused any damage. She gazed at the man from Denver and said, "I hear you're moving the Coldwater site soon."

"Yes, yes." The man smiled and nodded. "And once we do, we're going to get a trailer up there. Man it twenty-four-seven."

"Why are you moving it?" Allie asked. She'd already heard but wanted to end the Bezymianny discussion.

"To allow more accurate laser measurements. The spot is about nine hundred feet higher than Coldwater I and about two and a half miles closer."

"But isn't that more dangerous?" Allie's colleague asked.

"We don't think so. Coldwater I and II were both checked out for evidence of previous eruptions, and they cleared."

"Isn't it inside the danger zone, though?" Allie asked.

"The blue zone but not the red. It's about five-point-seven miles from the summit."

Allie's stomach dropped, and she turned to Nova. "Are you going to have to take overnight stints up there?" The thought of Nova sleeping so close to Mount St. Helens sent chills through her body.

Nova shook her head. "No, it looks like Johnston's assistant volunteered for the job."

Allie breathed a sigh of relief. Something about moving closer to a bulging volcano gave her the willies. She smiled to herself. The willies wasn't exactly the most scientific of terms.

The gathering wound down as nearly half of the participants called it a night. Cano glanced over at

Allie, who yawned for what must have been the tenth time.

Despite the lively conversation, part of Cano's attention had remained on Allie, making sure she was faring okay. Allie's coloring was better than when she'd first arrived, and during the discussions, the pain in her eyes had diminished. Now her eyes just looked tired, bordering on exhaustion.

Cano weighed her options carefully. She didn't think Allie was in any shape to drive the hour back to Toutle, but she wasn't sure she could convince the fiercely stubborn Allie of that.

For the past ten minutes, Cano had sat back and waited for the perfect time to broach the topic. The time seemed right as Grant had risen and was saying his goodbyes. She knew that should someone overhear, it would be less likely that Allie would agree.

Cano leaned over closer to Allie. "You look like you're getting a little tired."

"I'm okay." Allie clamped back the yawn that had just started.

Cano raised her eyebrows. "Want to try a different answer?"

Allie laughed. "Smartass."

Good. If Cano kept Allie laughing, she was more apt to go along with Cano's request. "I've got a proposition."

Allie's eyebrows raised.

"Oh, shit. I didn't mean it like that." Cano's face burned.

Allie laughed again.

Another good sign. "The drive back to Toutle is gonna suck now that it's dark outside. Let me drive you home."

Allie shook her head. "I need to have my car."

"I'll drive your car. Then Johnny can pick me up in the morning. He's planning on checking out Coldwater II."

Allie's eyebrows shot up again. "So that means—"

"I'll sleep on the couch." Cano glanced around at the others. Nobody was paying them any attention, but she leaned in just to be on the safe side. "I promise, no kissing attempts."

Allie smirked. "Well, that's reassuring."

God, she was adorable. Damn it. Cano needed to stop thinking that way. *Friends.* She needed to preserve the friendship, and thinking of kissing Allie was not a good way to do it. "So will you consider it?"

Allie stifled another yawn, and the stubborn set of her jaw relaxed. She sighed. "I am a bit tired, and I'm not looking forward to the drive." Allie glanced at her cane. "I haven't gotten up from the table for a few hours. I'm thinking I've probably stiffened up." She looked down at the table. "That's why I didn't leave earlier when I started to feel the fatigue set in."

Cano narrowed her eyes. "I'm afraid I'm not following."

"Should I explain like you did with Grant earlier?" Allie winked.

"Ah, in other words, I'm being dense." Cano thought for a second and held up her finger as if a lightbulb had just gone on. "You don't want an audience?"

"Exactly." Allie gave her a sad smile. "Nobody needs to see me struggling like that. I didn't think people would hang around this long."

"I understand." Cano smiled.

"Thank you." Allie returned the smile. "But now

I've gotten myself into a pickle by sitting here too long."

"Does that mean you'll let me take you home?" Cano tried to hide the hope from her voice. Getting the chance to talk to Allie about the kiss, while they drove, was just what she needed.

Allie nodded. "I appreciate it. How long before this lot clears out?"

"Leave it to me." Cano stood. "Hey. We should settle the check and let the poor waiter have his table back. We've been here for hours."

Murmurs of ascension came from around the table as the scientists reached for their wallets.

"Simple," Cano said to Allie once she sat back down.

⁂

Cano glanced over at Allie, who had her arms wrapped around the sweatshirt she used as a pillow. Cano couldn't help but wish she were the sweatshirt. Allie leaned against the passenger side door, and her chest rose and fell slowly as she slept.

So much for having a talk on the drive, Cano thought. Even though Cano had pulled Allie's car out in front of the restaurant, it had been difficult for her to make it there from the back of the restaurant. No doubt, she could use her wheelchair, but Cano suspected she'd fight against it as long as she could. Finally, she'd accepted Johnny and Cano's help, and they'd practically whisked her out to the car, but the walk had taken whatever energy she had left.

Cano averted her eyes from the road again and stared at Allie's peaceful face. The air in the truck seemed to be too thin, and Cano struggled to breathe. What if having Cano in her life caused Allie's MS to act up? Would she have to walk away from Allie again?

When she pulled up to a stoplight, she studied Allie's face. As she did, the pain in her chest worsened. Allie's silky blond hair fell across her high cheekbones, which Cano also thought was her sexiest feature. It was too dark for her to see the tiny freckles at the top of Allie's nose.

Allie shifted in her sleep, possibly sensing she was being watched. Cano snapped her gaze back to the road and waited for the stoplight to turn green.

Chapter Thirty

Days until eruption: 16
Friday, May 2, 1980, 6 a.m.
Toutle, Washington
Allie's house

Allie's eyes flew open. Her bed was shaking. *Shit.* This quake seemed stronger than most. Was this the big one?

She rolled over and searched in the dim light for her cane.

Before she could get out of bed, a loud rap sounded at her door.

"Come in," Allie said.

Nova rushed in, her eyes wild. "Did you feel that?"

"Yeah, it seemed pretty big." Allie sat up in bed and swung her legs over the side. Just with that little movement, she could tell she was still stiff.

Nova glanced from Allie to the door and back. "Um...would you like a little help?"

Allie thought of declining the offer, but it would delay her being able to call the university to see what magnitude they'd registered. "Sure. Could you grab my robe? It's a little chilly." Allie wrapped her arms around herself, wanting to hide the loosely buttoned pajama top that left little to the imagination.

Once covered, she was able to focus on Nova,

who wore a tight white tank top and a pair of white boxer shorts. Her lean and tanned body looked good in the all-white outfit. Her muscles rippled as she bent down and helped Allie to her feet.

Nova was solid, and whenever she supported Allie's weight, Allie had no concern that Nova couldn't manage it. She felt secure, safe, with Nova's arm wrapped around her.

"I'm afraid I'm having enough trouble walking." Allie chuckled. "Another tremor might cause me to tip over and not be able to get back up."

Nova's eyes widened. "And you find that funny?"

Nova's concern caused Allie to laugh again. "Dark humor. I use it to cope."

"You falling over in an earthquake is something to be amused by?" Nova's face still held a look of horror.

"Hysterical." Allie pushed Nova in the shoulder. "Just imagine it. You're the one that loves that crazy physical humor of Mork's, so you should love this." Allie placed two fingers on the bed and pretended they were legs as she walked them across the bedspread. With her other hand, she began to shake the bed as her original hand tipped over in a heap. Then she laughed—hard.

Nova's lip turned up, but she still didn't laugh.

"Aw, come on, lighten up," Allie said. "Fran says I get too dark for my own good. Says I'm terribly insensitive, but it's how I cope. I either laugh about it or cry. I choose to laugh."

"You're one warped woman." Nova smiled. "But I wouldn't want you any other way."

"Help me get up, so I can call and see what magnitude that was."

Cano flipped over the bacon and stirred the scrambled eggs. She'd been cooking breakfast for Allie the last two days. It was the only meal she could prepare with any success. After this morning's earthquake, she knew they'd both have a busy day, but she could still enjoy their remaining time together.

Today, Johnny would be here to pick her up. Yesterday, he'd refused. His argument that she'd taken little time off since she'd arrived did little to persuade her. It wasn't until he told her Allie needed her that she gave up her protest.

She'd spent the entire day with Allie, which only made Cano wish for more. It had been a quiet day, but in Cano's eyes, it was nearly perfect.

Allie had been fatigued and moved gingerly, but she'd insisted that they not just sit around, so they'd spent several hours analyzing the latest data. The bulge, which they found most worrisome, got the most attention. They'd calculated and recalculated the projected growth of the bulge. Cano had even drawn a crude map of the potential reach of the eruption should a pyroclastic blast occur. Later, when both had gotten tired of looking at numbers, they had driven Allie's car up to Timberline just to look at Mount St. Helens.

Cano rubbed her chest, hoping the ache would go away. She wasn't sure when she'd get back to see Allie once she left. She and Johnny would spend most of their day at Coldwater and then return to their hotel rooms in Vancouver tonight.

Fran was slated to arrive at Allie's later today. It

was Ben's annual golf getaway, so Fran and Allie had planned a girls' weekend. Three would definitely be a crowd, so it was good Cano was leaving. Besides, she didn't want to see the accusatory look on Fran's face when she realized Allie was having a flare-up. Maybe Fran's indictment of her would be right. Had the kiss caused it?

She glanced at the clock. Only an hour and a half before Johnny arrived. Her chest tightened further. They still hadn't talked about the near kiss. Whenever Cano considered bringing it up, the time didn't seem right.

Allie walked into the room, leaning heavily against her cane. Her hair was still wet from her shower. She'd insisted on doing it herself and refused to let Cano into the bathroom to help her with any part, even though it would have been easier.

Cano was secretly relieved. Although she would have handled it in a strictly clinical way, seeing Allie's naked body again would have been difficult.

"Ready for a feast?" Cano asked.

Allie sniffed at the air. "My god. Everything smells amazing. You're spoiling me."

"That was my goal."

"You've succeeded."

Cano motioned to the table. "Have a seat. Breakfast will be served shortly." Cano pulled the sizzling bacon from the pan and placed it on the paper towels she'd laid out to absorb the excess grease.

"Let me get the drinks." Allie shuffled toward the refrigerator.

"Sit. This is my last day to spoil you. So let me." Cano squinted. Had she imagined it, or had Allie looked sad before she smiled? Cano pointed at the chair again. "Sit."

Allie threw up her hand and feigned outrage. "Fine. I'm going." Allie pushed aside the papers they still had scattered all over the table. She held up Cano's map and chuckled. "I think you better leave the mapmaking to Mullineaux and Crandell."

Cano put on her best scowl before she turned back to the stove. "I thought it was a masterpiece."

"Better keep your day job. I'm afraid you'll never make it as a cartographer."

"Cartographers are boring. I'm more of an artist."

"Just like Dali." Allie shook her head and laughed. "Throw a couple melting clocks on your map, and you can call it impressionism."

"Exactly." Cano flicked her wrist as she ran the whisk through the eggs. "Did you get any news on how big the quake was this morning?"

"Yeah, they're saying it was a four-point-eight."

"Felt bigger." Cano grabbed the toast from the toaster.

"I thought so, too." Allie sighed. "I got some other news, too."

Cano glanced over her shoulder as she buttered the toast. "What's that?"

"Apparently, the citizens of Toutle are stirred up. Word on the street is that one of the scientists said that if the volcano blows, a hundred-foot wall of water could bear down on Toutle."

"Ouch. No wonder they're freaked out. I can't believe how many rumors are out there." Cano pulled the pan off the stove, turned off the burner, and scooped eggs onto the plates.

"It's not all rumors, though. It seems like there are more and more factions. Then they all talk to the press and scare the hell out of the poor residents."

"Well, some of them scare the hell out of me." Cano chuckled.

"Very true. I'm just worried that we're going to be caught flat-footed, and this thing is going to be deadly."

"That's what scares me." Cano piled bacon onto the plates.

"Me too."

"Enough of this talk." Cano held up the plates. "It's time for breakfast."

As they'd neared the end of breakfast, Nova had gotten quiet. Allie wanted to do something to ease the tension, so she piled her last bite of scrambled eggs on her last scrap of toast and put her last piece of bacon on top. "Perfection."

Nova grinned, but her eyes held sadness. "And you call me a child."

Allie wrestled with herself. Should she pretend not to notice Nova's change in mood? *Yep.* At least she'd try. She held up the bite. "It's a masterpiece. How can you not see that?"

"I stand corrected. Who am I to interfere with your perfect bite?" Nova crumpled up her napkin and threw it on her plate. She glanced at Allie one final time before she began to rise from the table.

Allie let the bite drop to her plate. The eggs and bacon toppled off the toast and scattered across her plate. She put her hand on Nova's arm. "Wait."

Nova met her gaze and lowered herself back into her chair but didn't speak.

"Why do I feel like all of the good feelings from the last two days are slipping away?" Allie asked.

Pain crossed Nova's face. She closed her eyes and took a deep breath before she turned her gaze to Allie. "It's been great being here, but don't you think we should talk about what happened?"

"No." Allie shook her head so hard that her hair whipped against her cheeks. "We got caught up in the moment." She pointed her finger at Nova. "I won't let a stupid mistake ruin the friendship we've been rebuilding."

Nova winced but then nodded. "Stupid mistake?"

"You know what I mean. This," Allie waved her hand between her and Nova, "having you around has been nice. Just because we couldn't make it as a couple doesn't mean we can't be good friends."

Nova looked down at the table and pushed her fork around her empty plate as if she were gathering up a bite. "It has been nice," Nova muttered.

"Exactly." Allie put more conviction in her voice than she felt. Part of her hoped that Nova would proclaim her love and beg Allie for another chance, but it was such a stupid wish. *Friendship was better.* That way, neither would get their hearts ripped out again. "Come on. Chin up. We've got a volcano to watch and a friendship to enjoy."

Nova gazed at her and smiled. There was still a hint of sadness around her eyes, but then her smile broadened. She nodded toward Allie's plate. "Looks like that perfect last bite is ruined."

"Nonsense." Allie made a show of gathering the ingredients back on her tiny piece of toast. Once completed, she held it up. "Restored perfection."

"Is a perfect last bite like a shooting star?"

Allie narrowed her eyes. "Shooting star?"

"Yeah, do you make a wish on it?"

"Hmm." Allie rubbed her chin, pretending to contemplate Nova's question. "Have you ever tried wishing on a perfect bite?"

Nova shook her head. "Not only have I not wished on one, but I've never had one."

"Never?" Allie let her mouth drop open in mock surprise. "We have to change that. What if I share mine?"

Nova raised her eyebrows. "Would it still be a perfect bite?"

"I believe it would be. More like the ultimate perfect last bite."

"Ultimate? How do you figure?" Nova's eyes danced with amusement. Allie had always loved her playful side.

"Sharing something with someone always makes it more special." Allie froze. That was a loaded sentence. She gazed at Nova, but she didn't seem to notice, so Allie continued. "Shall we?"

"Okay, but we both can't take the last bite."

"Sure we can. I'll take a bite and then hand it off to you."

"But then you won't have the last bite, I will." Nova smirked.

"Mine will be the penultimate bite then."

"So your bite will be better than mine? That's not fair."

Allie shook her head. "Good thing you're a scientist not a linguist. Penultimate means the second to last."

"No way. You're just making shit up. Penultimate is like the end-all and be-all of the extra special ultimate."

"Wow, you add one little prefix, and you came up with all that?" Allie laughed. "Pen is Latin for almost and ultimate the last, so it is almost the last."

Nova crossed her arms over her chest, cocked her head, and studied Allie. "Damn, you're good. That almost sounds believable."

"Because it's the truth. If I had a dictionary here, I'd show you. Look it up."

"I will."

Allie grinned. She knew as soon as Nova found a dictionary she would be rifling through the pages. "Let me know what you discover."

Nova nodded at the bite that Allie still held. "Will it still be perfect if the food gets much colder?"

"You've got a point. We better do this soon. Ready?"

Nova nodded.

Allie took a bite and handed the other half to Nova. "Now put it in your mouth," Allie said around the bite already in her mouth. "Then we chew and swallow on three. Don't forget to make a wish when you do."

Nova popped the bite into her mouth.

"One." Allie chewed. "Two." Chew. "Three."

They both swallowed at the same time.

"What did you wish for?" Nova asked.

Allie scowled. "I can't tell you, or it won't come true."

Nova gave her a crooked smile. "I'll let you know if my wish comes true."

"I'll do the same," Allie said, knowing they were getting dangerously close to flirtation. Another attempted kiss was out of the question. She didn't want another setback. Besides, they'd established that neither was willing to risk their renewed friendship. "What time will Johnny be here?"

Nova glanced at the clock and frowned. "Twenty minutes. I better get my mess cleaned up."

"I can get it later."

"Nonsense." Nova stood. "I want you to be able to report to Fran that I took really good care of you."

"I'll be sure to let her know."

"She still scares me." Nova grabbed the two pans off the stove and carried them to the sink. "So please put in a good word for me."

Allie bit back her words. She wanted to tell Nova that she'd miss her, but it wouldn't be fair. Some things were better left unsaid.

Chapter Thirty-one

Days until eruption: 8
Saturday, May 10, 1980
Toutle, Washington
Allie's cottage

Allie poured her first cup of coffee of the morning and breathed in the heady aroma. She didn't mess with cream or sugar; today called for black. The steam rose from the cup, so she blew on it a few times before bringing it to her lips.

She'd just swallowed the first sip when the phone rang. For a split second, she considered carrying her coffee in one hand, while she used her cane in the other. With a sigh, she set the coffee back on the counter. After a final look of longing at her cup, she turned toward the living room and the phone.

"Hello," Allie said.

"What the hell's going on down there?" Fran asked.

"It's nice to talk to you, too." Allie tried to hide the smile in her voice.

"Ah, sorry. But what the hell is going on?"

"You may need to be a little more specific since you just took me away from my coffee." Allie slipped into the chair next to the phone.

"Did you hear about the meeting in Toutle last night?"

"Of course I heard about it. I was there."

"What?" Fran's voice raised. "Why didn't I know about it?"

"Because I figured you'd classify it as nerdy scientist stuff."

"You have a point." Fran chuckled. "Normally I would, but the story is all over the news this morning."

"Oh, god, what did they say?"

"It depends on what paper I read. One paper said the scientists put the residents of Toutle at ease. Were there really a hundred and thirty people in attendance?"

"Probably. The gym seemed pretty full. I'd have to ask Nova. She's better at estimating that stuff than me."

"Is she there?" Fran's voice rose an octave.

"No, Snoopy. Her team had a powwow in Vancouver first thing this morning, so she drove back last night."

"Are you two sleeping together?"

"What? Seriously? No!" Allie paused and collected her thoughts. "Why in the world would you say something like that?"

"Just making sure."

"Well, get your mind out of the gutter. We're *just* friends." Allie didn't want to continue this conversation. "Back to the reason for your call."

"Oh, yeah. Another reporter kinda made you guys look bad."

Allie's mouth dropped open. "Me and Nova?"

"No. You told me that I couldn't talk about her." Fran huffed. "The reporter made all scientists look bad."

Allie groaned. *Typical.* "It doesn't help that

some of my colleagues like to air their disagreements in public. The reporters eat it up. What did the article say?"

"Let me find my favorite lines." All Allie heard was the sound of crinkling newspaper. "Here it is. This is a quote from one of the sheriffs. 'Pinning scientists down is like trying to corner a rat in a roundhouse.'"

Allie laughed. "He does have a point, but I think for the most part, the people walked away feeling better. Although Nova was pissed."

"Why?"

"They led the crowd to believe they'd have at least a two-hour warning should something happen. Neither of us thinks they'd have nearly that much time."

"It's only going to get worse."

"Aren't you a ray of sunshine?"

"I hear more at the university than I let on." Fran let out a deep breath. "From where I sit, it seems like things are getting political."

"Getting? It has been. With tourist season coming, it'll be hard to keep people out. It's been over a month and a half, and things have quieted down on the mountain. I fear that's a bad combination."

"Maybe the quakes have, but what about the bulge?" Fran asked.

"Nobody seems to want to talk about it. Something's pushing the side of the mountain out, and it's moving farther every day."

"Ugh," Fran practically yelled. "Enough. Let's talk about something fun. Your fortieth birthday."

It was Allie's turn to react. "No. I'm skipping my birthday this year."

"Too late. I've already invited Cano and Johnny

to the bash."

"And where will this bash occur?"

"Likely right where you're at now."

"Let me get this straight," Allie said, trying to keep the grin out of her voice. "You're throwing a birthday party for me, but it's at my house."

"Bingo. Scientists are so smart."

Allie rolled her eyes, which was, of course, lost on Fran over the phone. "And when will this occur?"

"Your birthday."

"Friday?"

"Duh. That's your birthday."

"Why not Saturday?"

"Sorry." Fran sighed. "We've got our niece and nephew for the weekend. Ben's brother is the best man in a wedding. He and his wife are spending the weekend in Portland, so we have the kids. They're leaving Saturday morning. I'm sorry."

"No, don't be. I wasn't even planning on celebrating. Am I cooking, too?"

"Don't be silly. We'll bring pizza and beer."

"Classy affair." Allie chuckled.

"Only the finest for my best friend."

Allie smiled. Fran truly was a blessing and always knew how to cheer Allie up, but she also could read Allie like a book, so she needed to be careful how she worded the next question. "You said you invited Nova? She didn't mention anything about it last night."

Fran laughed. "I was testing her. See if she could keep her mouth shut. I didn't tell her it was a surprise, but I didn't tell her it wasn't, either."

"You're terrible. When did you invite her?"

"Um...I called her...I don't know Tuesday or

Wednesday. She was all over it. I certainly didn't have to ask her twice."

"It'll be fun." Allie wanted to ask more questions about Fran's call with Nova but knew Fran would pick up on her interest, and she didn't have the strength for Fran's inquisition today. Besides, she wanted—no, needed—to get back to her coffee.

"I gotta scoot. Ben's bellowing from the other room. Probably lost something again. I swear that man loses everything."

"Tell Ben I said hi."

"Will do. I'll call you next week."

"Bye." Allie put the phone receiver back on the cradle.

If her coffee wasn't calling her, she'd sit here and try to figure out her life, but the coffee wasn't getting any warmer. When she got to it, it was tepid at best. She glared at her mug, wishing she were at home, so she could heat it up in her new microwave. Her parents had refused to buy one, insisting the waves would cause cancer.

She sighed and poured her coffee into a pan to reheat it. The thought of the party left her with mixed emotions. Even though she tried to ignore it, Nova was becoming part of her life again. Being here to celebrate her fortieth birthday solidified it more.

It wasn't a big deal, she tried to convince herself. Besides, Nova wouldn't stick around forever, she'd have to return to Menlo Park eventually. The thought caused Allie's chest to ache. *Shit.* This was so not good. After her birthday party, she'd need to put some distance between her and Nova.

That should fix the problem. Allie rolled her eyes. She didn't even believe it herself.

Chapter Thirty-two

Days until eruption: 2
Friday, May 16, 1980
Toutle, Washington
Spirit Lake Highway

Cano gripped the clutch and shifted up. The air still held a nip, but it felt good on her face. She'd been riding her bike back and forth from Vancouver to Mount St. Helens for the past week, and it made her feel alive.

She'd considered hitching a ride to Toutle with Johnny, but today, she needed time alone. For some reason, this party had her on edge, and riding her bike always put her at ease. With a twist of her wrist, her bike surged.

Despite her increased speed, she couldn't outrun the thoughts of Allie. For better or worse, Allie was firmly stuck in her mind and etched in her heart.

There was no denying her feelings. She was falling in love with Allie. She snorted. Who was she kidding? She'd never stopped loving Allie but had just been forced to move on. If she could call the way she'd lived the past four years moving on. It hadn't felt like living, especially now that she had the last couple of months to compare it to. She couldn't risk losing Allie again, even if it meant they could only be friends.

A car pulled out from a side road and nearly

sideswiped her. She swerved and gunned the bike. She stuck up her middle finger at the driver, who'd slammed on his brakes and sat parked in the middle of the road. Hopefully, he'd have to clean out his shorts after the close call. She needed to put Allie out of her mind and pay better attention since people didn't watch out for motorcycles.

The ride had left her colder than expected, so she left her leather gloves on as she walked up the sidewalk to Allie's place. Fran and Johnny's vehicles were already parked out front, so she was the last to arrive. *Great.* She hoped Allie wouldn't think it meant she didn't care.

Cano clutched the small package, wrinkling the blue and silver wrapping paper. She loosened her hold. No way would she give Allie a present that looked like it had gone ten rounds with Muhammad Ali.

When she knocked on the door, it immediately flew open. She jumped back in surprise.

"Jumpy much?" Allie asked. "Didn't you think I'd answer?"

"Yeah, but not so quickly. Were you standing on top of the door?" Cano hoped she'd been awaiting her arrival.

Allie pointed at the closet behind the open door. "I came in to get my jacket. It's a little chilly out back." Allie's eyes widened. "You must be freezing."

Warmth spread through Cano's body as Allie touched her face but not because of the heat from her hand. Cano held up her gloved hand. "I dressed for the weather."

"Well, get in here and warm up." Allie motioned her inside.

"I thought you'd never ask." Cano smirked.

Allie shrugged. "What can I say? I'm old now." She tapped her head. "The mind isn't as sharp as it once was."

"Oh, yeah. Happy birthday." Heat rose in Cano's cheeks. She couldn't believe she'd forgotten to say it first thing. "Sorry. You threw me off when you opened the door so fast, and I'm afraid I've yet to recover."

Allie put her hand on Cano's arm. "I'll let it pass as long as you promise to sing extra loud during my birthday song."

Cano laughed. Allie knew she couldn't carry a tune to save her life. "You asked for it." Cano pulled the package out of her pocket. "Oh, hey, I forgot." She held the present out to Allie.

A flash of amusement danced in Allie's eyes at the crumpled wrapping paper before she reached out for it. "Thanks."

"It got a little," Cano pointed, "messed up in my pocket."

"It's perfect," Allie said as she smoothed out the wrinkled paper. "I'll put it with the other gifts. I'll open them after dinner."

The back door banged open. "What the hell is taking you so long?" Fran called. When she entered the living room, she stopped and glanced at the gift in Allie's hand. "Um, sorry. I didn't realize." Fran took a deep breath. "I've lost my manners. Hi, Cano."

Good sign. Fran had been a much kinder and gentler version of herself since the barbecue, and Cano was happy to see it continue. Her fear that Fran would blame her for Allie's setback had been unfounded. "Hello, Fran." Cano smiled.

"Thanks for coming to celebrate this old lady." Fran put her arm around Allie's shoulders and squeezed.

"Says the woman that's six months older than me."

"But I look damned good." Fran fluffed her hair. "Don't I, Cano?"

"Absolutely. You both do forty proud."

Fran pointed at her. "Good answer."

"The boys are probably wondering where we are," Allie said.

Fran snorted. "I doubt they noticed. They were busy reliving the Lakers' championship win."

Cano's ears perked up. "Great game last night. That Magic Johnson is the real deal. It's insane that a twenty-year-old rookie was the MVP."

Fran clamped her hands over her ears. "Stop! Go outside and talk to the guys before my ears start bleeding. Allie and I will get the drinks together."

Allie nodded. "Go."

Cano wasn't going to argue and slipped from the room.

"Thanks, babe," Ben said as he took the beer from Fran. He pointed toward the sky. "What's with all the helicopters?"

Allie glanced up before she sat in one of the patio chairs. She didn't notice them anymore since they'd descended on the area. "Mixed bag. Mostly news helicopters."

"Vultures then?" Ben said.

Johnny shook his head. "They've actually been extremely useful. They've been pretty good about flying scientists up to the summit." He nodded toward

Nova. "Cano got to go up a couple of days ago."

Nova's eyes lit up like a kid at Christmas. "It was so cool. Got to look right down into the crater."

"Isn't that dangerous?" Ben asked.

"If she erupted, it would be."

Allie shivered at the thought of Nova near the summit in a helicopter. She'd not been back up since her first time. It made her nervous, so she hadn't pushed for another opportunity. She'd been a wreck the entire time Nova was gone, but she'd not shared that with anyone, not even Fran.

"So why would you go up there?" Ben asked.

"To collect samples." Nova said. "To put eyes on it, so we can see if anything has changed."

"They've pledged to help out with evacuation if it were to erupt," Allie added.

"Which is a relief to the guys working on Coldwater II," Johnny said.

"Unless it's a lateral blast." Nova's face was strained. "Then they can kiss their asses goodbye. No way would they have time to evacuate."

"Seriously?" Fran's eyes widened. "Allie, don't you go up there sometimes?"

"Not as much as I used to. I've been keeping the students a little farther away." Allie put her hand on Fran's. "Stop looking like you're going to throw up."

Fran pointed at Allie. "If you get yourself blown up, I will haunt your ass."

Allie laughed. "Um, I think it would be me that would be haunting you."

Fran flicked her hand toward Allie. "Details."

The others laughed.

"I think you're all crazy," Fran said. "No way would you get me up there."

"Speaking of crazy people," Johnny said. "Did you hear what they're doing this weekend?" When nobody responded, he continued. "They're letting people go up to their cabins to check out their property."

"No way," Allie said, sure that shock registered on her face. "Into the red zone?"

"It's true," Nova said. "Talk about shitty timing. At the meeting in Vancouver today, I heard the sheriff's office has sent a new map to the governor, trying to get her to move the boundaries back after the huge earthquake on Thursday."

"Oh, god, I forgot to tell you." Johnny practically bounced in his chair as he turned his gaze to Nova. "They've requested a tank for Coldwater II. I guess the official term is an M113 armored personnel carrier."

"Stop shitting me," Nova said.

"I'm not." Johnny held up his hands. "I swear."

"I heard it, too," Allie said.

"Ugh." Fran put her hand against her forehead. "What is wrong with you people? You *scientists*. If you need a tank up there, it's probably not a good idea to be there in the first place. I think you all should—"

Another helicopter flew over, cutting off her words.

After the helicopter had moved away, Nova said, "I've got a really bad feeling." Her brow creased, and a frown played on her lips. "Ever since the earthquake yesterday, I've felt…I don't know, creeped out."

"Foreboding?" Allie asked

Nova snapped her fingers. "That's it. I've had a feeling of foreboding."

"I'd listen to your instincts," Fran said. "You educated types might not like it, but give me a good gut feeling over data any day."

The others laughed.

"Spoken like a true layman." Allie winked at Fran, who glowered.

❧❧❧

Since it was starting to get dark, they'd moved inside after Fran had heated up the pizzas. Cano wouldn't admit it to the others, but for the last couple of weeks, the sound of helicopters flying over gave her an uneasy feeling. Even though she'd been thrilled to get a look inside the volcano, the thought of a helicopter being hit by a blast made her shudder.

"Damn, that was good pizza," Johnny said.

"We couldn't tell." Cano chuckled. "I'm telling Rosaria that you ate three-fourths of a pizza all by yourself."

"I did not." He scowled at Cano.

"Um, sorry, honey," Allie said. "But this time, Nova is right."

"No." He glanced around the table.

Fran and Ben nodded, too.

"Well, I'll be damned. It's all the good conversation. I lose track of what I'm eating."

"That's it." Cano smirked. "Still not as good as Allie's pork chops. Oh, by the way," she looked at Allie, trying to appear nonchalant, "what's the secret spice?"

Allie rolled her eyes. "That was a pretty lame attempt."

Cano shrugged. "I've tried just about every other method." Cano felt her face redden. She'd opened the door for Allie to embarrass her.

A mischievous smile played on Allie's lips. "I recall one way in particular."

Shit. Allie went there. Cano tried not to smile, remembering the time she'd threatened to withhold sex until Allie told her. Cano had lasted almost a week.

Fran put her chin on her hand and leaned forward. "Do tell."

Allie smirked at Cano before she turned to Fran. "She offered to cook for an entire month if I told her."

Cano breathed a sigh of relief. She'd done that, too, but by the teasing look on Allie's face, she suspected she was thinking about the other time.

"Why didn't you take her up on it?" Ben asked. "Sounds like a pretty good deal."

Allie shook her head. "You've never eaten her cooking."

Johnny laughed. "That was your mistake, Cano. You should have promised her you wouldn't cook."

Cano crossed her arms. The teasing felt good, but her chest still tightened. She missed Allie and moments like this more than anything.

"Hey, what's that look for?" Allie patted Cano's hand. "We were just teasing."

Shit. Cano didn't realize what she was feeling showed on her face. She needed to save the moment, so she put on a huge smile. "And the winner is...Cano. Oscar-worthy performance, I'd say."

Allie shot her a look that said, *Bullshit*, but then she said, "You're such a ham."

Fran clapped her hands and stood. "Shall we do cake and presents? Ben and I have to hit the road soon."

"I'll grab the presents out of the other room." Cano jumped to her feet.

"Don't forget you promised to sing the loudest," Allie called after her. "So don't think you can hide in the living room until the singing is over."

Cano smiled but didn't look back. When she arrived at the presents, her stomach did a flip-flop. Her present was stupid. Why had she thought this would be a good gift?

Instead of picking them up, she glared at her tiny box sitting on the larger ones. Maybe she could pocket hers and pretend she'd left it at home. Then she could buy Allie a better gift. *No.* Allie had already seen it.

She could save it for when the others were gone, but that seemed almost worse. The group would shelter her from her discomfort. She snatched the boxes off the end table and trudged back to the kitchen.

"About time." Fran held the cake in one hand and had a lighter poised over the candles.

"Um, sorry." Cano set the boxes on the table and slid into her seat.

"Oh, no, you don't," Allie said. "You're leading this song."

Cano groaned. "You just said I had to sing loud."

"You have to do that, too, but I changed my mind." Allie stuck out her bottom lip. "It's my birthday. You're not going to say no, are you?"

"Fine." Cano faked outrage as she stood. She turned to Ben. "Do you have a fire extinguisher ready? Just in case. You never know with all those candles."

"Keep it up," Allie said. "And you won't get a piece."

Fran and Cano both turned to Allie with wide eyes.

"Of cake." Allie's cheeks were bright red.

Cano stifled her chuckle, but Fran nearly dropped the cake as she laughed.

"Just light the damned candles." Allie frowned, but her eyes gave away her amusement.

As Fran flicked the lighter, Cano stood and spread her arms out wide in a conductor's pose. "Okay, team. When the last candle is lit," Cano glanced at the clock, "which should take about five minutes with the number of candles." Allie catcalled, but Cano continued. "The singing will commence."

"Last one," Fran called. "Let's do this."

Cano swept her hands down and started, "Happy birthday to you..." she practically yelled in her less-than-melodic voice.

Thankfully, the song came to an end. Allie was laughing so hard at the singing; it took her three times to blow out all the candles.

"You know," Ben said. "Blowing all over people's food is a strange custom. A little gross actually."

Fran rumpled his hair. "I'll make sure to give you the one with the most spit."

"Eww," Allie said. "Enough, you two."

Allie cut the cake into enormous pieces, but Cano wasn't complaining. She refused the ice cream, preferring to give her cake the entire stage to itself.

"Holy hell," Allie said. "This is so sweet my teeth hurt."

"Isn't it great?" Cano smacked her lips before shoving another bite in her mouth.

"I'm going to need another piece of pizza after this," Fran said.

"Oh, no, you'll be in the endless sugar and salt loop." Allie grabbed Fran's hand in mock horror.

"Sign me up." Fran laughed.

Once the cake was devoured, Fran pushed the wrapped gifts toward Allie. "Looks like you've raked in some loot."

"I still can't believe you brought gifts when I told you all not to." Allie shook her head. She grabbed the biggest gift first. The one from Fran and Ben. She started to shake it, but Fran stopped her.

"Um, it might be breakable."

Allie stood and ripped into the paper. "Oh, my god, they're so cute."

The large box showed a set of mushroom canisters. They had bright orange raised mushrooms on the side, but it was the lids that were shaped like mushroom caps that stole the show.

"Open the box." Fran grabbed a knife to cut through the tape. "You have to see them."

After removing the packing material, Allie lifted out the largest. "Oh, look at this lid. Isn't it adorable?" She passed it to Johnny.

He took it and held it at arm's length. One would think Allie had passed him her underwear by the look on his face. "Um, sure. Cute." He quickly handed it off to Ben.

"Give me that." Fran laughed and snatched it from Ben, who stared at it as if he'd never seen a canister before. "You men are so dense." She started to hand it off to Cano but shook her head. "I'm sure you won't appreciate it, either."

When it was back in Allie's hands, she pulled off the lid and slammed it back down. Then she stuffed the canister back into the box.

Cano stared. What was up with everyone and the canisters? She understood the men's reaction, but now Allie was acting strange.

"Do you like it?" Fran grinned and winked at Allie.

Allie stood and wrapped Fran in a hug. She whispered something in Fran's ear, but Cano couldn't make it out. Fran chuckled at whatever Allie said.

Once Allie sat, Fran handed her the present Johnny must have brought. Cano was impressed; he hadn't asked her for a gift suggestion.

Allie brought the perfectly square package up to her face and gazed at Johnny. "Can I shake this one?"

He grinned. "Go right ahead."

Allie shook it several times, but no sound came from the box. "Hmm. Whatever it is, it's solid." She carefully unwrapped it and squealed. "Oh, it's one of those Rubik's Cubes. I've seen some of the kids on campus with them."

"What do you do with it?" Fran asked.

Allie held it up. "You mix up all the colors and then you have to put it together again."

Fran gave Allie a superior grin. "That should be simple."

"Be my guest." Allie mixed up the cube and then handed it to Fran with a snicker.

Cano watched with amusement as Fran put on a determined scowl before she began twisting the cube.

"No pressure, Fran," Cano said. "But I heard there are like forty-three quintillion combinations."

Fran glared. "Quintillion. That's not even a number."

"It is," Allie chimed in. "Million. Billion. Trillion. Quadrillion, and then quintillion."

"How the hell do you know that shit?" Fran shook her head at her friend. "You're such a geek. Where does gazillion come in?"

Cano tried not to laugh, waiting for how Allie would handle the question.

"Honey," Allie started out. "I'm afraid I'm going to have to break this to you. Gazillion is a made-up number. It's not real."

Fran threw her hands in the air. "Jesus. Quinstillion is a number, but gazillion isn't?"

"Quintillion, not quins."

"Whatever." Fran dropped the cube on the table. "Way too many possibilities for me to solve the damned thing."

Cano laughed, but her chest tightened when she glanced down at the table and saw the tiny box left. She'd been stupid. Why had she decided to give Allie this gift?

Allie picked it up off the table. Her gaze met Cano's, and she smiled. "The best things come in small packages."

Yes, they do, Cano thought.

"Spoken like a short person," Fran said.

"Bitterness doesn't become you," Allie teased. "It's not my fault you don't have the patience to solve a puzzle with a mere forty-three quintillion possibilities."

Fran crossed her arms over her chest. "Just open your damned present."

Allie didn't ask Cano if she could shake it; instead, she tore at the wrapping paper. Once she'd freed a corner, she pulled out the cardboard jewelry box. She glanced at Cano before she lifted the lid.

Allie's eyes widened, and she turned to Cano. "Is this...this isn't," she stammered.

Cano smiled and nodded.

Allie leapt from the table and wrapped her arms

around Cano's neck, the jewelry box still in her hand. Cano returned the hug, enjoying the feeling of having Allie in her arms.

When Allie let go and stepped back, Fran said, "What the hell is all the commotion about?" Fran took the gift from Allie's hand. Her nose turned up as she stared into the box.

Fran gave it to Ben. His expression was equally as puzzled as Fran's. He shrugged before he handed it off to Johnny.

Cano saw the recognition in Johnny's eyes as he turned his gaze from the box to her. "Wow," Johnny said. He looked toward Allie. "Now I know just how special you are to her."

"Would someone tell me what the hell it is?" Fran put her hand on her hip. "You know I hate it when I'm not in the know."

Allie ignored Fran and turned to Cano. "This is too much." Allie fingered the piece of pumice hanging from the necklace. "You can't give this to me."

"I want you to have it." The lump in Cano's throat made it hard for her to speak. Maybe it signified too much, but she wanted to give it to Allie.

"But your grandma." Tears welled in Allie's eyes.

Cano chuckled. "She probably picked it up in a gift shop somewhere. It probably isn't even real."

"Doesn't matter." Allie cradled the stone and ran her finger along the rough surface.

"What does some bumpy black stone have to do with Cano's grandmother?" Fran said, her voice even louder than before.

"It's pumice," Allie said. "The pumice her grandmother gave her."

When Cano saw the puzzled look on Fran's face,

she said, "Lava. My grandma claimed to have gotten it when she was in Italy."

"Not just anywhere in Italy," Allie said. "Pompeii."

"Even I know about Pompeii." Fran smiled. "Your grandma picked it up there?"

Cano shrugged. "Possibly. At least that's what she told me, but I've always wondered. I was half tempted to have it analyzed to see."

Allie scowled. "And I told her not to. It's magical just the way it is. No sense ruining that."

"Wow," Fran said. "Look at you. What happened to the practical and logical scientist? I've never known you to be dreamy."

"I'm multifaceted." Allie grinned and turned to Cano. "And this is the sweetest and most magical gift I've ever gotten." She rolled the stone in her hands. "You always carried it in your pocket. When did you have it made into a necklace?"

Heat dotted Cano's cheeks. "Last week."

"So you had it made for me?" Allie put her hand on her chest.

Cano nodded. "My grandmother gave it to me when she gave me my nickname. Said it would ward off all the bad." Cano gave the others a sad smile. "That's when I was getting in fights all the time because of my name. She gave it to me and said it would protect me." Cano looked down at the floor. "I thought maybe it could help protect you."

Allie wrapped her arms around Cano again. "It's absolutely perfect. If you're sure you want me to have it, I'll wear it proudly."

"I'm positive. I wouldn't have given it to you if I didn't want to."

"Would you put it on me?"

It was as if no one else was in the room when Allie spoke those words. Cano's gaze locked on Allie. "Sure," Cano said, hoping her voice didn't come out as nervous as she felt. She took the necklace from the box and went around behind Allie. Carefully, she put it around her neck and pushed back Allie's hair. "There. All set." Cano let Allie's hair fall back over the chain. She couldn't help but take in the fresh scent of Allie's shampoo. Not wanting to get caught sniffing Allie's hair, she took a step back.

Allie clutched the necklace and held her hand against her chest. "It's beautiful."

Cano knew her cheeks must be bright red, but she didn't care as she gazed at the stone around Allie's neck.

Chapter Thirty-three

Days until eruption: 2
Friday, May 16, 1980
Toutle, Washington
Allie's cottage

It was almost midnight, and the others had been gone since ten. Cano should probably be going, but she didn't want to. Every time she looked at Allie with the stone around her neck, she couldn't help but smile.

Since she'd arrived at Mount St. Helens nearly two months ago, she'd tried to convince herself she only wanted a friendship with Allie. Tonight, there was no denying she wanted more. She wanted to touch Allie like she once did. To feel Allie's smooth skin against her own when they lay naked in bed.

"Penny for your thoughts?" Allie said.

Shit. "Um...I was...um...just thinking how much I like seeing you wearing that necklace." It wasn't a lie. Just not the entire truth.

"I love it." Allie beamed. "I've...um..." Allie jumped up from the sofa. "I've got to go to the restroom."

Cano stared at the empty room. What in the hell was that? Since the others had gone, Cano swore she'd felt tension in the air, but she couldn't quite put her finger on it. It was most likely wishful thinking. Allie had made it clear she only wanted to be friends—

nothing more.

Cano stood and walked into the kitchen. She should wrap things up and hit the road; instead, she began cleaning up. The dishes from earlier were still piled in the sink, and the table hadn't been washed down. Allie had refused to let anyone help, despite Fran's loud protests.

It wouldn't take her long. She closed off the drain, turned on the hot water, and squirted dish soap into the sink. While the sink filled, she gathered up the loose wrapping paper and discarded it into the garbage. She dipped a rag into the dishwater and ran a cloth over the table, cleaning off the leftover crumbs that littered it.

After she was satisfied the table was finished, she dipped her hands into the water, searching for the first plate. She'd hoped she could get the dishes done before Allie returned and refused to let her do them. She glanced toward the door. Allie had been gone awhile.

Allie stared at herself in the mirror; her gaze locked on the necklace. Tears threatened. She needed to get herself under control before she rejoined Nova. The gift had opened something inside of her that she wasn't sure she could close.

It had been so nice to have Nova back in her life, so why couldn't she just be happy with the renewed friendship? Why did she want to throw herself into Nova's arms and kiss her so hard that both would forget the past? Or maybe it would make them remember the past.

She sighed. How long had she been in here, staring at herself in the mirror? Surely, Nova would wonder what she was doing. But instead of leaving the sanctuary of the bathroom, she studied her own face. Tiny wrinkles were beginning to show at the corner of her eyes. Would her MS make her age quicker?

Lately, she'd felt good, but she knew a relapse could be just around the corner. Then she might end up in a wheelchair. That was why they'd broken up in the first place. Now at forty, the likelihood of her having more complications from her condition increased.

She steeled her eyes and spoke into the mirror. "You cannot do this to Nova. It's not fair." Her chest tightened. Obviously, her heart didn't agree with her words.

With a firm set to her jaw, she turned away.

She found Nova in the kitchen with her hands buried in the dishwater. "And what do you think you're doing?" Allie asked, sure that her words came out sharper than she intended.

Nova jumped. "Shit. You scared me. I wanted to help you clean up."

"Didn't I tell you that I'd take care of it tomorrow?"

"It's your birthday, so I decided not to listen." Nova nodded toward the dish towel. "You can dry if you'd like."

"Gee thanks." Allie picked up the dishtowel.

"So how long are you going to keep the rules on?" Cano stared into the dishwater.

"Rules?"

"The ones that say we can't talk about the past?"

Allie's heartbeat quickened. "Do you want to

talk about it?"

Nova rinsed off another plate and set it in the opposite sink. "I think I do."

"I see." Allie picked up the plate and ran the towel over it. "Do you really think it's a good idea?"

Nova shrugged. "I don't know." She finally met Allie's gaze. "But I think I want to, anyway."

"I'm not sure what there is to talk about."

"I never got over you."

Allie wasn't expecting Nova to jump right to the point, so her breath caught. She wasn't sure how to respond, so she decided infusing humor was the best plan. She pretended to look Nova up and down. "I'm sure you have women all over you. You're damned cute."

"Thanks," Nova said but didn't smile.

"Why so glum? I just told you that you're adorable, and you should have women falling at your feet."

Nova turned and locked her gaze on Allie. The intensity caused Allie to look away. "I don't want any other woman," Nova said in a soft voice.

"Come on." Allie had heard rumors about Nova's conquests. She wasn't sure why people felt the need to tell her about the news from Menlo Park, but they had. "I've heard about your exploits."

"My what?"

Either Nova was a great actress, or she was honestly surprised. "All of your success with the ladies," Allie said.

Nova snorted. "Don't believe everything you hear."

Why was she allowing herself to have this conversation? She should end it right now. Instead, she said, "So what's the truth?"

After Nova rinsed off the final plate, she pulled the plug on the drain. As she dried her hands, she said, "Do you really want to know?"

Did she? Allie could call foul and stop the conversation, but they'd already come this far. Maybe getting a good dose of reality would wake her up. "Yes."

"Once I left Seattle and settled into my life in Menlo Park, I cruised the bars."

Allie stiffened, not sure if she wanted to hear any more.

"Are you sure you want to hear this?" Nova asked.

Allie nodded, afraid her voice would betray her.

"I picked up a woman." Nova grimaced. "I don't even remember what she looked like, but I went back to her house. She took me into her bedroom and started undressing me." Nova looked down at the floor. "My whole body started to tremble, and the next thing I know, I'm sitting on her floor sobbing." Nova looked into Allie's eyes. "Needless to say, that was the end of the date."

"I'm sorry." Allie dried the final plate and put it into the cabinet. She tossed her towel on the counter. "Surely, you fared better another time."

"Worse." Nova shook her head. "I decided there was no way I could do it sober. Since the only woman I could think of was you."

"Oh" was all Allie could manage. Her heart ached.

"So I got hammered, and we took a cab back to her house. I thought I'd found the solution. Clothes came off without any tears. I jumped into bed, and the next thing I know, I'm puking all over her sheets."

"Ouch." The visual flooded Allie's mind. She

wasn't sure if she should laugh or cry.

"Ouch is right," Nova said with a sad smile. "She told me to get the fuck out. I didn't even know where I was, so I'm putting on my clothes begging her to call me a cab. By then, I'm starting to sober up. I ended up having to take a bus home. It was the ultimate in the walk of shame."

"You had to have found your groove eventually."

"I did."

Nova's words were like a gut punch. She didn't revel in Nova's pain, but she didn't want to hear about her conquests, either. It was too late now.

Nova held up her hand and wiggled her fingers. "This has been my date ever since."

Allie's eyes widened. "You mean there's been nobody?" The revelation shocked her. Nova had so much confidence, so much sex appeal, Allie couldn't believe she'd been with no one. "Why did everyone tell me there was?"

Nova put on her sexiest smirk and pointed at her face. "I put on the crooked grin and let people believe what they wanted. Nobody ever asks, and their assumptions serve me well. Not too many straight people want to know about my *conquests*. Works to my advantage. What about you?"

Allie waved her off. "You don't want to hear about that."

"Are you serious?" Nova glared. "I just bared my most embarrassing secret, and you won't talk."

Shit. This was the last thing she wanted to tell Nova about, but it wasn't fair since they'd come this far. "I don't think you *really* want to hear this."

It was evident by Nova's reaction that she was experiencing the same gut punch Allie had felt a few minutes ago. "We might as well put all our cards on the table," Nova said, her face the color of chalk.

"I went the opposite direction."

Nova shrugged. Allie suspected it was to make her look unconcerned, but instead, it looked as if she had an unnatural tic since her shoulder rose and fell two more times. "Lots of successful sex, huh?"

"God, no!" Allie practically shouted. "Nothing successful about it."

"You mean you didn't even try?" Cano said, the hope heavy in her voice.

"I didn't say that, either." Allie continued to back herself into a corner.

"I'm afraid you're going to have to spell it out for me. I'm not getting it."

Allie stared down at her thumb, suddenly interested in her cuticle. "I switched teams for a while."

"Men?" Nova's voice rose two octaves.

If the situation wasn't so uncomfortable, Nova's reaction might have been comical. "Afraid so."

"Unsuccessfully?"

"Depends on who you ask." Allie tried for a carefree smile but was afraid she hadn't pulled it off. She'd felt humiliated, but she'd done it to herself. Dr. Pappas had done nothing wrong. "He seemed to have a good time."

Nova recoiled.

"Your reaction is pretty much how I felt about myself." Allie fought back tears. She would *not* cry.

"I'm sorry. I didn't mean anything by it." Nova took a step forward. "You just took me by surprise. You'd said after you'd tried it in high school that... never again."

"I meant it at the time. Circumstances change."

Allie was having more trouble keeping her tears at bay as she gazed into Nova's concerned eyes. The eyes that melted her from the moment they'd met.

Nova took another step closer and put her hand on Allie's arm. "Care to elaborate?"

Allie couldn't maintain Nova's gaze, so she looked past her at the set of mushroom canisters sitting on the countertop. The cheerful design temporarily pulled her from the heaviness of the conversation.

When Allie didn't speak, Nova moved in closer and lightly squeezed her arm. "You don't have to talk about it if you don't want to."

Allie shook her head. "That's not fair. You shared your story, which I'm sure wasn't exactly comfortable."

"Not my proudest moments."

Since Nova stood so close, it was difficult for Allie to look anywhere else, so she settled on Nova's chin. "Let's just say my foray into trying a man was a bad decision."

Nova's eyes flashed. "Did he hurt you?"

"No, no. Nothing like that."

"Why...why did you? I mean..." Nova paused and looked toward the ceiling as if trying to find the words there.

"Turns out it was stupid logic."

"Stupid logic? Isn't that an oxymoron?"

Allie nodded. "I suppose it is. Maybe I should've said faulty logic." Allie was relieved to be stuck in a semantics loop, so she didn't have to finish her story just yet.

"And your faulty logic was?"

"I was lonely. I didn't think anyone would ever want me, but he did." Allie shifted her gaze from

Nova's chin to the middle of her chest. "I let him take me to bed one night. I thought maybe it would be easier that way."

Nova's throat bounced as she swallowed hard. Her face turned crimson. "Oh." Nova picked up the dishrag, wrung it out, and placed it over the faucet to dry. Then she grabbed the towel and began to fold it.

Allie stepped forward and placed her hand on Nova's. The dishtowel hung loosely between them, and their gazes locked.

"Are you disgusted?"

"No," Nova answered immediately.

"Then what are you?" Allie took the towel from Nova and set it on the counter before she took both of Nova's hands in hers.

"Surprised. Confused. Heartsick."

"It was a huge mistake. I hated it." Allie looked up into Nova's eyes, and this time, she didn't look away.

Nova shifted her gaze to the left, but Allie reached up and touched her face. "Please, look at me. I want to see what you're thinking. What you're feeling."

Nova blinked twice before she complied. She took a deep breath before she spoke. "I never thought... never thought after we split that you'd turn to men. It surprised and confused me. I'm having trouble understanding why."

Allie let go of Nova's hands and wiggled her own fingers. "As you know, sometimes my body stops working. I couldn't...you know...But with a man, I thought it would be easier. Less physical for me."

"And that's why I feel heartsick," Nova said. For emphasis, she rubbed her chest.

"It wasn't like I was assaulted, so you don't have to look at me with such sadness." Allie fought back her ire. "I know you aren't meaning any disrespect, but it's beginning to feel like you're pitying me. And I don't like it."

"No. Not pitying. If anyone deserves pity, it's me." Nova attempted a smile. "I'm the one puking in someone's bed. It all just seems so pointless. So unnecessary."

"I'm sorry you feel my choices were unnecessary," Allie said with a bite in her tone.

"I feel both of our choices were unnecessary," Cano replied. "It didn't have to be that way."

"But I couldn't give you what you needed." Allie's voice came out in little more than a whisper.

Cano's eyes narrowed. "You gave me everything I needed. And more."

Allie shook her head aggressively and backed away. "Don't lie to me. I know."

"Know what?" Nova took a step forward, but Allie sidestepped her and hurried from the room.

Allie wanted out of the conversation. She wanted Nova to leave. They never should have gotten into this discussion. Her birthday had been perfect up until this point. She clutched the pumice stone around her neck. She felt Nova's presence but didn't turn; instead, she stood facing the front door.

"Allie?" Nova's voice held concern. "We need to talk."

Allie spun around. "What is there to talk about? I know what you did."

"You keep saying you know. I don't understand." Nova's voice rose. "Would you just tell me?"

"Fine." Allie's jaw clenched. "I know I couldn't

satisfy you. I know you faked it. That you sneaked into the bathroom to finish yourself off because I couldn't."

Nova's jaw dropped, and her eyes filled with tears. "I didn't know what else to do. You wouldn't—"

"Oh, so it's my fault now?" Allie wasn't sure if she wanted to scream or cry.

Nova looked down at the floor and shook her head. "No. It was mine." She looked up and met Allie's gaze.

"Goddamn it, stop taking responsibility for everything. Hold me accountable for my shit," Allie yelled, knowing she was being irrational but not caring.

"I should have told you." Cano crossed her arms over her chest.

"And I should have let you buy a vibrator, but my pride got in the way. I thought I could find a way to satisfy you."

"But you did." Nova started to take a step toward Allie but seemed to think better of it when she met Allie's gaze.

"Not all the time." Tears rolled down Allie's cheeks. "Not when my body gave out on me."

Nova couldn't hold her gaze any longer and looked away. "But I should have tried harder to make you understand instead of faking it. I didn't realize you knew."

"It was humiliating."

Nova sat down hard in the nearest chair and buried her head in her hands. "That's why you left me? Because I wasn't honest?"

Allie's heart broke. It wasn't fair to put all of it on Nova, even though she knew Nova would carry the entire burden herself. Hell, she'd carried it for the past four years. "Why did you let everyone believe that you left me?"

"Because I thought that's the way you wanted it. Everyone I met assumed I'd left you and ran away to Menlo Park."

"So you took all the judgment and all the blame. Everyone thinking you were a terrible person for leaving your girlfriend with MS." Allie stared.

"I thought it was what you wanted." Nova shrugged. "I never understood why you dumped me. I figured I must have done something wrong."

"That's what you thought? That I dumped you?" Allie asked.

"How could I not? That's what you did, isn't it?"

Allie shook her head. "I set you free."

Cano wasn't sure how to respond to Allie's revelation. *Set her free?* Cano hadn't wanted to be set free. She'd wanted to spend the rest of her life with Allie.

The pain in Allie's eyes stabbed at Cano's heart. All she wanted to do at that moment was to erase the pain. Without thinking, she moved toward Allie.

She didn't have the words to tell Allie everything she felt. How much she'd missed her. How empty her life had been. Didn't they say actions spoke louder than words?

From the moment Allie had told Cano that she was leaving to live with her parents, Cano had been passive, letting Allie call all the shots. Studying Allie now, she doubted all her decisions. They'd lost four years because of her timidness. *No more.*

Somehow, she needed to find her five minutes of confidence before she ran from the room. She approached Allie and put her hand against Allie's wet cheek.

Allie's tears continued to stream down her face as Cano gently cupped it and tilted her head upward. Cano bent and kissed Allie's eyelid and moved to the next. "Please, don't cry. We can figure this out."

Allie shook her head and gasped for breath but didn't say anything.

Confidence. Cano pushed herself forward, hoping not to be rebuked by Allie as she put her arms around her. She held on loosely, giving Allie the choice to return the embrace or slip away.

Allie wrapped her arms around Cano and held on tightly. It was all the encouragement Cano needed. She hugged Allie with all her might, hoping her embrace could speak to Allie in ways her words hadn't been able to.

Cano wasn't sure how long they stood clinging to each other or who initiated bringing their lips together. But the instant their lips met, Cano's entire body responded.

Allie's kiss started out sweet and tender, but the longing—the desperation—came through as the kiss intensified.

Cano slid her tongue between her own lips and slowly ran it the length of Allie's top lip.

Allie moaned and pulled Cano closer.

Cano repeated the gesture, only this time running her tongue along Allie's lower lip.

Hungrily, Allie sucked Cano's tongue into her mouth.

Electricity ran through Cano's body all the way

to her center. She wasn't sure she could kiss Allie much longer without wanting to take her to the bedroom, but was that what Allie wanted?

Despite the ache between her legs, Cano had to ask before it went any further. "Allie," Cano said as she pulled back.

"Hmm," Allie practically purred.

"What does this mean?"

"It means we're both horny as hell." Allie's eyes were unfocused when she gazed at Cano.

Disappointment rose in Cano's chest. "Is that it?"

"I don't know." Allie's eyes focused, and sadness filled them. "I can't answer that. It wouldn't be fair when I'm on fire like this." Allie moved her leg rhythmically between Cano's thighs.

Cano gasped at the sensation but tried to concentrate on the conversation. "I want you so badly, but I don't know if I could take it if it meant nothing more than a release."

"We can't turn this into that Meatloaf song." Allie continued to rub against her.

"Meatloaf?"

Allie nibbled on Cano's neck and let her tongue trail upward. With her mouth next to Cano's ear, she said, "*Paradise by the Dashboard Light*. Where he swore forever because he wanted to fuck her so bad."

"Is that what this is?" Cano stepped back. The throbbing between her legs was almost painful, but she couldn't do this.

"I don't know what this is, but I know I want you."

"Now? Or forever?"

"Nova, please. I can't answer that right now."

Allie took a step toward her.

"No." Cano backed away farther. "I still haven't recovered from the first time we broke each other's hearts. I know I wouldn't be able to survive it again. Could you?"

Allie choked back a sob, and she ran both hands through her hair on each side, pushing it behind her ears. "Just go if you don't want to have sex with me."

Cano looked at the floor. "You're right. I don't want to have sex with you."

Allie's gaze lifted, and her eyes filled with anger. "Then get out," Allie shouted.

Cano went to the closet, pulled out her leather jacket, and slipped it on. She stood at the front door, her hand on the doorknob as her heart broke. She didn't move, waiting for Allie to look her in the eye.

When Allie's fiery gaze finally met Cano's, Cano said, "I wanted to make love to you. Not have sex. And I wanted it to mean forever."

Allie stood and stared with an unreadable expression on her face.

"I love you, Allie," Cano said before she turned and walked out the door.

Chapter Thirty-four

Days until eruption: 2
Friday, May 16, 1980
Toutle, Washington
Allie's cottage

Allie struggled to breathe, so she wrapped her arms around herself and squeezed. She stumbled to the couch and fell onto it. As hard as she tried, she could no longer hold back the tears. The roar of Nova's motorcycle was like a knife cutting into her soul.

Damn it. Nova had no business riding her bike this late at night in the state she was in. Allie said a prayer, asking God to protect Nova. She brought her knees to her chest and hugged them against her.

What just happened? She'd blown it and not been able to tell Nova the truth. Why hadn't she admitted that she, too, wanted forever? *Fear. Terror.* Nova didn't understand. Allie couldn't risk promising something she couldn't deliver. She couldn't guarantee that her body wouldn't fail her. Or that her MS wouldn't leave her unable to give enough to Nova to make her want to stay.

Nova acted so damned sure of what she wanted, but it was only because she didn't know any better. No way did she understand how far Allie's body could decline. What a burden she might become. *No.* She would not do that to Nova.

Being older, if she were honest, most times, she'd been in control of the relationship. Nova listened to her. Looked to her for guidance, but the dynamic would change when Allie became helpless.

Pity would creep in, and she would see it on Nova's face. Then the pity would turn to disgust. Allie's stomach roiled. *No.* She never wanted to see that reflected in Nova's eyes. She'd spend the rest of her life alone before she allowed that.

She curled into the fetal position as the past flooded into her mind.

November 26, 1975
Seattle, Washington
Allie and Cano's home

Allie jammed more clothes into her open suitcase. She'd already filled one and was well on the way to filling the second. She wasn't sure why she'd saved her clothes until last. Maybe packing them made it real, and she wasn't prepared for that yet.

She'd already loaded the car with her books and important papers. Everything else could stay, for now. She glanced at her watch and cringed. She only had another hour.

Her hand trembled as she closed the lid and fumbled with the zipper. *Damn it.* She hated the disease. She hated her body more. After the third attempt, she grasped the zipper and pulled. Despite the shaky movements, she finally got it closed.

She dropped to the bed and put her hands over her face. The urge to curl into the fetal position and sob nearly overwhelmed her. *No!* She was stronger than this; she had to be. She steeled her jaw and stood. Before, she would have hefted both suitcases and carried them to the car, but now she wasn't sure if she could even manage one. Why hadn't she thought of that before she packed them so full?

Her cane taunted her from across the room. She'd have to use it if she planned on carrying the suitcases without risking a fall. Her legs tingled and ached, making it hard to move, but she must. The last few days, as she made her plans, her body rebelled. Likely, she'd be in a full-blown relapse by tomorrow.

With great difficulty, she'd taken one suitcase into the living room and was in the middle of carrying the other when the front door swung open. Allie stopped in a panic and stared.

Nova burst into the house with a huge grin on her face. "Honey, I'm home."

"Um...you're home early." Allie hoped her voice didn't come out as shaky as it felt.

"I am." Nova held out a bouquet of flowers. "I left early. I wanted to spend a few hours with my girl tonight. Just the two of us."

Allie looked at the flowers but didn't take them. "I wish you would have told me."

Nova's face dropped. "Doesn't telling someone you're surprising them defeat the purpose?"

Allie had to avert her gaze. This would be hard enough. Just seeing Nova's dejected look melted her heart. She could only imagine how hard it would be after what was about to happen.

When Allie didn't speak right away, Nova continued. "I just thought we could have a nice dinner." She held up a bag. "I picked up ingredients to make a homemade pizza." She must have noticed the expression on Allie's face because she said, "I'll cook. I know you've been having some struggles. You can curl up with a book while I make dinner. And *Starsky & Hutch* is on tonight."

"It's not that" were the only words Allie could get out.

"Are you freaking out about going to your sister's? I know I have to be the *roommate* since her kids will be around. I understand. It just hurt my feelings, but I understand."

Allie shook her head. "It's not that, either."

Nova's brow furrowed, and she glanced at the two suitcases. "Jesus, aren't we only staying one night? Did we really need two big suitcases?" Nova smiled. "Oh, I get it. You wanted to hide the kids' gifts. Smart. They won't mess with our suitcases."

Allie shook her head again. She'd already been shaky enough, but standing in the middle of the living room was proving to be difficult. As she took a step toward the chair, her knees buckled.

Nova reacted quickly. She dropped the flowers and grabbed Allie around the waist. "Whoa. It looks like you've overdone it."

Allie wanted to push Nova away, but she needed her help to get to the chair, so she allowed Nova's strong arms to support her into her seat. Her chest tightened, but she couldn't back down. "I've loaded the car."

Nova squinted and glanced at the suitcases. "Are you sure you're okay? The luggage is right there."

"I've loaded my things in the car."

Nova pointed. "You mean that's all mine? How many clothes do you think I'll need?"

"No!" The word came out louder and harsher than Allie intended. "The suitcases are mine, too. I was trying to get them to the car before you got home."

"Oh." Nova nodded and smiled. "You want me to pack my own suitcase."

"Damn it, Nova. You're not going with me."

Nova's face fell. "I'm not? Why?" Before Allie could respond, Nova said with a hurt look, "I thought your sister likes me."

"She does." Allie's heart raced. This conversation was *not* going as she intended. "It doesn't have anything to do with my sister."

"Your parents?"

The horror on Nova's face made Allie want to hug her, but she knew she couldn't. "No. It's me."

"They're upset with you?" A protective look flashed in her eyes. "What happened?"

Allie put her hands on her head and pretended to pull on her hair. She took a cleansing breath. She'd already messed things up, so she needed to get it out now before she made it any worse. "I need you to listen to me without asking any questions."

"Okay." The fear in Nova's eyes broke Allie's heart.

"Could you please sit down?" Allie knew the moment Nova winced that she'd chosen the wrong words. "It's just I don't like you towering over me."

Nova backed away and lowered herself to the sofa but didn't speak.

"I've packed some of my things, and they're already in the car. I wanted to have everything loaded, so this wouldn't be awkward. But since you're home early, I'm afraid I didn't get it finished." Allie scowled at her legs. "I'm not moving the best today."

Nova started to rise, but Allie pointed toward her and motioned for her to remain seated. A look of indecision danced in Nova's eyes before she dropped back into the sofa.

Allie cleared her throat. "This isn't working out. I'm going to my sister's alone this weekend. Then I'll be staying with my parents."

"What isn't working out?" Nova's face showed that she suspected what Allie meant but wasn't ready to face it.

"You and me." Allie delivered the line with no effect. "I'm going to live with my parents. They can help me when," Allie slapped her leg, "these things don't work."

"But...but that's what I'm here for. That's what people in love do for each other." Nova's voice had a pleading tone, and she'd slid to the edge of her chair. "I don't want you to go."

"I've made up my mind," Allie said, putting more authority into her voice than she felt. "It's time for this to be over. It's best for both of us."

"No, it's not." Nova raised her voice. "It's not fair you made this decision without me. I should have some say."

Allie shook her head. This was what she'd expected from Nova, so she'd prepared for days. "It's bad enough that I'm ten years older, but—"

"Nine," Nova said through clenched teeth.

"Fine, nine. But still now it's more like twenty." Allie let out a derisive snort. "Hell, who am I kidding? More like thirty. I've always been concerned that I wouldn't be able to keep up with you as we aged, but now I know I won't be able to."

"For god's sake, I don't even know what that

means. What are you trying to keep up with?"

"We had dreams." Allie willed herself not to cry. "Hiking the Appalachians. Visiting the volcanoes in Hawaii. Seeing the pyramids. But now..."

"Why can't we still do those things?"

Anger rose in Allie. "You're either stupid or in denial."

"Wow." Nova glared but said no more.

Allie waved her hand. "I didn't mean it to come out like that."

"So you didn't mean to call me an idiot?"

"*No.*" Exasperation rose in Allie's voice. "That was wrong of me to say. Mean. I just can't have this conversation any longer."

"Of course not. Because you've made all the decisions for us as a couple without consulting me. Do you think I'm too stupid to participate? Or maybe I'm just too young, and I need the guidance of my *elder.*"

"Now who's being mean?" Most of the energy Allie had left was draining away.

Nova looked at the ground. "I'm sorry. I just feel helpless. You're making all these decisions without consulting me. I love you, and that's all that matters. If we can't do everything we talked about, it's not the end of the world because we'll be together."

Allie shook her head and narrowed her eyes. "You say that now, but you aren't ready for what this disease will likely do to me. You'll be trapped."

"Being with you will *never* make me feel trapped. Damn it, you're making this bigger than it needs to be."

Nova's words hit a button, and Allie's face burned. She tried to stand to give Nova a piece of her mind, but her legs weren't going to allow it. *Fuck.* This was exactly why she had to do this. Imagine how bad she'd be in five years. Ten. Her life might be over, but she wouldn't let Nova stay in this trap. Allie loved her too much. She knew she needed to deliver the knockout punch before things got any worse. "I'm glad you think I'm overreacting, but you try living in my body for a week. Then come and spew that shit at me."

"That came out all wrong. I know it's a big deal. I wasn't trying to minimize how hard it is on you. I just want you to understand I'll be by your side. I'll help you through this."

"I'm not a charity case," Allie snapped. Guilt washed over her. She'd been intentionally overreacting to everything Nova said. This argument was too much, and she just needed to extract herself from it.

"Argh." Nova put her hands over her face. "I don't mean to say all the wrong things. Maybe you just need to clear your head. Go to Thanksgiving without me. I'll just stay here. Then when you get back, we'll talk. It'll give us time to calm down."

"No. There's nothing to talk about." Allie crossed her arms over her chest and sat up taller. "I'm going to my parents to live. And that's final."

Nova's face dropped, and tears welled in her eyes.

Allie wanted to collapse onto the floor or grab Nova and hug her, but instead with sheer force of will, she pulled herself to her feet with the help of her cane. She walked to where the suitcases were and bent to lift one. Her hand shook as she picked it up and unsteadily made her way toward the door. Her muscles screamed, and she wasn't sure she could make it to the car.

Nova stood and took the suitcase out of her hand and picked up the other. "I'll carry them for you."

Allie thought of protesting but knew she'd never get them to the car, especially in the state she was in. "Thank you."

Nova's puppy dog eyes gazed at Allie before she turned away. Without a word, Nova walked out the front door with the suitcases.

Allie grabbed her coat and keys before she followed Nova outside, the pain in her chest nearly unbearable. Although she'd wanted to set Nova free, this had been a hundred times harder than she'd thought it would be. It took every ounce of her willpower not to throw herself into Nova's arms. *No.* She loved Nova too much. This was for the best.

Put one foot in front of the other was what she needed to do. Get to the car, drive away, and give Nova back her life.

After putting the suitcases into the trunk, Nova stood, waiting for Allie to make her way down the sidewalk. Her face had lost all expression, and she stared, not offering any further assistance until Allie stumbled and nearly lost her balance.

Nova sprang to life and grasped Allie's elbow.

When they arrived at the car, Allie opened the door and fell into the driver's seat, thankful she was able to sit. "I'll continue to pay my portion of the rent until our lease is up."

Nova shook her head. "And that's what you chose to say to me."

"It's best for you."

"Go ahead and believe that if it helps you sleep at night. But I'm here to tell you that you're wrong, and I will be here when you come back."

Allie steeled her eyes. "It's over. I'm not coming back."

Chapter Thirty-five

Days until eruption: 2
Friday, May 16, 1980
Toutle, Washington
Outside Allie's cottage

Cano ran out of Allie's house toward her motorcycle. Her insides churned, just like they had years ago when Allie had told her it was over. How had she been so stupid to think that Allie might want her back?

She knew this late at night, she should take the pickup, but her bike called. Maybe the cold air rushing at her would freeze the pain away. Her heart ached, and all she wanted to do was stop it.

She jumped onto Beulah and punched the kick starter with her foot. It sputtered, so she stomped down again, willing it to start. The engine roared to life. Cano pulled the clutch and shifted into first gear as she twisted her wrist to give it gas.

Cano shot from the driveway and roared down the street. The night was dark, but she didn't care. Her headlights couldn't keep up with her speed, but she didn't care about that, either. The vibration between her legs would hopefully quench the fire that Allie had caused.

As she rode wildly into the night, not caring about her own safety, she realized she felt the same way she did the last time Allie had broken her heart. She gunned the engine, just wanting to forget everything, but the past flooded her thoughts.

November 26, 1975
Seattle, Washington
Allie and Cano's home

Cano stumbled to the house as Allie pulled out of the driveway. Too stunned to cry, she entered the house and collapsed onto the sofa. Surely, Allie would come back to her.

The past month had been tough on them both. When Allie was diagnosed, they'd been ready to fight the disease, but something had shifted. Cano couldn't figure out what. All she knew was Allie had become more and more distant, even on her good days. Cano had tried in vain to get her to talk about it, but Allie would have none of it.

Cano rolled off the couch and wandered into the kitchen. Disappointment washed over her as she studied the contents of the refrigerator. Three beers. A carton of eggs. Bologna and a package of American cheese.

Three beers wouldn't be enough to take the pain away. Not even close. Allie's eyes had been so cold—full of steel. The wall had crashed down between them. No, Allie had erected the wall, and Cano knew there was no talking to her once she'd built it. How long had she been planning this? It had to have been awhile.

Anger mixed with her pain. Why did Allie get the right to make the decision without consulting her, without taking her feelings into consideration? She'd been trying so hard to do the right thing. To say the right thing, but obviously, she'd gotten it wrong. Allie left her anyway.

Cano angrily swiped at the tears that escaped and threw open the cabinet where they kept the bottles of hard alcohol they'd received as gifts. Whiskey. Vodka. Rum. Tequila. She pulled down the rum and tequila. Neither was opened, so she had to twist the caps hard to break the seals. She poured a generous splash of each into her glass.

She took her drink into their bedroom, feeling lost. Allie was her person; she knew it, so how could Allie have done this? She took a large gulp of the liquid that burned all the way down. She coughed and nearly choked. It was awful, so she took another drink. Rarely did she drink, so this was a bad idea.

She set the glass on the dresser and went to the closet. She pulled out her suitcase and began cramming her clothes into it. Allie had lived here for several years before Cano moved in, so Cano had little in the apartment. It wouldn't take her long to pack.

Once her suitcase was full, she went to the kitchen and grabbed garbage bags. Without thinking, she crammed the rest of her belongings into the sacks. She threw her books in with her toiletries and her photo album in with her shoes. Everything piled on top of each other without a plan.

After she'd hauled her stuff to the van, she hitched her motorcycle trailer to the back. With tears streaming down her face, she returned to the house for one more sweep before she left. As she walked through, Dali's melting clocks caught her eye. *The Persistence of Memory,* a present from Allie. Carefully, she removed the painting from the wall.

Chapter Thirty-six

Hours until eruption: 22
Saturday, May 17, 1980, 10:30 a.m.
Toutle, Washington
Allie's cottage

Allie rolled over and felt moisture on her face. *Gross.* She soaked up the drool with her shirt. She stretched out her aching legs. The old lumpy couch had done nothing for her back, which spasmed as she pushed back her shoulders.

The fog began to lift from her mind. *Dumbass.* What time was it, anyway? It had been after three a.m. when she'd last looked at the clock. Falling asleep in such an uncomfortable position wasn't good for her already ravaged body. Stress didn't help, either.

She should get up and go to bed. She blinked a couple of times. *No.* There was something wrong with that thought, but she struggled to figure out what it was. Then she noticed the sunlight streaming in through the window. It looked too bright to be sunrise.

She tried to sit up, but her body revolted, so she fell back against her pillow. What had she done to herself and to Nova? The thought of Nova sent shivers up her spine. Nova's motorcycle always made Allie nervous, but riding it in the middle of the night, as upset as she was, terrified Allie.

The pain in her heart was worse than the pain in her body, so she closed her eyes and willed herself to go back to sleep. The phone had other ideas. Even though it was on the other side of the room, the ring shattered the quiet. *Nova?* She should get up and answer it, but she doubted she could get to it before it stopped ringing.

After ten rings, it went silent. She'd give it to Cano for being persistent. The phone pealed again. With a burst of energy, she pushed past the pain and sat upright. She shuffled to the phone, catching it on the eighth ring.

"Hello," she said breathlessly.

"Allie, it's Johnny."

"Johnny? Is Nova okay?" Allie's heart raced.

"I was hoping she was with you."

"No." Allie drew in a deep breath. "She's not at the hotel?"

"Nope. I went to the staff meeting in Vancouver, but Cano never showed. I thought maybe she'd stayed with you. I went to her room and pounded on her door. When she didn't answer, I let myself in with the spare key she'd given me. The bed was still made up. I checked with housekeeping. They hadn't been in yet this morning."

"Oh, god, Johnny. She left here on her motorcycle."

"What? Why?"

Allie could hear the panic in his voice. She weighed her words but then thought better of it. Now wasn't the time to withhold information when Nova was missing. "We got into a fight," Allie said softly.

"Ugh. And Cano did a Cano and roared out of there on her bike."

He'd said it as a statement not a question, but she answered anyway. "Yes. I never should have let her leave." Allie's voice cracked.

"It's not your fault. Nobody stops her when she doesn't want to be stopped."

"But it was my fault. I upset her."

"Allie, she's an adult. Upset or not, it's not your fault that she stormed off." Johnny took a deep breath. "I don't mean to intrude, but..."

Allie waited for him to finish, and when he didn't, she said, "But?"

"Would you be willing to share with me why... what might have upset her?"

When Allie didn't respond right away, Johnny said, "Sorry. I shouldn't pry. I better let you go, so I can see if anyone else has seen her."

"No!" Allie practically yelled into the phone. "I'm just embarrassed."

"I shouldn't have asked." Johnny paused. "I just thought it might give me an idea of her state of mind, which might help me figure out where to look for her."

"I'm scared." Tears rolled down Allie's cheeks. "What if...what if—"

"No, we aren't thinking that way. You know her. When she's upset, she runs away and hides. It's my guess that's what she's doing."

If something bad happened to Nova, she'd never be able to live with herself.

"Are you okay?" The concern was evident in Johnny's voice.

"I broke her heart—again."

"Again?"

"I should never have let her back into my life. It wasn't fair after I broke up with her the first time."

"Wait. What? You broke up with her?"

"Yes." Allie sighed. "She didn't tell you, either?"

"I'm afraid I'm lost. I always thought she'd run away because of your...um...your..."

"My MS."

"Yes. That isn't true?"

"No. I left her."

"Wow. I can't believe she didn't tell me." There was disappointment in his voice. "I didn't think her ego was that big that she couldn't admit it."

"I don't think that's the reason. I think she did it to protect me."

"I'm afraid I'm not following."

Allie took in a deep breath. "I know this will sound crazy, but she has a twisted sense of honor. I think she wanted me to be the sympathetic one."

"So she let herself be the bad guy?"

"I think so. She's never really said. Did she ever tell you she broke up with me?"

"Hmm. You know, now that you mention it, I don't think so."

"And I never told anyone I broke up with her." Allie ran her hand through her hair and rubbed her scalp. "I'm not sure how it became an unspoken agreement between the two of us."

"Fran doesn't know?"

"I think she suspects by things I've said, but I never told her."

"My mind's blown," Johnny said. "So what happened last night?"

"We kissed." Allie stopped, not sure how to explain the rest.

"And she ran out?" Johnny sounded confused.

"It wasn't like that. Um...I wanted her to stay."

"I would've thought she'd jump at the chance," he said. "She never stopped loving you."

His words hit her like a slap. "She wanted me to promise it was something more...more than...just a one-time thing."

"She wanted you back?"

Tears streamed freely down her face, and she couldn't speak.

"But you didn't want her back?" Johnny said.

"I did. I do. I want her back more than anything in the world." Allie's voice cracked. "But I can't."

"Can't what?"

"I can't want it. I can't put her in that situation. Not with my MS."

"Allie, I mean no disrespect, but don't you think that's her decision to make?"

Allie bit her tongue. She. Would. Not. Sob. "I know," she said in the firmest voice she could muster. "Please, Johnny, find her."

"I'll do my best. Before I head up to Coldwater, I'll spread the word to keep an eye out for Cano. Don't you run out looking for her. You need to stay by the phone. Maybe try calling around and check if anyone has seen her."

"Thank you," Allie said, her voice not much louder than a whisper.

Allie stared at the phone once she hung up. Fran was busy with her niece and nephew this weekend, but she needed to talk to her friend. Fran would settle her nerves and get her back on the right track.

She was just about ready to hang up on the tenth ring.

"Hello," the breathless Fran said.

"Fran?"

"Allie."

"Did I catch you at a bad time?" Allie asked, hoping to keep the tremor out of her voice.

"What's wrong?" Fran said.

"Am I that obvious?"

"Yep. Are you having a flare-up?"

"Not yet." Allie answered honestly without editing herself.

"Hold on," Fran said.

Allie could hear Fran yelling for Ben in the background. There were other voices she couldn't make out, probably the children, although the voices sounded older. *Crap.* Ben's brother and sister-in-law were probably there dropping off the kids.

Fran's voice came back on the line. "Allie, I'm going to change phones, so we can talk. Ben will hang it up when I pick up in the bedroom."

"Okay" was all Allie managed to say.

"Got it, Ben," Fran yelled. "You can hang up now."

There was a click, and the commotion disappeared.

"Sorry," Fran said. "It's utter chaos down there."

"Damn, you're in for a wild weekend if they're that loud."

"You didn't call to talk about my dysfunctional household. Something's wrong."

"Nova's missing."

"Missing?"

Allie swore she wouldn't break down, but her hands began to shake. "We had an argument, and she sped out of here on her bike at midnight."

"So she's not really missing then. She's just not there anymore." Fran's voice was patient as if she were using logic with a child.

"She's missing. Johnny called. She didn't make it back to her hotel last night."

"Oh, shit. I'll come down."

"No. You have your niece and nephew. I just needed someone to talk to. No, I needed *you* to talk to. I feel like I'm going to vomit or sob or maybe both."

"It's okay, honey. I'm sure she's fine. Tell me what happened."

Allie took a deep breath. She needed to tell this like a logical scientist, not an emotional wreck. With little emotion, she chronicled what happened the night before. Unlike when she'd talked about the breakup, she didn't leave anything out.

"Thank you for finally telling me the truth," Fran said when Allie finished.

"I always..." Allie couldn't finish the words she was about to say. She couldn't tell Fran she didn't lie, although in technical terms, she hadn't.

"Lies by omission," Fran said, obviously knowing what Allie was about to say.

"Yes." Allie dropped her head into her hand. "You knew all along?"

"Just about." Fran sighed. "I'd say within the first couple of weeks. Scientists aren't the only ones that can figure out puzzles, you know."

Allie shook her head, and a slight smile played on her lips. "What gave me away?"

"A few things. First, Cano worshiped the ground you walked on. I always wished Ben looked at me the way she looked at you. I saw her after your diagnosis. If anything, she loved you even more, not less. But for a little while, I thought maybe she cracked and ran away."

"So why did you let me get away with it?"

"You needed me to."

With that sentence, the tears that Allie had been holding back poured down her cheeks. She didn't speak because she was sure it would come out in sobs.

Fran continued. "You're my best friend. You were dealing with some heavy shit. You'd just gotten a life-changing diagnosis. It couldn't have been easy for either of you. Then after she left, you spiraled. Remember?"

"How could I forget? I didn't know if I'd ever get out of that wheelchair."

"But you did." Fran's voice was full of conviction. "You fought back."

"I wanted to tell you after I got back on my feet, but the time never seemed right. Then too much time had passed, and I didn't want to dredge it up." Allie cleared her throat. "But if you knew, why were you so angry with her?"

"You needed me to be, so I did it for you." Fran sighed. "I felt guilty about it sometimes. I ask Ben all the time if I did the right thing, especially lately. I did what I thought was best."

"Oh, Fran. I didn't mean to put you in such a bad position." Tears continued to roll down her cheeks. She'd been horrible to two of the people she loved most in the world. What did it say about her?

"I didn't know what to do. You seemed so fragile. My strong, stubborn friend fell apart, rightfully so, you're entitled. I just didn't have a frame of reference, so I followed your cues. If you needed for me to believe that Cano left you with a broken heart, then that's what I was going to pretend to believe."

"She did leave me with a broken heart, but I'm the one that told her to go." Allie's breath caught in her throat, so she could barely get the rest of her words out. "And now, I've pushed her away again. What have I done?"

"I swear it's the strong ones that don't know how to bend when a powerful wind comes up, so they get blown over for a while. Until they figure out how to right themselves."

"You're saying if I'd let myself be vulnerable and not been so stubborn, I would have come through it easier."

"You said it, I didn't." There was a smile in Fran's voice. "Seriously, it was—it is—a hard situation. Everyone did the best they could. Even Cano."

"No, especially her." Allie took in a big gulp of air. "All these years, she's never told anyone. I still don't understand why."

"She loves you."

"If something happened to her, I don't know what I'll do."

"She's probably off hiding somewhere. That's her M.O. She's licking her wounds."

"I'm such an idiot." Allie's tears started up again. "Why couldn't I just open myself up to her? I wanted to. I really did, but..."

"It was too scary. You might have to give up a little control."

"Ouch. That hurt."

"Was it true?"

"Maybe."

"Here's the deal." Fran cleared her throat. "I made the mistake once, treating you like you're fragile. I won't make it again."

"Meaning?"

"I'm calling you out from now on. You've come

to terms with your illness. Of course, it will always be horrible and scary and everything else that goes with it, but it's the hand you were dealt. No more coddling you."

"Maybe just a little," Allie said with a smile.

Fran chuckled. "Okay, a little, but I'm going to tell you this."

"Uh-oh. Should I feign a bad connection?" Allie made a gurgling sound, trying to mimic static.

"Good try. This is what I'm going to tell you, and I'm going to continue to tell you this every day from here on out. Cano was the best damned thing that ever happened to you. She loved everything about you and was committed to spending her life with you. She had no doubts. It was you that decided your age and illness were something she couldn't handle. It was never her. It's time to stop being a dumbass."

"When you take the kid gloves off, you do it all the way." Allie smiled. "Thank you for being you."

"That's what best friends are for. Now I want you to get up and get a shower and stop moping around. I'm going to pack a bag and should be there in a couple hours."

"No, you have your niece and nephew." Allie steeled herself, wanting to make sure her voice came out strong. "I'll be fine. Johnny wants me to stay by the phone and make some calls."

"I'm coming anyway." Fran lowered her voice. "It'll give me an excuse to get away."

"But you love it when the kids are there," Allie protested.

"But not when my in-laws are. My mother-in-law decided she needed to be here with the kids, and she brought her new husband along."

"Ugh." Allie knew how condescending Ben's mom was, always insinuating that Fran was beneath him. "Then I insist you come sit with me."

"And that's exactly what I'll tell Delores."

Even though her chest still ached, after talking to Fran, Allie felt hopeful for the first time. She needed to listen to Fran and get a shower. If the numbness in her legs was any indication, it was going to take her awhile to get herself together.

She bent and picked up her cane from the floor. *No more.* She had to accept that she would always have to live with MS, but that was the point she'd been missing the last couple of years. She'd stopped living and let the condition rule her. Sure, it would knock her on her ass sometimes, but she'd grab her cane or a wheelchair and keep moving forward. No more sitting on the sidelines, being afraid, and feeling sorry for herself.

She gripped the cane, and with a determined push, she rose to her feet. *One step at a time.*

Chapter Thirty-seven

Hours until eruption: 19.5
Saturday, May 17, 1980, 1:00 p.m.
Toutle, Washington
Allie's cottage

After Allie finished her shower, she'd paced the house. The ends of her hair were still wet since she'd not blown it dry. The stiffness in her legs had subsided as she circled the rooms, but she still used her cane to steady herself.

When the phone rang, she hurried to it. "Hello," she said eagerly, hoping it was Nova.

"Allie, it's Johnny."

"Anything?" She clenched her fists.

"Not yet." Johnny said, dejection evident in his voice. "I just finished up at the roadblock. It's a zoo up there. Today's the day they're letting people visit their cabins, so it's been hard getting answers from anyone. So far, nobody's seen her. I'm headed up to Coldwater I and II. It'll be awhile before you hear from me again. What about you?"

"Nothing." Allie sighed. "I guess it's good. I tried all the police departments and hospitals from here to Vancouver. Nobody has reported any motorcycle accidents."

"Thank god."

"I hope I never have to make another call like

that again."

"Are you doing okay?"

"Trying. Fran should be here soon. She insisted on coming."

"Good. I'll find her. The dumbass probably doesn't even realize she has us scared shitless. Back in Menlo, she used to disappear on her bike all the time. Said it was no big deal since she didn't have to report to anyone. I suspected it was more of her bravado."

"That would be our Nova." Allie smiled despite the ache in her chest.

Hours until eruption: 18
Saturday, May 17, 1980, 2:35 p.m.
Toutle, Washington
Allie's cottage

Fran and Allie sat at the kitchen table trying to make small talk, but the later it got, the harder it was for Allie to concentrate.

When the phone rang, Fran bolted out of her chair and grabbed the receiver off the kitchen wall. "Hello." Fran nodded. "She's right here." Fran held out the phone to Allie. "It's Johnny."

Allie hoisted herself up from her seat and made her way to the phone as quickly as she could, which wasn't fast enough for her liking. "Hello."

"Nothing yet," Johnny said.

Her shoulders slumped. She'd been hopeful that Nova had gone to Coldwater. "Oh, Johnny. This is so scary."

"I know. I talked to a photographer up at

Coldwater I. He's been up there awhile. He hadn't seen her. Then I went to Coldwater II and saw Harry Glicken. He'd been there all night. Said he hasn't seen her for several days."

"Now what?"

"David's supposed to be up at Coldwater II sometime soon."

"Where are you?"

"I drove back down to the roadblock. Still couldn't find anyone that's seen her."

"Maybe she didn't go that direction." Allie clenched her fists. "Maybe she went back to Menlo Park."

"I thought of that, but I can't see her leaving here, can you?"

"No. Not really. But she was pretty upset, so who knows."

"Well, I'm going to—holy shit," Johnny practically yelled into the phone. "Hold on."

"What's the matter?" Fran said. Her eyes widened.

Allie shook her head. "I don't know. Maybe he spotted her."

After what seemed like an eternity, Johnny said, "Sorry. That was a leg splitter."

"Earthquake?"

"Yeah. Um...two forty-two. You'll have to see what that one measured. I'd say it had to be in the high fours. I bet the people pulling stuff out of their cabins just got a shock."

"No doubt."

"I'm getting kinda used to the quakes since I'm up here so much, but that one even shook me," he said.

"I'm not sure I'll ever get used to them, but then

again, I'm not up at Coldwater as much as you are."

"This one rattled my teeth."

"Well, hopefully, it rattled some sense into Nova, and she'll surface. Someone's watching for her in Vancouver, aren't they?"

"Yeah. I talked to the hotel staff, and Grant is keeping an eye on things there."

"Now what? Do you think she followed one of the cabin owners in? It would be just like her to help out."

"That's what I thought, too. It's why I keep checking in at the roadblock, but so far nothing. I would've stayed up at Coldwater and waited for David, but I couldn't just sit there. Since he's tight with some of the helicopter pilots, I thought maybe he could check with them."

"Great idea. I'm scared, Johnny." She didn't want her voice to crack, but it did anyway.

"Me too. But we'll find her. No news is probably good news. I'm gonna go now."

"Goodbye." Allie hung up the phone and dropped into the nearby chair. "I hate this," she said to Fran.

Hours until eruption: 17
Saturday, May 17, 1980, 3:35 p.m.
Toutle, Washington
Allie's cottage

"Hello," Allie said.

"David saw her up at Timberline." Johnny skipped the usual pleasantries.

Allie's heart raced. "Is she okay?"

"She was when he saw her. I need to get up there before she takes off, but I wanted to at least let you know. So maybe you can worry a little less."

"Thank you. Go get her. Please."

"I will. I'll talk to you soon."

The line went dead. Allie hadn't realized that tears of relief rolled down her cheeks until Fran handed her a tissue.

Allie grabbed Fran's hand and squeezed. "Thank you for being here. I can breathe for the first time today."

Tears overtook her. Fran stood and put her arm around Allie. Normally, Allie would pull away and become stoic, but this time, she let Fran pull her in.

Chapter Thirty-eight

Hours until eruption: 17
Saturday, May 17, 1980, 4:30 p.m.
Mount St. Helens
Timberline parking lot

Cano gazed out at the mountain. Her eyes were gritty. A combination of the ash that covered everything and the tears that she'd spilled. Now there were none left in her.

She'd been here for hours, staring at the mountain and wondering how she'd gotten things so wrong again. She should get going, so she didn't have to travel in the dark, but her feet didn't seem to want to move.

When she heard the low rumble of an engine, she didn't turn. There had been a couple of visitors to Timberline today, but for the most part, it had been quiet. Other than David, most had taken one look at her and made a beeline to the other side of the lot.

David had been his typical friendly self, not commenting on what must have been her unsightly appearance. She'd not showered, and she suspected she was smudged with ash, but she didn't care.

Pathetic. Apparently, she was going to wallow in her self-pity. She had been sure Allie felt the same way she did, but apparently not. How could she have been so stupid? Allie just wanted a roll in the hay.

Maybe Cano should have given in. Perhaps it

would have sparked something in Allie and made Allie want her again. She'd been playing with fire since she'd arrived here, now she had to suffer the burns.

No! She picked up a handful of ash and threw it. Then she picked up another and another. After throwing several more handfuls, her shoulders slumped. *Real mature.*

The roar of the engine became louder. *Damn.* Whoever it was had to be driving fast to be making that kind of noise. *Dumbass.* Probably someone who sneaked past the roadblock during the commotion, just like she'd done.

She stared at the mountain, or more accurately, the bulge, and shivered. The past week, whenever she gazed at it, an uneasiness settled over her. She didn't like the way it looked. Sitting up here quietly most of the day, she'd tuned herself into the mountain. She knew people would think she was silly, but she swore she felt the swelling.

About an hour ago, there'd been a big one. She feared that her bike would be knocked off its kickstand, but it held. She'd almost shoved her hand into the open bag of Doritos next to her when she noticed her hands. *Shit.* Without much thought, she ran her right hand down the length of her pants and marveled at the streak it left. Satisfied it was clean enough, she reached in and grabbed a handful of chips.

The engine cut off behind her, but she still didn't glance over her shoulder. Maybe whoever it was would leave her alone if she pretended not to notice. A door slammed.

"Where the hell have you been?" a familiar voice called. *Johnny.*

She didn't turn. Maybe he would go away, too.

He'd ask too many questions. Ones she wasn't prepared to answer.

"Goddamn it. Answer me." His footsteps were muffled as he stomped across the ash.

She debated with herself and settled on calling out without turning. "Hi, Johnny."

"Seriously? 'Hi, Johnny,' is all you have to say when I've been looking for your ass all damned day."

"I didn't ask you to." She crossed her arms over her chest like a sullen teenager. Gauging by his irritation, he must have talked to Allie. "You've found me. Now go away."

"Knock your shit off." His voice grew louder. He was likely only a few yards from her.

Her ire rose. "What the fuck did I do to you?" She leapt to her feet and spun around.

He stopped in his tracks and gasped.

If she weren't so pissed, his reaction would have been funny. "What? Are you expecting me to look like a fucking beauty queen?" *Lame.* It wasn't one of her bests, but she'd have to own it, so she glared at him.

"Have you been rolling around in the ash?"

"Where's my manners?" She snatched the bag of Doritos off the ground and held it out to him. "Care for a snack?"

"I have a pretty good idea where this hostility's coming from, but I think it's misguided."

When he didn't take the bag, she thrust her unclean hand inside and pulled out a large handful of chips. She shoved several in her mouth.

He turned up his nose in distaste, but he didn't say anything.

She shoved the rest in her mouth and chewed with exaggerated gusto.

He took the bag from her hands and rolled it closed. "Want to talk about it?"

"I'm just sitting up here minding my own business. Eating my lunch. I don't recall inviting you."

"I've raised teenagers, so I can do this all day, or you can cut the crap and talk to me." His body shuddered, and he looked around the area. "This place is giving me the creeps." He ran his foot through the ash. "After that last earthquake, I'd prefer not to be up here."

"You can leave any time." Cano knew she was being an asshole, but with her heart aching so badly, she didn't care.

"I see. So we're going to do this then?" He pointed to the ground where she'd been sitting. "Do you want to sit here, or do you think we can sit on the tailgate?" He motioned toward the truck.

Her jaw hardened. She considered making him sit in the ash where she'd been most of the day but knew he didn't deserve it. "The truck is fine," she muttered.

"Progress." He smiled and motioned for her to lead the way. "After you."

She picked up the sack with the rest of her lunch before she moved toward the truck. Neither spoke as they shuffled through the layer of ash built up around the area. The volcano had been spewing off and on for nearly two months, so ash covered everything.

Intentionally, she dragged her feet as she walked and kicked up clouds as she went. Somehow, it gave her a sense of satisfaction. *Yep.* She'd officially turned into a juvenile. When they arrived at the truck, she vowed to herself to behave better.

Johnny pulled down the tailgate and encouraged

her to sit. "I have a couple Cokes in the truck. Want one?"

"Got anything stronger?"

"Afraid not. Do you want the soda or not?"

"Sure."

He returned with the cans, pulled both tabs, and handed one to her. He jumped onto the tailgate and sat beside her. Their shoulders were only inches apart.

They sat in silence for several minutes and stared out at Mount St. Helens. Cano let the cool liquid roll down her parched throat. She'd likely inhaled more particles than she realized, so she greedily took in more of her drink.

"I've got another one in the truck if you finish that one."

"Thanks."

After a few more minutes, he said, "Mind telling me what's going on?"

"It's Saturday. Just doing my own thing."

"Try again."

"You talked to Allie?"

"Yes."

Cano ran her hand through her hair, unsure which was grimier, her hand or hair.

"What did she tell you?"

"Everything."

Cano's head snapped around, and she met his gaze. "Everything?"

"She told me about last night. She told me about the past. That she left you, not the other way around."

Cano's jaw went slack. "Why?"

"She was worried about you. Said it was time to come clean."

So many thoughts rushed through Cano's mind

that she had trouble sorting them out. She'd not expected this and wasn't sure how to respond. The numbness she'd embraced since she'd cried herself out threatened to be overtaken by pain.

"Why didn't you ever tell me?" Johnny asked.

"I was ashamed."

Johnny shot her a sideways glance. "Because Allie left you?"

Cano shook her head. "No. Because I ran away."

"You blame yourself?"

"Who else?" Cano kicked out her foot that dangled from the tailgate.

"Allie."

"No," Cano practically yelled. "It wasn't her fault. She was hurting and scared. For god's sake, Johnny, her whole life just got turned on its head, and at the first sign of trouble, I ran away."

Out of the corner of her eye, Cano could tell Johnny was studying her. "You believe that, don't you?"

"Did she tell you what happened?" Cano turned and met Johnny's gaze.

"No, just that she was the one that broke up with you."

Cano turned away when tears welled in her eyes. "It was right before Thanksgiving. I came home early from work, and she was trying to get the car packed before I got home." She ran her hand through her grimy hair. "I was stupid and didn't realize what was happening until she told me she was leaving me."

"Must have been hard." Johnny patted Cano's leg. "But I still don't understand why you're blaming yourself. It sounds like Allie made her wishes clear."

Cano shook her head. "She'd been struggling. I knew it. I couldn't get her to go to her support group or talk to any of the counselors Dr. Antioch recommended. She just kept stubbornly saying she'd figure it out. I felt so useless."

"You can't force someone to do what they're not ready to do." Johnny's voice was full of compassion, which was making it harder for her to fight back her tears.

"But you can support them. You can be there for them." Cano met Johnny's gaze and held it. "Last night, she told me she set me free. Deep down, I think I knew it all along. That's why I blame myself."

"I'm afraid I'm not following."

"Ever hear the saying, if you love someone, set them free?"

"If they come back to you, they're yours—"

"And if they don't, they never were." Cano put her head in her hands. "She was scared and in pain. She didn't want to be a burden, so she set me free." Cano's chest ached, but she still looked up at Johnny. "And I was a coward. I ran and left her to deal with it all on her own. The night she told me she wanted to break up, I packed my bags and left town. I didn't put up a fight. I didn't try." Cano's voice had dropped to a near whisper.

"Oh," Johnny said.

Cano snorted. "Yeah, oh."

"But you never stopped loving her?"

"Never." Cano's voice came out strong. "But I didn't deserve her."

"But you came back to her now."

"Four years later. Only because of Mount St. Helens."

"I'll never believe Mount St. Helens was the only reason you came back."

"Doesn't matter. She made her wishes clear last night."

"Just like she did four years ago?" Johnny said, his voice raised. "Are you going to go down that same path again?"

A slight tremor rattled the ground, but it was nothing like earlier, so she continued. "I'm not strong enough to have it happen again." She turned to Johnny, and her shoulders slumped. All her energy left her body. "The first time nearly broke me. Maybe it did break me."

"Have you slept?"

Gratitude coursed through her. Johnny understood that she needed a break from the heaviness of the conversation. "A little."

"Where'd you go?"

Cano sighed. "After I left Allie's last night, I drove toward Coldwater, but the higher I went, the colder it got. My fingers would barely work, so I had to turn around. I didn't want to pick up my truck at Allie's, so I headed to Vancouver. I got to Castle Rock. I've never been so cold in my life, so I checked into a hotel there. Rented it for the weekend, so I could get away and think. I woke up at eight and couldn't get back to sleep, so I drove here."

"You've been here all day?"

Cano nodded.

"What were you trying to do?"

"I just sat in the ashes, watching the mountain. I hoped it would swallow me up. But then you showed up and pulled me out of the ashes."

Johnny smiled. "I think it's Allie that needs to pull you out of the ashes."

"I don't think she will."

"You might be surprised. She's been a mess."

"She knows I'm here?" Cano sat up straighter and turned to Johnny.

Johnny nodded. "After Johnston told me he'd seen you here, I called her before I drove up."

"Thank you. I didn't mean to worry her."

"Do you think we should go see her?"

Cano shook her head. "No. I'm a mess." Cano glanced down at her ash-laden clothes and her ash-smeared skin. "I'm not up for it." She put her cold hand on Johnny's arm.

He flinched. "Holy hell. You're a block of ice." He jumped off the tailgate and opened the pickup. He returned with a sweatshirt. "Put this on."

"I have my coat on my bike. I don't want to mess up your shirt."

"Put it on." His tone left no doubt this was an argument she'd lose.

She slid it over her head. "Thanks," she mumbled.

"Have you eaten anything other than Doritos today?"

"M&M's."

"High nutrition." Johnny smiled. "What say we load your bike in the back of the truck, get you some real food, a hot shower, and some sleep?"

Cano sighed. Her body hurt. Her mind was fuzzy. And her skin felt disgusting. "Okay. You'll let Allie know I'm okay?"

"You could do it yourself." She could hear the encouragement in his voice.

"No, I can't." She was too raw.

"Okay. First you take care of yourself. Then things will look better."

"I hope so."

Chapter Thirty-nine

Hours until eruption: 14.5
Saturday, May 17, 1980, 6:00 p.m.
Toutle, Washington
Allie's cottage

Allie had been pushing spaghetti around on her plate for the past twenty minutes. Fran had been kind enough to make her dinner, but Allie had no appetite. She'd hoped that if she wrapped it around her fork a few times, it would give the appearance of her having eaten some.

The phone rang, and she jumped from her seat. "Hello."

"Hi, Allie," Johnny said.

"Did you find her?"

"Yep. I'm at a payphone, and she's sitting in my truck."

"Where's her bike?" Panic rose in Allie's chest. Nova wouldn't leave her motorcycle. "Is she okay?"

"Physically, yes." Johnny paused but then didn't go on.

"Where was she?"

Johnny relayed a brief synopsis of where Nova had been and what she'd been doing. "I've seen her looking better. She needs a shower, a meal, and sleep."

"Will you bring her here?"

"Afraid not." Johnny's voice was strained.

"Why not?"

"She doesn't want to."

The gut punch hit Allie hard. Nova didn't want to come to her house. *Think.* Of course, Johnny had said she was a mess. She wouldn't want Allie to see her that way. "If she's all covered in ash, she'll need some clean clothes. I have clothes here that will fit her."

"I'm a dad, so I'm always prepared."

"I thought that was Boy Scouts," Allie tried to put levity into her voice.

"I was one of those, too." Johnny chuckled. "Before I came looking for her, I grabbed some things out of her room, figuring she'd likely need a change of clothes."

"Can I talk to her?"

"I'm sorry, Allie. She doesn't want to talk."

"You mean she doesn't want to talk to *me*?" Allie bit down on her lip.

"Uh, yeah. But she's barely strung together two sentences since we left Timberline. She's spent."

The gut punch turned into a battering ram to her chest. "Okay." She wanted to slam down the phone, but instead, she took a deep breath. More than likely, this was how Nova felt last night. *Rejected. Pushed aside.* "I understand. But could you tell her something for me?"

"Certainly. But...just don't..."

"Just say it." She hoped her words didn't come out as impatient as she felt.

"Don't give up on her. She's exhausted and not thinking clearly. But she loves you. That's one thing I'm sure of."

The constriction in her chest loosened. "I haven't blown it forever?"

"I don't think so. Both of you just need to stop blaming yourselves and talk."

"Nova blames herself?"

"Yes. But I don't want to say more. It's for you and Cano to talk about. Tomorrow is another day. Things will look brighter."

Allie's heart raced. She knew Johnny was right, but an urgency gripped her. *No.* It had been four years, so one more day wouldn't be the end of the world. "I understand. You'll take care of her tonight?"

"I'll get her some food other than Doritos and M&M's. Make her take a shower. And tuck her into bed."

"But you'll be with her?"

"She wants to stay in her room at Castle Rock, says she's too tired to go all the way back to Vancouver with me. I'd like to go to church in the morning, so I intend on driving back to Vancouver tonight if I think she's doing okay. Don't worry. I'll stay with her if I need to."

"You're the best." Allie put her hand on the necklace Nova had given her. "I never meant to hurt her."

"I know." Johnny's voice was low. "I should get her to the hotel. What is it you wanted me to tell her?"

"Tell her I love her." Tears rolled freely down Allie's cheeks. She ran her hand across her face and marveled at the drops on the back of her hand. She thought she'd run herself dry.

"I'll tell her. And, Allie, I might be speaking out of turn, but I'm going to say it anyway. I know she loves you, too."

Allie held the receiver against her chest after they disconnected. Fran gently took it from her and replaced it on the cradle.

"She's okay?"

Allie nodded.

"Then what's that look for?"

"Nothing." Allie blinked back tears. "It's just been a long day."

"Bullshit." Fran scowled. "Be honest with me this time."

Allie bit her lip. "Johnny says she still loves me."

"Duh." Fran rolled her eyes. "That's not a big revelation."

Allie decided to ignore Fran's comment. "And she blames herself for what happened."

Fran snorted. "That's obvious, too. You both need to stop blaming yourself and each other."

"I don't blame her."

"Yes, you do." Fran's tone was matter-of-fact. "You blame her for running away, instead of fighting for you."

Allie cringed, and then she picked up her half-eaten plate of spaghetti and dumped it into the garbage before she took her plate to the sink. "But she tried to make it right, and I blew it."

"Nonsense."

Allie spun around. "No, it's not." Her voice rose. "Four years ago, I dumped her and broke her heart, and then I hurt her again last night." Allie jabbed her finger into her own chest. "It's all on me."

"Things can be different." Fran held her gaze. Fire burned in her eyes, almost daring Allie to say more.

"Not after all I've done to her, the idiot...." Allie marched to the table and picked up Fran's empty plate. It clanged against the other plate as she slammed it into the sink. "The sweet idiot stood in my living room, willing to give her heart away to me again. Only for me to step on it. No, I stomped on it. So now, I want her to lay it at my feet again, so I can take a kill shot?" She glanced at the dishes, considering whether she should wash them but instead turned and walked toward the living room.

"Wait, Allie. You can't—"

Allie threw up her hand but didn't turn. As she left the room, she said, "No, there's nothing to talk about. I did this to myself. And I'll have to live with it."

Chapter Forty

Hours until eruption: 2.5
Sunday, May 18, 1980, 6:03 a.m.
Castle Rock, Washington
Cano's hotel room

Cano sighed and stared at the water-stained ceiling. This place certainly wasn't the Ritz, but the bed had been comfortable. She'd slept like a log. She glanced at the clock on the nightstand. Just after six a.m. She'd slept for nearly nine hours.

She put her arms over her head and brought her hands together as she stretched. It felt good as her back cracked and popped. She twisted and stretched again. *Ahh.* Another twist in the opposite direction brought on a few more pops.

She inhaled and held it for several beats before releasing it. Her body felt better than she'd expected after how cold she'd gotten. It took her nearly half an hour in the shower to fully thaw out. Now she felt overheated.

No wonder. She smiled at the covers Johnny had piled on her. She'd have to apologize to him. He'd handled her insolent child behavior like a pro. Instead of reacting in anger, he'd channeled his fatherly skills and made her feel less broken, but it was the message he'd delivered from Allie that had truly lifted her spirits.

If she weren't so exhausted last night, she would have run to her. Cano's heart raced. What if Allie rescinded her words this morning? She took a deep breath. *No.* If her words were true, then she would give Cano the time she needed to recover.

She'd been speechless when Johnny told her that Allie loved her. In the state she was in, all she had done was stare at him dumbfounded. It had been the words she'd wanted to hear for the last four years.

How early would be too early to show up at Allie's house? She chuckled. Six thirty would likely be too early. *Seven?* Sleep had done her wonders. The heaviness that gripped her yesterday was gone, replaced by a sense of hope.

Cano kicked the covers off. She needed to get a shower, so she'd smell nice for Allie. She shook her head, but a goofy grin played on her lips.

She peeked in the garbage bag Johnny had placed her clothes in. Her eyes widened. *Wow!* Looking at them now, she couldn't believe she'd worn them. They probably should just be thrown away, but she'd see if she could get the ash out. They looked as if she'd rolled around in the debris. *Out of the ashes.* She'd definitely rise.

After she finished her shower, she debated on her clothing choice. She wanted to look good for Allie. As she rummaged through her suitcase, she said a silent thank you to Johnny, who'd had the forethought to bring her clean clothes. Likely a dad thing.

When she'd mentioned it, he'd jokingly told her it was self-preservation. He didn't want to be around her when she hadn't showered or changed her clothes in two days. No matter what his reasons, it served her well.

She removed her only pair of Calvin Klein jeans from her suitcase and held them up. She'd gotten compliments on her ass when she'd worn them. *Good choice.* The selection of a shirt proved to be slightly more difficult. After trying on several shirts and making a halfhearted attempt at refolding them, she settled on the steel gray T-shirt that hugged her body and showed off her muscular shoulders.

The anticipation of seeing Allie soon caused her to move quickly through her shower. She stepped out of the hotel at six thirty-four. That should give her time to swing by McDonald's and grab a breakfast sandwich.

As she walked toward her bike, she gazed at the mountain. A shiver ran through her, and the hair on her arms stood up. While it was a little chilly this early in the morning, her reaction seemed excessive. What was it her grandma used to say? *Someone walking over her grave.* She narrowed her eyes. *Weird saying and even weirder feeling.*

Nothing could ruin her day, though. Once and for all, she'd be able to profess her love for Allie. She just had to hope that Allie would return her feelings.

Hours before eruption: 1.5
Sunday, May 18, 1980, 7:06 a.m.
Toutle, Washington
Allie's cottage

Cano had driven around the block a couple of times, not sure she should show up at Allie's house so early, but she couldn't wait any longer.

She pulled off her helmet and laid it on the seat. With one hand, she straightened her hair, while she unzipped her leather jacket with the other. Maybe it was silly, but she wanted to look good. Likely, Allie would be blurry-eyed with sleep, but Cano would think her beautiful regardless.

Cano squared her shoulders and marched up the sidewalk. Not giving herself time to think of all the reasons she shouldn't do this, she rapped on the door.

She waited a few minutes without an answer before she knocked more forcefully this time.

"Hold your horses," a gruff voice called from inside.

Wow. It had been a while since she'd woken up next to Allie, but Cano didn't remember her sounding this rough in the morning.

The door flew open, and she came face to face with a very disheveled Fran. Her normally perfectly styled hair splayed out in every direction, and her eyes held a hint of unfocused question.

Eventually, recognition dawned on Fran's face, and she smiled. "Cano. Um, what are you doing here at seven o'clock in the morning?"

"I came to see Allie." Cano couldn't help the grin that parted her lips.

"No shit." Fran's voice dripped in sarcasm.

"Is she still asleep?" Cano continued to grin.

"How the hell should I know? I just rolled out of the sack myself." Fran opened the door wider. "Get your ass in here, and I'll get her."

Cano stepped inside.

"Nice outfit." Fran looked her up and down. "Trying to impress someone?"

"Maybe." Cano smirked.

"I think she'll like it." Fran winked. "Let me rouse her," Fran said over her shoulder as she made her way down the hallway.

Fran returned a few moments later with a puzzled look on her face. "She's not here."

Cano's heart lurched. "What do you mean not here?"

"Gone. Bed's been made." Fran held up a finger. "Hold on." She disappeared into the kitchen.

Cano glanced around the room, willing herself to remain calm. Maybe Allie couldn't sleep, so she'd made a doughnut run.

Fran returned holding up a piece of paper with Allie's distinctive handwriting scrolled across.

"Looks like I have the answer."

Cano looked over Fran's shoulder as they read it together.

Fran,

I couldn't sleep. Every time I closed my eyes, I saw Nova's face. I needed to get out of here before the walls closed in on me.

I'm going to run up to the roadblock and get a closer look at Mount St. Helens. I might go on to Coldwater.

Hopefully, a little fresh air will do me good. Clear this messed-up brain of mine.

Love ya,

Allie

Cano's hands clenched into fists, and her heart raced. "I don't like it. I've been getting edgier and edgier the closer I get to the mountain."

Fran put her hand on Cano's arm. "Me too. I

had some funky dream about the damned thing. It was spewing a steady stream of Dr. Pepper and M&M's."

Cano laughed. "Wow. You have some interesting dreams."

"Tell me about it."

"Do you want to stick around and wait for her to come home? I could whip up some breakfast."

"As tempting as that is, I want—need—to find Allie."

"I understand. Get the hell out of here, so I can go back to bed," Fran joked.

"Aye, aye." Cano saluted her. "I'll hopefully see you in a bit."

Cano walked to the door and had her hand on the doorknob when Fran said, "She loves you, but she's scared."

Cano turned back. "I'm scared, too."

"I know you are, hon." Fran's eyes were filled with more compassion than Cano had ever seen Fran direct toward her. "Just pour your heart out, she'll respond better this time."

"I can do that." Cano rubbed her chest. "I won't let anything hold me back." She smiled and jokingly said, "Not even Mount St. Helens could keep me away from her."

Fran flicked her wrist at Cano. "Then get the hell out of here and stop flapping your jaws at me. I have a warm bed calling my name."

Cano laughed. "Thanks again. For everything."

Chapter Forty-one

Hours until eruption: 0.5
Sunday, May 18, 1980, 8:04 a.m.
Spirit Lake Highway
Near Mount St. Helens roadblock

Allie pulled her car to a stop behind an old pickup that had seen better days. *Unbelievable.* She thought she'd be alone this early on a Sunday morning. The revelers had decreased, but the volcano still drew people to it. Word had gotten out that the roadblock was only sporadically manned, which allowed thrill seekers who wanted to get as close to the volcano as possible to slip through.

She suspected the area would be teeming with people later since they intended to allow the cabin owners back in to check their property. She couldn't claim it was crowded, but she felt two people were two too many.

She didn't turn her car off, weighing her options. She could drive on through the roadblock and head up to Coldwater II. David was there, so she could check in with him. But wouldn't it be worse interacting with someone she knew? At least here, everyone was a stranger and might leave her alone.

Allie put her head on the steering wheel and closed her eyes. What possessed her to come up here when she'd gotten so little sleep? She'd tossed and turned most of the night; she finally gave up and got out of bed at five thirty. Her nerves were raw, and the walls seemed to close in around her until she couldn't take it any longer.

With a sigh, she put her car into drive and drove toward the roadblock. A couple sat on the roof of their car taking pictures. They waved as she passed. When she pulled closer to the roadblock, she glanced at the cars parked on each side. None blocked her path.

She sat in her car and stared at the barrier. A shiver ran through her, so she pulled her coat tighter around herself. The air still held a bit of a chill this time of the morning, but she suspected her body's reaction was unrelated to the cold.

An internal debate raged. *Coldwater or go back down the mountain a ways?* She grasped her gearshift, still not sure if it was the right choice.

She popped the gear into reverse and hit the accelerator. The cars on each side gave her plenty of room for a three-point turn, which she did on the first try. *Whew.* She'd been self-conscious with the audience around her, but she'd pulled it off, and now her car faced back down the mountain.

Maybe she should have gone on to Coldwater II. *No.* She'd made the right decision. Besides, she didn't want the others to think she was drunk turning around and then turning back around again. She'd drive a bit down the mountain, so she could find a place to be alone with her thoughts.

She drove past the first side road, not liking the incline or the muddy entrance. By the time she'd found an offshoot she liked, she was nearly five miles from the roadblock. Even though there was no traffic, she flicked on her turn signal and pulled down the dirt road. She drove her car about twenty yards down the path and pulled to the side in case someone needed to pass.

When she opened the car door, she reluctantly grabbed her cane. The lack of sleep and stress had left her legs numb and tingly. She couldn't take the chance as much as she wanted to leave the cane behind.

Her cane scuffed along the dirt as she unsuccessfully tried to pick up her pace. She slowed. It wasn't going to happen today. When she emerged from the side road, she turned left, which took her toward the summit. She'd walk back a little, so she could see more of the mountain.

She lost track of time as she shuffled along. Her thoughts were filled with Nova and the mess she'd made of things. Somehow, she'd find a way to repair the damage she'd caused. With her concentration elsewhere and fatigue setting in, she stumbled and nearly fell. Her cane was the only thing that kept her from crashing to the pavement. She glanced back and realized she'd walked farther than she'd thought.

She glanced at her watch. *Eight twenty-one.* She'd been walking for nearly twenty minutes, but it only felt like a couple. Just as she was about to turn back, she caught the roar of an engine. Her heartbeat quickened. It didn't sound like a car. *Motorcycle?*

She glanced at Mount St. Helens one last time. The roar became louder, and her heart raced faster. She stood up straighter before she turned.

Cano gunned the engine when she saw the figure stop on the road ahead. The long blond hair cascaded to the woman's shoulders. The slender body leaned into the cane in her right hand. It had to be Allie.

She forced herself to slow her bike, so she didn't roar up and slide to a screeching halt. When the woman turned, Cano saw the face that still made her heart skip a beat. Cano couldn't hide her smile. Allie returned the smile as Cano pulled to a stop beside her.

"Hey." Cano grinned. "Imagine running into you here." She dismounted from her motorcycle and pulled off her helmet. She resisted the urge to smooth her hair.

"Imagine." Allie took a step toward her. Her enormous smile made the fatigue in her eyes disappear. Without another word, she wrapped her arms around Cano.

Cano stiffened, surprised by Allie's reaction, but then she let herself relax and returned Allie's embrace. She refused to cry as she held Allie.

Allie's body trembled. Was she crying, or was it her MS causing the tremor? While Allie continued to hold on, she whispered into Cano's ear, "I am so sorry."

Cano increased the pressure of her hug. "Nothing to be sorry for."

"Sure there is." Allie started to pull away.

"Nothing that can't be solved by having you in my arms."

"Oh, Nova." Allie let herself fall back into Cano.

Movement from above caught Cano's eye, and she looked skyward. "Holy shit. That looks like a Cessna."

Allie glanced to the sky, too, and backed a few steps away from Cano. "I heard that a couple scientists were going to fly in from Yakima to take a look at the crater."

Cano shuddered. "I swear the hair on the back of my neck just stood on end. Is it me or does the air feel oppressive up here this morning?"

Allie met Cano's gaze and raised her eyebrows. "I thought it felt electric."

"There is that element." Heat rose in Cano's cheeks. She glanced back at the mountain before meeting Allie's gaze. "I think we need to talk."

"I'd like that." Allie put her hand against Cano's cheek. "I'm sorry."

"And I'm sorry, too. I finally understand that we both panicked."

Allie put her hand against her chest. "But it was my fault."

Cano reached out and touched Allie's cheek. "No. We both have regrets, but we aren't going to make the same mistake again." Cano smirked. "At least I'm not."

Allie smiled. "Does that mean that I will?"

Cano gave a nonchalant shrug, happy to see the smile on Allie's face. "You're pretty stubborn, so who knows."

"Jerk." Allie laughed and put her hand on Cano's arm. Her legs buckled, and she grabbed Cano's arm tighter.

Cano reacted quickly and helped support her weight. "Whoa. You okay?"

Allie's face reddened. "I'm fine."

"Let's get somewhere more comfortable to talk." Cano took another glance at the mountain. "It's making me nervous here, anyway. I can take you back to your car."

Allie's eyes widened. "On your bike?"

"No, on my back." Cano laughed. "Of course, on my bike."

"I can walk down."

Without thinking, Cano's gaze shifted to Allie's legs. If things were going to turn out better for them, Cano couldn't keep cowering from hard topics. "No offense, but I'm not sure your legs are going to hold up."

"I know." Allie sighed. "I didn't realize how far I'd walked."

"Was something on your mind?" Cano gave her a crooked grin.

"Maybe." Allie returned the smile.

Cano handed her helmet to Allie. "Here, put this on."

Allie frowned. "We're going less than a mile."

"Don't care. No passenger of mine will be without a helmet."

"What about you? You won't have one."

"Passenger always gets the helmet." Cano held it out toward Allie.

Allie took it. "But you need something to cover your eyes. You don't want a bug flying into them."

Cano flipped up the seat. "I've got goggles right here," Cano said as she pulled them out.

"Okay." Allie put the helmet on her head, and Cano helped her secure the straps.

Cano secured her goggles, hopped on her motorcycle, and jammed the kick starter toward the ground. The engine roared to life on her first attempt. She patted the gas tank. Her baby hadn't embarrassed her in front of Allie.

"What am I going to do with my cane?"

"I'll go slow. You should be able to hold it."

"Do you need help getting on?" Cano asked.

"I think I've got it." Allie grabbed Cano's shoulder and swung her leg over the seat.

"You're like a pro."

Allie laughed. "I just didn't want to embarrass myself and fall on my head. It's been a while since I've ridden back here." Allie put one arm around Cano's waist and scooted closer.

Cano's heart lurched into her throat as Allie pressed against her back. *Control.* Nothing was certain yet. They still needed to talk, so she couldn't get her hopes this far up. But damn, it felt good having Allie behind her.

They made it just about to the turnoff where Allie's car was when Allie squeezed Cano and put her mouth near Cano's ear. "I dropped my cane."

Allie's breath on her neck almost caused Cano to veer off the road, but she managed to pull to a stop. She engaged the kickstand and was about to dismount when the bike began to shake.

"Holy shit," Allie said behind her as the tremor shook for several more seconds.

Cano's eyes widened. "That was a big one." She twisted in her seat to look up at the mountain. "You're gonna have to call the university to see what it registered as."

Allie had also turned and was gazing at the mountain.

Something gave Cano pause when she stared at Mount St. Helens. The hair on the back of her neck stood up, and then as if in slow motion, the top of the volcano disappeared. Cano stared slack-jawed, trying to make sense of what was happening. The plume rose silently from the summit.

"Oh, my god, Nova. It's erupting."

Cano's mind raced. How could it be erupting? There was no sound. *Holy shit.* The sound waves had to be compressing. "I think it's a lateral blast."

Allie's eyes widened in terror. "Then it's coming our way." Her brow furrowed, and she closed her eyes. Cano knew the look. She was doing math in her head. Her eyes popped open. "It's going to be on us in four minutes. We need to get back to my car."

"We don't have time. We have to go on the bike." Adrenaline surged as Cano stared at the rising almost black cloud coming from Mount St. Helens.

"Can you outrun it?" Allie's voice held a note of fear.

"It's our best chance." Cano peeled her gaze away from the mesmerizing eruption. Gaping would lose them valuable time. "Hold on." Cano waited to feel Allie's grip tighten around her waist before she twisted the accelerator.

"There's people at the roadblock. We have to warn them," Allie said.

Bile rose in Cano's throat. "We can't. Riding toward the blast would be suicide. We'd never make it out alive." Cano refrained from saying there was no certainty they'd make it out as it was. Her chest tightened at the thought of not warning the people, but there was nothing more they could do. If they turned back, she would only be signing Allie's death certificate, something she wasn't prepared to do. "Hold on."

Allie tightened her grip and yelled. "Cumin."

Cano spun out, picking up speed. *Cumin?* Did she hear Allie right? "What?"

"My pork chops. Cumin is the secret ingredient.

In case something happens."

Cano was picking up speed, and they'd be unable to communicate soon. "I can't believe that's the first thing you thought to say. You're an interesting woman," Cano yelled as the wind rushed past.

"And I love you." Allie yelled. "I love you more than anything in this world."

Cano's heart soared. Allie's words gave her all the reason she needed to ride her motorcycle like she'd never ridden it before. "I love you, too. With all my heart," Cano called out before she increased her speed to a point where nothing else could be said.

Allie gripped Nova around the waist and held on. This was insane. Who tried to outrun a volcanic blast? But this was their best option. Likely, if they could get another ten miles from Mount St. Helens, they'd survive. When she peeked over Nova's shoulder, the speedometer read seventy-five and climbing. Allie did another quick calculation in her mind. It would likely be the longest and shortest eight minutes of her life.

She glanced behind them as the gigantic ash cloud continued to rise and move outward toward them. If she didn't understand how deadly it was, she would find it beautiful. She feared the people at the roadblock would be so enthralled by the blast they'd be stuck in it. They wouldn't have the scientific foresight to recognize the dangers. All she could do now was pray for them.

Allie's heart went out to Nova. At times like this, ignorance would surely be bliss. More than anyone, Nova understood the risks. Allie contemplated whether the hurricane-force winds or the ash posed a bigger threat. Near the summit, the winds would be nearly three hundred miles per hour, which would make riding a motorcycle nearly impossible, but how severe would the winds be as they got farther out?

Nova's stomach muscles tightened under Allie's hands. She was using her entire body to guide the motorcycle around the curve as she leaned into it. Allie followed Nova's body position and looked over her inside shoulder as Nova had taught her years ago. Being a passenger was quickly coming back to Allie, and she hoped it would help Nova control the bike.

When they came out of the curve, Allie took the opportunity to glance over her shoulder. The giant gray cloud seemed to be closer to them than the last time she checked. Maybe it was her imagination, but by the way Nova increased their speed, Allie didn't think so.

She closed her eyes. Now she understood the saying there were no atheists in foxholes. The Lord's Prayer flooded her mind, so softly she whispered, "Our Father, which art in heaven—"

A sudden wobble in the bike cut off her words. *Shit.* Did Nova almost spill them? Wind buffeted Allie's back and caused her jacket to billow wildly. The air suddenly felt heavier and darker. The clear day was quickly being engulfed by the volcanic ash spewing out of Mount St. Helens.

Allie took a deep breath, trying to calm herself. At this point, the eruption wasn't the only concern. While it would be unlikely to affect her and Nova, the possibility of melting snow caps and mudslides grew greater.

She squeezed Nova just a bit to make her

presence known, without distracting her as a driver. They had to survive this. They had four years of lost time to make up for.

As they came out of another curve, Cano took the opportunity to glance in the side mirror and then wished she hadn't. Every time she looked, she swore, the enormous ash cloud appeared closer. The blast held a majestic beauty, despite the deadliness. She shifted her gaze back to the road where her focus needed to be.

The bike shook a little. Partially due to their speed, but also because of the blast winds that had begun to catch them. If they stayed steady, she was confident she could ride through them, but she was less sure if they turned gusty. It was so easy to compensate hard for the wind, only for the bike to become unsteady when the winds changed intensity.

She pushed the scientific thoughts from her mind and tuned into Allie's arms wrapped around her waist. It was this feeling that made her more confident. She'd gladly take on a volcano if it meant having Allie back in her life.

The next curve was quickly approaching, so she forced all other thoughts away. She'd need her entire concentration for this one. "I can do this," she said under her breath as she leaned into the curve.

Even though her heart thumped out of her chest, Allie found comfort when she focused on numbers.

By her calculations, they'd been traveling about four minutes, which put them at the halfway point. If they could stay upright and maintain this speed, they might survive.

Her stomach lurched. There would likely be others who weren't so fortunate. Her heart immediately went to Coldwater II where David likely was. Tears welled in her eyes. Despite wanting to convince herself that everyone would be okay, the scientist in her knew better. She shivered. She'd almost gone to Coldwater II. It was amazing how many thoughts ran through her head. *Focus.* She needed to follow Nova's lead and not let the rushing thoughts distract her.

Nova slowed slightly and swerved around a piece of debris in the roadway. *Crap.* Ash and debris had begun to fall from above. She glanced up. The entire sky was being overtaken by the dark cloud. Day was quickly turning to night.

The trees flew past. She didn't want to know how fast they were traveling, or she'd likely panic. She longed to hug Nova tighter but didn't want to distract her, so she gently increased the pressure around her waist.

Cano hoped Allie couldn't see the speedometer from where she sat. Earlier, she'd pushed the bike up to nearly one hundred on the straightaways, but she'd pulled it back as the darkness set in. Unbelievable that it was morning. If she didn't know better, she'd think it was twilight.

The poor visibility was only part of her problem. The ash and debris falling around them made it seem as if they were driving through an insane snowstorm. If the ash became too thick, it would pose the same danger as wet leaves on the pavement. What if it clogged Beulah's engine? It might slow her down or make her stall out.

She didn't want to slow her speed in fear the gale-force winds would overtake them, but she also didn't want to crash. Going this fast, the results would likely leave them badly injured if not dead. Just as the thought stuck in her mind, another blast of wind shook the bike, causing them to fishtail before she righted it.

Allie squeezed her more tightly.

Cano wished she could turn around and see how rapidly the eruption was approaching, or maybe she was lucky she couldn't. The tiny side mirrors made it difficult to see the full scale of what they were trying to outrun.

Holy fuck. When she glanced back, she caught sight of a car careening around the curves they'd just left. The fool must be doing at least a hundred. Hopefully, the driver would see them despite the diminishing visibility.

She wasn't going to beat the explosion only to be taken out by an out-of-control driver, so her only choice was to outrun them. Cano let out a breath and said a quick prayer before she gunned the engine even harder.

Jesus. Why did Nova just speed up? Allie could no longer make out any of the trees. They were a green blur. She took a quick peek over her shoulder, trying to figure out what caused Nova's reaction.

Headlights. It couldn't be. She'd noticed what looked like lightning flashing in the cloud last time she looked, so maybe it was just lightning, but it surprised her to see it this close to the ground. She shivered as her senses went on overload. She shifted her focus back on the road ahead. At this speed, it became even more important to mimic Nova's body movements.

They'd survive this. They had to. There were too many things she needed to say to Nova, to apologize for, that they couldn't die like this.

It may have been her imagination, but her skin felt gritty as if the ash had seeped into her pores. They must be nearly six minutes out. By her calculation, they only needed a couple more before Nova could slow to a safer speed. The ash would continue to fall, likely hundreds of miles away, but hopefully not enough to get into their lungs and suffocate them.

Wasn't her life supposed to be flashing before her? Why did she have to be fixated on the scientific possibilities when she should be reliving the best moments of her life? A slight smile parted her lips; most would involve Nova.

For the first time in several minutes, which seemed like hours, Cano's spirits lifted. A little farther and they'd have ridden away from the worst danger. The hurricane-force winds wouldn't reach this far out, at least she didn't think they would.

How far should they go before she slowed? When did the excessive speed become more of a danger than the blast?

It unnerved her that they still heard no sound from the eruption. Ironically, the roar of the wind helped ground her to the reality of what was happening. She allowed herself one more glance in the side mirror. While the cloud wasn't shaped like a mushroom, it still gave her the same vibe. The unfathomable size of the rolling and swirling mass almost didn't look real, but she knew it was. She pulled her gaze from the mirror.

She let off on the accelerator slightly and reduced her speed to seventy-five. The worst was likely over, but she didn't plan to stop until they got another ten miles away.

The tension in Nova's shoulders relaxed, which in turn relaxed Allie. She'd also slowed. Did that mean they were almost out of danger? Allie thought so, but if she were Nova, she wouldn't take any chances.

She'd hoped the sky would lighten, but if anything, it continued to get darker. It was a wonder Nova could see anything. She shuddered. Their speed must have exceeded the limits of the motorcycle's headlights, but somehow, Nova had done it. Or at least she'd gotten them this far.

As their speed slowed, Allie pushed against Nova's back, needing to feel the connection between them. Now that the imminent danger had passed, Allie realized that her heart had been racing, so she took several deep breaths, hoping to slow her heart rate. Her hand held a slight tremor, and her legs were more tingly than they had been earlier. Likely, she'd need Nova's help once they stopped since she'd lost her cane.

As she slowed the bike, Cano glanced toward the darkening sky. Ash continued to flutter toward the ground and clung to the pavement. It was getting slicker under the tires, so she decreased her speed further. They'd survived, so she certainly didn't want to dump the bike on the ash.

She longed to get a good look at the volcano, which she couldn't do in the tiny side mirrors. It was too dangerous to look over her shoulder, or she might miss something in the road ahead of them.

The headlights were rapidly approaching again, as the car continued roaring down the highway. Cano moved the bike to the far-right side of the lane and prepared to drive off the road should the car not see them. She kept her gaze on the mirror and saw the car swing out to pass them. It must still be going ninety, so she was glad to get out of their way. She wished there was some way to tell them that it was safe to slow down a little.

Ash kicked up as the car flew around them. Cano shifted down again. She leaned back against Allie and yelled, "Hey." She hoped Allie would lean in farther, so she didn't have to yell. She'd prefer not to get a mouthful of ash if she had to open her mouth too wide to be heard.

"Hey," Allie said into her ear. It came out muffled because of the face shield.

"You okay?"

"I am. What about you?"

Cano briefly took her hand off the handlebar, and it trembled. "I think I have a little adrenaline surging through me." She put her hand back on the grips.

Allie raised her hand and rubbed Cano's chest above her breasts. "That was some pretty impressive riding you pulled off."

"Don't remind me. I'm gonna have nightmares for years."

"Do you think we should pull over and regroup?" Allie glanced over her shoulder. "And get a glimpse of her for ourselves?"

"I'd like that. Stretch my legs, too. I was gripping the bike so hard with my thighs that they're like Jell-O." Cano pulled off onto a dirt side road but didn't cut the engine. "I'm not sure what this ash is going to do to her engine, so I'm thinking I won't shut her off."

Allie sighed and looked down at her legs. "I might need some help. I was already pretty shaky this morning. Now I don't have my cane, and that ride was something else."

"Certainly." Cano pushed the bike onto the kickstand and swung her leg over the gas tank. She held out her arm to Allie. "May I help you off your chariot?"

Allie smiled. "I'd like that."

They walked only a few feet from the bike. Allie leaned against Cano, who happily supported her weight.

They gazed back at Mount St. Helens and the massive cloud that rose into the sky. Cano was in awe of the sheer enormity of the blast. "I'm not sure I can wrap my brain around how big this eruption truly is. You'd think after studying them all these years, I wouldn't be standing here slack-jawed."

"I don't think any of us were prepared for this. Mother Nature at her most violent."

"Terrible and beautiful all at the same time."

"But I worry. How many people do you think didn't make it out?"

Cano put her hand on her chest. "Johnston. I was so busy thinking of our survival that I didn't think of anything else. David is…was up there."

Allie nodded. "Was. I don't think there's any way he could have found shelter or escaped it." Allie's voice cracked, and she blinked back tears.

Cano's mind raced. How many other people were too close? "Thank god it's Sunday, or there would have been a forest full of loggers, too."

"I don't even want to think about it." Allie reached out and wiped a piece of ash off Cano's face. Then Allie's face fell. "Shit."

"What's the matter?" Cano gripped Allie's arm tighter, afraid she might be struggling to stand.

"Fran."

Cano's eyes narrowed. "What about her?"

"She has to be worried sick. She knew I was going up there."

"And Johnny probably knows, too. We should check in."

Allie took one last look at the plume over the summit, turned away, and gripped Cano's arm tighter.

Chapter Forty-two

Hours after eruption: 1.5
Sunday, May 18, 1980, 10:05 a.m.
Toutle, Washington
Allie's cottage

Cano down-shifted as she turned onto Allie's street. Her hands ached from gripping the handlebars so tightly. She'd not driven more than forty-five miles per hour during the rest of their journey, but she'd grasped the handlebars with all her strength. Between the darkened sky and the ash, the past half hour had seemed like two.

The only thing that made it bearable was having Allie pressed against her back. No doubt, she could endure anything with Allie's arms wrapped around her. Allie rested her head against Cano's back and held her tighter around the waist. Cano wanted to pat Allie's hands or squeeze her leg, but given the road conditions, she didn't dare risk riding one-handed, even for a short time.

So many questions ran through her mind, and she was anxious to get answers concerning the blast. For now, her biggest concern was to get Allie home safely, then she'd think about the bigger picture.

As she turned into Allie's driveway, she glanced toward the house. Fran sat on the front step and leapt from her perch when she saw them approach. Cano pulled the bike to a stop, killed the engine, and pushed the kickstand into place. She took a deep breath and willed her tight muscles to relax.

Fran sprinted down the sidewalk toward them, yelling both their names. Allie still gripped Cano around the waist and made no move to let go. As Fran approached, Cano could see the tears streaming down her face.

Cano put her hands on top of Allie's hands that still gripped her waist. "Do you want to get off first?"

Allie shook her head. "I think I might need a little help."

When Fran reached them, they'd yet to get off the bike. She wrapped her arms around them and pulled them against her. "Thank god. We thought you were dead." Fran's body shook as she held on to them.

The reality of Fran's fear crashed down on Cano. How horrible it must have been for her. "It's okay, Fran," Cano said and grasped Fran's arm. "We're good."

"You two scared the shit out of me." Fran's voice cracked. "What the hell happened?"

"What do you say we get Allie off the bike, and then we can talk about it inside?" Cano said and made eye contact with Fran.

Despite her distress, Fran seemed to know exactly what Cano was trying to convey and stepped back. "Who gets off first?"

"Me," Cano said and swung her leg over the bike and stepped to the ground. Her legs were shaky from spending the last hour squeezing her bike with her thighs, willing it to stay upright. After a quick shake of her arms to get the blood flowing, she held out her hand to Allie, while Fran did the same. "Careful. My legs were a bit wobbly when I first climbed off."

Tentatively, Allie swung her leg over the seat and slid to the ground. Cano moved up alongside her on the left, while Fran slid into position to her right. "After that ride, I'm not as unsteady as I thought I'd be." She pulled off her helmet, shook out her hair, and set the helmet on the seat.

Cano studied Allie for the first time. Her hair was plastered down on top from the helmet, while the bottom bushed out. The normal sheen of her blond hair was muted by the ash clinging to it. Despite the helmet and face shield, her face held a gray pallor from the ash with a few smudges that were nearly black. Cano didn't want to know what she looked like since she'd had neither.

"Are you okay?" Fran grasped Allie's arm.

"I think I am, physically." Allie turned to Fran with a pained expression. "But I'm afraid that anyone too close couldn't have survived. Have you heard anything?"

Fran shook her head. "I tried to watch TV, but I couldn't. I came outside to wait for Johnny, instead. He called from Vancouver when he couldn't reach Cano at the hotel."

"Did he know anything?" Cano asked.

"I'm not sure. As soon as he heard that you two were up there, he said he was on his way, so we didn't talk about much."

Cano looked to the sky. "Let's get inside and away from whatever's in the air."

Allie shivered as she stepped under the stream

of water. She'd protested when Fran and Nova insisted she take a shower, but now she was glad they did. As much as she wanted to know more about the eruption, her body needed to warm up. Her adrenaline must have kept her from feeling the cold while riding on the back of Nova's motorcycle.

The hot water cascaded off her skin as she lifted her face to the showerhead. Her tears mixed with the water as she allowed herself to release her tension. They could have died. Had Nova not come up to look for her, Allie never would have made it back to her car in time. She would have been buried under ash and debris if she weren't blown apart. The thought sent another chill through her body.

The ashy water pooled around her feet. She hadn't wanted to think of the repercussions of the blast, but here alone with her thoughts, she could think of nothing else. How many people weren't able to escape? How many animals perished? Her stomach roiled.

As she ran shampoo through her hair, she thought about the mudslide predictions she'd studied and wondered how accurate they would be. She quickly finished washing, so she could get answers to the questions swirling in her mind.

Once out of the shower, she had to sit on the edge of the tub to towel off. Her muscles were suffering the effects of the last couple of hours, or more accurately, the last couple of days.

She dressed as fast as her body allowed and ambled into the living room. Nova and Fran sat next to each other on the couch. Their faces sported similar expressions—a combination of fascination and horror as they listened to the radio reports.

"What did I miss?" Allie asked.

Nova looked up at her. Although she'd washed the ash from her face, her hair had a gritty film on it. Nova moved down and patted the seat between her and Fran. "I think it's going to take me awhile to process all this."

Fran reached across and squeezed Nova's hand. "You're the reason my girl Allie is here. Thank you."

Nova blushed. "I can't claim heroism. It was pure animal instinct."

Allie lowered herself to the sofa, hoping neither Nova nor Fran noticed her stilted movements. "Well, I for one am happy that you're an animal." Allie winked at Nova.

Nova and Fran both laughed, briefly lightening the mood in the room. It didn't last long as they listened to the frantic reports on the radio.

"Don't you think you should call the university?" Fran asked.

Allie shook her head. I'm sure they're being barraged with calls. They don't need me bugging them just to assuage my curiosity."

Before she could say more, a loud pounding cut off further conversation. Fran rose to answer the door, but before she could reach it, the door flew inward. Johnny pushed inside. When his gaze landed on Nova and Allie, the tightness in his jaw relaxed. "Thank god. I saw Cano's ash-covered bike out front, and I prayed that it meant something good." He stood up straight and backed up a few steps. "Um…sorry. I guess I just barged in." His eyes widened. "I'm normally not in the habit of bursting into people's homes without an invitation. I apologize."

Allie smiled. "Extenuating circumstances. No

need to apologize."

"How the hell did you get here?" His eyes narrowed. He pointed between Allie and Nova. "Apparently, you both didn't come from the same place."

"We did." Nova grinned. "Allie took a shower, but I didn't."

"Always the grandstander." Johnny shook his head. "Wear your ash like a badge of honor, is it?"

"Damned right. I didn't think you'd believe me if I didn't look the part." Nova winked.

"Do not tell me you rode your motorcycle out of a volcano blast."

Nova smirked. "They don't call me Cano for nothing."

The next several minutes, Allie and Nova told Johnny and Fran of their escape from the blast. Both sat quietly with their eyes wide as the story unfolded.

"Holy shit," Johnny said when they'd finished. "You two are lucky to be alive."

"Yeah." Allie sighed. Her chest tightened. "I'm afraid everyone isn't going to be so fortunate. Did you hear anything about David?"

Sadness filled Johnny's eyes, and he nodded. "I went to early Mass and then stopped in at headquarters in Vancouver shortly after the eruption. David had radioed right after it happened. He said, 'Vancouver, Vancouver, this is it!' That's the last words he said. Never responded to anything else."

Allie didn't try to blink back the tears that welled in her eyes. The thought of what must have happened sickened her. "Any word on how many others might have been in the area?"

"There might be now." Johnny glanced at Nova. "As soon as I talked to Fran, I jumped in my truck and drove way too fast to get here."

"Aww, he does like me," Nova said.

Johnny glared. "I was worried about Allie."

Nova smiled. "What happens now? There might be people alive but injured."

"I should give Vancouver a call and see what's happening," Johnny said.

"We need to go help." Nova stood. "I can't just sit here doing nothing." Nova's head whipped around toward Allie, and her mouth dropped open, but she didn't say more.

"It's okay." Allie took Nova's hand. "I know what you meant. And I know my body isn't going to allow me to participate."

"I'll stay here with you." Nova sat back on the couch.

"No." Allie continued to hold Nova's hand and looked into her eyes.

"But I don't want...We can't do this again...I just—"

"I need to go make that call," Johnny rose from his chair. "If you'll excuse me."

"Um...I need to...um...go with you," Fran muttered. They both hurried from the room before Allie or Nova could speak.

Allie smiled. "I guess we know how to clear a room."

"No doubt." Nova returned the smile.

"You were saying?"

"I know we have things to talk out, and I'm afraid the next few days aren't gonna lend itself to that."

Allie shook her head. "Not likely."

"I just want you to know that I love you. I never stopped loving you, and I *won't* let you push me away again, and I won't run away."

Allie's chest filled with warmth. She wanted to wrap Nova in her arms and never let go, but there were things that needed to be done. A crisis to handle first. "I love you, too. And I don't want to push you away anymore, but—"

"No buts." Nova's eyes filled with tears. "Not this time."

Allie smiled and touched Nova's face. "I meant, but you need to go help with the rescue. I won't be responsible for you sitting on the sidelines. I know you would for me, but you shouldn't have to."

Nova's eyes filled with hope. "And you'll still be here when I'm done?"

This was Allie's moment of truth, but this time, she didn't hesitate. "I will be. I was wrong. Wrong about so many things. I hurt you, and I am so sorry." All the emotions she'd choked down for the past four years threatened to erupt just like the volcano had earlier.

"It's okay." Nova gently put her hand against Allie's cheek. "We'll rise out of the ashes. Together."

"I love that." Allie threw herself into Nova's arms and rested her head against Nova's chest, no longer able to keep her tears at bay.

Nova held her and rubbed her back, but neither spoke. Allie wanted nothing more than to take Nova's hand and lead her to the bedroom where her body could say what her words couldn't, but that would have to wait.

Allie wasn't sure how long they held each other before Johnny and Fran wandered back into the room.

"Get a room," Fran called out in a brassy voice.

Allie let go of Nova and wriggled her eyebrows.

"I have a room. I just don't have any privacy."

Nova's face reddened, and Allie had to choke back a giggle. *Damn.* She was so adorable when she was flustered.

"I think that's our walking papers," Johnny said.

"No. I just like to throw Fran off her game every now and then." Allie looked toward Fran.

Nova squeezed Allie's hand before she stood.

"You can pick your jaw off the ground now," Allie said to Fran.

Fran crossed her arms over her chest. "My jaw is just fine, thank you very much."

"Then why is your face so red?" Nova said with a grin.

Fran pointed. "Damn it. Don't you start on me, too, or I might have to rethink being happy that you're back in Allie's life."

Nova looked Fran directly in the eye. "I'm just glad you've always stood beside her. Even if it sometimes put me in the line of fire." Nova swallowed hard. "I always knew Allie would be taken care of, which made it slightly more bearable."

"Come here." Fran pulled Nova in for a hug, and Allie's chest filled with warmth.

When Fran and Nova separated, Johnny stepped up and looked down at Allie. "And I'm glad you're back in this one's life." Johnny motioned toward Nova. "She's a handful, so I'm thankful to have someone else to help me keep her in line."

Allie laughed and reached her hand out to Johnny, who helped her to her feet, while Nova glared. She hugged Johnny. "Thank you for being there for her. She's not as tough as she acts, so I'm sure you pulled her through some tough times."

"Do you think maybe you guys can stop having this conversation in front of me?" Cano stood to her full height.

Johnny and Allie's gazes met, and at the same time, they said, "Nope."

"When you're done, we need to come up with a game plan." Nova met Allie's gaze. "I think you and Fran should go back to Seattle."

Allie's glowered. She knew Nova was right, but she hated to admit it.

"I think that's a good idea," Johnny said.

Allie sighed. "Okay. Although, I hate it."

Cano took Allie's hand. "I know you do, but you'll be able to help out at U-Dub. Besides, you don't need to be here with all the ash falling, and we don't know how all the melting snow and avalanche are going to affect the rivers."

Fran's eyes widened. "Could we end up underwater?"

"Unlikely," Allie said. "We're far enough from the river, but I wouldn't want a house too close to it." She took Nova's hand. "Where will you go?"

Nova glanced at Johnny. "What did you find out?"

"Rescue efforts are underway. First responders are mobilizing. It sounds like groups are gathering in the fields at the high school."

"In Toutle?" Nova asked.

"Yep."

"What are we waiting for? Let's go."

Chapter Forty-three

Hours after eruption: 2.5
Sunday, May 18, 1980, 11:15 a.m.
Toutle, Washington
High school

The parking lot was teeming with people when Johnny pulled to a stop. The air was still heavy with ash, blocking out the sunlight. Two helicopters had touched down, and another had just flown off. It took off low and stayed at that altitude.

Cano watched in fascination, figuring visibility must be limited from higher up. Johnny pushed her shoulder. "Hey, are you listening to me?"

"Huh?" Cano peeled her gaze from the activity around them. "What did you say?"

"I didn't think so." He shook his head. "I said, should we go see where they might need us?"

"Um, yeah, sure." Cano took a deep breath. "Sorry, it's just a lot to take in."

They exited the vehicle, and Cano assessed the scene. There were several groups gathered, and people were moving about in a frenzy. She glanced at a pocket of people assembled around one of the helicopters. Just as she started to turn, someone called her name and waved.

"Cano," the man called. "Johnny?"

Johnny glanced at her. "Do we know him?"

Cano narrowed her eyes and stared at the ashen man. Then she raised her arm over her head and waved. "Tom." She turned to Johnny. "Tom, my friend from the roadblock. Let's go see what's going on."

Johnny and Cano hurried across the expanse toward the helicopter. Tom's face was covered in ash, but there was no mistaking his smile when they approached. He hurried toward them. Suddenly, he narrowed his lips as if he feared smiling at a time like this would be insensitive.

"Thank god you're okay," Tom said. "I was afraid you might have been up at Coldwater this morning."

Cano shook her head. "Nope, but I was near the roadblock."

Tom's eyes widened. "Holy shit. But obviously, you made it out."

Cano waved her hand at him. "That's a story for a different day. We came to help."

Tom pointed over his shoulder. "You might be able to hitch a ride with one of those guys. There are several news copters around, but they don't know much about volcanoes. I bet they could use some expertise, so they don't get themselves into trouble."

"Driving up, I swear the sky was full of helicopters. All news crews?"

Tom shook his head. "Weyerhaeuser has several birds in the sky, too. Apparently, there's an Air Force Reserves group training around Mount Hood that should be on their way. Rumor has it that a National Guard troop is at Yakima, but I haven't heard definitive confirmation yet."

Cano pointed. "I think that's the pilot I went up with the other day. Great guy if it is."

"Come on. Let's go see." Tom turned and trotted toward the helicopter.

Cano and Johnny hustled to keep up.

In times like these, social convention flew out the window, so introductions were kept to a minimum. It turned out the pilot Marcus was the one who'd flown Cano a few weeks back. He and his cameraman were the only two assigned to his helicopter.

As they talked, a sheriff wandered over to the group and spoke quietly to Tom before he addressed the others. "I hear you want to help," the sheriff said.

"Yes, sir," Johnny said. "We'll do what we can."

"No offense, but I'm not sure we need *scientists* right now." His lip curled as he said scientists. "We need rescue workers, not someone measuring gas and ash."

"No offense taken." Johnny grinned. "I spent some time in Korea, so I'm pretty sure I can be of use."

The sheriff's face lost its hard edge, and he clamped his hand hard on Johnny's shoulder. "I'll be damned. I did a tour in Korea, too."

As Johnny and the sheriff talked, Tom leaned over to Cano. "I think you're in." He turned to Marcus. "Are you up for it?"

"I'm ready."

Soon they were secured in the helicopter with headsets on. Cano's stomach fluttered as they rose from the ground. When she woke up this morning, she never would have predicted this would be where her day took her. Apprehension rose inside of her as she tried to imagine what they would encounter.

"We're going to fly low," Marcus called out. "Too far up and we won't be able to see a thing. I'm going to start out following Spirit Lake Highway to get my bearings."

Cano didn't realize her fists were clenched until her nails dug into her palms. *Shit.*

"You okay?" Johnny patted her leg.

Cano nodded, even though her stomach told her otherwise. "Gonna be weird seeing our escape route."

"That's what I figure." Johnny gave her a warm half-smile. "It'll likely hit you hard. Just let it."

Cano was thankful when the cameraman lifted his camera and began taking footage. "Holy hell." He pointed ahead. "Looks like we're flying into a dust storm."

"I hope to stay under the worst of it," Marcus called out. He pointed toward the road. "Don't think I'm drunk. I'm gonna follow the curve of the road the best I can. Some of the other guys that had already been up said the destruction is unbelievable. Easiest if I try to focus on landmarks."

They flew for several miles in silence as they all gaped out the windows. They passed the large trees that Cano had driven past many times on her way up and down the highway. While an ashy residue appeared to cover them, they still stood. As they flew on, the destruction worsened.

Johnny pointed. "I think we're near where the roadblock was."

The pilot slowed and dipped the helicopter a little lower.

"Look," the cameraman shouted. "A car."

It was nearly buried in debris. Bile rose in Cano's throat. It wasn't far from where Allie's car had been parked, but this one looked as if it were on the road.

"Should we check and see if there's anyone we can help?" Marcus flew lower and a cloud of ash kicked up, erasing their visibility. "Shit. We can't set down here."

Johnny shook his head. "Nobody survived that. I don't think we need to stop."

"He's right," Cano said. "They would have been dead in minutes, possibly seconds."

Marcus pulled up and rose away from the car and moved on toward the location of the roadblock.

Pockets of steam rose from the ground, likely from tiny pools of water. Lightning continued to streak in the clouds ahead.

"Damn, check that out," the cameraman said. "How thick is that shit?"

They were likely almost on top of the roadblock, but it was impossible to tell for sure. The rocks, downed trees, and ash covered the entire road, so it was no longer discernible.

"It's likely hundreds of feet deep. But it's hard to tell until we can get out here and measure it, and that'll be a few days," Cano said.

"Hey, there's another helicopter." The cameraman pointed to the northwest and raised his camera.

"I'm guessing that's somewhere near Weyerhaeuser's camp," Marcus said. "Do you think anything is left?"

Cano gazed off in the direction of the camp and then back at the ground. "I think it's far enough back that it likely escaped the brunt of the blast."

"Should we go check it out?" the cameraman said.

"I don't think so," Johnny answered. "Weyerhaeuser's team is likely all over it. If you don't mind, could we go check out Coldwater?"

"Nothing's going to be left," Cano said as she

looked into Johnny's sad eyes.

"I know. I just want to pay my respects."

Cano nodded. "Understood."

As they flew on, nothing was left. Where there once was trees and green was now flat and gray. They couldn't be sure where Coldwater had been, but she was sure nobody could have survived.

Cano glanced over at Johnny, who had his eyes closed. His lips moved in prayer, and he made the sign of the cross. She looked away, not wanting to interfere in his private moment.

"Where's Spirit Lake?" the cameraman called. "I'd like to get a shot of it."

Marcus called over his shoulder, "Do you think we should go that close? Is she going to let rip with a bigger blast?"

"She'll continue to spew," Cano answered, "but nothing like the pressure she released on the first blast."

"So it's safe?" Marcus asked.

"Safe-ish. We're dealing with a volcano," Johnny said. "But I wouldn't worry unless something changes."

"I'm trusting you." Marcus banked the helicopter to the left.

Cano gaped at the terrain that all looked the same. The lush Washington landscape was now barren. She trained her eyes on the ground as they passed, knowing she was being ridiculous hoping to see survivors.

"Jesus," Marcus said. "How the hell could I not be able to find a huge lake?" He tapped on his gauges. "I swear it should be around here somewhere."

The cameraman gasped. "Is that it?"

Cano peered out the window in the direction he'd indicated. "Holy shit. I think it is. If you look really hard, you can see hints of water through all the downed trees."

Johnny edged nearer to Cano to get a better look. "Damn. I think you're right." He shook his head. "I can't even comprehend how many trees must be in there."

Cano stared, certain that they were flying over Spirit Lake. If she didn't know it was there, she'd never be able to spot it. The trees were so tightly packed in the water that one could easily miss it.

"Unbelievable." The cameraman kept his lens trained on the ground. "How can something that large be consumed like that? How big is it, anyway?"

Cano gazed at where the lake likely was. "I believe it's around four-point-five square miles, about twice the size of Castle Rock."

The cameraman whistled. "Shit."

Marcus pointed. "That's around where Harry Truman's house was." He sighed. "I liked the old guy. I got the opportunity to fly him a couple times. What a character. I hope he didn't suffer."

"Doubtful that he did," Johnny said. "He would have been bl...um...gone before he knew what hit him."

Cano caught Johnny's stumble but doubted the others had. She guessed he was about to say he would have been blown to pieces, but she was glad he chose not to voice it aloud. She gave him a quick nod of understanding before she said, "Mother Nature isn't someone to mess with. That's for sure."

After circling Spirit Lake a few times, they went back the way they'd come. "Hey, over there," Cano called out. "It looks like a car."

Marcus banked the helicopter toward the vehicle. As they got closer, Cano could see a man lying on the roof. "Someone's out there," she said excitedly.

The cameraman trained his camera on the car as they flew nearer. "Um, I'm not feeling good about this."

The blades of the helicopter stirred up dust as they descended. "Shit. I can't land her here," Marcus said.

"What about over there? To the right," Johnny said. "It looks like a wet spot. Might not kick up as much ash."

"I'll try."

Marcus hovered a couple of feet from the ground. "Did you guys want to go check it out?"

Johnny was already at the opening of the door. Cano sprang up and followed. They jumped the short way to the ground, landing about thirty yards from the car.

"Careful," Johnny said. "Watch where you're stepping."

They walked gingerly across the debris. Pieces of mountain rock and tree parts were covered in ash, making each step an adventure. They didn't talk other than to point out the best path, as they made their way through the rubble.

By the time they were within ten yards, it was apparent the man was no longer alive, but something compelled them forward. It was hard to make out much about him since he was covered in ash. He could have been twenty or sixty, but it was impossible to tell.

"Should we search for an I.D.?" Cano asked.

"Probably want to get his name if possible, so we can alert the authorities."

Cano reached out to wipe the grime off his face to get a better gauge on what he looked like. His skin sloughed off at her touch. She recoiled. Her stomach lurched. "Oh, fuck," she said as she backed away.

"You look green. Why don't you let me finish up here?"

Normally, Cano would have protested but not this time. She turned away and willed her stomach not to rebel. The last thing she wanted to do was vomit next to the corpse. Somehow, it would seem disrespectful. She fought the urge to run back to the helicopter. It was safer if they walked back together.

It didn't take Johnny long before he said, "Got it. Let's head back."

Cano felt like a zombie as she trudged toward the helicopter, following their earlier footsteps. She scolded herself for her reactions.

Johnny must have known because he put his hand on her arm as they approached the helicopter. "You're a geologist not a medical doctor. Give yourself a break."

Cano nodded before she climbed inside.

Once back in the air, Marcus said, "We need to run to Kelso to refuel. Are you guys done, or do you want to stick with us?"

Johnny glanced at Cano, indicating he would let her make the call.

"We're in," Cano said with more conviction than she'd felt.

"Good," Marcus said. "While you were out there, I got word that they need help up along the Toutle River. Mudslides. They're trying to evacuate people in the path. They say it'll likely take out everything in its path."

After refueling, they'd flown back toward Mount St. Helens. While they were on the ground, Johnny had been able to get in touch with someone from Vancouver and confirmed that the 304th Squadron of the Air Force Reserves had arrived to aid in the rescue, and the 116th Cavalry of the Washington State National Guard would arrive soon.

Relief flooded Cano. Trained rescuers would know better what to do than she and Johnny would. She rubbed her hand along her pants again, even though she'd washed them so hard they were nearly raw. The feeling of flesh falling off the man's body might haunt her the rest of her life.

Helping people evacuate a mudslide and flooding would hopefully prove easier, but she braced herself for the potential horror. Cano sat back in her seat while they flew toward the devastation. She had a little time to collect her thoughts before they arrived in the thick of it. She closed her eyes and brought Allie's face into focus in hopes of calming her frayed nerves. She tried to keep the smile off her lips, not wanting the others to think she was cracking up.

Johnny tapped her leg. "Getting close."

She opened her eyes, not sure how long she'd been lost in her thoughts. "Thanks" was all she managed to say.

Helicopters filled the sky as they neared the Toutle River.

"I'm gonna fly in a ways to get a lay of the land

before we try to pick people up," Marcus said.

They swept out away from the river and flew off toward Mount St. Helens. After a bit, he circled back toward the river, so they could fly the length.

"I'm such an idiot," the cameraman said. He pointed at Cano's tattoo. "I expected to see red and orange lava flowing down the side of the mountain, but all we have is chocolate milk."

"Looks more like chocolate syrup to me," Marcus called. "Certainly not what I expected."

Cano held back a chuckle. They were right. The mudslide did resemble hot fudge running into the river. From above, it looked to be moving slower than it likely was. Whole trees and other debris bobbed in the mixture. She glanced at her arm, definitely nothing as pretty as her tattoo. The bleak browns and grays were depressing.

Several places where a bridge should have been, there was none. They came up to a standing bridge, so Marcus pulled back on his speed. "I don't think she's going to hold much longer."

Felled trees piled up around the footings of the bridge, as more piled in behind the others. With each surge of the muddy water, the bridge seemed to shudder more.

Johnny pointed. "That end is about to break loose."

The words were barely out of his mouth when the entire bridge twisted sideways. Cano imagined the sound it must have made as the metal ripped away from the foundation. "It's trying to hold on."

With one final rush, the other end of the bridge popped loose and joined the trees as they continued down the river.

"Damn. It ripped that bridge out like it was made of toothpicks," Marcus said.

Cano shivered. "Let's go rescue people."

"Certainly," Marcus said.

They flew past Weyerhaeuser's camp, which was already half overrun by the mudslide. Heavy machinery—tractors and trucks—had been toppled. Likely in a short time, there would be nothing left of the camp.

"Just got radio word," Marcus called. "People need picked up at Kid Valley. Finally, maybe we can do some good."

Cano's heart clenched as they approached Kid Valley. People stood out in their yards with suitcases packed. "Marcus, can we stop there?" She pointed at a family with two small children standing with their suitcases. The little girl clutched a teddy bear to her chest.

Chapter Forty-four

Days after eruption: 2
Tuesday, May 20, 1980
Seattle, Washington
Allie's house

Allie paced from the kitchen to the living room and back again. When she entered the kitchen, her stomach growled at the smell of the lasagna baking in the oven. Nova would be there shortly.

Allie hadn't seen her since she and Johnny left to help with the rescue effort. She'd talked to her once on Monday and then again a few hours ago when she told Allie she was on her way home. *Home.* When Cano uttered the word, it had set off a firestorm of emotions in Allie.

She wandered into her bedroom and looked at herself in the full-length mirror. Even though she knew Nova would be covered in grime, she still wanted to look good for her. Her tight blue jeans hugged her small frame. She smiled. Nova never could resist the way her butt looked in a snug pair of jeans. Her red silk shirt was tucked into her jeans. *Power color.* It would hopefully make her feel more confident than she felt. She chuckled as she undid another button of her shirt. *Yep.* Her cleavage would make it difficult for Nova to concentrate on dinner, which was exactly what she hoped for.

While Allie had been busy at the university, she'd still had time to think about their reunion. She'd resisted the urge to give herself some relief, but her body screamed out to her now. She chastised herself. Nova would likely be exhausted, so her plans might have to wait until tomorrow.

They'd have all the time in the world when Nova arrived tonight. Nova didn't plan on returning to Mount St. Helens for a while. The rescue efforts for survivors had ended and had moved to the recovery of bodies. With the professionals on the scene, Nova had decided that her services were no longer needed. Allie suspected that Nova didn't have the stomach for this phase of the search, after hearing the pain in Nova's voice when she'd called.

Despite feeling guilty and a little selfish, Allie couldn't help the rising excitement she felt with Nova's imminent arrival. She took one last look at herself in the mirror. *Not bad for forty.* She flicked her curls a couple of times to give them more body before she turned from the mirror.

A moment later, a knock sounded at the front door, causing butterflies to dance in her stomach. *Get a grip.* It wasn't like this was a first date, but in some ways, it felt like it. She smoothed the front of her shirt, even though there were no wrinkles.

Her eyes widened when she opened the door. *Damn.* Nova looked amazing. Instead of the tired, grubby woman she expected, a bright-eyed freshly showered Nova stood in the doorway. And she smelled good, too. *Polo.*

"Hi." Nova had a goofy grin on her face as she waved.

"Hi, yourself." Allie tried to appear casual but couldn't help but stare. Nova sported a well-worn, light brown leather bomber jacket over a billowing white button-down shirt. The chunky silver chain Allie had given her several years ago rested on Nova's chest.

Allie let her gaze travel downward. Nova wore a pair of tight shiny black pants that sported multiple zippers. The pants tapered into a pair of white high-top tennis shoes. She needed to stop staring, so she moved aside and motioned for Nova to enter.

Allie's focus immediately went to Nova's tight little buttocks. She'd always loved Nova's ass, but damn, the pants made it look even better. "Nice pants," Allie said without thinking.

Nova turned with a smirk. "Liking what you're seeing?"

"Um..." Allie's cheeks tingled with heat. "The pants are interesting." Allie ran her hand along Nova's leg. "Interesting material."

"They're called parachute pants." Nova turned in a complete circle with her hands raised above her head, so her jacket rode up, clearly revealing her entire backside. "I've seen a bunch of teenagers wearing them around Menlo, so I decided to get me a pair."

Allie moved in closer to Nova. "I like them." She ran her hand down the length of Nova's thigh. "Smooth."

Nova smiled and ran her hand the length of Allie's silk shirt. "I could say the same about you. Smooth."

A shiver ran up Allie's spine. Just having Nova touch her arm sent shock waves through her entire body. "I'm not sure we should be touching like this. It might ruin our dinner."

Nova sniffed the air. "The food smells divine, but you look even tastier." Nova put her hand against Allie's cheek and gazed into her eyes. "You're a beautiful woman."

Allie put her hand over Nova's that lay against her cheek. She brought Nova's hand to her mouth and lightly kissed her palm.

Nova shuddered. "Damn. I felt that in places I didn't even know were still functioning."

"Do you want me to stop?" Allie's tongue trailed across Nova's palm to her wrist where Allie nibbled on Nova's soft skin. She'd not intended things to happen this way, but her libido had taken over. Every time she moved, her tight jeans pressed against her crotch, making her more turned on.

Nova moaned. "That depends on whether you want dinner to burn."

"It's done cooking. I can switch the oven to warm."

"You might need to shut it off and reheat it later." Cano pressed against Allie. "I've been waiting for this moment for four years, so it just might take a while."

Allie straddled Nova's leg and moved in closer. As she rubbed her sex against Nova's leg, she said, "I'm thinking the opposite. This isn't going to take long at all." Allie shot Cano a seductive smile.

"The first one won't." Nova put her hands on Allie's buttocks and pulled her closer. "But I plan on making sure every inch of your body is explored, worshiped, and satiated."

"I like the sound of that." Allie gazed up into Nova's eyes.

Nova bent and brought her lips to Allie's. Nova's lips brushed Allie's and moved away, only to brush them again. Allie moaned. She fought against herself. Part of her wanted to grab Nova and devour her mouth, while the other part wanted to take this slow and savor the moment.

Nova flicked her tongue out and parted Allie's lips. The motion was driving Allie insane, so she placed her hand against the back of Nova's head and pulled her in. Allie thrust her tongue in and out of Nova's mouth.

She'd missed the taste of Nova and couldn't get enough. It was as if she'd been deprived of her favorite candy for too long. All she wanted to do was ravage Nova and let Nova ravage her. "Please," Allie said between kisses.

"Please what?" Nova gave her a crooked grin.

"I need to have all of you. Now."

"All right then. Who am I to argue?" Nova stopped. "And here I got all dressed up for you, hoping it would convince you that you wanted to let me make love to you, but now I've wasted a good outfit for nothing."

"Trust me, it won't be for nothing. I'm going to enjoy peeling those clothes off you." Allie wasn't sure where her newfound assertiveness was coming from, but she wasn't going to question it since her body was more than ready for Nova's touch. "Meet me in the bedroom. I need to turn off the oven."

"Sure. I need to freshen up, too."

"Is that code for 'I've had a long drive, and I need to pee'?" Allie smiled.

"Um. Maybe. But it didn't sound very romantic or sexy."

Allie ran her hand through Nova's hair. "Anything you say sounds sexy."

Nova playfully pulled away. "Stop, or I might pee myself."

"Okay, I take it back." Allie grinned. "Nothing sexy about that."

Nova chuckled. "Some people might find it sexy."

"Eww. Not this girl. But to each his own, I suppose."

Cano stared down at her shaking hands as she washed them. This was really going to happen. What she'd wished for the past four years. What if something went wrong?

She violently shook her head. *No.* She couldn't go into this thinking that way. But what if Allie struggled again? Should she fake it or tell Allie the truth? *Ugh.* Her thoughts weren't helpful. She needed to let go and let things play out naturally. Having Allie in her arms was all she really needed.

Cano glanced at herself in the mirror one final time and took a deep breath. She could do this.

Cano knocked on the half-closed bedroom door. "Can I come in?"

"You better," Allie answered, her voice full of flirtation. "Or I will hunt you down."

Cano pushed open the door. Her breath caught at the sight of Allie. She was still fully clothed, but she'd unbutton her shirt, so it was open to her navel. *Get a grip.* She needed to act cool but suspected Allie saw right through her. "Hunt me down, huh? When did you get so aggressive?"

"Since I haven't had a proper orgasm in four years." Allie moved toward her. "Do you think you could help me with that?"

"I think I'm the woman for the job."

"So do I." Allie reached out and touched Cano's face. "I'm crazy in love with you."

Cano's pulse quickened. "And I'm crazy in love with you, too. It never stopped. Never went away."

"For me, either." Allie's eyes filled with tears. "I'm so sorry what I did to us. To you."

Cano reached out and brushed the tear from under Allie's eye. "No sadness. We both had something to learn. And now we have. It'll only make us stronger for our next chapter."

"But what if we…I…mess up again?"

"You won't," Cano said with conviction.

"I wish I had your confidence." Allie looked down at her feet.

Cano lifted Allie's chin, so she met Cano's gaze. "The moment I saw you again, I knew…hell, I've known the last four years. I never want to be without you again."

"But what if I go stupid again? What if I let my MS win?" The despair on Allie's face made Cano want to wrap Allie in her arms.

"That's where I come in." Cano smiled and rubbed Allie's cheek with her thumb. "When you told me to leave, I acted like I was fine. Typical Cano, strutting around like nothing was wrong, while all the while my heart was ripped out." Cano shook her head. "Now I know. I should have jumped up and down and refused to let you push me away. Deep down, you wanted me to fight for you, and I didn't because I was scared."

"No, Nova. Never blame yourself. It was all my fault." Allie put her hand against Cano's cheek.

"What do you say we agree that both of us could have done better? There's no blame in love. We're two imperfect people trying to do the best we can."

"Are you sure?" Allie's eyes were full of hope.

"Positive. Your diagnosis threw us both for a loop. Just in different ways. But I need to say this to you now."

A crease lined Allie's forehead, and her eyes held caution. "What?"

"I want to spend the rest of my life with you. For better or worse. In sickness and in health. Whether you're moving around like this." Cano swept her hand toward Allie's body. "Or you need a wheelchair. It's you I want."

Allie grinned. "Was that a proposal?"

Cano laughed. "I suppose it was. That's if we could actually be married."

Allie laughed. "Like that will ever happen in our lifetime."

"Well, we can still spend forever with each other. Married or not."

Allie smiled. "We're jumping right in? No dating? No seeing how things go?"

Cano stood taller, and her jaw tightened. "I've waited four years for this. I don't want to wait another minute. I don't need any of those things. Do you?"

"No." Allie wrapped her arms around Cano. "Absolutely not. I just wanted to make sure." She pulled back and looked into Cano's eyes. "Will you stay here? Can you with your job?"

"Yes and yes. And if I can't, I'll find a new job." Cano brought her lips to Allie's, and this time, there was nothing slow about it.

Allie sucked Cano's bottom lip into her mouth and flicked her tongue over it. Cano moaned. Cano pulled Allie tighter against her and returned the kiss.

Cano wasn't sure how long they'd been kissing, but her lips felt swollen and other parts of her body screamed for attention. She ran her hand over Allie's smooth stomach and enjoyed the way it quivered under her fingertips.

She fought against herself. Part of her wanted to yank all their clothes off and fall into bed, but the other half of her wanted to savor the moment.

Allie didn't seem to be having the same debate since she'd pushed Cano's coat off her and tossed it onto a nearby chair. She already had nearly all the buttons on Cano's shirt undone.

Cano considered slowing the action but decided against it. Tonight, she'd let Allie set the pace. Allie's shirt was nearly unbuttoned, so Cano finished with the last two buttons, and her hands played over the smooth silk.

Allie let the shirt slip to the floor, and in one motion, she unhooked her bra and let it fall on top of the shirt. "Sorry I took the shirt away from you. I know how much you love the feel of my silk shirts." Allie smiled and took Cano's hand and put it against her breast. "But maybe this will make up for it."

Cano's hand trembled as she touched Allie's ample breast. She cupped it in her hand and gently kneaded it. "Yeah. I'll take this over silk any day."

Touching Allie like this caused Cano's breath to catch in her throat. Allie was beautiful. She'd never get tired of exploring her body, but she still needed to slow down. She fought her urge to pick Allie up and carry her to the nearby bed.

With her thumb, Cano teased Allie's nipple. In response, the nub became rock hard. "Should I stop?" Cano teased.

"You better not, Nova Kane."

"Ouch." Cano chuckled. "Low blow." She lowered her mouth to Allie's breast.

Allie gasped, and her back arched. "Now who's guilty of a low blow?"

Cano released Allie's nipple from between her lips. "Payback."

Before Allie could respond, Cano sucked the tip back into her mouth and flicked her tongue over it.

Allie's knees buckled.

"Oh, god." Cano grabbed Allie around the waist. Her eyes widened. "Are you okay?"

"Don't freak out." Allie laughed. "That one was all on you, not my condition. You know how sensitive my breasts are."

Cano smiled. It was true. It wasn't the first time Allie's knees had buckled when she'd given special attention to Allie's nipples. "To be on the safe side, do you think we should get into bed?"

"I'd like to finish undressing you first. It's been a long time since I've seen your body, and I want to feast my eyes on the whole enchilada."

"Enchilada?" Cano raised her eyebrows. "Are you sure you don't want to eat dinner first? Sounds like you're hungry."

"Ah, I see. Getting cocky now that you caused my knees to buckle."

Cano smirked. "I'm known for my swagger."

"It's been known to get you into trouble, too."

"True." Cano gave Allie a sad smile. "Can I at

least keep some of it?"

"I was teasing." Allie put her hand on Cano's chest. "I never want you to lose your cockiness. It makes you, you. Just don't let it get in your way."

"Deal." Cano broke out a huge smile. "Now do you think we can have a little less talking and a little more kissing?"

Allie stepped back. "Wait. I need to get something."

Cano gaped as Allie hurried from the room. She must be losing her touch.

Allie's heart raced as she marched through her house naked. She needed to do this before she lost her nerve. Her hand rested on the closet door as she debated with herself. *No.* There was no time for second guessing or letting things derail like they had last time.

She pulled open the door and grabbed the box from the closet shelf. She thought of taking her surprise out of the box but decided against it. She shivered, which reminded her that she wore no clothes.

With a decisive set to her jaw, she kicked the closet door shut and hugged the box to her chest. She scurried across the room back to the bedroom.

Nova sat naked on the bed. Her expression held a mixture of puzzlement and concern. "Everything all right?"

"Yum," Allie said, ignoring the question. She ran her hand over Nova's shoulders. Her fingers danced across the rock-hard muscles. "You've been working out."

"About the only thing I could do to release some of my sexual frustration."

Allie smirked. "Remind me to cut you off every now and then."

Nova drew Allie to her. "Are you going to tell me what's in the box?"

Allie let her hand holding the box fall to her side. With Allie still standing, Nova's face was at chest level.

Nova licked her lips. "How can I concentrate when you give me this view?" Nova ran her tongue between Allie's breasts, making circular motions as she did.

Allie shuddered. The sensation of having Nova's mouth on her was making it hard for her to concentrate on anything else, but she needed to give the gift to Nova.

Reluctantly, Allie stepped back and broke contact. "You need to stop that." Allie smiled. "I can't talk to you about this," Allie held up the box, "when you're doing that."

"Um…do you think this is really the right time to exchange presents?" Nova reached out and brushed her hand across Allie's breast.

Allie jumped back farther. She wagged her finger at Nova, but the smile remained on her face. "Here." She held the box out to Nova.

As Nova read the outside of the box, her eyes widened. "Is this what I think it is?"

"Yep." Allie suddenly felt exposed and unsure of herself. Maybe this was a bad idea.

"But you said...you said…" Nova fumbled with her words.

"I know what I said, and I was wrong." Allie took

the box from Nova and yanked open the lid. "You shouldn't have to be in a position to fake an orgasm or finish yourself off in the bathroom afterward."

"But you said it would ruin everything. It wouldn't be natural."

"I was feeling sorry for myself." Allie pulled out a machine with a long handle and a large rubber head on the end. "There's no shame in using one of these. My ego just got in the way."

"You've had it all along?"

"No." Allie's face heated. "Did you notice at my birthday party? When I shoved the canister set Fran gave me back into the box?"

Nova's brow furrowed. "Yeah. It was weird." Nova burst out laughing and pointed. "Fran gave it to you?"

Allie joined Nova's laughter. "Yes. The asshole. Embarrassed the hell out of me with the guys in the room—and you. I hid it as fast as I could."

"Priceless." Nova shook her head but stopped and tilted her head. "Why did she give it to you?"

Allie shifted her gaze away from Nova. "She wanted to give me the push she thought I needed."

Nova's eyes widened, and she put her hand against her chest. "She knows about...our problem?"

Fear and relief washed over Allie at the same time. She wanted everything on the table with Nova, but she wasn't sure how she would react, either. "Yes. She's my best friend. I told her everything."

"Except that you dumped me."

Allie gave Nova a sad smile. "Except for that."

Nova reached out and grabbed Allie's hand. "Sorry. I shouldn't have said that. It came out wrong. I was just shocked that you told Fran about our sex life."

"Are you angry?"

"God, no. It just took me a minute to process. I'm glad you can talk to her. I doubt if I'll be sharing any of this with Johnny."

"Please don't." Allie laughed, thankful that Nova made the joke. It told Allie that everything would be okay. "I'd like to be able to look him in the eye when I see him."

"So Fran gave it to you on your birthday? Was she expecting something to happen?"

"I think that was the idea. It was her way of telling me she was okay with us being together."

"I see." Nova smiled and nodded toward Allie's hand that held the vibrator. "Are you going to tell me what you've got?"

Allie smiled and held up the machine. "It's called a magic wand."

Nova laughed. "Seriously?"

"Yep." Allie waved her hand along the base up to the large head. "This is for massages. Not sexual pleasure."

"Really? So do my muscles look too tight?" Cano flexed her chest, and her pectoral muscles danced.

Allie playfully pushed Nova's shoulders. "Stop that, or I'm going to ravage you right now."

"About time," Cano said with a grin. She took the vibrator from Allie. "Seriously, are you okay with this?"

Am I? Allie rolled the thought around in her mind for what must have been the thousandth time, and then she nodded. "I am. I want to spend the rest of my life with you. And I don't want you walking around frustrated half the time, if my body isn't working the way I want it to on some days."

"We don't have to. I mean...we don't have to on the days things aren't working one hundred percent."

"Screw that." Allie winked at Nova. "My body might go through stages of not working for months. I'm not willing to keep my hands off you that long." To demonstrate, Allie moved toward Nova and ran her hands through Nova's hair and then raked them down the side of Nova's body before she straddled Nova on the bed.

Nova tossed the magic wand onto the bed next to her, wrapped both arms around Allie, and nuzzled her neck.

Between moans, Allie said, "Don't you think we should plug it in?" Allie motioned toward the vibrator.

"Something tells me you aren't going to need it for the first round."

Allie raised her eyebrows. "First round? Are you planning on there being more than one?"

"Uh-huh," Nova said as she ran her tongue along Allie's jawline to her earlobe.

Allie's entire body reacted, and a fire burned between her thighs. "Exactly how many are we talking about?"

"Let's leave that open," Cano said right before she sucked Allie's earlobe into her mouth.

Allie's mind went blank. She had no more words. Tonight, she wanted to feel every part of Nova. Gently, she pushed Nova against the bed, and her mouth found Nova's.

Chapter Forty-five

Days after eruption: 2
Tuesday, May 20, 1980
Seattle, Washington
Allie's house

Cano fell back against her pillow, panting. "Jesus. I told you that you wouldn't need any magic wand when you have a magic tongue."

Allie laughed as she crawled up beside Cano and dropped her head to Cano's chest. Her breathing was labored as she snuggled against Cano.

Cano pulled the covers over Allie and wrapped her arm around her shoulder. "I love you." Cano lifted Allie's chin, so their gazes met. "I love you so much."

Allie squeezed Cano and draped her leg over Cano's midsection. "I love you, too. I believe that was the sweetest orgasm I've ever had."

"Sweet?" Cano frowned. "I was going for hottest."

Allie pursed her lips and then smiled. "You'll have to try for hottest the next round. For me, that was sweet. You were so tender with me."

Cano puffed her chest out. "You mean I've already lost my swagger?"

"Just the opposite. I think it's swaggerful to be tender with the woman you love."

"Um, I don't think that's a word. Shouldn't it be full of swagger?"

"Swaggerful or swaggerness. Take your pick." Allie ran her finger around Cano's nipple. "But there will be no full of swagger choice."

"Swaggerful it is then." Cano smiled. She fought the urge to let out a loud laugh since smiling wasn't enough. Happiness flooded through her, and she didn't know how to let it all out. Running through the neighborhood naked and screaming with euphoria would likely be frowned upon.

"What are you thinking?" Allie asked, studying Cano's face.

"Running through the neighborhood naked, screaming about how much I love you."

Allie scowled. "Seriously, what were you thinking?"

"That's the truth." Cano felt her face flush. "I was thinking about how happy I am and how much I want to scream it to the world."

"Let's wait until you at least have some clothes on." Allie smirked and ran her hand over Cano's shoulders. "I don't want anyone else getting a glimpse of this body, or they might try to steal it."

"Or I might get arrested."

"That too." Allie adjusted herself, so she could look into Cano's eyes. "Are you going to tell me about the rescue missions before round two starts?"

Cano put her hand on her own stomach. "As much as I would love to lay here with you all night, all I ate today was a breakfast sandwich, and with all the calories we just burned, I'm starving."

"Oh, god." Allie bolted upright. "How insensitive. I had a nice big lunch at the university today."

"Rub it in," Cano teased. "I want to hear all the news from U-Dub, too."

Allie rolled out of bed and slid into Cano's button-down shirt. *Damn.* Allie in nothing but Cano's oversized shirt made Cano's pulse race. "You've lost it now." Allie sported a mischievous smile as she modeled the look. She pointed toward the dresser. "I've got some T-shirts in there that I know will fit you."

"I'll be happy to wear a T-shirt since you look so damned sexy dressed like that."

Allie pulled out a pair of sweatpants from one of the drawers and pointed at Cano. "I'm *not* going to wear this shirt and nothing else."

Cano wriggled her eyebrows. "Maybe later? Round two?"

Allie smirked. "If you're good."

"Trust me. I can be *really* good."

Allie laughed. "Yep, you've still got your swagger. Get dressed, and we'll eat." Allie winked at her before she left the room.

It didn't take long for the lasagna to warm up. Allie scooped a generous helping from the pan, careful not to touch the sides with her bare hands. If it tasted half as good as it smelled, she would consider it a successful meal.

Nova arrived in the kitchen wearing a pair of black sweatpants and sporting Allie's AC/DC T-shirt. Allie suspected it wasn't for the music but because it was slightly too small on Cano and hugged her chiseled frame.

"Are you into AC/DC now?" Allie raised her eyebrow.

Nova put her hand in the air with her pinky and

index finger raised. Her thumb jutted out, instead of being tucked against her other fingers. "*Dirty Deeds Done Dirt Cheap.*"

"I love you, too," Allie said, trying to hide her smirk.

Nova looked at her hand and then back at Allie with a puzzled look.

Allie laughed and held up her hand. "If you're going for devil horns, it's like this." Allie held up her index finger and pinkie, while placing her thumb over the fingers resting against her palm.

"Devil horns? I don't want devil horns. I was going for the rock sign."

"That's what the rock sign is called. You just gave me the I love you sign." Allie shook her head. Another reason she loved the tough girl so much. The inside didn't match the outside. "I think you better stick with the Carpenters and John Denver."

Nova glared, but her eyes twinkled. "Let's not go sharing that story with anyone."

"Not even with Fran?"

"Especially Fran." Nova smiled. "You can tell her about our sex life but not something as embarrassing as this."

"Johnny would love the story. I bet he knows it since he has teens."

"Don't you dare." Nova glared.

Allie motioned toward the bottle of wine sitting on the counter. "Why don't you put your rocking self to work and open that?"

"I've got this." Nova lifted both hands over her head in the sign of the devil and bopped her head up and down as if she were moving to the beat of heavy metal music.

"You're such a dork." Allie picked up the two plates and carried them to the table. "When you're done jamming out, dinner is ready."

Cano's knife glided through the thick piece of lasagna. Cheese strings clung to her knife as she pulled it away. "This looks and smells amazing." She brought a bite to her mouth and closed her eyes. "Damn, this is almost as good as my orgasm."

"I aim to please." Allie took a bite herself. "Not bad. Tell me about the rescue efforts. I saw on the news there were more people than I suspected who were saved."

Nova's head bobbed. "There were some real heartwarming stories." Her gaze shifted to her plate. "And a couple tragic ones."

"David?"

"Among others."

"How about you tell me the happy stories tonight?"

"I like that." Cano smiled. She didn't want to think about the things that would likely give her nightmares for years. "Did you see the news about the youngest survivor that we found yesterday?"

"I heard rumblings about it, but I figured I misheard."

"Nope. You didn't. Terra Moore. Age three months."

"Tara? Like in *Gone with the Wind*?"

"No. Terra. Like in earth. T-E-R-R-A."

"What a beautiful name."

"I thought so." Cano smiled. "I still can't believe the family was only thirteen miles from the blast but managed to survive."

"Wow. Thirteen?"

"Yeah. They hid in an old elk hunter's shack and used tarps, blankets, and wet socks to keep the ash out of the baby's lungs."

"Genius." Allie touched Cano's hand. "That had to make everyone feel good when they were rescued."

"At times, it was tough being there, but stories like that made it bearable." Images of the devastation rushed through Cano's mind, so she shook her head to clear it.

As if reading her mind, Allie said, "I've seen the footage on TV. It's unbelievable."

"It was even more unbelievable from the air. It's indescribable. The pilots were having a hell of a time because there were no landmarks left. Just scorched earth."

"I would think Spirit Lake would be easy to spot."

"It's gone." Cano ran her hand through her hair. The unbelievable images etched in her mind gave her pause. "Not exactly gone, but it's full of trees and ash. That land will never look the same. Or at least it won't for a very long time."

"The geologists at the university are saying more than two hundred twenty-five square miles were destroyed in a matter of minutes." Allie shook her head. "I'm sure it'll take us weeks, if not months, to come up with an exact figure."

"That's huge." Cano looked toward the ceiling, trying to figure the size in her mind.

"It translates to the size of about ten Manhattans."

"Fuck." Cano set down her fork and took a gulp of her wine. "That's insane."

"Wanna hear something else even more insane?"

Cano cocked her head. "Lay it on me."

"They're estimating that the blast was somewhere around five hundred times more powerful than the bomb dropped on Hiroshima."

"Whoa." The statistic was a stunning reminder of the power they'd narrowly escaped. Cano took another sip of wine. "After seeing it, I believe it. We'll be studying her for years."

"Maybe it will help us be more accurate in our predictions next time."

"And people will listen to scientists."

Allie nodded. "And we'll be in more agreement. In hindsight, there's a lot we could have done better. Then so many people wouldn't have had to die."

Cano stared down at her lasagna. Although she was famished, her stomach roiled at the thought of the loss. "Last I heard, the count is over fifty."

"It had to be horrible to see." Allie put her hand on Cano's. "I shouldn't have brought it up at dinner."

"It was." Cano picked up her fork. "But there were other amazing stories, too. The rescuers saved a ton of people."

Allie smiled. "Care to define a ton?"

"Last I heard, we were approaching a hundred fifty. I'm not sure when the total counts will come out."

Allie touched her own chest. "It has to feel good that you were able to help."

Cano forced a bite of lasagna into her mouth and chewed. Once she'd swallowed, she said, "It does."

"Were you involved with the couple that got

swept up by the floodwaters?"

Cano shook her head. "No, but I heard about them. I saw a bridge get ripped out like it was made of Tinkertoys. I'm still shocked they survived. As if the blast wasn't bad enough, Barry Voight was right, the ice melt and mudslides were devastating."

"I'll never forget that cloud." Allie met Cano's gaze. "Or that ride out. I didn't think we were going to make it."

"Me neither." Cano held Allie's gaze. "Want to hear what kept running through my mind?"

"Sure."

Cano studied Allie's beautiful face before she spoke. The face that she'd longed for the past four years. "I thought...if I was going to die, at least I would die with your arms wrapped around me."

Allie's eyes welled with tears. "That may be the most romantic thing you've ever said to me."

Cano narrowed her eyes. "Then I better work on my sweet talking." She grinned. "Something that doesn't include death in the declaration of my love."

"Finish your dinner." Allie's eyes danced. "You can work on your lines during round two."

Cano raised her eyebrows in mock surprise. "You're horny already?"

"Yep. And I might just have to try out my wand."

Cano dug into the lasagna with gusto. "Who am I to stop a magician at work?"

Chapter Forty-six

Four months later
Saturday, September 13, 1980
Seattle, Washington
Allie and Cano's home

Allie hurried into the bedroom. Cano doubted she'd ever get tired of the sight of Allie's naked body. Her long blond hair, still wet from the shower, made her look even sexier.

"Would you stop gaping and get your ass out of bed?" Allie said as she rummaged through her dresser drawer. She pulled out two balled-up pairs of socks and lobbed one at Cano.

With ease, Cano plucked it out of the air and launched it back at Allie. "What's the hurry? They won't be here for a couple hours."

"Try one." Allie glared. "You fell back to sleep."

"Really?" Cano blinked and rubbed her eyes before she glanced at the clock. "Well, shit, I guess I did."

"And you're in charge of getting the pork chops ready."

"Cumin." Cano grinned.

Allie glowered. "I still can't believe I gave away my secret in a moment of weakness."

"You call a volcano eruption a moment of weakness?" Cano shook her head. "I still can't believe that's the first thing you decided to say."

Allie stepped over to the bed, bent, and brought her lips to Cano's. When she pulled back, she said, "I told you I loved you afterward."

"That you did." Cano smiled.

"And every day since."

Cano gently pulled Allie toward her. "Want to tell me again?"

Allie put her hand on her hip and backed up. "Nova Kane, you will not seduce me again. We have guests coming in less than an hour. You need to get your butt up." Allie pointed toward the bed as she walked back to the dresser. "And don't forget to put away your wand."

Cano held back a chuckle. What a difference three months made. The first few times Allie needed the help of the wand, she'd fought back tears, and Cano had had to comfort her. Now she was casually telling Cano to pick up her toys.

When Allie turned back to the drawer, Cano grinned at the wand. She stifled a giggle as she flipped the switch, and a low buzzing sound filled the air.

Allie spun around. "Would you turn that thing off?"

"Killjoy." Cano flipped the switch.

"I think you had plenty of joy earlier to last you for a while."

Cano sat up in bed and swung her legs off the side. She held her thumb and forefinger about an inch apart. "Maybe a little while."

Allie finished hooking her bra and held her thumb and forefinger much farther apart. "Try a long while."

"Fine." Cano stood and stretched, reaching

her arms to the sky. When she brought her arms back down, she noticed Allie staring. "What are you looking at?"

"Um, nothing." Allie rifled through the drawer and pulled out a T-shirt.

"Ha." Cano sidled up next to Allie. "You were checking out the goods. Weren't you?"

Allie pulled the T-shirt over her head. She glowered at Cano when her head popped through the hole. "Didn't we discuss your need to curtail that cockiness?"

Cano put her arm around Allie. "You like it, and you know it."

"I'd like it more if you'd strut your ass into the shower."

"Like to join me?" Cano wriggled her eyebrows. She'd never get tired of teasing Allie.

"No. Have you been listening to me?"

"Were you talking? I was blinded by your beauty."

"Since when did blindness cause someone to be unable to hear?"

"Damn. Got me on that one."

Allie pulled a pair of jeans from the closet and went to put her leg into the leg hole. She wobbled and grabbed onto the door frame.

Cano moved quickly and wrapped her arm around Allie's waist, supporting most of her weight. Allie had been a little shaky the last several days as the new school year approached. She worked too hard preparing and hadn't slept well, either.

Cano decided not to say anything and instead braced for Allie to become upset with her body.

"Thanks." Allie leaned against Cano and took a

deep breath. "I need to be more careful. I'm a little unsteady today."

Cano hoped the surprise didn't show on her face. Since they'd gotten back together, Allie had become more accepting of her condition, but Cano still feared for the worst. "Is there anything I can do to help?"

Allie didn't speak as she studied Cano's face. "You still worry, don't you?"

Cano glanced at the floor. "A little." She'd vowed never to hide things from Allie again. "You've done great. It's just me being afraid that you'll not handle things well."

"I'm doing my best to react better." Allie put her hand against Cano's cheek. "I don't want you cringing every time I'm struggling physically."

"I'm trying not to." Cano put her hand over Allie's hand.

"I can't promise that I'll never react out of frustration. But we're in this together." Allie locked gazes with Cano. "Out of the ashes."

"That's all I needed to hear." Cano brought Allie's hand to her lips and slowly kissed each knuckle.

"What I need to hear is the shower running." Allie swatted Cano on the butt. She glanced at the clock. "You know Fran and Ben are always early."

"So are Johnny and Rosaria." Cano smirked.

Allie opened the door and smiled at the two couples standing on the porch. As predicted, they'd both shown up fifteen minutes early. "Please. Come in." Allie swung the door open wider.

Fran and Rosaria entered, followed by Johnny

and Ben. They exchanged hugs and small talk as Allie accepted a bottle of wine from Fran and a homemade pecan pie from Rosaria.

"Oh, my god, this looks delicious," Allie said. She leaned in and whispered. "I'm going to hide it, or Nova will insist on eating dessert first."

"Speaking of," Johnny said. "Where's that rascal?"

Allie shook her head. "Still in the shower."

"Figures." Johnny laughed. "She never arrives on time for anything."

"Including her own party, apparently." Allie smiled. "Maybe we should have the pecan pie first and tell her she was late, so she missed out."

"I like the way you think." Rosaria put her arm around Allie. "I'm so glad you're back in Cano's life. I couldn't believe how much better she was doing the last time we were here." Rosaria shook her head. "It broke my heart how sad she was before. You put the spark back in her eyes."

Allie's cheeks burned.

"I'd say it was a two-way street." Fran winked at Rosaria. "Allie here's got a spring back in her step, too."

"Whose step is springing?" Nova said as she entered the room.

Johnny's face lit up as she walked toward them. Nova went to him first and wrapped her arms around him before she moved on to the others.

Allie leaned over toward Rosaria and handed her the pie. "Quick. Make a dash for it before she sees it."

Nova's eyes twinkled, and she sniffed the air. She turned her gaze on Rosaria. "Do I smell pecan pie?"

Rosaria laughed and wagged her finger at Nova. "You will keep your hands off my pie until after we eat dinner."

"Yes, ma'am." Nova smirked. "But I could carry it into the kitchen for you."

"Not a chance." Rosaria shooed Nova away.

"I can't wait for those pork chops," Ben said.

"Someone," Allie pretended to glare at Nova, "was supposed to make the rub for the chops. Dinner might be delayed."

"No." Fran's eyes widened, and she put her hand on her hip. "You mean all someone has to do is sleep with you to get the secret ingredient?"

Nova laughed. "No, you just have to throw them on the back of your bike during a volcanic eruption."

A puzzled expression settled on Fran's face as she looked between Allie and Nova. Allie bit her tongue, trying to keep her laugh at bay.

"What aren't you two telling us?" Fran asked.

"She certainly isn't a hopeless romantic." Nova pointed at Allie. "You'd think in a life-or-death situation, she'd profess her undying love for me. Instead, the first thing she does is yell out the secret ingredient."

Fran's face turned bright red as she laughed. "You're joking, aren't you?"

"Afraid not." Allie smiled. "Although, in my defense, I did profess my love after that."

Nova put her arm around Allie and kissed the top of Allie's head. "What can I say, she's such a charmer."

Cano leaned back in her chair and patted her

stomach. The dinner conversation had been lively and full of laughter. Mount St. Helens had certainly changed her life. Less than a year ago, she spent most of her time alone, but now people she loved surrounded her, which included the woman of her dreams.

She watched as Allie told Rosaria a story. *God, was she beautiful.* Her hair billowed in the light breeze, and her smile lit her entire face.

Johnny nudged Cano, bringing her out of her trance. "So is your transfer permanent?"

Cano shrugged. "I'm not certain, but I'm planning on staying."

"Damn right she is," Fran said, joining the conversation. "You're not letting her get away again, are you, Allie?"

"Absolutely not." Allie took Cano's hand. "She's mine, and I'm not sending her back. Sorry, Johnny."

"That's okay. Now that Hector, our oldest, is starting at U-Dub next week, I'm sure we'll be around Seattle much more."

"You two are welcome here any time. We have plenty of room," Allie said.

"Thanks," Rosaria said. "That's so kind."

Cano leaned in toward Rosaria. "Don't tell Johnny, but I'll miss the grumpy old man."

"Hey now." Johnny sat up straighter. "I resemble that remark. But seriously, is the boss going to let you stay on here?"

"Yep. It'll take years to discover all we can about what happened and how we can do better in the future to know when a volcano might erupt."

Rosaria put her hand on her chest. "Thank god only fifty-seven died. Still a lot, but Johnny said if it hadn't happened on a Sunday that there could have been nearly three hundred loggers in the forest."

"Absolutely. The thought terrifies me," Allie said. "We should never underestimate the power of nature."

"What are you working on at the site?" Rosaria asked.

"Right now, I've been taking lots of measurements. Figuring out the numbers. For instance, did you know that the mountain is thirteen hundred feet lower after the blast?"

"Holy shit," Ben said. "That's over four football fields."

Cano pointed at Ben. "I might steal that. Everyone is always asking how much thirteen hundred feet is."

"Puts it in perspective," Johnny said. "There are days I still can't believe it happened and that we witnessed it."

"Something none of us will ever forget." Allie's eyes filled with sadness.

"Enough!" Fran said. "We're here to celebrate."

"What are we celebrating?" Cano asked.

"Duh." Fran frowned and thunked Cano on the back of the head. "The two of you. It only took four years and a volcanic eruption for you two to pull your heads out of your asses."

Warmth filled Cano's chest as everyone laughed. She was home, and her heart filled with love. She reached for Allie's hand at the same time Allie reached for hers. Their gazes met. In that moment, Cano knew that no matter what life handed them or how Allie's condition progressed, they'd survive since their love had risen out of the ashes.

About The Author

Rita Potter has spent most of her life trying to figure out what makes people tick. To that end, she holds a Bachelor's degree in Social Work and an MA in Sociology. Being an eternal optimist, she maintains that the human spirit is remarkably resilient. Her writing reflects this belief.

Rita's stories are electic but typically put her characters in challenging circumstances. She feels that when they reach their happily ever after, they will have earned it. Despite the heavier subject matter, Rita's humorous banter and authentic dialogue reflect her hopeful nature.

In her spare time, she enjoys the outdoors. She is especially drawn to the water, which is ironic since she lives in the middle of a cornfield. Her first love has always been reading. It is this passion that spurred her writing career. She rides a Harley Davidson and has an unnatural obsession with fantasy football. More than anything, she detests small talk but can ramble on for hours given a topic that interests her.

She lives in a small town in Illinois with her wife, Terra, and their cat, Chumley, who actually runs the household.

Rita is a member of American Mensa and the Golden

Crown Literary Society. She is currently a graduate of the GCLS Writing Academy 2021. Sign up for Rita's free newsletter at:

www.ritapotter.com

IF YOU LIKED THIS BOOK...

Reviews help an author get discovered and if you have enjoyed this book, please do the author the honor of posting a review on Goodreads, Amazon, Barnes & Noble or anywhere you purchased the book. Or perhaps share a posting on your social media sites and help us spread the word.

Check out Rita's other books

Broken not Shattered - ISBN - 978-1-952270-22-2

Even when it seems hopeless, there can always be a better tomorrow.

Jill Bishop has one goal in life – to survive. Jill is trapped in an abusive marriage, while raising two young girls. Her husband has isolated her from the world and filled her days with fear. The last thing on her mind is love, but she sure could use a friend.

Alex McCoy is enjoying a comfortable life, with great friends and a prosperous business. She has given up on love, after picking the wrong woman one too many times. Little does she know, a simple act of kindness might change her life forever.

When Alex lends a helping hand to Jill at the local grocery store, they are surprised by their immediate connection and an unlikely friendship develops. As their friendship deepens, so too do their fears.

In order to protect herself and the girls, Jill can't let her husband know about her friendship with Alex, and Alex can't discover what goes on behind closed doors. What would Alex do if she finds out the truth? At the same time, Alex must fight her attraction and be the friend she suspects Jill needs. Besides, Alex knows what every lesbian knows – don't fall for a straight woman, especially one that's married…but will her heart listen?

Upheaval: Book One - As We Know It - ISBN - 978-1-

952270-38-3

It is time for Dillon Mitchell to start living again.

Since the death of her wife three years ago, Dillon had buried herself in her work. When an invitation arrives for Tiffany Daniels' exclusive birthday party, her best friend persuades her to join them for the weekend.

It's not the celebration that draws her but the location. The party is being held at the Whitaker Estate, one of the hottest tickets on the West Coast. The Estate once belonged to an eccentric survivalist, whose family converted it into a trendy destination while preserving some of its original history.

Surrounded by a roomful of successful lesbians, Dillon finds herself drawn to Skylar Lange, the mysterious and elusive bartender. Before the two can finish their first dance, a scream shatters the evening. When the party goers emerge from the underground bunker, they discover something terrible has happened at the Estate.

The group races to try to discover the cause of this upheaval, and whether it's isolated to the Estate. Has the world, as we know it, changed forever?

Survival: Book Two - As We Know It - ISBN - 978-1-952270-47-5

Forty-eight hours after the Upheaval, reality is beginning to set in at the Whitaker Estate. The world, As We Know It, has ended.

Dillon Mitchell and her friends are left to survive, after discovering most of the population, at least in the United States, has mysteriously died.

While they struggle to come to terms with their devastating losses, they are faced with the challenge of creating a new society, which is threatened by the divergent factions that may tear the community apart from the inside.

Even if the group can unite, external forces are gathering that could destroy their fragile existence.

Meanwhile, Dillon's budding relationship with the elusive Skylar Lange faces obstacles, when Skylar's hidden past is revealed.

Thundering Pines – ISBN – 978-1-952270-58-1

Returning to her hometown was the last thing Brianna Goodwin wanted to do. She and her mom had left Flower Hills under a cloud of secrecy and shame when she was ten years old. Her life is different now. She has a high-powered career, a beautiful girlfriend, and a trendy life in Chicago.

Upon her estranged father's death, she reluctantly agrees to attend the reading of his will. It should be simple—settle his estate and return to her life in the city—but nothing has ever been simple when it comes to Donald Goodwin.

Dani Thorton, the down-to-earth manager of

Thundering Pines, is confused when she's asked to attend the reading of the will of her longtime employer. She fears that her simple, although secluded life will be interrupted by the stylish daughter who breezes into town.

When a bombshell is revealed at the meeting, two women seemingly so different are thrust together. Maybe they'll discover they have more in common than they think.

Betrayal: Book Three - As We Know It - ISBN - 978-1-952270-69-7

Betrayal is the exciting conclusion to the As We Know It series.

The survivors at Whitaker Estate are still reeling from the vicious attack on their community, which left three of their friends dead.

When the mysterious newcomer Alaina Renato reveals there is a traitor in their midst, it threatens to tear the community apart. Is there truly a traitor, or is Alaina playing them all?

Dillon Mitchell and the other Commission members realize their group might not survive another attack, especially if there is someone working against them from the inside. Despite the potential risk, they vote to attend a summit that will bring together other survivors from around the country.

When the groups converge on Las Vegas, the festive

atmosphere soon turns somber upon the discovery of an ominous threat. But is the danger coming from within, or is there someone else lurking in the city?

Before it's too late, they must race against time to determine where the betrayal is coming from.

Whitewater Awakening - ISBN

Can two lost people find themselves, and possibly each other, halfway around the world?

After a tragic accident, Quinn Coolidge leaves everything behind, hoping to find solace in a secluded life in the Ozarks. Her solitude is disrupted when her best friend unexpectedly shows up with a proposition she may not be able to resist.

Faced with a series of failed relationships, Aspen Kennedy is left wondering why she can't find true love. With each new partner, she immerses herself in their interests, hoping to find the connection she's been missing. That should make her the perfect girlfriend, shouldn't it?

Come along with Quinn and Aspen as they travel to Africa to take on one of the most grueling whitewater rafting courses in the world. With the amazing Victoria Falls as their backdrop, the pair will have to look deep inside to discover what holds them back. Will the churning waters of the Zambezi River defeat them, or will it lead them to a whitewater awakening?

Made in the USA
Monee, IL
11 March 2023